WRATH

&

MERCY

Also by Jessica Rubinkowski

The Bright & the Pale

WRATH

&

MERCY

JESSICA RUBINKOWSKI

Quill Tree Books
An Imprint of HarperCollinsPublishers

For the angry girls of the world

Quill Tree Books is an imprint of HarperCollins Publishers.

Wrath & Mercy
Copyright © 2022 by Jessica Rubinkowski
All rights reserved. Printed in the United States of America.
No part of this book may be used or reproduced in any manner whatsoever
without written permission except in the case of brief quotations
embodied in critical articles and reviews. For information address
HarperCollins Children's Books, a division of HarperCollins Publishers,
195 Broadway, New York, NY 10007.
www.epicreads.com

Library of Congress Control Number: 2021949284
ISBN 978-0-06-287155-8 — ISBN 978-0-06-324610-2 (special edition)

Typography by David DeWitt
22 23 24 25 26   PC/LSCH   10 9 8 7 6 5 4 3 2 1
❖
First Edition

ONE

Once there was a girl who was gifted the powers of a god. Filled with a righteous fury, she tore down the Czar's army and ripped apart the curse that had held her village in an icy grasp for a decade.

She did it for love.

She did it for power.

But mostly, she did it for revenge.

IN THE OLD TALES, THE ones grandmothers tell in hushed whispers around dying fires, villains are creeping, evil things full of malice and deceit. It is a familiar story, one that children have heard all across the frozen country of Strana for hundreds of years. Once, humans warred among themselves, knowing nothing of industry or peace. Seeing the destruction being wrought on the land they so loved, the Brother Gods, one Bright and one Pale, fell to the earth. They did so willingly and with no expectation. They wished only to help. For years, there was prosperity, a utopia the world hasn't seen since.

But gods and mortals were never meant to live side by side. As the Brother Gods remade humanity, so too were they changed.

Before their fall, the Brothers knew nothing of jealousy, hate, or fear. These were mortal emotions meant for humans alone. Slowly, these sentiments sowed seeds of discord between the Brothers, choking their benevolence until they were consumed only by their envy of one another. The Bright God wished to wield his brother's power over frost, snow, and stone, while the Pale God wanted the light and life that came with his brother's might. In the end, their jealousy devoured them.

The war they waged lasted a decade, destroying mountains, lakes, and woods, decimating the very world they sought to protect. At the end, when both were exhausted and bleeding, the Bright God made his final, desperate blow. He struck down his brother, burying him deep beneath the earth, entombing him in frost and bone and stone, until there was nothing left but a mountain. A monument to a former god.

But wars between brothers are bitter, volatile things. They were not content to let their battle end there. From their secret, hidden places, they chose mortal champions, humans destined to wage war against one another until death claimed them. The battles would play out as the original had, with the Bright champion casting down the Pale. A repeating cycle that never seems to end.

Until now.

I will be different.

The sky reels as the last claws of sunlight disappear behind Knnot Mountain at my back, as if my hatred of the Bright God alone forced twilight upon the world. With the dark comes a wave of dizziness, the edges of my vision going black and fuzzy, the world no longer as certain as it had been mere moments ago when I commanded the Pale God's power. My arms ache, the scalding heat of Alik's body is too much for the ice filtering through my veins. I can't stop the tremor that rolls up my spine and down my arms, losing my hold on Alik, who falls to the powdery snow.

Alik slowly rights himself, his gaze going to the field of destruction before us. Bodies bedecked in the black-and-gold uniforms of the Storm Hounds, Czar Ladislaw's personal army, lie sprawled and broken across the icy field between Knnot and the small village of Ludminka. Kosci's monsters still lope among them, ripping into limp bodies to eat their fill. Pools of ice form along the areas where Matvei, the Bright God's champion, pulled rays of sunlight from the sky in an attempt to kill me, cooled by the nipping wind of night.

All of it—the death, the blood, the monsters with wide, unseeing eyes and a maw of teeth—had been me. Instead of despair, a strange warmth brews in my heart like a storm, thunderheads of pride and vindication building in my chest.

"Valeria?" Alik's voice is hoarse as he reaches for me, brushing warm fingers along my cheek so softly it's as if he isn't there at all. "Are you okay?"

The eyepatch over his left eye is stained with blood, some still leaking from the corner of his mouth. A bloom of deep maroon mars his chest, a hole torn in his shirt where the bolt went into his heart. I healed it. I brought him back. Yet looking into his face, with its pale cheeks and jagged scar from hairline to nose, I see nothing but the specter of death. I lost him for a second time, and it had been all Ladislaw and Matvei's fault.

A familiar mantle of rage falls across my shoulders as I stumble to my feet, pushing away from Alik's pinched face. I will never bow to the people who forced me to my knees, no matter what it will cost me. I do not care what I have to do to kill Czar Ladislaw. I will leave a river of red all the way to his palace in the capital. If Matvei seeks to destroy me, I will kill him first. No one will stop me.

Czar Ladislaw sent his Storm Hounds to trap us in Knnot. He let Matvei round us up like sheep to slaughter just so he could get his hands on lovite, the magical ore deep within Knnot's heart. And Luiza helped.

Luiza, who claimed to love me. Luiza, who saved me from the streets when I was just a little girl, lost and alone after frost had devoured my family. As if that meant nothing, she betrayed me, and it almost cost me the only thing in this world that I loved.

I stagger toward Ludminka, ignoring Alik, who calls after me as snow swallows my boots. I have to keep going, I have to move toward Rurik and the palace and the Czar. If I don't, they will come, they will take and conquer and kill. I can't let them step foot onto Zladonian soil again.

I slip forward on a patch of ice, my exhausted body giving way, but a set of warm arms catches me before I collapse. I blink up into Alik's face to find a single wide, panicked eye, the rest of his face dissolved into a pale blur. He hugs me tight to his chest, keeping me upright by will alone. I tell my body to fight, but it doesn't respond, the last vestiges of Kosci's power trapped in the pendant around my neck leaking away, one heartbeat at a time.

"It's over," Alik says into my hair, his breath almost too hot against my cheek. "It's over, Val. Let them go. Send the creatures away."

I open my mouth to say it isn't over, it won't be until Ladislaw is dead at my feet, but I release a strangled sob instead. The threads of magic twining from the pendant into the monsters and people in the village pull at the interior of my mind, siphoning energy with each breath they take.

Slowly, I relinquish the tight hold on the pulsing power coursing through me. First, from the creatures, who look in my direction before slinking back toward the gaping mouth of Knnot, to hide in their pit of darkness until I have need of them again. I turn my attention to the droning buzz of the village.

I can't leave them to walk their ruined streets full of bodies with no explanation, not when my family is among them, too. The world changed as they slept in their cocoons of frost, and they've a right to know why. Vaguely, so softly that I almost don't catch it, Kosci murmurs in the back of my mind, like a thought I don't remember thinking.

Order them to the square.

At first, I have no idea how I am supposed to do that. I know nothing of Kosci's power or how to wield it. After I accepted his deal to plant his heart somewhere it could flourish in exchange for his power while I wore it, I let my rage and sorrow overtake me. It had been as simple as breathing then. Now it's like trying to dig through frozen ground. Plaintively, Kosci attempts to guide my mind, pointing it toward the threads tugging at his heart trapped around my neck. I think a single word, "square," before every last one of the strings snaps from my control.

The feeling is visceral, like a spring trap exploding into my chest. I sag against Alik, who catches me with a soft huff.

"Alik, I need—" I start to say, and it's like speaking through water. "I need to get to the village square."

"You need to sit down," Alik says, his arms still the only thing holding me upright. With every last bit of strength left within me, I force myself away from him once again. I wobble but remain standing, the edges of my world going murky and dark.

"I have to go to them," I say. I'm not certain if Alik hears me, but I don't wait for his response. I struggle forward, concentrating on putting one foot in front of the other. I trip over something, an arm or leg, I don't know, but someone is there to grab me. Alik slips his arm beneath my left, while Chinua, one of the few to make it out of the mines of Knnot alive, appears and takes my other arm. Her long black braid sits in disarray, but her mouth is determined.

Neither speak as they help me toward Ludminka, which sits eerily quiet as we are swallowed by the brightly colored houses of the main street. Shutters bang against the sides of cabins, forgotten, decade-old clothes flapping in the empty alleys between the buildings. When I'd freed Ludminka, I'd expected life to flow into the streets again, not this empty husk of what used to be.

At last, we break out into the city center, finding a small crowd dotting the snow-dusted cobblestones of the square. I scan each face, searching for my parents or brothers, but their features bleed together in a blanket of icy white. My family is out there, though. I can feel it.

The silence deepens as Chinua and Alik slow to a stop in the center of the square. In the gloom of winter dusk, the citizens of Ludminka are more ghost than people, but I can feel the slip of their eyes over my face like a warm wash and I disentangle myself from the others, determined to stand on my own before the people I freed.

"People of Ludminka," I cry out as a dull ringing begins in my ears and sweat pools on my brow. "I know you are confused. You likely have no memory of what happened here. I hope I can provide you with the answers you seek, though I will warn you that what I am about to tell you will seem unbelievable. For the past ten years, all of Ludminka has been trapped in ice. Strana has long since believed you dead and the mines within Knnot unreachable."

I don't think I imagine the collective inhale. I forge ahead, the world spinning rapidly around me now.

"Everyone outside Ludminka within the Zladonia region fell to plague, their bodies withering away until their hearts gave out. Czar Ladislaw, whom you only know as a benefactor, refused us all sanctuary. He claimed we would bring disease and ruin to Strana. He imprisoned Zladonians, one by one, and holds them captive still. The world you remember is no more. Zladonians are hated. Hunted. And we will continue to be until either Ladislaw is dead or we are."

As my words sink into the sea of people before me, whispers begin, quickly changing to mutters, then shouting. Their voices blend together in a symphony of fear and worry until it beats against my eardrums. I raise a hand to silence them before the tide of their voices can pull me under. To my surprise, the cacophony cuts off completely.

"I know you don't want to believe me," I say into the silence. "It sounds impossible, like something out of a legend. But I'm here to tell you that's exactly where you find yourself, in the middle of a myth. My name is Valeria, daughter of Ivanna and Nicklaus, and I am the Pale God's chosen champion."

Not a single person moves. I'm not certain they even breathe. The weight of my new title settles into my body, sending cold goose bumps up my arms. I attempt to wet my lips as tension crawls through the crowd.

With the very last dregs of Kosci's power, I raise my hand and release his magic. It curls along my palm in frozen fractals, spiraling along my fingers until it creates a small, diamond-shaped shard in the middle of my hand. Some gasp, others silently gape, while still others surge forward to get a better look. Their faces come into startling focus for a single heart-beat before my vision collapses into darkness.

TWO

I'M NOT CERTAIN HOW LONG I'm unconscious, occasionally drifting to the surface long enough to hear furtive whispers or soft lullabies sung by a voice I almost recognize. But it is different than before. Sleeping, dreaming, it was all something for me alone, somewhere I went to relive memories or rehash nightmares. Now, another heart beats beside mine, a spark of blue-veined mist in the abyss. It's comforting thump is what I follow out into the real world.

A dull throb beats behind my eyes as I attempt to open them, still gritty with sleep and aching like every other muscle. Bright light pierces my vision and I blink, taking a few breaths to force the pounding in my head to dim.

A pitched ceiling I don't recognize sits above me, warm yellow light from a small fireplace to my right throwing shadows against the ridge beam. Red curtains rest closed before the window over my bed, a small washstand in the corner near a partially opened door. With each new detail, a small link of fear connects to another, forming a chain of panic. I have no idea where I am or who I'm with. I struggle to push myself up, but my arms fold beneath me, pinning me in place.

A soft sigh emanates from my right and I look over, instantly wishing I hadn't as the world spins in flecks of golden brown. I blink them away to find my mother asleep in an armchair. Behind her, leaning against the wall, is Alik. He straightens as I shift up onto my pillow, but instead of reaching out, he places a hand on my mother's shoulder and shakes her softly.

"She's awake," he whispers, but in the quiet of the room it feels like a shout.

Matta startles awake and my throat constricts as her eyes flit from one of my features to another, her mouth pressed into a line impossible to read. I beg the gods to let her recognize me, to force her arms to bring me to her chest, but she does no such thing. A dull sheen covers her eyes before a single tear slips out to collect in the small divot between her nose and cheek. She hurriedly wipes it away.

"I'll go get the others," Alik says.

My mother says nothing as the door closes and a strained hum of silence carves between us until I can't stand the quiet. When Luiza first took me into the guild, I dreamed every night of my mother knocking on the door, asking to take me home. It wasn't until Alik and I created our space in the attic that the dreams slowly stopped. Now, the very person I spent nights dreaming of sits before me and I can't speak because I don't know what to say. Nothing seems big enough.

"Matta?" The word slices against my throat, and I swallow against the dryness there. "It's Valeria."

Color drains from my mother's face. Slowly, so slowly that I could've counted every beat of my heart, she reaches for my hand across the navy duvet, curling her fingers around my own, turning over my hand to expose my wrist.

A bright scar sears across the inside in the very place Kosci grabbed me years ago and accidentally marked me as his champion. She swallows a quick gasp before her head comes up once more.

"It really is you," she whispers, running a gentle hand along my hair, tears slipping down her cheeks in earnest. "My Valeria."

Matta pulls me hard to her chest, and I wince against the sudden movement, my body aching more than ever. My mother's shoulders shake, and I force my arms around her as wetness leaks down my own face.

As if the very act sealed something between us, she holds me tighter, and I bury my head into her shoulder, just like I used to when I was a little girl scared of the wind howling in the pines outside our house. She smells like I remember, bits of fir wood and yeast from days spent baking bread for

Ludminka. A sob catches hard in my throat, and she crushes me tighter.

I want to tell her how much I have ached for this moment; how long I spent dreaming of her hugs and my father's laugh, of what it was like to think they were dead. It all bubbles to my tongue, but not a single word falls. I can do nothing but cling to her and try to stuff ten years of longing into one moment.

The door swings open, hurried footsteps clattering into the room. My mother sniffs and pulls back, pressing a kiss to my forehead before helping me lean against the headboard. As she pulls away, I find the previously empty room full. My father hovers near the foot of my bed, my brothers on either side of him. Alik stands beside the half-open door, clearly not sure if he should stay or go. I wipe at my eyes and don't fight the slow smile spreading across my mouth.

"I've missed you." My voice breaks on the words. I swallow several times to stop the knot forming in my throat from choking me. "I didn't think I'd ever get the chance to see you again."

My father steps forward, studying me just as my mother had, before sitting heavily on the edge of the bed, staring at the floorboards between his feet.

"You are really our Valeria. I had hoped . . . I didn't think . . . Ten years?"

His gaze finds my face once more, and I nod slowly.

"And all this time you've been alone?" Matta asks, voice thin, on the verge of breaking.

"Not completely," I say, finding Alik. "I had friends, a place to live . . ."

My eyes don't leave Alik, and I realize he is the only thing I have left from that time. I want to call him to me, or for him to cross the floor and sit by my side. Neither of us acts. Time stretches between us for a long moment before he gives me the smallest of smiles and slips from the room, closing the door behind him. I clear my throat and face my family once more.

"I wasn't . . . someone you would be proud of," I say, picking at the blanket. "I was alone, desperate for food, I didn't know what else to do."

Before now, I had never been ashamed of what I did to survive. Luiza offered me shelter and food in exchange for a pair of sticky hands. To seven-year-old me, it had seemed like a fair trade. Staring into the faces of my parents somehow makes me feel ashamed.

It is my father who breaks the silence.

"Whatever happened, *Milaya*, we love you. Not a one of us can say we would've done differently in your place. If your words of the world are true, Strana is a cruel place now."

Pressure releases from my chest like a frayed cord snapping. Until this moment, I hadn't realized how afraid I'd been they would push me away or chastise me for everything I had done. If I didn't have them, I had no one in the world at all. The realization makes tears well in again, and I take a long, steadying breath before starting my tale.

"I made it to Rurik somehow. I don't remember a majority of the journey, only that I had to get away from the frost. A woman found me there trying to steal food from her stores." I pause, waiting for admonishment. When it doesn't come, I continue. "She said her name was Luiza and that I was just what she needed for her guild. Luiza helped me from the cellar and showed me a warm bed and even warmer food. When she offered me a room, food, family, in exchange for becoming a thief in the guild, I couldn't say no."

I wet my drying mouth. "It's what I've done for the past ten years, the entire reason I came back to Knnot in the first place. I was to help steal the lovite left in the vaults within the mine and return to Rurik. I never expected . . . all of this."

"I doubt many people expect to become a champion to the gods," my eldest brother, Gregori, says with a half smile. "Don't tell me you always knew you were destined for greatness, Val. We all remember the way you couldn't carry a bucket of water from the well."

A shocked laugh falls from my lips and Gregori's smile spreads. He looks like our father when he grins, with his broad forehead and wide mouth. Freckles sprinkle his nose from days spent in the sun, and his long, white hair sits tied at the nape of his neck.

"Of course she did," Anton, my middle brother, says,

taking a step forward so he is shoulder to shoulder with Gregori. Anton and I look more alike, sharing wide-set eyes and arched noses. "She used to demand we carry her through the streets so she didn't muddy her boots. Only godly champions would do that."

"Boys," Matta chastises, but a tiny smile spreads across her mouth. It all is so heartbreakingly familiar that my chest squeezes tight.

I'd forgotten how my brothers teased, how my mother always found a small bit of humor in their words despite trying to hide it. How had I ever believed I had found family with Luiza? For years I wanted her affection, her attention, attempting to kindle a semblance of the warmth in this room now. Fresh tears well in my eyes and I bury my face in my hands before anyone can see.

I start as warm arms circle me, my mother's judging by the smell. Another set follow, strong and sure, my father's. Anton and Gregori fall on either side, completing the family. They all hold me tight as tears silently fall.

I'm not certain how long we all sit like that, but no one makes to move until my chest stops heaving. They pull away as I wipe at my eyes, both embarrassed and comforted by their presence. The soft crackle of the fire is the only sound in the room for a long moment before Gregori shifts.

"What's Rurik like?" he asks.

"Yes, tell us," Anton says leaning on the sturdy wood of

the foot of the bed. "Not even Matta and Papa have seen Rurik."

A soft laugh escapes my lips even as the idea sticks somewhere deep in my mind. Out of everyone in my family, I am the one who saw Strana, who experienced things. It's a core part of my being they will never understand, no matter what words I use to describe it. As I look at each of their expectant faces in the warm firelight from the hearth across the room, I realize I have to try. I want my family back.

"Well, the first thing you always notice is the smell. Rancid, sweet, and wet in the slums, hot cinnamon buns and onions in the trading square," I say, and Gregori grants me a laugh. I give a tentative smile before letting my memories unspool.

I tell them of the guild, of Luiza's rigorous trainings and the best way to cut purse strings. Gregori and Anton found it particularly interesting, but Matta made them stop asking questions after that. From there I told them about meeting Alik and growing up with him, of our training together and our first mission into the Pleasure Quarter to steal petty coin from people passing through.

Not a single one of them breathes as I tell them of my return to Knnot, and they stop moving completely as I finish my story at accepting Kosci's deal. I press a palm to my chest, relishing the cool bite of Kosci's pendant still resting there. My family tracks the movement, their faces falling from ruddy-cheeked happiness to taut, hollow masks.

Gregori worries at the inside of his cheek. "What do we do now?"

I look to my parents, expecting them to answer as they always have. Their faces are slack, the crease between my father's brow deepening and Matta's fingers twisted into knots. They have no answers, and as much as I wish they could fix the wrongs of the world, they can't. My mother turns her watery blue eyes in my direction and I swallow hard, something heavy and hot landing in the base of my stomach. They don't want answers from Valeria, their lost daughter and sister, but from Valeria, champion of the Pale God. Iron brands clamp down on my chest as I realize no one in all of Ludminka knows what to do. They will look to a leader, and the most natural one is me.

That is what you wanted, isn't it?

The sound of Kosci's voice nearly makes me jump. His heart bites cold against the skin of my chest, sending a subtle pulse of power through me. I let the cool surety of it pull the panicked pieces of my soul back together.

I don't know what I want anymore.

Yes, you do, Kosci's voice slithers out from the deepest reaches of my mind. *It is what you wanted when you accepted my deal. You want to destroy the Czar, Luiza, my brother. You want to ruin Strana for what it did to Zladonia. To your Alik. That fire still burns inside you, no matter how much you wish to ignore it now.*

I want to deny it, to pretend I have everything I want now

that my family surrounds me, but it isn't true. I *want* Ladislaw dead. I want his blood spilled across the snow at my feet. I want Zladonians freed and back in their homes. I want it more than hugs from Matta or jokes from Gregori and Anton.

Suddenly, the room is far too hot, the weight of the quilt across my legs trapping me too tightly. I fling it back, startling my father, who helps me sit fully upright on the edge of my bed. I steady myself on his arm before letting go and brushing imaginary dirt from my shirt. I've had my time with my family, now it's time to make good on my promise to Ladislaw.

My mother stares as if she doesn't recognize me and, with a hard jolt, I realize she doesn't. Not really. None of them do. I can't be their little girl and soak up the warmth they offer, hoping they can right the world. I have to be a girl born of blood and steel, readying myself and all of Ludminka for a war I know the Czar will bring to our doorstep.

I need a reason to gather all of Ludminka together once again, this time without Kosci's help. I have to ask them all to pick up blades they've never wielded and find the will to fight for all of Zladonia. The Czar won't simply be content to let us be. Not when Knnot and all the lovite he needs to make Strana wealthy again stands open at our backs. Despite having a god twisted around my neck, I cannot win against Ladislaw on my own.

THREE

IT TAKES ME A FULL day to recover enough to hobble down the stairs of the cabin I now call home. Using Kosci's magic stole every bit of my strength, and each new movement leaves me sweaty and aching. Even now, as my feet contact the lower level, beads of sweat trickle along my lower back. I ignore it as I take in the oak door and the small window beside it offering a view of a low stone wall framing a front garden covered in snow. I don't recognize the view and I frown as I turn from the front door toward the kitchen.

A large stove takes up the farthest wall, the same familiar bright-white brick I'd seen as a child in my parents' house. The wide chimney slopes up toward the ceiling, the slow incline serving as a small bed full of pillows and blankets in the coldest of months. A cast-iron pot already rests on the cooktop, steam curling from a small gap between the lid and pan. At the table in the center of the room sits Chinua and Sera, both bent over wooden bowls of porridge. My foot stalls at the sight of them. A large part of me expected them to be gone. After all, they had no real reason to stay. They had the lovite they were promised by Ivan, our expedition leader on the way to Knnot, and they owe me nothing aside from gratitude for getting them out of Knnot alive.

We'd all been lost within those dark mines for days on end, certain we'd never find our way out, hunted by gaunt creatures with mouths full of teeth. We had no way of knowing they were Kosci's, sent to herd us toward the exit, toward him. I swallow the memories of those cold, dark halls and step into the kitchen. They both look up, features nearly completely opposite of one another. Sera's blond hair lies over her shoulder in a braid, her icy eyes pinned on me, thin lips pulled taut. Chinua breaks into a smile, dark-headed with high cheekbones and deep-brown eyes. She stands and hurries to help me to a worn armchair beside the hearth. I collapse into it with a sigh, legs already wobbly from the descent.

"How long have I been out?" I ask, attempting to break the tense silence.

"Two days," Chinua says, going to the small samovar beside the hearth. She fishes around the fire for an ember, plunking it down into the base before settling the teapot on top. I lean my head back. Two long days I'd given to the Storm Hounds I released into Strana to warn the Czar of what was coming to him.

"I'm surprised you both stayed," I say after a long moment. Chinua's brow crinkles, her mouth turning down. Sera remains unchanged, as if she isn't sure why she is still here either.

"In the mountain, you promised me I would make it out when I was certain I wouldn't. You did absolutely everything you could to make good on that promise. In return, I gave you my loyalty when asked for it. I did not lie that day." Chinua looks up at me. "If not for you and the deal you struck, we would all be dead or in the hands of Storm Hounds right now."

I swallow at the unexpected fervor in Chinua's voice. Sera pushes herself from the table, lifting her chin.

"I have nowhere else to go. I knew if Ivan failed his foolish mission to Knnot I would be marked a criminal. Ladislaw made it perfectly clear that no one was to travel to the mines without his consent. I am a wanted woman now, whether I agree with what you are doing or not." Sera doesn't look away as she hefts a breath. "But I *do* believe what Ladislaw has been doing is wrong. Clearly all that happened here was not the Zladonian's fault. I can't ignore all I've learned even if I wanted to. So here I stay."

It isn't the same pledge Chinua made, but it is more acknowledgment than I expected from Sera. She didn't trust me on our way to Knnot, and I'm not sure she does now, but at least she isn't running to Ladislaw to tell him everything she knows. I give her the briefest of nods, which she accepts as her cue to leave and swiftly exits the kitchen before either Chinua or I can speak.

"Don't mind her," Chinua says, going back to the cup of tea before her. "She's been angry since the Storm Hounds rounded us up."

"I think she's been angry her entire life," I say.

"Then you should both get along," Chinua responds, a small smile falling across her lips.

I chuckle as I turn to the window behind me. Through a whirl of frost I make out the bright-red side of a fabric shop, a small, circular sign swinging slightly in the breeze. I still can't place where in the village we are, and it sends an uncomfortable twinge through my gut. I don't know whose home we've commandeered, perhaps someone who lost their life to the Storm Hounds while controlled by Kosci. A bitter taste crawls its way up my throat as Chinua presses a cup of warm black tea into my hands. She follows my gaze to the dirt street beyond the garden wall. Small figures peer into the cabin, little mittened hands clamping hard on the stone of the garden wall. I lean forward to get a better look at their faces, but the children let out strangled squeaks and dive behind the wall. Chinua snickers.

"They've been out there since your display in the square," she says. "When Sera and I went out to gather food, I heard them whispering about who could get close enough to touch you. The children seem to think it will bring good luck."

"I can't do that," I say into my cup.

But I don't know if that's the truth. I have no idea what I

can do or how to wield the power granted to me. There wasn't a way to know. Champions are rare, Pale ones even more so. I can count on a single hand the tales I remember of Kosci's past champions. The tragedy of Inna the Blighted, who became champion to heal an unstoppable sweating sickness from decimating Strana three hundred years ago. She healed all she touched but took on the illness herself until she was nothing but boils, pus, and fever. She died only six months after being named champion by the Czar at the time.

I suppress a huff. Ladislaw will never grant me the honor of being named champion. I'd be written as enemy and pretender only. The children beyond the gate are the only hope I have at being remembered the way I want to be. Any hope I'd harbored of being welcomed back into the fold of Ludminka as if I'd never left dissolves, replaced by the cold reality that I am no longer daughter, friend, or neighbor to anyone in the village. It may be free from the ice, but Ludminka is not my home. It hasn't been since the day I left.

"Don't worry," Chinua says, resting a hand on my shoulder. "I am sure they will find you perfect."

"Perfect." I mutter the word. "You've a lot of faith for someone who didn't want to agree to Kosci's deal."

"So sour," Chinua says, releasing my shoulder. "Should I sweeten the tea for you?"

I laugh, passing the cup back for extra sugar. She dumps another teaspoon in, reminding me of the many times Alik has done the exact same thing for me. I straighten as Chinua hands the cup back. "Have you seen Alik?"

Chinua's smile falls. "He hasn't been here much. I think he's burying Ivan."

"Oh." The word falls pathetically from my lips.

Ivan had been the one to plan the expedition to Knnot, but he had also saved Alik from certain death at the hands of the Storm Hounds. For the year I believed Alik dead, Ivan had nursed him back to health, teaching him to walk again on his wounded leg, aiding him in learning how to navigate a world with a single eye. Ivan may have only been an ex–Storm Hound to me, but he was everything to Alik.

"I think he is near Knnot," Chinua hedges, "if you want to look for him."

I tap my thumb for a few moments before nodding and pushing to my feet. It takes far longer than I would like to dress and get myself outside, but as soon as the icy wind bites against my cheeks and worms its way down the front of my coat, it jolts every one of my senses into awareness.

Ice-topped snow crunches beneath my boots as I make my way from the cabin onto the dirt road leading to Knnot. The few children still hiding behind the wall fall in step behind me, a silent, wide-eyed mob that follows me as I walk through town, only stopping when I stride beyond the edge of the village. They hover in the shadows between the houses, watching as I continue down the worn path toward Knnot.

I scan the horizon, searching for Alik's familiar figure, and find only a pile of carcasses. I move steadily toward it as if guided by an unseen hand. Storm Hounds still dressed in their livery pitch high above my head, their faces icy white, lips bloodless. I had known, vaguely, what I was doing when I accepted Kosci's power. It had felt good, righteous. Now, however, there is nothing but buzzing apathy.

"Valeria?"

I jump and spin, coming face-to-face with the very person I'd been looking for. Dirt and sweat streaks Alik's forehead and a bruised circle hangs beneath his eye. My heart gives a horrible lurch as memories spring up one after the other—his breath rattling through his chest, bright blood cooling on the snow, the feeling of it, hot and viscous oozing through my fingers. I believed seeing him would bring me some semblance of normalcy, but all it's done is remind me of how close I'd been to losing him. Permanently this time. A strangled silence stretches between us and I open my mouth, intending to break it, only to realize I have nothing to say.

"I'm glad to see you out of bed," he says, his mouth twisting into a sad smile. It hurts to see, but I return it anyway.

"I'm glad to see you," I say. "I haven't since I woke up."

Alik gives a half shrug. "I wanted to give you time with your family. I know how much you wanted to see them again."

I take his hand and give it a squeeze. "Thank you."

His mittened hand circles around mine and holds tight.

Despite his effort to appear nonchalant, grief and exhaustion cling to his body.

"Let me help," I say.

"You don't have to do that," he says.

"You're not doing this alone."

Alik studies me for a long moment before nodding, swallowing hard. Together, we gather the linen-wrapped form of Ivan's corpse and begin toward the thick pine forest at the western edge of the plain. My arms burn with the weight, but I remain silent as Alik maneuvers through the forest. Sweat pours down my back and my arms shake by the time Alik finally stops before a lone fir tree overlooking a rolling foothill. Scraggly branches hover above a shallow grave, broken shovels scattered around the rim. The earth had been far too cold and rocky to dig more than a few feet. It would do nothing to protect Ivan if wolves came prowling.

"Wait," I gasp.

We stumble to a stop and lower Ivan's body to the ground. I push sweaty hair from my face before slipping into the grave. It barely reaches my waist and likely isn't long enough for me to lay flat in. Ivan will never fit, and I won't leave him out in the open. I inhale the scent of sharp snow and wet stone as I close my eyes and press my fingers to the pendant, as if the action alone will wake Kosci.

Help me, I think. A thin feeling of acceptance filters through me, and I place my hands on the frozen dirt walls, hoping

Kosci can see what I want.

As if my thought alone controlled the earth before me, the permafrost and stone slowly fall away, tumbling onto my feet and burying me to my knees. Alik hops in, grabbing the end of a broken shovel, and slowly disposes of the earth I manage to move. We work silently, me carving away snow and dirt, him shoveling it out, until the grave's lip hovers at my temple. Alik places a hand on my shoulder and my movements stall, bones already aching and cold with the use of Kosci's power. Alik cups his hands and helps boost me from the grave, and then I turn to help him up the side.

Wind bites my cheeks as Alik and I gather Ivan and lower him into his grave. They are numb completely by the time Alik and I stand side by side, staring down at the hump of earth that will be the only memory of Ivan. Alik closes his eye, mumbling something under his breath. Whether it is a prayer or promise, I don't know.

"I am sorry you lost him, Alik."

"Me too," he says dully as he scrubs at the wetness on his cheeks. "Why didn't you save him, too?"

The words aren't said as an accusation, instead they are full of broken desperation. It shreds at the already worn bits of my heart.

"I wish I could've," I say, surprised to find that it's true. "I didn't have the strength. The power I used to bring you back was the very last I had."

Heaviness settles into the space between us, buffered only by the breeze tangling in the branches high above. Old, hard snow spits at us on its way down from the boughs as if determined to remind me this is a cold, hollow end.

"He was the first one to really care for me since my mothers," Alik whispers. "Luiza never did. And you," he looks over at me, "well, you were just a kid, too. It isn't the same."

"It isn't." I agree.

I'd believed Luiza loved me like a daughter, that I'd found a new home by her side, but it was no home and she was no mother. Alik had been my only bulwark, but we were children trapped in the same sort of misery, taking care of one another as best we could because no one else would.

Bitterness warps through my chest as I stare down at the dull, crumbled earth of Ivan's grave. What is the point of all this power if I can do nothing to protect the people I love? I can do nothing to help Alik. Words feel useless, and there is no magic I can perform that will mend the slivers of Alik's soul.

I take his hand and, when he doesn't resist, I pull him closer to me, wrapping my arms around his middle. With a second's hesitation, he pulls me tight to his chest, burying his head into my hair. He inhales once before letting it out in a shudder, the edges of his breath ragged. I curl my fingers into the fabric of his coat, hoping it conveys everything I wish I could say. That I'm sorry, that I wish I could fix it, that he didn't deserve to hurt so badly.

"Why doesn't it ever stop?" he whispers into my hair. "Why is it always hiding or running or dying?"

"I don't know. But we are ending it," I say, holding his unwavering stare. "I will kill them all if I have to. Strana will no longer suffer. Not while there is something I can do."

FOUR

TWO DAYS LATER, THE SKY hangs a hazy black as snow tumbles down in fat flakes to land on my nose. Laughter and chatter spill from the small sliver between the doors of the village hall, yet I stall on the steps. The gathering had been my idea, but now that I'm here, doubt creeps into my mind like an unruly bramble.

I let out a sigh and smooth the front of the deep-blue sarafan Matta brought me earlier in the day. She'd tailored some of her old clothes to fit, so I would look the part of the Ludminkan girl I claimed to be. Already the woolen skirt beneath the sarafan makes sweat gather behind my knees. Or maybe it is nerves. I try to take comfort in the delicate stitching on the bust of the sarafan, a crimson clover, but all it does is remind me this is no longer my world. I haven't worn clothing like this since I ran from Ludminka, instead wearing the tunic and trousers Luiza preferred.

You aren't alone. Kosci's voice rings unbidden from the back of my mind. I let my hand brush along the curve of the pendant and release a long breath. With Kosci's help, I pushed Matvei back from Knnot and destroyed the Storm Hounds threatening Ludminka. If I can do that, I can speak to a group of people.

Before I lose my nerve, I fling the door open and step into the glowing yellow light of the hall. It's not much more than a wide floor with a raised platform at the opposite end, a pitched ceiling arching high overhead with iron chandeliers clinging to exposed beams. The babble slowly dies as the crowd realizes I'm trudging toward the stage. Parents pull their children toward them, clasping their hands around their chests as if I might swoop in and devour them if given half the chance.

They fall completely silent as I hike up the small set of steps and turn to them. My tongue dries as I consider their upturned, tense faces. They expect answers and leadership, but all I've done for the past ten years is follow orders given by Luiza. How do I go from follower to leader? I scan the crowd for my family, almost as if they will have the answer for me. They stand toward the center, just as curious as everyone else.

Give them what they need, Kosci whispers, pulling me away from my spiraling thoughts and into the present. *Let them remember a time before the world fell apart. Once they remember, they will fight. They will want to reclaim what they've lost.*

His voice seeps away, leaving me alone with the crowd. Heat beats down on me from the chandeliers above, and when I open my mouth, the words catch, stuck in the desert of my throat. I wet my lips before trying again.

"I know none of what you've learned has been easy. You have doubts." In the silence, my voice sounds like a storm. "The world is darker than the one you remember, full of danger and fear. I wish I could shield you from the things that are coming for Ludminka, but we are the only thing that stands between Ladislaw and Knnot."

This isn't what I would call hopeful, Kosci says, a wash of agitation itching over my skin. I bat him from my mind. Candied words won't force them to fight.

"I asked you all here tonight to remember the times before the freeze, yes. But I also ask that you take up arms against Ladislaw so we can have one hundred more nights just like this. We can't leave our families to rot in the Czar's prisons, and we can't let Ladislaw harm us again. So please, I ask, who will join me in ridding Strana of Ladislaw once and for all?"

Gregori lets out a cheer, raising a fist over his head, but no one answers it. He looks around before slowly lowering his hand, pausing only to give me a small, apologetic shrug. I swallow down the flush creeping up my neck.

"No one is willing?" I ask.

"We have no weapons," a man says.

"We have no armor or stamina. The Czar's army would cut us down," another woman says.

"You don't even have a plan," another voice calls.

I hide a wince as I scramble to placate them.

"We have all the lovite we could ever want and we can forge armor and weapons with it. We can scout and make a tactical decision on how to proceed," I say, but the vigor leaks from my voice with each word. I'm a girl begging to be heard, not a general commanding an army.

People shake their heads and turn to one another, new conversations already beginning that had nothing to do with Ladislaw or the battle I know is coming. The urge to scream nettles through my chest. I *need* them to listen or Ladislaw will kill us, no matter how much power I have. A hard knot sticks in my throat as the crowd begins to disperse, moving toward the tables laden with food along the back of the hall. My family lingers, trading glances before I motion for them to join the rest.

My cheeks burn hot as I descend the stage, keeping my head low. I've failed. And what's worse, they're right. I don't have a plan. I don't even know how to wield the power granted to me.

The pressure of the world returns, squashing me like a bug beneath a boot. There's no way I can do this alone. I know nothing of tactics or warfare. How was I to lead an army when I'm not sure how to train one?

Do you not have someone in your party who knows exactly those things? Kosci says.

My eyes spring open and I scan the crowd. Chinua and Sera stand near the back corner of the hall, half hidden in shadow. They turn toward me as I approach, Chinua open and warm, Sera full of a cool indifference.

"I need your help," I say, my gaze cutting to Sera.

"Just realizing that now?" Sera asks, raising a brow. Chinua elbows her in the ribs.

"Stop," she says. "Why would you need us?"

I glare at Sera like it will make my embarrassment disappear.

"We know the Czar won't ignore us for long. He wants Knnot, and Matvei wants to kill me. If we don't do something soon, it will be a slaughter, but I know nothing of war. My life has always been knives in the dark and traded secrets. That's why I've come to you." I turn to Chinua. "Your parents are tacticians for the Khan, right?"

Chinua blinks several times before nodding. "Yes, but they're trapped in Adaman. I've no way to reach them."

"I don't need them when I have you," I say.

Chinua's brows rise. "Me?"

"You're their daughter. Surely you learned things from them."

"Yes," she says slowly. "But I'm no general. I can't help with arming or training these people. Not to mention I'll need to know everything from numbers to geography if you want me to do anything truly useful."

I let out a long breath, looking to Sera. "And that's why I need you. You know Strana better than anyone. You spent years crossing it as a navigator, right?"

Sera nods, her brow furrowed.

"Together, the three of us have the skills needed to cobble together a revolution," I say, words running together as pieces of a plan begin to take shape. When Chinua and Sera remain silent, I reach for both of their hands, holding them tight. "Please."

They exchange a glance before Sera slowly smirks.

"I see you've learned how to swallow some pride."

I let her hand flop back to her side. "Does that mean you'll help?"

Chinua laces her fingers through mine and gives me a firm nod. "Of course we will, Valeria."

Relief tumbles over me in a palpable wave as I toss my arms over Chinua and squeeze her tight.

"Please don't do that to me," Sera says with a sniff.

I laugh, turning to do just that when a piercing scream echoes through the hall. Instantly the chatter dies, everyone looking for the source. A loud clang echoes off the doors, and my eyes snap to them just as the wood bows forward, as if hit by something. I shove my way toward the doors, ignoring the protesting and shuffling of those I pass. The doors remain latched tight, but a buzz flutters along my senses, setting every one alight.

The doors release another bang and a long crack splits the wood, sending shards in every direction. Wind whistles through the new opening, sputtering candles and casting the hall into semidarkness. I peer into the night with my breath held, searching. Flakes of snow tumble in from outside, melting as soon as they touch the floor. A flash of gold catches in the remaining light, bright brass buttons appearing in a sea of black. My heart clenches hard and fast.

Storm Hounds.

"Everyone back," I yell, but the people around me either don't hear or are too stunned to move.

Another crack rings out and the doors fly open, Storm Hounds spill into the hall with shields raised as if they expect a volley of arrows. My breath gets stuck somewhere between my lungs and mouth as vivid images of their uniforms circling us outside Knnot, of one of them releasing the bolt that sank deep into Alik's heart, slice through my mind. This is my fault. If I hadn't let two Storm Hounds run out of the village, or let Matvei escape after our battle, they wouldn't be here now.

A hard beat of power rolls through my body, and Kosci's strength surges into my muscles. I am not the weak, helpless girl I was in Knnot.

"Stop at once, or I will personally make sure you regret it." My voice reverberates off the walls, louder than even the solid clink of Storm Hound boots across the floor.

Some of the Storm Hounds stumble to a halt, their blades half raised as if surprised someone would dare command them. A broad-chested man with a long beard pushes his way forward, his lips curling into a sneer as he rips a girl from the crowd by her hair, resting his blade against the pale flesh of her neck.

"I don't think you're in a position to demand anything," the Storm Hound says. "We are under orders to take this village. If anyone stands in our way, we are to slaughter them, so why don't you stand down before you hurt yourself."

The smug smile, his hands so steady on the blade, so sure I will cave like every other person before me, all of it draws a pool of rage so vast and deep even I don't know how far it goes. I put my hand to where my throwing daggers typically rest but come up empty. I'd stopped wearing the belt Luiza gave me sometime in the mountain.

When I don't retaliate, the captain nods curtly and the Storm Hounds snap their blades out in bright arcs of gleaming silver, catching waists and arms. Screams echo around me, swallowing me with their desperation. These are my villagers. I won't have them taken from me. Not when I just freed them.

My vision wavers as Kosci answers my unasked cries for help. I blink as the world goes black before the room comes back into focus. The hall is nothing but dusky outlines, white orbs of light blooming inside the shadowed figures. Some beat rabbit quick, while others slowly dim as blood pools around cooling corpses. My stomach lurches hard as I realize they are heartbeats. I search for the Storm Hounds in the chaos. Their hearts manifest as muted grays, the thumps slow with surety, like they've destroyed countless towns before.

They probably have.

That single thought breaks whatever reservation I have. If they want to kill, I will more than happily answer.

I pull at the loose threads of Kosci's power, fumbling along the strange strands of light emanating from inside the Storm Hound's bodies. One by one, I take hold of the strings until every single one is gathered in my hand.

Then I squeeze.

There are no gasps. No cries of pain. Their lights simply blink out. Heavy thuds slam to the floor one after the other. Silence follows, long and deep. The strange film covering my eyes lifts and the world spins around me, too bright for a moment before returning to stark clarity. People who had just been in Storm Hound hands stare down at their bodies with shock. I scan the floor, finding more Ludminkans than I want. Even more bodies to bury, more Storm Hounds to burn. I'm not as exhausted as the first time I used Kosci's power, but life leaks from my very fingertips. I take a deep breath as all eyes shift to me. They want words, but what sort, I don't know. Nothing will make this right.

Nothing but revenge.

"This," I say, but my voice is hoarse. I clear my throat. "This is what the Czar does. He captures and kills like we are nothing but prey to him. He gathers up our families and leaves them to fester in prisons across Strana. I refuse to let this continue. We deserve more than to cower in our homes, praying one day things will get better. I will ruin the Czar for what he has done. I won't let Zladonians suffer any longer."

No one speaks as I force myself to take steps toward the fallen Zladonians who were unlucky enough to stand beside the door. I kneel in congealing blood, closing the eyes of an old woman, rage and guilt twining around themselves in my heart until they are nearly indistinguishable. If only I'd acted sooner, this woman would still be alive. I stand, my legs shaky, and turn toward the crowd.

"The Czar will never let us rest. He's already painted Zladonians as the people to blame for the fall of our nation. Stranans won't so much as blink an eye if he destroys all of Ludminka this time. Especially not now that he has the Bright God's champion by his side. It will seem like a divine right." I curl my fingers into a fist as strangled gasps echo around the hall. "I know you aren't skilled warriors, but you can fight this. *We* can fight this. If we do not, Ladislaw will sweep over our town like a flood, killing and maiming where he sees fit. That is why I ask you now to take up arms and protect your home. If we don't fight, Ladislaw will kill us. Of that, I have no doubt. Together, we stand a chance at freedom. What say you? Will you fight beside me?"

Do not let them doubt your power this time, Kosci whispers. *Show them, woo them, give them no choice but to believe.*

Closing my eyes, I whisper to Kosci, giving him pictures of ice, jagged and sharp, a row of teeth to circle the village in an unbreakable wall. I show him the sheen of it in the sun, the way the tips will tilt toward the sky like blades ready for the war I know is coming. He gives an answering nudge, and I kneel once more, placing my palm to the old boards, warped and knotted by age.

The candles in the room flutter and a thrum resounds through the hall, so loud the ground begins to tremble. Shouts ring out, but I smile.

It always pays to have a bit of showmanship, Kosci whispers.

A sharp crack rends the air. People clutch their partners as the ground rolls. Chairs and cups clatter to the floor and still I push more power into the earth, forcing large blades through the frozen ground. A wave of dizziness rolls over me and my body tumbles backward, but instead of hitting the ground, icy air kisses my cheeks.

I blink and find myself staring down at Ludminka. Tiny candles flicker in windows, almost like stars in the blanket of night. I hover above it all, watching as great shards of ice burst forth from the dirt. Showers of dirty snow and gravel cascade to the ground as each new blade forces its way up.

Power oozes from my body, bleeding into the ground and

leaching away my strength, but I don't stop. I raise shard upon shard into the air until a wide circle of jagged teeth wraps around Ludminka, just as unbreakable as the ice that covered it ten years ago.

I crash back down into my body, wobbling slightly before someone catches my arm. I follow the line of the arm, surprised to find Alik at the other end. His mouth is taut, but he holds me steady as I rise and face the waiting crowd. The candles flicker back to life slowly, as if prompted by my movement.

"Now," I wheeze, "we have defenses."

FIVE

PEOPLE STAMPEDE PAST ME AND their fearful, awe-struck shouts echo through the night as they spot our new defenses. I don't need to see their faces to know I've succeeded.

My power is undeniable.

Fine work, I think to Kosci.

That was you. I just gave you the ability to do it, he says. *I am but the ember to your flame. I feed you the power, but you mold it to your will.*

"Me?" I whisper aloud. Exhaustion clouds my eyes as the shattered doors bang in the wind.

"You okay?" Alik asks, bracing my elbow as I lean danger-ously to the side.

I barely manage a nod. "Just tired."

His brows furrow, and I know he's trying to figure out how

Kosci and I work together. I wish I had an answer for him. He doesn't speak as he helps me to my feet, catching me as my legs buckle.

"Let's get you back to the house," he says.

We slip away unnoticed through the crowd, Alik taking most of my weight. We've done this so many times it almost feels like we could be back in Rurik, slinking through streets to return to Luiza after a mission gone wrong. My entire body aches as I stumble along. At last, the tiny house we claimed as our own comes into view and my body sags with relief.

We stagger across the threshold, and Alik unlaces my boots and slips them off. He slings my arm over his shoulder once again, leading me to the soft fabric chair beside the oven and covers my legs in a thick knitted blanket. My head falls hard against the back and tension leaks down my neck as I close my eyes.

"This is just like last time," he says softly.

I open a single eye to find him fiddling with the samovar. "That's not true. I'm conscious this time."

Alik doesn't smile. "This isn't much of an improvement. You should see yourself, Val. The color leeched from your cheeks and lips. You look like a corpse." He looks up at me. "Will it always be like this?"

"I don't know," I say. "I really don't."

Alik frowns and returns to making tea, movements rigid. The warmth of the fire loosens my tightened muscles and lures me into the comfortable embrace of unconsciousness. I almost think I'm dreaming when a warm hand brushes my face. I blink, fully awake and Alik drops his hand to press a mug of tea into my palms.

Silence and tension stretch between us as his eye trails across my face, lingering on the pendant at my neck, before going to my trembling fingers around the mug. My very bones ache, pulsing with the beat of my heart, and it takes everything in me to lift the cup and inhale. The sharp scents of clove and cinnamon reach my nose and a sigh falls from my lips. "My favorite. You remembered."

"Of course I did." Alik runs a hand through his hair before straightening again, like he can't bear to stand still. "I don't like this, Val. You can barely hold on to your tea. You can't keep doing this to yourself."

I take a sip of the scalding liquid, willing it to warm the ice that seems to have settled into my veins.

"I couldn't even if I wanted to, and I think you know that."

"That's the worst thing of it all," he shoots back, shoving his hair away from his face again. "I wish you'd never taken that deal."

Bitter fury rolls from his body in waves, and I tighten my hold on the mug, narrowing my eyes. "You can't mean that."

"I do," he says vehemently.

I surge from the chair despite my aching body, ignoring the wave of darkness hovering at the edges of my vision.

"Don't you dare say that," I spit. "If I hadn't, you would be *dead* right now. All of us would be. You expected me to watch that happen?"

Alik's jaw tightens, but he keeps his mouth closed. My body slumps as my shoulders fold in on themselves, anger leaking away as a pang begins in the back of my throat. My breath hitches as I gesture helplessly.

"I watched you die, Alik. Do you have any idea what that's like?" I shake my head. "I wanted the strength to ruin this world for what it did to me. I will not regret that decision. I watched you die once and did nothing and *hated* myself for it, just like I did for surviving the freeze. I couldn't do it again. I wouldn't."

He collapses onto the stone ledge of the hearth, cradling his head in his hands. I sink beside him slowly, giving him the opportunity to move if he wants to. His leg bounces rapidly, and I place my hand on his knee to still it.

"In all of Strana's history, there have only been a handful of times there has been a Bright and Pale champion at the same time," he says into his hands. "And every time, they go to war. It will extend across the country and you will be at the helm. That can't be what you wanted. My life isn't worth a war."

When I remain silent, he raises his head to search my face, his own open and perfect in the flickering firelight.

"Oh," he whispers. "It *is* what you wanted."

Warmth sweeps across my cheeks as shame settles into my

gut. I force my eyes to the fire, refusing to give in to the feeling.

"Strana has suffered long enough under Ladislaw. Do you think it will get any better with Matvei by his side? How many others have stories like ours, Alik? How many others have watched the life leak from those they love and been helpless to stop it? This is bigger than us. It always has been." I look back to Alik. "I can't keep watching it happen."

"But did it have to be you?" His voice cracks, rough and ragged, over the words.

I give him a helpless shrug. "There was no one else."

He kneels before me, taking the mug and putting it to the side before collecting my hands into his and holding them tight. His eye darts across my face, and the overwhelming urge to bring my lips to his consumes my mind. Slowly, he rests his forehead against mine, releasing an exhale that tickles along my lips.

"I don't want to lose you, Valeria," he says quietly. "I would sacrifice myself a thousand times over if it meant keeping you alive. It's the choice I made a year ago, and it's a choice I will make again. This world means nothing to me if you aren't in it."

I swallow hard and slip a hand from his, placing it on his cheek.

The heat of his body chases away the horrible memories of his cold corpse, the feeling of blood hot and sticky between my fingers. He is alive and whole and here because of the deal I struck.

"I feel the same way," I say, painfully aware of the scant inches between us. "I did this to protect the people I love. To protect you. You won't lose me. I promise."

"That isn't a promise you can keep," he whispers, our bodies already leaning toward each other.

I don't want to remember him dying anymore. I want to remember him how he is now, alive and wholly mine. I close the last inch between us and gently let my lips brush his. He releases a soft sigh before pulling me closer.

Our lips meet again, this time hungrier. A cool fire builds in my chest and ripples through my arms as my fingers tighten their hold on the back of his neck. His lips sear along mine as his hand cups my face. I open my mouth to his, wanting more and not sure I can have enough. He gives me a single, deep kiss that warms me all the way to my toes before he leans back onto his heels, never releasing my hand.

"For you, I will fight," he says, brushing stray hair behind my ear. "For us."

I exhale as relief washes along my body. Until this very moment, I hadn't realized how afraid I was that I'd chosen a path Alik wouldn't follow. He has always favored careful strategy and a few well-placed pieces of evidence over open battle, but we couldn't think our way out of the mess of the world.

Carefully, I slip down to the floor beside Alik, twining my arm and his and resting my head on his shoulder. "For us."

★ ★ ★

The following day I find myself back within the village hall. Gone is the cheery warmth of the night before, replaced by people on their knees, watery blood frothing beneath their fervent scrubbing. Seven bodies in total lie against the far wall, tightly wrapped in clean linens awaiting burial. No doubt their families had traveled to the cairn piles on the outskirts of town that Ludminka has always used as a grave site. A raw ache opens in the pit of my stomach as I study each one, forcing myself to remember what my hesitation cost.

A warm hand slips onto my shoulder, startling me from thought. My mother stands beside me, her face unreadable, hair impeccably braided around her head as always. I ache to divulge the hurt festering inside my body for the harm I'd caused. Or the roaring fury that demands I answer the wrongs committed. I remain silent, unable to put meaning to the jumble of words stuck in my throat. I don't know how to. She isn't Luiza, who would've wanted a brisk, efficient report without a drop of emotion. But she also isn't someone I really know anymore.

"This isn't your fault," she says. I glance over, surprised by her voice. Her hand slips around mine, just like it used to in dark, thunder-filled nights. "None of this is."

"But if I'd—"

"No buts, Valeria. You didn't make those men violent. You didn't command them to kill innocents. This was the Czar's doing. We all think so," she says with a nod around the hall. "We've no doubt that you tell the truth. Nothing could've made it clearer. We are ready to do what is necessary to keep our home safe."

Again, that horrible, weighty mantle returns to my shoulders. I'd wanted a war. I'd declared it to Alik just last night, but looking down at the blood-soaked linens around the corpses, the true cost of it unfolds before me. There will only be more shrouded bodies, more grieving families in the hills.

There isn't a war in history that's been won without casualties, Kosci's thought whispers through my mind. *I've seen the game played hundreds of different times over a thousand years, and no matter what I do, they suffer. Through it all I've learned it is better to die on your feet than in the mud. I cannot see another loss. I will not survive it.*

I more than hear Kosci's words, I *feel* his pain. So sharp and real I'm almost not sure if it's my own. The Pale God is said to devour the suffering of the world, to take it from mortal shoulders and burden himself instead. It's what the Vestry always taught, and I never fully believed them.

Try as he might, Kosci can't hide every memory of his from me. Just as I can't from him. I see flashes of war, gruesome and bloody, of famine and gaunt children. Kosci could take their suffering, but he was helpless to stop it. He watched it all, only able to reach them at the end. I don't know how he didn't go mad.

Who says I didn't? he whispers.

His words chill me further, and I focus on my mother's hand in mine. It's the only relief I allow before I force myself back into the champion I must be.

"I wish there were another way," I say. "But I will not lead Zladonians into a war they can't win. We will end Ladislaw's rule. Together."

Matta gives my hand a squeeze before releasing it. "Your brothers and father are already going door to door asking for volunteers. By nightfall, you should have the beginnings of an army. With any luck, next time we will be ready."

Next time.

Those two words slam one after the other into my soul. Because there *will* be a next time, no matter if I build warriors or comfort grieving villagers. Ladislaw wants Knnot. He always has. Between him, Matvei, and Luiza, Ladislaw will get what he wants eventually. Right now, only I stand between the Czar and his lust for control of Iovite. And in the end, there will be bloodshed, no matter the path I take. Just as Kosci said, I would rather die defending what I love. I have to hope Ludminka feels the same.

SIX

A DAY LATER, I FIND myself on a high bluff just outside
Ludminka, the village sprawling beneath in a patchwork of
brightly painted houses and woodsmoke. Sweat pours down
my back even as wind howls through the trees, tugging bits
of snow from their branches. They pelt my face, promising yet
another winter storm, but still I stand, forcing myself to concentrate on Kosci's voice.

Again.

I open my palm and imagine threads of magic twisting
down my arm, coalescing at my fingertips to form a long
sword. It is like yanking on a stuck rope, but slowly, crystal
after crystal grows on top of one another, forming a shimmering blade of translucent ice. I slice it through the air and smile
as a high-pitched whine rings out.

Good, Kosci says. *Now imagine something bigger. Truly grasp the threads swimming through your body and follow them out into the world. Strands of magic dance around you even now, waiting to be manipulated by your hands. Stop hesitating and open yourself to my power.*

Since the attack on Ludminka, all I have done is work on the bluff with only Kosci's voice in my mind. With each hour I practice, the toll magic takes on my body leaks away, as if it is a muscle I only have to exercise. The exhaustion that clung to me after I'd first accepted Kosci's deal has ebbed, leaving behind only a dull exhaustion.

I release a long exhale as I attempt to do as Kosci says. I can barely make out the curls of magic worming their way out of Kosci's pendant and into my chest.

I push past the discomfort and follow the lines working through my body down to my fingertips. I lift my free hand and imagine a tornado of snow forming before me. My body thrums with the idea, and the ice-crusted snow begins to sprinkle up, as if it is snowing in reverse. The particles swirl in the air, attempting to form my thought.

Kosci's heart begins to vibrate, sending tremors down my body and into my head. Instantly, the sword melts and the swirling snow flutters to the ground. Hot annoyance not my own flickers through me as the magic recedes.

Why do you still fight it? Kosci's voice cuts cold.

"I am *trying,*" I say. "I don't know how much more you

expect of me. I've already given you the use of my soul, and you sit in my mind every time I put on this necklace. It's not like I can turn into a god."

I kick at the tree stump before me, dully aware of the pain through my boot.

Allow me to rephrase. You have to trust me. You clearly don't, even if you won't admit it. I can sense it in your mind. If you fight every time I give you power, you will never be more than a host. I can't control you all the time.

"You can't just tell me to trust you and have it be done," I snap. "Trust is built, not demanded."

What more can I possibly do? I brought your boy back from the dead, slayed Storm Hounds, and freed your village. Is that not enough?

"You did those things for yourself," I say through gritted teeth. "You wanted to give me a taste of magic and show me what we could do together to ensure I would hold up my end of the bargain."

I brought the boy back for you. I assure you, it would've been much easier for me if he'd stayed dead, Kosci says flatly. *And you cannot make good on your promise if you are dead.*

The crunch of footsteps yanks me away from Kosci's words. My hand goes for the pendant even though I know I don't need to grasp it to use Kosci's power. The cold of it bites hard against my fingers, but I relish the feeling, as if it is a reminder of what we can do. Instead of the nameless threat my mind had conjured, Alik stands a few paces away, brow raised.

"Why are you always wearing that thing?" he asks.

I stare down at it, taking the small, veined piece of lovite into the palm of my hand. The clusters of blue twisting through the milky white of the stone pulse softly, beating in time with my own heart.

"This is his heart," I say, angling my hands so he can see. "I have to be wearing it to access his power. I'm helpless without it."

Alik shuffles closer, peering down at the stone like it might explode at any moment. The soft blue beat of light illuminates the angles of his face, catching on the edges of his scar. He closes my fist over it.

"You should take it off," he says. "You won't need it to meet the militia."

I tighten my hold on Kosci's heart. "You have no way of knowing if that is true, or when we will be attacked again. I need to be ready."

"Val, you've made Ludminka a fortress. I don't think there is a soul in Strana who could break through those walls."

"Matvei could," I say. Alik stills at my words. "We both know he is coming. Even if he weren't Ladislaw's hound, he would track me down and destroy me anyway. I am a Pale champion and a threat to his power. You said it yourself. When there are dual champions, the world goes to war."

"Don't you have a way of knowing if Matvei is nearby?"

I open my mind to Kosci despite desperately wishing I

didn't need him. He ignores the feeling, his voice taking on a lofty air.

I do not. The Bright God Zoltoy, he grinds out the name like it is a sin to say, *has always had a way of hiding himself from me. We are veiled from one another, weaker when we are apart. I will not know where Zoltoy is until he is within striking distance.*

I blink away Kosci's words to find Alik evaluating me. "What did he say?"

"How did you know I was talking to him?" I ask.

"Your face goes slack, and your eyes don't focus on anything," Alik says.

I tuck the information away for later. I can't make it obvious when I am listening to Kosci. It leaves me too vulnerable to attack.

"He says he has no way of knowing when his brother is nearby. Some facet of his magic keeps Kosci blind to his whereabouts."

"He seems so useful," Alik says sarcastically.

And he seems insincere.

I push Kosci away and slip my hands into my pockets. "I assume you came up here for a reason?"

"The villagers are ready for you. I've come to take you to the training grounds." He gestures back the way he came. "It isn't much, but Chinua did what she could."

Moments later, I stand behind a straggling crowd, Alik and Sera at my back. They line up unevenly before piles of salvaged

Storm Hound armor and weaponry.

I scan the volunteers slowly. They span all ages and genders, some as young as I am, but all share the same grim determination on their faces. My father stands before the crowd, a withered old man hovering over his left shoulder. He catches my eye and nods once before he begins.

"The goal of sword fighting is to deal a killing blow without taking one. Sounds simple enough, but the true task is far from easy." My father looks at the crowd, mouth flattening at what he finds. "We will start with the proper grip."

Kosci lets out a long sigh as the old man hobbles down to begin correcting forms, moving each foot into position almost painfully slow. He wears the frayed uniform of a Knnot militia officer, a post made necessary by the numerous raids Knnot suffered each year.

Why are we doing this again? he asks, annoyed.

They need to learn how to fight, and this is the only way. I only know throwing knives and daggers. My father was on the patrol route for Knnot more often than not.

That's not what I mean. Why bother teaching them at all? he whispers. Flashes of the villagers breaking free of the ice completely wrapped in my power enter my mind, hacking and slashing at everybody they come into contact with. *It would be as simple as that.*

I recoil and consider ripping the pendant from my neck.

I will not remove their will.

Why waste time training mediocre soldiers when I could grant you the ability to control them all at once?

I refuse to turn them into thralls whenever I need an army, Kosci. This country will not be won by more choking control. We need their hearts and their minds and their determination to free the people they love. I won't have you meddling and controlling them.

Fine. He huffs. *At least allow me to give them memories of learning the basics. Just help this dolt correct their stances with a touch and I'll be able to lend them this boon.*

I roll my eyes. *You are truly magnanimous.*

I know that was sarcasm. He sends a strange flick through my body, almost as if I missed a step at the bottom of a staircase. I suppress a sigh as I make my way to the first person in line, a spry woman with a long braid down her back.

Gently, I adjust her back leg and her arm. A cool, numbing wave courses down my fingers and drips into the woman's arm. She shifts into the correct stance as if she'd spent years doing it, oblivious to the fact she didn't know how to a moment before. One by one, I correct every person in the crowd, each drop of power siphoning my strength. By the time I reach the boy at the end who can't be more than fourteen, my arms are sluggish and slow.

There, Kosci whispers. *Your army.*

That *was sarcasm,* I shoot back.

A wave of agitation courses down my spine, and I lift trembling fingers to my neck, removing the pendant and sticking it deep into the pouch at my hip. I refuse to argue in my own mind.

I wobble back to my spot behind the crowd as my father begins the process of running them through their strikes. Both Sera and Alik look over at me as I take up post between them.

"All right?" Alik asks.

I nod, not trusting my voice.

"You look like you've been drained of blood," Sera says flatly. "I wouldn't call that okay."

"What did you do?" Alik asks.

"Kosci gave them memories of the basics so we wouldn't fumble while the Czar gathers his army."

"Smart," Sera says.

At the same time Alik says, "Really?"

I can't understand the tone in his voice, and my tired brain doesn't want to make the effort to unravel it.

"Can we just go back to the house? I don't want anyone to see me like this," I say.

They nod, neither one asking why I felt the need to hide. They know as well as I do that a leader can only be seen as capable. I must be strong, unbreakable, determined. The village doubted me once. I can't afford to have that happen again.

Exhaustion tugs at me by the time we reach the cabin and I fumble through the doorway. Alik catches my elbow as I sag on the first step, aiding me the rest of the way up to the bedroom I'd claimed as my own.

"Tell me truthfully. Are you okay?" he asks as we reach the door to my room.

I do my best to give him a smile.

"Yes, of course."

"You're not in front of the crowd now. You don't have to pretend," he says quietly as he opens the door for me.

My heart gives a strange double beat as heat pricks at my eyes. I collapse onto the foot of my bed and press my head into my hands to stop tears from falling.

"Just . . . tired," I say at last.

Alik lets out a soft hum above me, but I can't force myself to look up. Gently, he trails fingers along my shoulder before pulling away one of my hands. He cocks his head slightly as our eyes meet.

"Why are you trying to do this alone?" he says. "I'm here for you. So are Chinua and Sera. Don't shut us all out. Wars aren't won by a single person."

I take a shuddering inhale. "I know."

"Do you?" he asks softly.

I let him gather me against his shoulder. I press into his familiar smell and hate that I can't do this alone. I'm not just risking my life anymore. It's everyone, all those faces I trained one by one today; my father, my brothers, and I'll only add more.

While I don't like the idea of bringing more people into the fold to die, I also can't stand the thought of them languishing any longer in the Czar's prisons. The soft curl of anger heats my gut at the thought of Ladislaw's cruel face as he forced children into the *tyur'ma* in Oleg.

I grasp the burn of my anger and hold it hard. This is what I need. To remember why I started, why I accepted Kosci's deal. Ladislaw killed and imprisoned Zladonians after the freeze ten years ago. He deserves the weight and heat of my fury. All I have to do is fan the flames and let it armor me as it always has. I steady my breathing and pull away from Alik.

His face wrinkles slightly, but he makes no move to hug me again. The slow circles my mind had been making come to a standstill. I feel adrift because I am. I have no idea what Ladislaw is planning or where Matvei and Luiza are. The three of them together are a nearly unstoppable force. I can make ready an army, but it will do no good without a plan. And to make a plan, we need information.

"I need you to do something for me," I say.

"Anything," he says.

"You were one of the best in the guild at getting information. We need it if we hope to best Ladislaw at his own game. I need numbers, locations, missives with orders to march, and anything about the *tyur'mas* you can find, all information on Matvei. Everything."

"How do you expect me to do that?" he asks, raising a brow.

"I don't know," I answer honestly. "That's why I gave the

task to you. Luiza never favored me for information gathering, and when we became a pair, it was always you. Can you do it? Please?"

His face softens, and he brushes the side of my cheek with the back of his hand. "Of course."

SEVEN

THREE WEEKS BLEED BY IN a blur of weapons training, organizing food stores, and a slow start of a strategy. A
surprising amount of food and iron had been saved during the
freeze, easing my fears of taking care of Ludminka during the
deep cold of winter. Once the snowstorms come, we won't
have a chance to requisition more.

Well, that isn't completely true. There is always Kosci.

His power is boundless, limited only by my ability to wield
it. Every day, I head to the top of the hill above Ludminka
and force myself to use Kosci's power. I craft the ice blade, and
throw ice daggers, but anything more than that and it trickles
away like water. It only makes the idea that I am not meant to
lead grow from a seed to a sapling. The only good thing about
my constant training is that each day my body grows stronger.

Kosci's power taxes me less and less until I hardly feel the pull of it all. It should prompt some pride, but all it does is make me realize all the potential I am wasting.

It wouldn't be a waste if you'd stop being afraid of what you can do, Kosci hisses. *You wanted this power. You wanted to ravage this land and set fire to any who stood in your way. What happened to that girl?*

"She realized the weight of war," I say.

Despite my words, his thoughts rankle me. What *had* happened to that girl? The one so determined to march to Rurik and slit the Czar's throat? I need her. She is the me I want to be, the one who took what she wanted and didn't think of the consequences because she knew what was right. I've done nothing but doubt myself, and it bleeds into every single aspect of my life.

I see the workings of your mind, Valeria. I am not blind to your guilt, your exhaustion, your suffering. I share it with you. This world is not kind to those who seek to change it. Reformation is a violent act in and of itself, whether over hundreds of years or the slip of a millisecond, whether by nature or by mortal hands. You are the change Strana needs. Think of those who suffer in Ladislaw's prisons. Would you leave them there?

You know I will not.

Then you know your mind, even if it doesn't please you. Your determination to seek vengeance on Ladislaw for all he has done has never wavered, even in your uncertainty of yourself. Kosci's voice takes on an almost delicate tone. *There will be a cost, yes. But the reward . . . it will be more than the weight of lives lost. You will be free.*

You speak as if you know the burden of confinement, I think back bitterly.

Don't I? I languished within Knnot for centuries, watching as people chipped away at my bones, helpless to stop it. With each nugget mined, I grew weaker, only capable of feeling the growing strength of my brother as I waned. When you accepted my deal and I was released from the cavern where Zoltoy imprisoned me, it was as if I were breathing for the first time. No one deserves that fate.

I stare up at the stony sky swirling high above, considering Kosci's words. There has been precious little sun since I released Ludminka, the town always swathed in the dim gray of snowy clouds. He is right. No one deserves to wither away locked from sunlight and air. I owe it to Ludminka, to all the Zladonians, to release them from Ladislaw's grasp. No matter the cost.

Why do you hate each other so much? I ask. My reasons for hunting down Ladislaw and Matvei are translucent, but I have never understood Kosci's. This was a mortal problem, something below the notice of a god.

The suffering of mortals has always been my concern, Kosci says. *It was the task I chose when Zoltoy and I fell to earth. It seemed righteous then. Mortals had done nothing but fight and die to survive. And while my brother thought they needed warmth and light, I thought they needed the burden of their lives removed. At first, our tasks were balanced. We were both admired for what we could do, and we basked in their reverence. That's how we get our power, you know. The more prayers whispered to us, the more belief poured into our names, the more we are able to do. Zoltoy grew jealous when my power grew larger than his. We were supposed to be equals, brothers in all things, but the mortals valued what I could do above what he could.*

This started your war? I ask.

No. Jealousy brewed in Zoltoy's chest, while pride grew in mine. I liked being considered better than my brother. I liked the attention and wanted to keep it. It wasn't until Zoltoy started whispering his rumors that I paid any mind to what he was doing. He told mortals I caused them to suffer, that I was the one who created famines and wars so I could grow fat from their heartbreak. It wasn't true, but he had sowed enough doubt for them to believe. I was the first to attack, furious he would take mortals from me to satisfy his ego.

But Zoltoy had grown stronger by then, his rumors whittling away at the prayers said to me without my notice. I couldn't tell you how long our personal war raged, but in the end, he was the one who succeeded. Kosci releases a wistful sigh. *Apart, as we are now, we are weaker. It was a cruel twist of fate neither of us realized. Zoltoy believes that if he destroys my heart, his full strength will be restored.*

And is that true? I ask, truly curious.

Kosci's voice dulls in my mind for a long moment, leaving only my own jumping thoughts and the slow crawl of cold lacing up my mittenless fingers. They were red and chapped with exposure, but I curled them into a fist, waiting.

Yes, Kosci says at last. *With it he would be unstoppable.*

The information bounces through my core, gaining momentum until my entire body is as taut as a razor wire. I wasn't just a threat to Matvei's and Zoltoy's power, I was a potential source.

Does that mean if I find Zoltoy's heart and destroy it we will be more powerful?

Kosci hesitates a single beat. *Yes.*

A call sounds from behind me and I whip around to find Chinua at the edge of the clearing, wind tugging wisps of black hair from the braid over her shoulder. She raises a hand in greeting.

"Alik said this is where you'd be," she says as she crosses to me. She whistles as she comes to a stop. "Quite the view. I can see why you come up here."

"To look down on my mistakes?" I bite out bitterly before I can stop myself. Not only have I put Ludminka at risk, but it is also pinned under Matvei's gaze. Now that Kosci's heart wanders free around Strana, easily taken from a girl who has minimal control over magic, Matvei could return any second for the thing he wants most. And he would not falter if a paltry village militia stood in his way. Ludminka is in nearly as much danger as I am.

Chinua turns a wide-eyed gaze toward me.

"All I see is a town free of its prison, a boy alive who shouldn't be, and a wall protecting everything you saved."

"And a girl trapped with a god around her neck who has an

impossible war to win." Two impossible wars.

"Not impossible. Highly improbable, but not completely impossible," Chinua says with a grin.

A surprised laugh bubbles from my lips, and Chinua's smile widens. She slings her arms over my shoulders, pulling me into a hug. I lean against her and let the warmth of her skin sink into the icy shell I've buried myself in.

"I've been meaning to thank you myself," she says without letting go. "You promised me I would see the sun again, and here I stand, in the light once more. I truly thought Knnot would swallow me whole. You made sure it didn't."

"I wasn't going to leave you in the dark or let Kosci's monsters devour you. I wouldn't even have let it happen to Sera."

Chinua laughs. "You know, she really isn't that bad once you get to know her. She's all hard shell, but inside she cares. More than you can imagine."

I study the side of Chinua's face as she talks. The corners of her lips turn up, eyes going soft. Something about it is almost vulnerable. I smile.

"You two must've gotten close if you know so much about her."

Chinua stiffens beneath me. "I mean, we talk. We have to. She's the navigator, I'm the tactician. We need to work together. It's just business."

Her words are hurried, slipping into one another like she can't get them out fast enough.

"If you say so," I respond, letting my grin widen. She

wrinkles her nose at me, nudging me in the side.

I stop my teasing as Chinua releases me and her eyes turn back to Ludminka. We study it together, and something akin to peace settles over my body. I've always been in love with the smoke piping out into the cold air, creating plumes of pine-scented clouds. When I was a girl, I would walk up here with my brothers to spy on the town below and build forts of broken timber. It is the smallest sliver of home, and I cling to the memories.

"They love you," Chinua says. My brows knit together but she continues. "They whisper about how you protect us, how you hone your power every day. Many believe you are a miracle worker."

Her words, which I am certain are meant to encourage me, only add to the mounting evidence that I am not just a Ludminkan villager anymore. I am a symbol, a general, a champion, but I am not Valeria. I want to tell her how it makes me feel trapped like a rat without a place to go. That I am both too big for Ludminka and too small for the world.

My words never come.

Alik has been my only friend for so long that I don't know how to be friends with anyone else. Would Chinua laugh if I told her? And I am her champion. I can't show weakness to those I seek to lead. I can't be transparent to her, no matter if I want to or not. Before she can say any more, I change the subject.

"Why were you looking for me?"

"You told us all to find you when Alik got the information you asked for. Well, he got it," Chinua says, lacing her fingers together behind her back.

"Why do you say it like that?" I ask slowly.

"It's best if you see for yourself," she says.

Chinua takes my arm in hers and ushers me down the slow slope of my hill to the back door of our cabin. We leave long tracks in the drifts, and I know it's only a matter of time before all of Ludminka finds a way into the hills to watch me practice magic.

Chinua sneaks me through the small back door, avoiding the large group of people collected around the front gate. They've been coming in larger numbers recently, all of them determined to catch even the smallest glimpse of me, as if I can bring them luck by sight alone.

We slip into the darkened room at the end of the hall and the silence of it sets me on edge. Since we announced the plan to go to war, people have been pounding the door down with something to offer—weapons, food, their skill at sewing, or their ability with herbs and tinctures. It hasn't been truly quiet in weeks.

Chinua slips off her shoes and starts toward the front of the house, drawing all the curtains as she goes. I nod my thanks and follow the soft voices echoing from the kitchen. Alik, Sera, and one I can't quite place. It tickles the edges of my memories, almost familiar with its deep, gravelly timbre and notes of humor.

Chinua and I step into the room and are greeted with a broad frame and a mass of shaggy dark hair. My heart drops to my toes. I summon the ice blade I'd practiced with so many times and raise it to the newcomer's throat.

"What are you doing here?"

EIGHT

THE TEMPERATURE IN THE ROOM drops, sending the kitchen fire to sputtering embers. The boy lifts his head and looks down the blade at me with a raised eyebrow. His high cheekbones and full lips are far too familiar. He was one of Luiza's, the only Adamanian guild member she ever employed. He raises his hands before him as if to signal he has no weapons, even though he must. Luiza would never let him go without.

"And here I thought you *wanted* to see me, Valeria," he says with a small quirk of his mouth. I narrow my eyes.

"I never want to see a single member of the guild again," I say, letting the tip of the blade sink a little farther into his neck. "You can't be trusted."

"Val." Alik steps forward and pushes the sword from the boy's throat. I turn my rigid body toward him, blade poised to slash if the guild member makes a move.

"You asked me to get information, and Bataar brought it," Alik hisses. "He's come to pledge himself to our cause."

"I asked you for intelligence and expected a report, not for you to let a guildling walk right into our base. We have absolutely no way of knowing if his allegiance is true. He could've been sent by Luiza. You know better than to trust anyone loyal to her."

"I would really appreciate it if you stopped talking like I'm not in the room," Bataar says. I raise the sword back to his throat. "I assure you I have absolutely no allegiance to Luiza. Not anymore."

Silence hangs in the air as I wait for him to elaborate. He doesn't.

"Are you going to explain yourself or force me to figure it out on my own?" I ask.

"I'm waiting to see if you're going to kill me," Bataar says, that half smile never falling from his lips. "Since you've yet to lunge, I'll take it you're still making up your mind."

"Your witticisms aren't going to help you," I almost growl the words. "The next time you open your mouth, you better tell the truth."

My words only make him smile wider, but he dips his head in acceptance.

"Luiza has gone absolutely mad. She has everyone doing bizarre missions to gather material for Ladislaw and his army.

We aren't thieves and spies anymore; we're errand runners and cannon fodder. She throws us into battle arenas with untested weapons against Storm Hounds and runs us to exhaustion. When someone complains, she takes a finger for impertinence. When someone questions the Bright champion, she lets him sear a brand into their flesh. We know he wants to destroy all of Zladonia and take back Knnot. I'd rather a zealot and a simpering Czar not rule the country if I can help it."

My chest squeezes hard and fast. Luiza had always been determined to keep the Czar in power. She mastered all information flowing in and out of the capital for years beyond counting. If she has turned the full weight of her devotion to Matvei, there is no telling what she'll be willing to do. I remember too well the fervor in her eyes the night she told me of the Bright God's champion, the way her entire body seemed to alight at the very thought of him.

"How do I know you're telling the truth?"

Bataar lifts a hand to display two missing fingers, the middle one freshly hewn with a bloodied bandage wrapped around it.

"You could've done that yourself," I say.

"Why would I do something to jeopardize my ability to blend in? It was the first thing Luiza taught us all, remember? Nothing to make you stand out. Now, I'll always be the Adaman with two missing fingers."

Kosci's interest perks in the back of my mind. I allow him to guide my power out, extending it to Bataar. My stomach twists as the inner workings of his mind become almost visible. I can feel the honesty rolling from him in waves. I yank Kosci back to myself before he can dig any further.

I lower the blade slowly. "Are you the only one turning?"

Bataar shakes his head. "At least half the guild wants out. We didn't sign up to be used as target practice. The other half are blindly devoted and get rewarded for snitching on the rest of us. It's no longer a haven for the unwanted of Strana."

My body goes rigid at his words. For most of us, the guild had been our only salvation, the one thing that kept us from freezing or starving on the streets.

"Very well," I say at last. "We can't do it all on our own without your information, anyway. Not against Luiza."

Bataar's shoulders relax as I allow the blade to melt away, turning to small droplets on the floor. His warm eyes study my hands, carefully considering my fingers, his gaze moving up to Kosci's scar barely visible on my wrist. I tug my sleeve down and slip my hands into my pockets.

"Can we move from the doorframe now that you're done interrogating people?" Sera asks loudly behind me.

I gesture for Alik and Bataar to sit at the table. Chinua, Sera, and I fill in the remaining seats. A wide, detailed map of Strana lies rolled open across the worn wood, tacked down on each corner. I trace with my eyes the slow path of the river cutting across the middle of Strana like a jagged scar, studying the strict separation of Zladonia from the rest of Strana.

Bataar's chair creaks as he leans back, forcing my gaze up.

"I had no idea what Luiza had done to the two of you. Not until the few Storm Hounds who made it out of Ludminka started spreading their stories. There had been whispers before, of course, but you know as well as I do you can't trust rumors in the guild. I am glad to see both of you alive."

"I'm glad you got my letter," Alik says.

"You *wrote* to him? Any number of people could've read the letter!" I say, folding my arms across my chest.

"It was all in Adaman," Chinua says. "I wrote it for Alik. If anyone came across it, they wouldn't have been able to understand it."

"Not even Luiza could read it," Bataar adds. "She never bothered to learn."

I press my lips together, biting back my growing agitation. It had been a massive risk. Luiza is the best in the game, and we were trained by her hand.

"Why don't you start by telling us everything you know," I say.

Bataar drops his chair back to the ground. "Ladislaw wants to take Knnot."

"Obviously," Sera drawls. "Perhaps try something useful."

With a roll of his eyes, Bataar begins to spin his tale, glossing over rioting in Rurik's streets against the draft and Matvei's promise to bless any who pledged themselves to Ladislaw before leading into the specifics he knew. By the time he's done detailing where the prisons are, he is mostly hoarse, and Sera has made heavy-handed ink stars across the map of Strana. Chinua passes Bataar some water as I walk my fingers to the closest star.

"You're certain there is a *tyur'ma* here? It doesn't look like more than an open plain," I say.

"An isolated plateau," Sera corrects. "Not many would ever travel in that direction. It's too close to the Adaman border."

"How long would it take to reach?" I ask.

"A good two days, at least," she says, and my shoulders slump. She goes on. "But it will likely have the least number of guards. They won't expect anyone to come from Zladonia, and the Adamans have no idea what's going on here, right?"

She looks between Chinua and Bataar, who both nod. Sera glances back down at the map.

"It *is* close to the border, though. I don't know if we should risk you being seen by one of the Khan's patrols," she says to Chinua.

"It's far enough out from where Khan sets camp this time of year. We should be safe enough," she says.

"That's why I recognize you," Bataar says from over his cup. "You're the girl who ran away. The one he was set to marry."

Chinua frowns. "I didn't run away. I came to seek glory for the Khan."

"No one believes that," Bataar says with a wave of his hand.

Chinua turns a steely gaze toward him.

"How is it I never saw you but you saw me?"

Bataar's lips twist into a lazy grin. "That's the power of Luiza's guild, to see but never be seen."

"If you know the workings of Adaman, then you know what has become of my family," Chinua says, her stiffened body coiled like a spring-loaded trap.

Bataar levels her with a stare, his face betraying nothing before he nods slowly.

"And?" Chinua's voice goes tight.

"They live," he says. "The Khan keeps them close; all are in Khurem for the winter. They wait for your return. You know they stand to gain much if you accept the proposal. He's promised positions as advisers to your father and two of your brothers."

"I know exactly what I left behind."

Bataar shrugs. "I'm not saying your choices are wrong. Just giving you the facts."

Our conversation drops, the low crackle of the fire the only sound. Chinua fiddles with a tattered edge of the map before Sera places one of her hands over Chinua's. Slowly, the girl removes it, curling her fingers hard into a fist.

"Do you want to go back and find them?" I ask. "I understand if you do. I won't stop you."

Chinua's cheeks color ever so slightly, but she shakes her head, keeping her mouth pressed into a tight line. "It will do no good. Not yet, at least. Khan Temujin does nothing unless he feels like he is getting the better end of the bargain. If I return, he will find a way to hold me."

I rub the scar at my wrist, tracing the rigid edges and the smooth center as I consider Chinua's drawn face. "If there is a way, I will get them back for you. I swear it."

You like to make grand promises, don't you? Kosci asks.

Hush, I say. He begins to protest, but I reach up and unclasp the necklace, allowing it to tumble into my hand before shoving it deep into my pocket. Kosci's murmurs fade away, and my mind is blissfully my own once again.

It takes a long moment to get used to the silence as everyone else around me buzzes in agitation. There is too much energy, and it needs direction.

"What do you know of the inside of the prisons?" I ask Bataar.

He reaches for a worn rucksack slung to dry on the oven's top. He riffles around, spilling Adamanian coins and a set of tin mugs onto the stone of the fireplace before finally pulling out a rolled bit of paper. Bataar unravels it, placing it atop the map of Strana.

It's a roughly drawn map, the lines wobbly and the measurements completed with question marks, but it is enough to make out the layout of the prison. Bataar traces the outer wall, tapping what I assume is supposed to be a turret.

"Four watchtowers at each corner. A guardhouse stands in

the center of the complex with windows circling the outside for complete visuals." He moves his fingers to a drooping hut in the center. "The Zladonians live in narrow houses near the guardhouse and aren't allowed to leave at night. There are around thirty guards a majority of the time, likely more in the prisons closer to Rurik."

Chinua inspects the drawing, lowering her head to get a better look. "Where did you find this? A child's room?"

"I drew it." Bataar frowns. "I'd like to see you do better without light and in a three-minute time frame."

"Every *tyur'ma* is laid out like this?" I ask before Chinua can retort.

"From what I could tell," Bataar says, leaning back against his chair once more. "Ladislaw is nothing but predictable."

I consider the layout of the prison before looking again at the closest one on Sera's map. It's far enough away from Ladislaw that if we strike hard and fast, it will be weeks before he notices what occurred. All we'd need is a few capable warriors and a bit of magic.

"Let's take the closest *tyur'ma*," I say.

"What?" Sera says, straightening in her seat, the orange firelight turning her skin rose gold. "We don't have the weapons, the training."

"What other choice do we have? We can't sit here and wait for the Czar to circle Ludminka and wait out the winter. Kosci's power is great, but not so magnificent he can conjure food from snow."

"If we strike, Ladislaw and Luiza will know we plan on taking the *tyur'mas*," Alik says.

"Not for weeks, if we're lucky," I cut in before he can continue to list all the reasons taking the prison is a bad idea. His doubt will only color my own decision. "I'm sure they don't send new guards to the nearest one often, especially not in the winter."

"It's risky," Chinua says.

"You would rather them rot in prisons? Or for Ladislaw and Matvei to amass an army three times the size of our own?"

"Of course not," Alik says, brow creasing hard, wrinkling the patch over his eye. "But we need better information, we can't go in blind. Luiza would never—"

The sound of her name grates hard on my nerves and I lean forward, cutting Alik off.

"And how to you propose we do that? Slip someone into the guard and hope they aren't found out and can report back to us the workings of the *tyur'ma*? That will take months, which is time we don't have." I sigh at Alik's taut face. "Listen, I know this isn't a great idea, but I made a promise when I accepted Kosci's deal. I won't leave them there, and the faster we strike at Ladislaw, the better. We can't wait for him to gather forces. He has us outnumbered, with the weight of Strana at his back. We need to show this country we are not people to be trifled with."

The table goes silent once more. Only Bataar looks unconcerned, his lips slightly quirked at the corners. Again, his eyes travel to my hands, and I resist the urge to curl them into fists.

"Valeria's right," Bataar says, and surprise flickers all the way to my toes. He was the last person I expected to break the tension. "None of you has ever seen real battle, and you need something small to test your skill. If she's promised to free the Zladonians, you can't ask for a better practice round."

"Lives are nothing to practice with," Chinua shoots back, crossing her arms. "We can't attack blindly and hope for the best. Our goal is to save the people inside, not slaughter them in a fight they had no idea was coming."

"We attack at night," I say, pulling Bataar's blueprint toward me. "Bataar says the Zladonians aren't allowed out, so we'll mitigate bystander casualties by descending on the Storm Hounds while they sleep."

Chinua digests my words slowly as she laces her hands atop the table. "A raid instead of a full assault? It could work. But we'd need a way to get inside quietly to make it effective. They probably have a protocol in place if the *tyur'mas* come under siege, and I doubt it's favorable to Zladonians."

"How many do you think we'd need?" I ask.

Chinua shrugs. "As many as you can get."

"I'll talk with my father in the morning," I say.

Sera shoves from her chair, sending the legs screeching along the floorboards. "This is insanity. We aren't ready!"

I glare up at her. "I'm only trying to do what is right."

"Are you?" she snaps back. "Because to me it seems like you are rushing into war with nothing but hope on your side. Do you really think any of the people Nicklaus is training are ready for a fight? Half of them can barely hold their weapons through the entire training session."

"They will never be ready," Bataar says, and it silences the entire table. "No one ever is their first time, no matter how well you think you've managed to prepare yourself."

An unreadable expression darkens his face for a heartbeat before it fizzles away, and he raps his knuckles on the table. "If we're done here, I think I will take that room you offered, Alik."

Alik stands, beckoning Bataar into the darkened hall, leaving me alone with Chinua and Sera. The latter fumes, her gaze hot on my face.

"I don't like this," Sera grinds out. "This is exactly like your plan in the caves, and look where it got us."

"Out of Knnot and in control of the lovite, alive and well?" I ask pointedly, and Sera looks away, her cheeks pink. "Your displeasure is noted, Sera, but this is my decision. If you don't want to go with us, I won't make you. Simply make us a map and we will be on our way without you."

With a frustrated exhale, Sera storms from the room, leaving her chair haphazardly against the wall and her maps spread across the table. Chinua sighs and begins to slowly roll them up, tucking them into Sera's map cases carefully placed along the counter at her back. Once done, she hesitates at the doorframe, casting a glance back as if she might say something. Instead, she shakes her head and lets the dark hallway consume her.

I stand slowly, banking the coals before clambering onto the long arm of the oven. I settle into the fire-warmed pillows before slowly pulling Kosci's pendant from my pocket. It casts waves of blue pulsing light along the walls, brighter than it had been when I'd first put it on. I watch the rippling light play along the oak ceiling before cupping the pendant and bringing it closer to my face. The veins of blue tracing through the stone mesmerize me, the gentle beat calling to my own heart.

I have no idea if what I'm doing is right, I think to Kosci.

Such is the weight of being a leader, he says, and light flickers softly along the veins. *But I believe it is right. We will take the* tyur'ma, *and the world will change once again.*

"I see I'm not the only one who can't sleep." Bataar's deep voice curls from the shadows before he steps into the kitchen.

I startle and snap my hand closed, dampening the light of Kosci's pendant.

"What are you still doing here?" The words slip out more harshly than I intend, my heart still racing.

"You know, I remember you being a little nicer in the guild." He leans against the doorframe, crossing his arms, followed by his ankles. I shove Kosci's heart into my pocket and swing upright, letting my legs dangle off the ledge.

"I'm surprised you remember me at all," I say, because I only have vague memories of him. He was two years my elder and almost never in the guild, always galivanting across

Adaman for one thing or another. Luiza spoke of him only when relaying the messages he sent about Strana's northwestern neighbor and to complain when he was returning, saying they would never get any useful information out of Adaman if Bataar didn't hold his station.

"You were Luiza's favorite. Of course I remember you."

His teeth catch the dull light of the fireplace as he smiles. He's undeniably handsome and seems more than aware of the fact.

My stomach does a strange flop, and I suddenly become very aware the samovar is my only weapon as I curl my fingers around it.

"Don't look so concerned. The last thing I wanted was the full weight of Luiza's attention. I liked my life in Adaman. I had no wish to come back to the freezing tits of Strana."

A shocked laugh tumbles from me. "And now you're all the way in Zladonia."

"Yes, this is much worse." Bataar shifts his gaze from the embers to my face. He sweeps over it slowly, almost as if memorizing it. "You know, Luiza has done nothing but talk of you since Ludminka was released from the ice. She told Ladislaw and Matvei everything about you, in detail. She made sure we overheard as well. Everyone knows every single thing about your life, every weakness, every strength."

My stomach grows tighter with each word. "You aren't doing anything to make me feel like you're not about to kill me."

"I don't think I would get the chance, even if I wanted to. Your power is quite the sight to behold," he says. His eyes stray to where my hand curls on my knee. His gaze doesn't hold fear or even shock, just thinly veiled appreciation.

"Besides," he says with a shrug. "You don't need me lining up to kill you. There are more than enough people waiting for the opportunity. In fact, Luiza has mentioned more than once they should assassinate you. Cut off the head of the wolf and all that nonsense."

"She should stop being a coward and do it herself, then," I say as I slip down from the oven top and fish for an ember to place in the samovar. Bataar folds himself on the ground beside me, taking the item from me and swirling it around once. I raise an eyebrow.

"Stranans can't make tea to save their lives," he says, smirking as he reaches for the canister of tea leaves above his head. He adds some, and a few pinches of Chinua's spices she keeps on the counter, before closing the teapot and settling it atop the samovar.

"You're being very nonchalant about your possible murder," he says. I sit on the other side of the hearth, crossing my legs and leaning against the warm stone.

"I've always known it was a possibility. I mean, she hoped I'd die in Knnot," I say. "Hard to be afraid of something you already knew was coming."

"She's opening up bids to Adaman, you know. Luiza will

infiltrate your camp. You can trust no one," he says.

"How do I know you aren't the assassin?" I ask. Bataar rolls his eyes.

"Alik told me what you did to my mind."

I blanch, but he waves a hand.

"I don't blame you. If I had the ability, I'd use it, too. It's the only way to know if someone is actually telling the truth. I'd *keep* using it, if I were you. Luiza has many eyes, and they are all trained on you."

"It doesn't bother you, then? That I took a look in your mind without asking?"

"It wouldn't exactly be a tool if you asked every time you went sifting for information," he says with another of his easy smiles. When I don't return it, he considers me. "No. It doesn't bother me. Growing up like we did, doing what we had to for a bed and some food, it doesn't leave a lot of room for morality. We do what we have to. Our lives depend on it. Some of us learned that lesson a little better than others."

Bataar says the last sentence hesitantly. I'm not sure if he guesses how Alik feels or not, but his words make it seem like he knows exactly why I asked. I let Bataar's words sink in. I did always understand the guild and its dance between right and wrong better than Alik.

Bataar seems to sense my souring mood because he softens and turns toward me.

"I don't envy you this position, Valeria, but I will help you, as much as I can. This I swear." He presses a closed fist to his heart, the same way Chinua had when she pledged her loyalty to me.

"You're very willing to sacrifice yourself to a cause that has nothing to do with you."

"Well," Bataar says, and looks down at his missing fingers, flexing the remaining ones slowly. "Luiza made it personal. Besides, I've always liked the longshot myself."

He gives me another smile, and I find myself returning it. It's no wonder Luiza always sent him to Adaman. His easy charm and open face had to loosen more than a few tongues.

"Won't you be missed if you stay here? Surely Luiza must know you are gone. You'll ruin your chance of being a mole before you've begun."

"I very much doubt Luiza cares what I do. She's made it abundantly clear I am no one of worth anymore. But she currently thinks I'm on an intrepid mission to Adaman to scout out how amenable they'd be to an alliance."

"What?" I straighten, swinging my entire body toward him so quickly it almost knocks over the samovar between us. "You didn't think to tell us this information *before*?"

He shrugs. "I have no intention of going to Adaman. Not only will it reveal that I've been a spy in their midst for years now, but I don't want Luiza to win. I'd kill her myself if I actually thought I'd get close enough to try."

As much as he's tried to hide how Luiza's punishment hurt,

it laces through his voice, bitter and angry as he looks down at his hands. That, more than any word that has come from his mouth, makes me trust him. I know the anger that comes with Luiza's betrayal. It's the same one that burns a hole in my heart.

"I believe you," I say. He glances over at me, his face devoid of emotion for the briefest of moments before the same cocky grin comes to his lips.

"Looking into my mind wasn't enough to convince you?"

I laugh. "It just told me you were telling the truth, not that you really believed what you said."

We fall silent, the soft hiss of the dying fire oddly comforting. The warmth of the oven leaks into my back, chasing away the freezing nip of the night. The moment is a brief sigh of calm in the storm of expectations and battle plans.

I should have known Luiza would want to kill me before I could incite a revolt. There was no other way the Czar would be able to keep control if the people saw another avenue to hope. I'm the one who controls the lovite. I'm the one who unlocked Knnot. She has to know how dangerous that is. I need more than the anger of the Zladonians to best her. People who already know their way around weapons and war. I straighten as an idea bolts into my mind.

"Do you think Adaman would ally with us instead?" I ask, looking over at Bataar.

"I'm not sure. You have lovite, which is what they've always wanted. Could you imagine an Adamanian army with unbreakable weapons? They'd conquer the world."

"But?" I ask.

"But they don't trust Strana. Never have, likely never will. Despite your determination to overthrow Ladislaw and your wealth of lovite, they will still be suspicious. They won't look at you and see someone who has suffered, someone who wants to right the wrongs done to her. They will see another Stranan vying for power and willing to do anything to take it." Bataar considers the belly of the samovar for a long moment. "Sometimes the Khan honors brutality, and sometimes he values honesty more. He will admire your strength, your skills with the blade, and your ability to wield magic. But when he looks at you, I doubt he will see a ruler."

"Because I'm a girl?" I ask, the words cold.

Bataar raises a brow. "Do you really know nothing about Adaman?"

"Do you really think Luiza took the time to teach me when she had you?" I ask.

"An excuse, but I'll accept it for now." Bataar removes the tea, filling two cups from the table without speaking. As he passes the first one to me, he shakes his head. "The Khan values women and not just as wives and daughters. Women are allowed to own land and divorce their husbands. They can join his army if they prove themselves adequate. Women are taught the same things as men. Khan Temujin believes that for society to flourish, all must participate in building it."

"If it's not because of what I am, then why?" I ask.

"You are young, untested in battle. To back you would mean he believes in your ability to be victorious in battle, and you've never seen war. If you can conquer, then you can control. Temujin won't support you if he believes the people will overthrow you the first chance they get."

I simmer at his words even as the thought of ruling over all of Strana buries its way to my core. I hadn't thought a moment beyond killing Ladislaw and Matvei, but the country would turn to me. I will be the one to strike the killing blow, and a champion of the gods. Who else would they believe should rule? I put the cup to my lips. Several different flavors spill across my tongue, sharp cinnamon and smoky cardamom. I take another sip, relishing the taste.

"You're right," I say, and look over at him. "You are much better at making tea."

Bataar smiles and I go back to the drink, willing it to ease the growing weight of the world falling onto my shoulders. Between Luiza's determination to have me killed, hunting Matvei and Ladislaw, and figuring out the future of Strana, I'm not sure how much more I can carry.

NINE

THE FOLLOWING MORNING, I TAKE the beaten
dirt path of Ludminka's main street toward my parents' home,
avoiding the frozen ruts crusted with smooth ice that always
twist my ankles. My father used to carry me when I was small
so I could avoid them. My heart gives a double beat as the
cheery roses on the window comes into view above the waist-
high drifts capped in a crystalline sheen. Smoke curls lazily
from the brick chimney, meaning they're inside. Half of me
hoped they wouldn't be here. We need warriors for the raid,
but I know who will be the first three to offer their lives. Papa,
Gregori, and Anton are some of the best in the militia, and no
matter how much I wish they would, they won't stay home.

I stand outside the door with my hand raised, not daring to
knock. This is the first time I've come to my parents' house,
too afraid that doing so would make me feel small and weak

again. I jump as the door swings open suddenly. Gregori stands on the other side, his blue eyes wide. He blinks at me before breaking into a smile and slinging an arm around my neck. He pulls me into a tight hug before mussing my hair with his other hand.

"I was wondering when you'd finally stop by! Anton, look, Valeria has deigned to visit her family at last." Gregori pulls me inside.

It smells just as I remember, wood smoke and the thick scent of yeast from the bread rising on the hearth. My mother wipes her hand on her apron before wrapping me in a hug. Her hair is pushed back with a red kerchief and a smudge of flour sits on her nose.

Anton comes next, giving me the briefest hug. Last is Papa. He stands from his spot at the table and the chair screeches beneath his weight as his face breaks into a wide grin. He smooths back my hair, fixing Gregori's mess.

"We're happy to see you, *Milaya*."

"Are you hungry?" Matta asks.

"No, I'm fine."

"You're hungry. Sit, I'll bring you some food," she says.

I remember enough of my childhood that I know I can't disagree. Papa leads me to the table and forces me into a seat. Gregori and Anton sit on either side of me with Papa at the head. The entire scene makes my head spin. It's so familiar. I remember nights spent just like this, laughing over a horrible joke from Gregori or complimenting a wood carving of

Anton's. It feels almost normal.

My mother places a bowl of warm stew before me and a thick chunk of brown bread covered in butter. Steam wafts from the bowl, and she stares down at me expectantly. She doesn't stop until I pick up my spoon and put it in my mouth. She smiles and settles beside my father.

"What is it you need?" she asks.

I take another spoonful to avoid answering right away. I glance between my father and brothers.

"I came to talk to Papa," I say. "I need warriors, as many as you can spare."

"What for?" my father asks, leaning forward on the table.

"I plan to take the closest *tyur'ma*." The table goes very still. Before I am overwhelmed by their questions, I explain the information Bataar brought and the plan to take the prison at night. My father nods along, his eyes unfocused as if visualizing it all on the wall behind my head.

"It's doable," he says. "Not sure how many of the recruits are actually ready. I can give you maybe twenty, counting myself and the boys."

My mother clutches her apron tight. "Isn't there anyone else?"

"No," Papa answers. "I wish for your sake there was, but most of them are still trying to understand the basics. I can't risk half-trained warriors."

I twist my fingers together and stare down at my stew, somehow feeling like I'm seven years old again and being chastised for hitting one of my brothers.

"If there were anyone else, I wouldn't ask. I swear to you, Matta."

She continues to twist her apron until my father's hands swallow hers, clasping them tight.

"We will be fine, Iva. I'll watch after them all and get us back safe."

Matta reclaims one of her hands to poke my father in the ribs. "Do not make promises you can't keep."

"I never have," he says with a smile.

The rigidity doesn't leave my mother's shoulders, but she allows herself to be collected to my father's side.

Gregori straightens, a grin tugging at his lips. "We'll be the first to hold those new weapons the smithy has been making."

"You just want an excuse to see his daughter," Anton says.

"Do not," Gregori shoots back, cheeks flaming.

"Boys," Pap cuts in. "This is serious, not a game you get to play."

Gregori and Anton wilt slightly, and I take in a shuddering breath.

"Don't do this because you feel like it's your duty to me as your daughter. I can't stress how dangerous this will be."

Papa lets a small, sad smile play across his lips.

"I've known since I saw you conjure a gem of frost that the world had changed. What we remember is dead, and if we ever want to flourish again, we have to take it by any means necessary," Papa says.

"And Papa isn't the only one who says that," Gregori says, leaning on the table to look over at me. "Everyone in Ludminka whispers it. You're a champion, Val. One the world hasn't seen in a century."

"We want our families back," Papa says. "Everyone in Ludminka understands the cost of that, even your mother and I."

It feels wrong to be talking of the world and death around the table where I used to eat breakfast as a child. Like we are telling a favorite legend to amuse ourselves while Matta readies bread. It doesn't feel as if I should be leading a rebellion against the Czar, who has been in power longer than I have been alive. In this little home, with its rising bread and carefully carved roses, I am a little girl again.

But I can't be that version of me. Not with Kosci's heart. Not with Luiza's eyes trained on my back. Just like I told Alik, I am no longer just Valeria. No matter how much I wish I were.

"We will leave at week's end. We want to go before the weather turns," I say, unsure of what else I can say.

Gregori whoops and stands up from the table. "Get your cloak, Anton, we're going to the smithy!"

Anton shoots me an amused look before rising from the table. Matta is the only one who doesn't move. She stares down at the knotted fingers in her lap.

"Matta," I start, then stop, not sure what to say. "I'm . . . sorry."

She releases a long breath. "I know."

My father brushes a kiss to the top of her head, pulling her into his chest. She sinks into him and they fit right together, as if they were made that way. I smile softly before forcing myself to stand.

Matta catches my hand as I walk past. "Is there anything I can do?"

"We plan to start making armor soon, if you've a mind to sew leather. But Ludminka needs your breads, Matta. It brings them normalcy, and they need that now more than ever. Soon there will be even more mouths to feed."

She settles back against my father, drawing his hand into her lap. She stares down at his fingers before glancing back up.

"We are proud of you. You know that, right? Somehow you managed to live while everything you knew faded. You've done everything you can to make our world seem right again. I am proud to call you my daughter."

I can't catch the tears before they begin to fall. Papa leans forward and brushes them away. My heart hurts at it all. For so long I'd tucked everything about them far away so it couldn't strangle me. Being here, being part of a family, it fixes something broken deep inside.

"I love you both," I say. I kiss my mother's cheeks and then my father's.

"I will gather the rest," my father says. "You'll have the warriors you need."

TEN

THE JOURNEY TO THE *TYUR'MA* is dark and cold, all reserves of autumn falling fully into winter. No one complains as we march through tundras and fir trees, our minds fixed on our quarry. Near the end of the second day, the prison rises out of the forest as the sun dies behind it, streaks of red illuminating the tall sides and fluttering flags at each turret. The small forms of Storm Hounds pace around the top, their backs to us. Their job has always been to watch the inside, not the outside. No one has ever attempted to break in, and they have no reason to believe anyone would.

We huddle deep in the boughs of a pine forest, the heady scent of fir and sap permeating the air. The walls seem impassable, made of solid wood at least four feet thick. I can barely make out the top of what looks like a house in the center of the prison. I turn back to the others.

We aren't an overly large or threatening-looking group. My brothers and father, bedecked in old armor we found in the back of the smithy, Sera, Chinua, and Alik all with lovite weapons and grim faces. Bataar wears a light, quilted gambeson that reaches mid-thigh, belted with Luiza's guild gear, a quiver strapped to his back and a longbow in his hands. The rest are dressed in the remaining vestiges we salvaged from the Storm Hounds who attacked us. The deep black of the armored uniform contrasts sharply with the ice white of their hair, making them appear more like ghosts of Storm Hounds past than Zladonians ready to fight.

"We should make our move as soon as the sun is down. With any luck, the shadows will hide us even if they do manage to reach their crossbows," I say.

"And how do you propose we climb those walls?" Sera asks.

"With magic," I reply, twirling my wrist so the snow at our feet twines around itself. Sera looks down at it as if I've done nothing more than step on a rat.

"Of course, magic. How could I have forgotten," she says.

"Come on, Sera," Chinua says, and bumps Sera's shoulder with her own. "Isn't it a little exciting to have legendary power at your side?"

"I'd be more excited if I could watch this battle from afar and not risk my neck on some half-baked plan," Sera says.

I want to argue, but I can't. I'm risking not only my life, but the lives of everyone around me for something I'm not even sure will work.

It will, Kosci says, and I nearly jump at the sudden clang of his voice in my mind. He'd kept mostly silent since I put his heart back on. I'd worn it sparingly since my talk with Alik in the kitchen, but the open plains of Strana brought back the fear of the Czar's eyes on us. I will not be caught off guard again.

You're always so certain, I say.

One of us has to be. There is a skeleton crew inside, not more than twenty men. You could win this easily, if you just allow me to control those with us.

No. I think the word as forcefully as I can manage. *They don't deserve to become puppets on your strings, Kosci.*

All mortals are puppets to gods. I thought you would have realized that by now. In life they pray to us and in death they come to us. What does it matter now if I take them?

I grit my teeth. *I said no.*

Very well, Kosci says airily. *I will be here to aid you, as always.*

"Val?" Alik says from beside me. He studies me carefully, worrying at his tongue as he does so. "You were talking to him again, weren't you?"

His question is quiet enough that only I can hear. The others mill at our backs, checking their weapons and tightening their paltry armor.

"Just trying to figure out if what I am doing is right," I say, keeping my voice low.

"And you think a god could tell you better than the people around you?"

"I would assume knowing the fates of men is one of his godly duties," I say, cutting a glare at Alik.

"What did he tell you?" Alik asks.

Wind scrawls across the open plain before the *tyur'ma*, churning the loose snow into a fine mist that falls as the gust dies. Flakes catch in Alik's hair, dissolving as soon as they reach the heat of his body. He looks so normal, even after greeting death for a second time. I don't spare a thought for the people around us or the prison before us. I reach out and grasp his mittened hand in one of my own and give it a squeeze, reminding myself he is alive. He is breathing and whole right now, in this perfectly imperfect place.

But how much longer would he stay that way?

"Maybe you should stay here, watch our backs, scout the roads to make sure no new shipments are coming or Storm Hounds are patrolling."

"What?" He rips his hand from mine. "Why would I do that?"

Heat pricks through my stomach and nestles into my neck. Instead of seeing Alik indignant and determined before me, I see blood leaking down the corner of his mouth, a bolt protruding from his chest. I swallow hard, squeezing my eyes shut.

It isn't real. It is a memory. Just like the memories of Ludminka that followed me after the freeze. Alik is alive. He *is*.

I repeat the words over and over again until they stick in my mind, but my heart continues to race faster, like a frightened rabbit in a snare. Alik is alive now, but I don't know what lies beyond those prison walls. Another bolt aimed for his heart? A sword to the neck? A dagger in the eye? I need to protect him. It's what I have always done, and twice I failed. Life will not grant me a third time.

Cool hands settle on either side of my face, and I force my eyes back open. "Take a breath, Val."

Alik's mittens lie discarded on the snowbank beside us, and he applies soft pressure to my cheeks, inhaling slowly as though he is teaching me to breathe. I fight to mimic him, but it's like trying to breathe underwater. Still, I gulp painful gasps, focusing on his face.

"I can't watch you die again," I say, my voice so thin and quiet it hurts my own ears. "I can't."

"You won't."

"You don't know that, Alik. You don't know anything."

"And neither do you," he says, his hands still cooling my burning skin. "Kosci doesn't know the future any more than we do. I will be fine. This isn't a desperate escape straight into a trap. We are the ones fighting this time."

I want Alik to be right. My entire being aches to believe, but I can't. This is a stupid, foolish idea and everyone here knows it. How could a handful of people beat back trained Storm Hounds and free a prison's worth of people? I'm no great general. I'm just a girl with too much anger in her heart.

And a god at her disposal, Kosci says. *I will not let you fall. You do not walk this path alone.*

I take in a deep, shuddering breath and nod once. Alik caresses my cheek once before his hands drop. The last stretches of sunlight claw their way across the sky, turning the air bitter, and I shiver at the lack of warmth on my face.

I have no more time to doubt.

My legs start to tingle as dusk grows over the forest, sending black shadows between the thin trunks. Storm Hounds still monitor the interior of the prison, their movements slow and precise as the sun fades to gray light.

"Ready?" I whisper.

I feel more than hear affirmation. I take the lead as we creep along the trees at the edge of the circular clearing. The long shadows beneath hide us, and our movements are muffled by snow and pine needles. Torches spring to life along the walls, spilling orange pools of light across the outer rim of the prison. The closer I get, the better I can make out the walls. The wood seems soft from years of water damage, and it groans beneath the weight of the guards atop it. If I were more powerful, I could likely break down the gates myself.

You could, Kosci agrees. *If only you'd stop fighting against your true nature, you could do anything your mind could imagine.*

You're not helping at the moment, I say as we slink ever closer to the back side of the prison.

Snow-covered stumps dot the terrain before sloping straight into the prison's thick walls. I scan the parapets, scrutinizing the Storm Hounds as they continue their slow patrol, waiting for the horn to ring out as it had in Oleg to signal a shift change. I turn back to the others.

"As soon as you hear the signal, run for the walls. Don't stop. Watch your step until you reach it. Wait for my order to climb and be ready for a fight as soon as we're inside." I scan the wan faces before me. "If anyone wishes to stay behind, back out now. We need to trust each other in there."

I look from face to grim face, heart in my throat, expecting someone to change their mind. Not a single one raises their voice and I take a steadying inhale.

"Very well," I say, and pull a leather helm over my head. My vision narrows, and my breath fogs into my eyes, but I bounce, readying to sprint.

Still your breathing, rely on your senses. You have done this before, Valeria. You can do it again. Kosci's voice swims in the back of my mind and settles my thudding heart.

I am powerful.

I can do this.

The horn blasts from the center of the prison, and I spring to my feet. I rush toward the walls without looking back, slamming into it first and pressing my spine hard into the freezing wood. The others soon skid through the snow beside me, all of them panting and wild eyed. In the shadow of the wall, we're nearly invisible. I take a deep breath and conjure the image of a ladder of frost and snow stretching up the side of the wall, frozen to the logs beneath it.

The vision solidifies, and I follow the snaking, heated pulse of Kosci's magic through my chest, chasing the thin strands of power I'd become accustomed to seeing out in the real world. The threads aren't as visible here, but I follow the nudge of Kosci's mind through the air, latching on to the magic in the snow.

A cool wind pulls at the ends of my hair, and I open my eyes to find particles of snow detaching themselves from the drift before me. They spiral around one another in tight circles, fusing and hardening as they go. With a soft crack, the first ladder solidifies, the torching light playing off the translucent ice. I inch down the wall to create another.

With soft snaps, ladder after ladder materialize from the snow like fallen soldiers raised from the dead. By the time I've made the last one, sweat beads on my brow and air wheezes in my lungs. I click my tongue twice and the others run to their ladders to begin their ascent. There is no time to wonder if we will succeed. There is only the top of the parapet and the slow thud of approaching footsteps.

ELEVEN

WE CREST THE TOP OF the wall in unison and slip silently onto the walkway. It creaks beneath our combined weight, and we all look out over the first *tyur'ma* any of us have seen.

The prison lies in rows of narrow houses, smoke curling from small chimneys. Near the wide front gate is a small, cobbled square leading to a circular, two-story guardhouse. Storm Hounds stroll lazily in and out, tossing waves and laughs with one another as they change shifts. I follow the lines of the snow-dusted roofs to the back of the prison, where a deep, circular hole sits in the earth, concentric spirals winding ever downward.

A salt mine.

For the past ten years, the people inside this prison have

been doing hard work for the Czar, sending salt instead of lovite. Rage burns in the back of my throat as I spin toward the others. I know by their faces alone they've seen it, too.

"What—" a voice calls from the far end of the walkway.

I snap my head in the direction of the yell to find a thin-framed Storm Hound with a long pike standing near a set of rickety stairs.

Before the boy can call out again, an arrow finds its way into his throat. Bataar stands with bow raised, his face hard as the Storm Hound crumples to the ground. It wasn't fast enough to stop the others from taking notice. A loud bell clangs, ricocheting off the ice-encapsulated buildings around us. Another answers from inside the guardhouse, and Storm Hounds begin to pour from its doors.

We can't afford to watch the scene unfold a moment longer.

"Watch your backs and protect your partners," I cry before I call on Kosci's power and step out into the open air.

There is a moment of weightlessness before my foot comes down on a pillar of frozen snow. I step forward again and the ground rises up to meet me like a personal set of stairs. The Storm Hounds in the courtyard watch my descent with open mouths, some of their weapons drooping toward the ground.

A twang sounds from behind me and another arrow snaps forward, catching a Storm Hound in the eye. The man cries out and stumbles backward into his compatriots. It breaks whatever trance my power had put the Storm Hounds in.

They scurry into formation as Bataar nocks another arrow, followed promptly by one from Chinua. They release simultaneously, both arrows clanging off the Storm Hounds' stout shields as commands are yelled from behind.

My feet kiss the ground, and I raise my hands. Instantly, blades of ice form before me, just as I had practiced in the clearing with Kosci. I throw them in a spray and they burst through the shields in front of me. Surprised cries sound from behind their defenses and I dash forward, pulling on Kosci's power as I go.

I grasp the familiar ice blade just in time to parry a blow from a guard over his ruined shield. He sends the shield forward. I dodge, thrusting the blade straight toward his open right side.

Don't look. Kosci orders as I shove the blade deep into his body. The man collapses to the ground without another sound.

I spin to face the others. An ax wheels through the air to bury itself in the chest of a Storm Hound attempting to run for the guardhouse. Sera stands to my left and swings her broad ax wide, catching one Storm Hound in the gut and another in the hip. Chinua dances through a Storm Hound's defenses to place a dagger in his ribs, while Bataar rains arrows down from above.

More cries sound as Storm Hounds rush from the narrow houses and into the dirt courtyard. My father takes a blow on his sword from the Storm Hound before throwing him backward with a push, Gregori and Anton on either side. Alik bars the door to the guardhouse, sweeping a long sword at anyone who tries to retreat.

Storm Hounds fall one after another, turning the courtyard into a churning mess of blood and snow. Two guards round the farthest corner of the courtyard, bows raised. I pull my hand inward and force it up. Kosci's power amplifies through my body, singing along my bones, feeding strength I've never felt before into my soul. A solid wall of snow forms just as their bolts leave their crossbows and the arrows thud uselessly into it before I let it collapse. I dart forward as they reload, giving them no chance to aim.

My blade slices through the air and I take off one's hand, whirling to strike the other in the chest. He topples to the ground, and I wrench my blade out as he falls. Using the momentum, I swing the blade toward his compatriot. He dodges the first swing and I round on him fully. He fumbles for the short sword at his hip, and I use the opportunity to slide in close and skewer his throat.

I whirl back to the others, letting my blade of ice melt and mingle with the blood pooling beneath the bodies before me. I thrum with power as I take in the courtyard. I expect to find the others as I left them, overthrowing their opponents with bloody strength. Instead, Sera is slammed into the wall, two Storm Hounds forcing their weight down on her, angling for her throat. Another one catches Chinua around the middle, pulling his short sword toward her. With a yell, I send out a flick of power. A rolling wave of ice catches the Storm Hound's blade before it can make contact with Chinua's exposed stomach.

The man reels back, releasing Chinua long enough for an arrow to catch him first in the right shoulder, then the left. I glance up to find Bataar still above us all, ripping an arrow from a nearly empty quiver and locating his next victim with fluid accuracy. A scream tears out, and I spin to find Anton bringing down his blade on the neck of one of the men holding Sera. The blow isn't strong enough. The Storm Hound only flinches forward before turning toward Anton with a growl. Before I can so much as blink, he shoves a small dagger into Anton's ribs.

"No!" The scream rips from my throat as my brother's face goes slack. He blinks at the guard before falling to his knees, his hand pressed to the skin beneath the dagger. Heat whirls up my legs and zigzags along my spine. I don't think, just fling all of Kosci's power at the man who wounded my brother. A lance of pure ice shoots from somewhere behind me, catching both men beside Sera and running them through. The force of it takes the bodies across the courtyard and buries them deep into the side of the guardhouse wall.

Gregori pushes a man off him and Papa runs the Storm Hound through. Alik wobbles as a soldier puts pressure on his weaker side, and I race forward only to stop short as an arrow finds its way into the back of the Storm Hound's neck. The world around me seems far too bright and clear; the blood-drenched courtyard, the sharp tang of copper suffused with fresh snow, the flickering torchlight making every shadow look like a Storm Hound about to strike.

I spin, looking for another person to hunt, another to destroy. I find no one. Not a single Storm Hound stands.

It feels as if it shouldn't be over. I'd expected a raging battle to last an hour. Instead, the Storm Hounds had been surprised and overwhelmed in a matter of minutes.

It almost doesn't feel like a victory.

Movement to my right catches my eye. I glance up to see a single remaining Storm Hound, crossbow raised directly at Alik.

I scream his name.

Alik's eye flicks to me, then up at the Storm Hound. The click of the crossbow echos throughout the silent courtyard. I scramble to catch my power, but it slips through my mind, unwilling to form to my panicked thoughts as the bolt travels straight toward his heart.

Alik throws his hands up and turns his face. Suddenly, a wide circle forms before him, crystalline and blue. The bolt sticks into the ice with a crack, the shaft poking out the back. Alik blinks and stares down at his hands, and the ice shatters and falls to the ground.

Bataar takes aim. His arrow flies through the air and

collides with the last guard. He clutches where it lands before falling backward over the parapet. My gaze flicks back to Alik.

I wasn't the one to save him.

Somehow, Alik had conjured the mirror of ice all on his own.

It takes me a few moments to move. Alik meets my stare across the body-strewn courtyard to him, his eye wide and mouth slack. I consider moving toward him for the briefest moment before Anton groans. I rush to his side, collapsing to my knees to catch the hand around the dagger.

His wide blue eyes find my face, his lips a bloodless white. He gasps and looks back down at the dagger.

"Well," Anton says, his words strangled. "It was bound to be one of us."

"You aren't dying," I say.

Without another word, I rip the dagger from his side. Blood bubbles to the surface and oozes over his armor, already beginning to freeze in the night air. I place my palms over it and almost feel the magic weaving through his punctured flesh, sewing it back together with quick tugs. Anton gasps in my ear but I don't stop. I won't until I'm sure he's fine.

"Valeria," he says. He grasps my shoulder, fingers digging into my flesh. "Stop."

I shake my head, tears hot in my eyes as the ice needle and thread work their way through sinew and muscle until the needle digs its way back out. Anton gasps again, rocking forward to collapse against my shoulder. I release my hold on Kosci's power and wrap my arms around Anton, sucking in shuddering breaths. He smells of blood and ice, and I tighten my hold.

He is alive, Valeria. He is. Let him go.

Kosci's voice walks through my mind until it reaches my numb ears. Slowly, I let my fingers curl off Anton's back, terrified to release him only to find him dead. Anton shudders as he lifts his head from my shoulder. He wets his lips and opens his mouth like he might say something. A shout sounds from behind the guardhouse, cutting him off before he has a chance to start.

I stumble to my feet, expecting another Storm Hound. Instead, people slowly filter out of their cabins. They scan the ground, jumping back from the blood freezing beneath the fallen Storm Hounds. I steel myself before slowly moving forward. They scurry back and I stop, holding my hands before me.

"We aren't here to hurt you," I say. I rip my helm off and expose my white hair, identical to their own. Dozens of eyes trail over my body, and the slow realization that I'm Zladonian sparks across their faces. "My name is Valeria Kowel, and I am the Pale God's champion. I have come to free you all."

Awed whispers roll through crowd, swelling slowly as more people venture from the houses, children caught in blankets and elderly wrapped in thick furs, their breaths clouding to mist before them. My heart thunders in my ears. They look to me like I am the only thing in the world that matters, hope and wonder scrawled across their faces. Something swells sure and vicious inside me. Power, but not Kosci's. Power all my own.

"We will see you to safety. Take the night to gather what you need. We leave at morning's light," I say.

At first, silence follows my words, and my heart hangs in my throat. Mutters build to a cheer as the news spreads through the hundreds of people before me packed into the tiny alleys between the houses. Some of the braver souls venture forward, taking in my face, my hair. I urge them to ready to depart, repeating that yes, I am a champion of the gods. They run their fingers along my exposed hair and my shoulders, crowding closer and closer until I am pinned in the center of the courtyard without a familiar face in sight. The weight of their reverence confines me, and I struggle free, gasping in bitter night air. A single woman remains at the edge of the crowd, tall and imposing with a thick woolen blanket around her shoulders. Her eyes aren't on me. They sit fixed just over my left shoulder.

I glance behind me to find Alik, mouth slack and eye wide.

"Alasha?" The woman before me whispers.

"Matta?" The word falls from Alik's mouth, little more than a breath.

The blanket drops to the ground and she bounds across the space between us, taking Alik's face in her hands, heedless of the muck and blood splattered across his clothes.

"Is it really you?" she asks.

Alik nods, his voice caught somewhere deep in his throat. The woman smooths back his hair and kisses his forehead and all the hard edges of Alik's body melt away. He leans into her, and she holds him tight, resting her head on his.

"Oh my love," she whispers, "what has life done to you?"

I look away. Alik hardly ever spoke of his mothers. It was always too painful for him to remember, even to me. Alik seeing her again, after watching her carted away by Storm Hounds when he was a child, was a moment for him alone.

I wade through the crowd until I find my father and brothers, no longer wanting to be alone. As soon as I sidle up beside him, my father throws an arm around me, hugging me tight.

"I would say you had yourself a successful first mission," he crows.

"Unless you count Anton's near-death experience," Gregori says.

My heart squeezes, but Anton looks down at his splattered clothing, brushing away a speck of mud despite the blood staining the rest.

"I would hardly call it near death. It was a scratch at best."

"Anton," my voice wobbles out.

He smiles. "I'm fine. Thanks to you."

"You wouldn't have been injured at all if it weren't for me," I spit, staring down at my boots, the ground beneath nothing but muddy snow and crumbling cobblestone.

An arm falls around my shoulders, followed by another from the opposite side. My brothers stand on either side of me and they squeeze tight. We stand there for a long moment before Gregori pulls back slightly.

"You know this is serious when Anton willingly joins the family hug."

"Shut up." Anton shoves him with his free hand. "I'm extremely lovable."

I laugh, but it comes out strangled and tearful. Papa joins us, filling in the gap between Anton and Gregori.

"This was a success, Valeria. We lost no one, suffered no grievous injuries. Even if you weren't here, Anton would've recovered. Look at the people around you. They have hope for the first time in ten years because you dared to lay siege to a prison."

My eyes prick and before I can stop myself, tears slip down my cheeks and I squeeze my brothers tighter.

"Thank you," I say. "For following me. For believing I could do this."

"We always knew you'd do great things, *Milaya*. I'm proud to follow you now," my father says, and my brothers nod.

"I'm so happy I have you back," I say. Papa leans forward and places a kiss on the crown of my head. Gregori lets out a long sigh.

"Now that we all know how much we love one another, can I let go? I'd love to get the smell of blood out of my nose."

We laugh and I shove him away, wiping the last of the tears from my eyes. As we part, the battlefield behind my brothers' shoulders comes into view.

Perhaps I should feel some sort of remorse for the broken and bleeding bodies strewn across the courtyard. They were people, after all. Ones with friends and families who laughed and teased just like mine did. I hunt through every crevice of my brain, but I can't find a crumb of empathy anywhere. They chose this path, and they died for their convictions. I'd reunited a family, freed hundreds of people from years of back-breaking labor.

I will never feel guilty about that.

TWELVE

WE'VE ALMOST MANAGED TO CARRY all the bod-
ies to the edge of the *tyur'ma* by the time Alik brings his mother
toward us. She appraises us slowly, her eyes lingering on me.

"These are the rest of our saviors, then?" she asks.

"Yes," Alik says, and introduces us one by one, leaving me
for last. "And this—"

"Is Valeria, the Pale God's champion. It's a pleasure to meet
you. My name is Irina," his mother says. "I wouldn't have
believed it if I hadn't seen it with my own eyes. I have you to
thank for the lives of everyone here, and for returning my Alik
to me."

I find my mouth dry, unsure what to do with the surge of
gratitude rolling from her. I nod slowly. "Truly, it was the least
I could do for the Zladonians. I won't let them linger in the

Czar's prisons. Not if I can change it."

"Alik says you plan to continue across the rest of Strana." Irina draws herself to full height. "I know I speak for each and every person here when I say we want the chance to fight. We've spent far too long under the thumbs of petty men. We want to join you, if you'll have us."

Again, that swell of power presses against my breastbone and something like pride wells in my soul.

"If you want the chance to fight, I will give it to you," I say.

"We want it more than you could ever know." Her face grows grim and taut, her eyes focused on something far away. Alik squeezes her hand, and she blinks back to the present.

"We have provisions enough to help those who need it and homes in Ludminka. Those who can't or don't want to fight will find sanctuary in our village," I say.

Irina nods. "I will let the rest know. We will see you at dawn."

She turns toward the narrow houses and the large knot of people forming in the now empty courtyard, small bundles of belongings strewn among them. Alik hesitates between his *matta* and me. I smile softly.

"Go with her."

Relief breaks across his face and he hurries after Irina, tossing an arm around her shoulders as he reaches her. My smile widens as I watch them go. At long last he finally found part of his family. Someone steps beside me. I look over to see my own father watching my face.

"You really care about that boy, don't you?"

A flush springs up my neck to curl around my ears. I clear my throat.

"I suppose I do." I stumble over my words, all the surety I had before the crowd of prisoners completely gone.

I never once considered what my parents would think of my relationship with Alik. No one has cared before. All Luiza told me was not to get attached, and it's all too obvious how well I listened. It seems such an odd thing to worry about. So . . . normal in the face of every other unnatural thing in my life.

"It looked like more than a 'I suppose I do,'" Gregori says, and nudges me.

"Oh, are we talking about Val's love life?" Anton says as he squeezes his way between Papa and I. "Tell us, have you kissed? What was it like?"

"Anton," I hiss, my face flaming.

"That's a yes if I've ever heard one." Gregori and Anton exchange a look over my head and burst into laughter.

"Boys," Papa admonishes, but it's half-hearted at best. He turns a grin toward me. "Please, we need to know how it all started."

"I don't think anyone *needs*—"

"I know!" Chinua says, suddenly at Gregori's elbow. I glare at her.

"I think we have far more important things to discuss," I say.

"What's a brief break between chores?" Anton says. "We don't have anything better to do."

"You could go wash the blood from your face," I shoot back.

Anton clutches his chest as if I'd shot him. "You wound me. I just want to know about my little sister's life. Is that so wrong?"

Gregori turns toward Chinua. "Since Val won't tell us, why don't you?"

"It all started on our way to Knnot. At least, what I saw. You should've seen the looks they exchanged when they thought no one was looking—"

"I'm not listening to this," I say, my body practically on fire. "I'm going to find a bath."

Laughter follows me as I stalk away. I can't believe I freed an entire prison and all they want to do is talk about love.

I stomp into the guardhouse, slipping off my disgusting boots at the door. The common area is dim but well appointed, with overstuffed chairs and thick rugs on the wall keeping out the winter chill. I sneer, doubting the prisoners had any such luxuries. I startle as I find Bataar standing beside the roaring fireplace on the eastern wall, warming his hands, fresh blood on the bandage where his middle finger had been.

"Nice shooting," I say, coming to stand beside him.

"I told you I had talent. You just didn't believe me."

I don't look over, but I can tell by the lilt in his tone he's smiling.

"I don't remember saying that. Just that you could be an assassin. Which, if anything, is a compliment." A grin tugs at my lips.

Bataar hisses as one of his other fingers catches the stump on his right hand. I turn toward him as he clutches it to his chest.

"Here, let me," I say, extending my hand.

Bataar searches my face for a single moment before willingly placing his hand on mine. I unwrap it carefully, and toss the bloodied bandage into the fire. What remains of the finger is raw and jagged, the muscle so red it could almost be paint. I grimace down at it before slowly letting Kosci's power ease into Bataar's hand, just as I had with Anton.

Small stars of snow and ice start to form, curling their way around the stump before sealing it away completely. Bataar takes in a single, sharp breath, and I release the magic, watching to ensure it recedes completely from his skin. I couldn't make the finger whole, but I healed it over, leaving behind smooth skin.

Bataar's hand trembles as he lifts it up. He turns it over, as if seeing his hand anew, before gently touching the stump.

"You . . . healed it."

I shrug, unsure of how to handle the obvious awe. "Sorry I

couldn't give you the finger back."

He laughs. "I think I'll take what I can get."

"Val?"

I jump at Alik's soft voice behind me and spin to face him.

"I thought you were helping Irina."

"I was, but there wasn't much left to do after we'd spread the word through the crowd." Concern hangs from every feature, his gaze only flickering to Bataar once. "Besides, I wanted to check on you. I know . . . I know Luiza never had us kill anyone before."

"They deserved their deaths." The words fall from my lips before I think. Alik's eyebrows climb, and my gut clenches. I already know what he will say before he opens his mouth.

"They were still people."

"People who have hurt and killed Zladonians at nearly every opportunity," Bataar says. I blink, surprised to find an ally in him and not Alik.

"I don't remember inviting you into this conversation," Alik says, not bothering to look at Bataar.

"Fine, fine," Bataar says, voice full of nonchalance. "I know a lovers' quarrel when I see one."

He walks away but pauses in the doorway, casting his gaze back to me. "Thank you, Valeria. Truly."

I grant him a wan smile, and he slips out of the barracks. The air in the room changes without his presence, almost harsh now that it's just Alik and me. Heat prickles along my neck as irritation festers at the mask across Alik's face.

"I'm not an idiot," I say. "I know they were people. I saw them bleed, but I don't care. I wish I did. I've tried, Alik, I really have, but I feel nothing. You lost your family because of *them*. We had to hide for years because of *them*. These prisons only work because of their blind loyalty to the Czar. They chose their path, and this was its ending."

"Ivan was a Storm Hound. Did he get what he deserved, too?" Alik says darkly.

I press my lips together. Ivan didn't mean the same thing to me as he did to Alik, but any response other than the one he wants will cause a rift between us I'll never manage to cross.

"You know I don't think that," I say.

"You don't know how many of those men were like him. They could've enlisted before the Storm Hounds were sent to round up Zladonians. They could've been pressured into it because their families were poor and broken. They all could've wanted out, too."

I shrug. I refuse to deal in might have beens. Of course they could've wanted to leave, but the fact was, they hadn't. They stayed right where the Czar placed them, valuing comfort over doing the right thing.

You don't have to find space in your heart to care, Valeria. They are the hands that caused the world to suffer. Vengeance is justified. He should see that.

"I thought you would understand," I say, Kosci's words

lingering in my mind. Why *didn't* Alik understand?

Alik reaches for my hand. I let him take it.

"I guess I can see your side. A little. And if you need to use that as your shield against the horror of it, then I understand." He releases a heavy breath. "But I can't stop seeing them fall, all the blood pooling around them." He pauses, eye unfocused. With a shake, he looks to me. "Just . . . don't get so caught up in revenge that you forget why you're doing this."

He softens at the look on my face and gives my hand a squeeze.

"I am proud of what you accomplished. Don't think I'm not. Don't think I won't ever be. I just wish it hadn't cost so much."

"This is war, Alik. It's nothing but suffering and bloodshed until the bitter end."

He sighs and tightens his grip on my hand. "I know."

Silence falls between us as we both stare into the flame. His hand is warm in mine, almost too hot against the new chill of my skin. A cold we should both share. I cast a sideways glance at Alik as the mirror of ice he'd conjured jumps to the fore-front of my mind.

Did you help him? I ask Kosci.

No. I have no ties to him. He shouldn't have the ability to access my power. I don't know how or why it's possible. Dark undertones filter through Kosci's words.

"Alik," I say slowly. "What happened out there, with the

ice? Did you know you could use Kosci's abilities?"

His brow crinkles as he stares into the flames. "That was the first time it has ever happened."

Doubt rolls through me, and I don't know if it's Kosci's or my own. It had been so precise, so perfect. I don't even know if I could do it.

I consider using Kosci's power to rifle through Alik's memories but stay my hand. If he ever found out, he would never forgive me. I want to believe him and yet . . .

Yet he has lied to you before. Kosci puts voice to the nagging worry in the back of my head. *He lied about Ivan being a Storm Hound. He lied about Luiza finding him in Oleg. How can you be certain he's telling the truth now?*

I know. I think the words far more forcefully than I intend. Kosci curls back from the heat and I take a steadying breath. In the end, my heart wins, as it always does.

"We'll figure it out," I say. "We always do."

The next day dawns bright and bitter. I stand at the edge of the courtyard, a pile of Storm Hound corpses before me. Others bustle around, requisitioning the sleigh the guards used to get to the prison and filling it with the elderly and the sick. We've taken from the prison every last bit of food, blankets, and weapons we can find. The newly freed prisoners are mostly in good shape, fed and cared for well enough so their duties never faltered. It seems a meager blessing.

Slow footsteps approach, and Bataar comes to a stop at my side. He eyes the pile with an impassive face before turning to me.

"What will you do?"

"I'm burning it to the ground," I say, my hand tightening around the tinder in my hand.

"Good," he replies. He shivers into his coat, letting the fur brush up against his nose, but he doesn't seem to regret what he said. It's such a stark difference from Alik's reaction last night that I almost don't believe it.

"You don't think we should have spared them?" I ask.

"So they could turn over information about your power to Luiza and use it against you?" He shakes his head. "No. They are better off dead."

The tension that had crawled its way into my heart at Alik's admonishment eases slightly. Someone, at least, understood. I pull myself up to full height as Chinua and Sera make their way toward me, oil lamps in hand, Alik and his mother behind them with more. I take the one passed to me and throw it across the bodies, dousing every inch. Sera flicks long lines along the wooden walls while Irina and Alik head into the narrow houses.

By the time we've finished, my brothers have managed to move everyone a safe distance away from the prison. I hold out the flaming torch to Irina.

"You deserve the honor," I say.

Her jaw firms as she takes the torch. With a yell, she buries it deep into the heap before us. The oil catches and flits along invisible lines across the bodies. The stink of burning hair wafts through the now empty courtyard, and I back away as the fire takes hold, hungrily moving to the walls smeared with oil.

We retreat to the edge of the forest with the rest of the freed Zladonians and watch it burn in silence, black smoke marring the beauty of the morning. I smile down at the wreckage. I will burn every single prison if I have to.

I will set all of Zladonia free.

THIRTEEN

IT TAKES TWO DAYS LONGER to travel back with the sleighs and the new additions to our team, but at long last, Knnot rises out of the foothills like a beacon.

Home.

A thrill runs along the new crowd as we cross the plain in a slow procession toward the tall wall of ice. They stare up at it with the same wonder they'd fixed on me at the prison as we pass into its shadow.

With a quick twist of my hand, I lower the wall and wait as everyone passes through. As soon as I'm certain everyone has entered the town, I raise it back up and lead the new Zladonians into Ludminka. Villagers still as we pass, children racing from house to house, banging on each door to tell everyone we have returned. The crowd swells until it bursts onto the cobbled village center before the inn. Knnot looms overhead, and some of the new Zladonians eye it nervously. Ludminkans hang around the edge of the square, silent and watchful for so long I fear I miscalculated in bringing the freed Zladonians here.

"Babushka!" A small cry comes from the west.

A tiny girl no more than eleven flings herself forward and races across the stone until she collapses into the arms of an old woman to my right. She falls to her knees and gathers the girl into her arms, tears running into soft wrinkles. She rocks the girl back and forth, pressing her nose into her hair.

It's all the invitation the others need. They tumble into the square to study the new faces; some clasp hands in greeting while others exchange tearful hugs and kisses. My heart swells with each meeting. This was more than I could've wanted.

I climb the steps to the front of the village hall, waiting for the tears and shouts to slowly die down. When, at last, everyone seems to notice me, I raise my hands to the crowd.

"We have suffered for ten long years under the Czar's reign." My voice echoes back at me from the houses rimming the square. "He marked us as the ones to destroy Strana, when in truth it was nothing but his own hand. Tonight, we will forget the past and celebrate what we have. We deserve the right to flourish and be happy. We will welcome our new villagers with a feast fit for the ages."

Bright cheers ring through the group.

"Soon, we will deal with the Czar. We will gather our strength, hone our rage, and bring it down upon Ladislaw. We will make him pay for what he's done. Together, as Zladonians are meant to be. What say you?"

Again, a chorus of cheers and whoops comes at my words. The crowd before me seethes with anticipation.

"Then let us feast! For tomorrow a new age will begin. One where we are the heroes!"

Roars rise at my announcement, and I back into the shadows of the village hall, shivering in the sharp drop in temperature.

"Nice work," someone says from behind me. I spin to find Bataar casually leaning on one of the columns. He shrugs off it and tosses me a smile. "You seem to have a knack for speaking to the masses."

"I wouldn't say that."

"I would, and trust me, I've seen my fair share of political posturing. Adaman is full of generals trying to find their way into the Khan's favor."

Bataar falls into step beside me as I descend the stairs, slipping to shield me from people as they try to reach out for me. Hands crash into his arm and side, but he stares straight ahead with a good-natured set to his mouth. The relief of being untouched as we make our way back toward the cabin is almost palpable.

"Have you escorted a godly champion before?" I ask, half joking as he intercepts another brush.

"No, but I've been a very decorated bodyguard. It seemed like maybe you could use a break. I'm not sure I saw you alone once on the return to Ludminka."

"That's because I wasn't," I say with a huff. "Someone even followed me to the latrine."

Bataar chuckles as we meander back toward the cabin, the crowd thinning until it disappears completely. By the time we stop before the low garden walls of the cabin, the sound of the crowd has died away completely, replaced only by the soft tinkle of fresh snow landing against frozen pine needles.

"I'm heading back tonight." Bataar turns to face me. "Any longer and Luiza will suspect something is wrong. What do you want me to do while I'm in Rurik?"

"Oh." The question catches me off guard. The entire reason Bataar is here is because we need someone inside Luiza's empire of spies and thieves, but somehow the why of his arrival had gotten lost in my mind.

"We need any and all information you can gather on Matvei. I would especially like you to find where he keeps Zoltoy's heart. It should look something like this." I pull Kosci's out from beneath my coat, and Bataar leans forward to study it. Blue light paints his face in long scars as he reaches out slowly, brushing the tip of his finger along it. A jolt runs through his body, and he snaps his finger back.

"Not very friendly, I see," Bataar says.

I'm a delight, Kosci replies sourly. *I just don't appreciate being prodded.*

I suffocate a snort as I tuck Kosci's heart back. "I also need you to find out where they are amassing their army, if they are training new recruits. It would be even better if you could worm your way in close enough to figure out their exact plans, but that may be too impossible a task."

"I'll do my best," he says with a solemn nod. The expression is almost foreign on his face.

"How do you intend to get information back to us?" I ask.

"I have a courier hawk gifted to me by a friend in Adaman. She flies in any weather and can reach the right spot if given the correct scent clues." Without another word, he pulls the loose scarf around my neck. "This should do just fine."

A bemused smirk comes to my lips. "A scarf?"

"How else do you expect her to find you?"

"You are the strangest person I've ever met."

Bataar's lips quirk. "You haven't met very many people then."

He makes to turn back to the cabin, but I catch his arm before he can. He looks over his shoulder with a raised brow.

"Be careful, Bataar. I don't want you to end up on the wrong side of a crossbow because of me."

He smiles, and his eyes turn a molten brown. "I'm always careful."

With that, he pulls away and steps inside, leaving me along the stone wall very certain he is lying.

The village of Ludminka doesn't disappoint in turning out for a feast to rival any of Ladislaw's banquets. Before the sun sets, the village hall is fit to bursting. Long tables and benches run the length of the building, each one full of people laughing and talking. A dozen different scents compete for dominance: burning pine branches, fresh brown bread, sharp air promising snow, and a multitude of other flavors rolling out on the steam rising from the food table along the far wall.

Someone had thrown cloths over the food table, turning it into a patchwork of bright yellows and whirling red stitching. Atop it sits everything the Ludminkans could make with a half day to prepare: cold cuts of fish; cinnamon taiga bread; pastila, a lovely sweet with berries and sugar that melts on the tongue; soups and lentil stews; cabbage rolls and potato kugel.

I squeeze into a seat beside Sera and Alik, passing cups of mulled red wine among us. Our plates are piled with food, and for the first time since I accepted Kosci's deal, I feel right. As if I finally found my place. I am their champion, their leader, their warrior, and if it means a dozen more nights like this, then I will gladly go to war. I raise my cup.

"To bravery and your willing friendship," I say.

Chinua, Alik, and Sera's cups clink against mine, and we all take a sip. I wrinkle my nose as the clove and cinnamon dusts my tongue, the sour tang of wine rolling down my throat. I've never cared for mulled wine and today proves no different. I set it aside and dive into my food, grinning at the others over pastries and roasted meat.

Before long, someone takes up a balalaika, the small three-stringed instrument favored in Ludminka. As a merry tune starts, people begin to clap, the braver souls twirling to their feet to dance. A man joins the woman on the balalaika with a set of panpipes. Chinua claps with the beat, her eyes trained on the whirling skirts of the women before us.

Sera returns with more drinks, and I sip mine, trying to hide my disgust. Chinua downs hers in one swig and holds her hand out to Sera.

"Let's dance," she says.

Sera raises a skeptical brow. "I really don't think you'd enjoy that."

"Don't tell me what I'd enjoy," she says, and gives Sera a playful yank.

Despite Sera's height and breadth, she tumbles after Chinua, laughing as the girl pulls her deeper into the ocean of skirts and twirling tunics. It's clear neither know what they are doing, but they whirl around anyway, beaming and red cheeked. I laugh as Chinua attempts to spin Sera, her short arms nowhere near long enough for Sera to move under.

Two more string instruments join, followed by a larger set of pipes. Music ricochets from the ceiling, setting the hall alight. Matta and Papa join in the dance, vaulting and spinning like they'd been doing it their entire lives. A very red-faced Gregori is tugged onto the floor by the blacksmith's daughter, and Anton dances along alone until a smooth-faced young man asks to join.

As the tune moves from a lively dance to a slower melody, a warm hand slips into mine. I look up into Alik's face. "Our turn."

I try to protest, but he grins and pulls me onto the floor anyway, curling an arm around my waist, pressing me closer. I rest one hand on his shoulder, the other caught in his own. He rests his forehead on mine, and the music swirls around us like a river. Part of me remains far too aware of the wandering eyes cascading over me. What do the villagers think of seeing their champion in the arms of a boy? Did it make me seem addle-headed and foolish? As if he can hear my thoughts, Alik brushes a kiss to my brow, stealing a small amount of air from my throat.

"For tonight, let's not worry about anyone else," he whispers, warm breath slipping along my ear. A rolling shudder runs up my spine, and I melt into him.

His hand finds its way to the small of my back, and the warmth of his body seeps into my chest, chasing away the icy frost that always seems to emanate from the pendant at my neck.

Alik's eye doesn't leave my face as we sway with the

music. It's as if he's transfixed, unable to see anything else. A cold heat blooms in my stomach, and I shift my gaze to his lips, lingering for a moment before finding something else to concentrate on. My body almost trembles with nervous energy, the scant space between us both too close and too far away.

He doesn't put too much weight on his injured leg, but we've sparred enough together over all our years that I know his body almost as well as my own. It feels like the most natural thing in the world, and I lose myself in the beautiful simplicity of it. I almost don't notice as we pull farther from the lights and the push of the crowd into a darkened corner.

He slows us to a stop, ignoring the tempo changing to something more exuberant. He runs a thumb along my cheek, until he barely traces my bottom lip. My breath catches and he lowers his mouth to mine.

We meet in the middle, his lips warm and tasting of cinnamon and wine. My mouth explores his as I lace my fingers around the back of his neck, following the hungry pull of his mouth. A loud beat on a drum startles me and I pull away, suddenly aware of the hundreds of eyes in the hall, all of which will eventually look for the Pale God's champion.

"Not here," I whisper.

Alik nods and takes my hand, pulling me into the cool night. My body thrums in anticipation, my heartbeat in my ears as his arm slips around my waist and we make our way back to the house we call home. I ache to turn into him, to feel his chest against mine, but I let him lead me all the way to the cabin without whispering those words into existence.

As soon as he swings the door open and we step inside, I spin to face him, lacing my arms through his and curling my fingers into the fabric at the back of his shirt. With a desperate exhale, I pull him into me, finding his mouth almost immediately. His lips sear along mine and I gasp against them, the want pooling in my body. Alik's hands dance along my sides, sending my muscles jumping at his touch. I clutch helplessly at his tunic, trying to get closer even though there isn't so much as a whisper of air between us.

Alik's fingers curl around the back of my neck, his thumb finding its home on my cheek and he opens his mouth to mine. I return in kind, letting his lips and his hands carry me far from the prisons and war, far from everything in the world that has changed.

We stumble a bit, my back slamming against the door jamb. I laugh against his lips and he smiles. Alik nudges my chin to the side, kissing along my jaw until he finds my ear. He takes it softly between his teeth and tugs. A soft sigh escapes my lips.

Alik laces his fingers through mine, holding tight before pulling me toward his room at the end of the hall. My heart hammers as I follow, lips warm with his kisses.

His room is dimly lit by a single, flickering candle housed inside a glass casing on his desk. The room sits like all the others in the house, but feels distinctly like him. It even smells like him, soft winter wind and pine. I cross to the twin bed against the wall covered in a small quilt and sit, apprehension suddenly rolling over me.

I tense as I slowly follow the planes of his body to his face. He bites the inside of his cheek, obviously just as nervous as I am. Something about that settles the flutters in my stomach. I reach out, deliberately giving him enough time to step away. When he doesn't move, I fiddle with the edge of his shirt before standing and pulling it over his head.

Alik's bare chest flickers with shadows, but the scars down his torso can't be more obvious. I'd seen them before, in the cave outside the Storm Hound encampment, what seemed like ages ago. A long, ridged scar trails from his shoulder across his chest, the skin pulled tight and white, while another crosses from his hip bone down. Just as it had in the cave, the desire to learn these new additions to his body laces through me. I place my fingertips on his shoulder at the start of the scar, and Alik shudders. Slowly, I run the length of it, memorizing the rough skin sliding beneath my fingertips.

I look up at his quick inhale, wondering if I should stop. He stares at the floorboards beneath our feet, cheeks pink. I take his chin in my hands, turning him to face me, and press a slow, gentle kiss to his lips.

"Do you want me to stop?" I ask.

No," he breathes against my mouth.

I trail my fingers along his face toward the patch on his eye he's never removed. I expect him to jerk away, but he lets me slip a finger beneath the strap and take it off. His eyelid droops over the empty socket, the scar starting at his hairline runs over it, nipping deep into the delicate skin of his eyelid all the way to his nose. I lean onto my toes and press a kiss to it, then to his cheek, then to his mouth. I pull away so he can see me.

"I love you. Just like this," I say softly in the space between us.

I kiss his shoulder, then his chest. Alik inhales sharply and his arms move from his side to pull my own shirt off. It falls to the ground beside his and Alik leans forward, catching me around the waist, finding my lips again. This kiss is different, his mouth soft and slow, almost reverential. His fingers curl harder into my side and it makes my body arch into his. Every place our bare skin meets feels like small starbursts, tingling and warm. Gently, he lowers me onto the bed. Alik's weight settles on top of me and I sigh again, sliding my hands to his back, needing to be closer still.

Alik's mouth moves from mine to my neck, where he stalls. He catches the pendant around my neck and we break apart. He leans onto his elbow and takes the loop of leather into his hand. For the briefest flash, I don't want him to take it off, but

I lean up, letting him slip it over my head. He drops it to the ground.

Alik leans back down, the warmth of him touching every inch of my cold body. Now, I'm furiously glad he took off the pendant. Tonight is for us and us alone.

FOURTEEN

THE NEXT TWO WEEKS FLY by, lost to planning our
next raid, training, and exploring the reaches of Kosci's
power. The biggest surprise comes from the people who
were freed. Led by Alik's mother, every able-bodied person
showed up at the small clearing on the outskirts of Ludminka
to train. Every one of them simmered, their rage pouring
into Kosci, feeding them and building our power until it
burned like an ember in my chest. It was easier to give them
the memories I had gifted my first volunteers, flowing into
their minds like it was always meant to be there. It's the only
thing I don't tell Alik.

I bounce down the stairs one frigid morning, expecting the
day to pass as they all have, only to find a capped falcon standing on the kitchen table. His long, elegant wings are coated in

ice, and it trembles as Alik unties a small parchment from its leg. I cross to the bird, reaching out slowly to pick it up. The hawk pecks half-heartedly as I move it closer to the warmth of the fire.

"A message from Bataar?" I ask as I gently break the ice from the falcon's wings.

Alik nods. "But it's all in Adaman."

"Here," Chinua says, moving from her spot at the table to take the parchment.

She scans the page quickly, brow furrowing with each word. At the end she lets out a long sigh, and I know before she even opens her mouth that whatever it is, we won't be happy.

"He says he hasn't seen the Bright God's heart yet and that their army numbers in the hundreds, new recruits being trained almost daily. Ladislaw has ordered everyone who has a sliver of lovite to bring it to the palace. Apparently they are melting it down for something, Bataar doesn't know what, but I'm willing to bet it's to make more weapons and shields to fight against your power." Chinua looks up at me, her face stony.

"That doesn't bode well for us," I say. "Lovite is our only advantage at the moment."

"There's more," she says.

"How can there possibly be more?" Alik asks.

"He says they are sending an envoy to Adaman. They're going to ask the Khan for help."

My stomach sinks hard and fast. It's no secret Adaman has some of the best riders in the world. Their skill had expanded their borders far beyond their original area. The only thing that has kept them from consuming Strana completely has been lovite. Ladislaw has always refused to give them the raw material which would grant them the ability to make weapons fine enough to destroy empires. If Ladislaw manages to secure an alliance, there will be absolutely no chance at winning this war.

Bataar's words about Adaman come back to me. The Khan would respect my strength and power, but he wouldn't ally with someone who had no victories. I had proven I was capable of moving against the Czar, and I was the one who controlled the lovite. With it, I could control the world. Even the Khan would have to see the sense of our alliance.

"Looks like we are going to have to go to Adaman ourselves."

"What?" Chinua's head snaps back up. "You can't be serious."

"I'm very serious. We can't let Ladislaw drip honey into the Khan's ear. We'll have absolutely no hope of winning if he manages to secure an Adaman army. We're closer to the border here, we will make it before any envoy from Rurik does," I say.

"We have nothing to offer. No reason why the Khan would want to see us, let alone agree to a deal," Chinua says, her voice growing thinner with each word.

"We're sitting on the world's largest deposit of lovite. He has every reason to listen to us." I take a step forward, closing a hand around Chinua's shoulder. "I'm not asking you to come with me. I don't want to put you in danger, but I promise I will try to get your family back."

"I have to go." Chinua's hands begin to tremble. "No one here knows Adamanian. Without a translator you won't get very far."

I try to find a way around the problem, but Chinua's right and Bataar is too far away to make it before Ladislaw. I can't ask Chinua to return to Adaman, not when I know what waits for her there, but if Ladislaw manages an alliance, every last person in Ludminka will be slaughtered.

Chinua squares her shoulders. "I can't run from Temujin forever, and if there is even a sliver of a chance to see my family, I want to take it."

"If you're sure," I say hesitantly, and Chinua gives a firm nod. "I will keep you safe in Adaman, just like I did in Knnot. I swear it. You won't return to the Khan if you don't want to."

Chinua's eyes flick to Sera, who has been silent and still by the oven since the conversation began, before bouncing back to mine.

"I don't," she says, her cheeks flushing a brilliant scarlet.

"Then we need to ready ourselves. The longer we wait, the more time Ladislaw's envoy has to get there."

Chinua nods again, this one more certain. "I'll start gathering the supplies. You'll need different clothing, something finer than what you've been wearing to make a good show of yourself."

"My matta should be able to help with that," I say. "I can speak with her. I need to talk to my father anyway. Just because we aren't here doesn't mean we shouldn't still push on with training."

Chinua beckons once to Sera, who immediately stands, half-drunk cup of tea forgotten, and they struggle into their fur-lined boots with furtive whispers. I resist the urge to slip my hand into my pocket and draw power from Kosci to hear what they are saying and cross to Alik who helps the hawk break more ice from its feathers.

"I never thought I'd see the day you'd choose diplomacy over action," he says with a teasing smile.

"I'm not always violence and rage," I say with a scowl.

"No, you are not," he says, and the way he says it warms me all the way to my toes.

"I need your help," I say, straying from the tempting curve of his lips. "You've always had a good eye for useful people. We need our own little net of spies. Bataar will only be able to maintain his position inside Luiza's circle for so long. I need you to find people she would've chosen for the guild. Become our master of spies, of a sort."

An even larger smile spreads across his face and one of his

arms curls around my waist.

"I've never been so flattered," he says. "It will be nice to be something other than a hindrance."

"You're not a hindrance. I couldn't do any of this without you."

Alik presses his lips together. "You would've been able to shake this world with or without me by your side."

I don't know how to respond, so I slip against his chest, hugging him tight. Whatever may come, I am glad to have Alik by my side. The stain of his deaths has slowly faded from my dreams. With each soft touch or gentle word, those horrible memories turn into bruises that may eventually heal.

After scrambling for supplies and mounts, we travel a fortnight through the stark, jagged mountains of Strana before descending into the rolling plains of Adaman. Wind dogged our every step, nipping at our faces and blowing so hard my ears ached. No scrubby pines or determined birches cling to the steppes we travel. It's nothing but snow and waving grass for miles upon miles.

Alik, Chinua, Sera, and I sit astride horses, a very small contingent of guards at our back, and stare down at the vast expanse of the Khan's winter home nestled in a valley beneath us. We can make out nothing besides tall, white-brick walls topped in red clay shingles. Tall watchtowers made of the same fine, white brick lance the air like knives, their tops coming to severe points. I've no doubt we've already been spotted.

I resist the urge to smooth the fine fabric of the *letnik* Matta and a couple other women in the village came together to make. It's icy blue in color, square-cut buttons of lovite running down the front. Wide wings of fabric, the same color blue, fall down my shoulders and along my arms, hemmed in tiny, crystalline beads that catch the weak afternoon sunlight. It's by far the finest thing I've ever worn and it feels as if it weighs hundreds of pounds. This isn't just a costume, like I'd put on for Luiza during guild missions. This is who Strana would come to see me as. It's who I had to be now, as I begged a ruler for his help.

"How big is this place?" I ask in an awed whisper.

"Larger than Rurik by far," Chinua says, doing her best to keep her horse steady beside mine. "The Khan isn't always here, but he retreats for the winter months to rest his men and prepare for their next advances."

My eyes follow the lines of the walls. They disappear over the horizon in misty smudges. I've never seen its like and I doubt I ever will.

"This is a fool's errand," Sera says from my other side.

I frown. "So you've said."

"We should be back in Strana, taking the next prison," Sera says.

"Perhaps you should've stayed, then," I snap back, tired of her complaining. "You had absolutely no reason to come with me."

With a movement so brief I almost don't catch it, Sera's eyes flit to Chinua before finding mine once again.

"I wasn't going to let you go off alone," she says, but she isn't talking to me.

A gust of wind whistles into the space between us, and the cold of it settles right into my bones, making Kosci's pendant beat at my throat. We are far from the familiarity of Strana.

I have little power here, he whispers and every single one of the hairs on my arms rise. *Adamanians do not pray to the Bright and Pale Gods. Aside from a few whispered prayers from your guards, I have nothing. Keep that in mind.*

You didn't think to tell me?

What good could it have brought you? Your ideas of allyship are good ones. Would you have made the journey so readily if you had known I wouldn't be much help?

What if I need to fight?

Do you plan to start a war with Adaman, too? Kosci asks. *You should have no weapons and should definitely not have use of them while meeting with the Khan. It is called diplomacy.*

What do you know about it? You've been stuck under a rock for centuries.

I don't think that jibe was necessary, Kosci sniffs and fades away, clearly done with me.

My hands tighten around the reins, and I take a deep breath. No weapons, no magic, just my tongue and a wish.

"Let's go," I say, nudging my horse forward. The walls stray ever closer, tossing dark shadows across the yellow grass. With each step, my gut tightens.

Our horses fall in line with other small carts and people meandering their way to the tall gates in the center of the wall. It rises up before us like a mountain, massive doors of lacquered wood thrown wide to welcome the approaching pilgrims. Most of the other travelers don't look up as they pass beneath the yawning gate, but my eyes go skyward, taking in the sharp, determined lines of the stone.

"How did they ever manage this?" I nearly whisper the question.

"Slowly and carefully," Chinua replies. "It took years for the walls to be completed. Khan Temujin's grandfather was the one to order their construction. They weren't complete until the first year of Temujin's rule."

The walls and gate fade away and the road empties onto a long street, squat buildings of brick lining it like a procession of soldiers. Most of them follow the same design, a long ridgepole, tiled roof coming off it, with arching windows facing the sun. People go about their business as we pass, not caring about the crowd slowly making their way into the city. My eyes swing from one building to the other. Happy faces poke out of front doors, trading laughs with their neighbors, some people sell food in small carts on street corners, all of which overflow with cheeses and yogurt, meat and dried jerky.

"I never knew it was so big," I say to Chinua as we follow the street leading toward a vast open field with multicolored yurts as far as the eye could see.

She smiles. "Just because Adamans prefer travel doesn't mean we don't put down roots occasionally. Korum is essentially our stronghold, the place where the Khan goes to regroup and relax."

Chinua takes the lead, turning down another long dirt road, keeping the field of yurts to our right. After two months in Ludminka, everything seems so *loud*. So many people jostling and talking, children running, and everyone . . . happy. That was the strangest thing to see. I'd stared into the forlorn faces of Ludminka for far too long. This is what I fought for, community, laughter, love.

The chatter of the city dies as the road opens onto another wide field, this one devoid of the tents and people that had studded the path behind us. Instead, it is full of statues and scrubby trees. A tall temple with sloped roofs, curving at the end, stands off to our right. Chinua leads us past it, turning in to another walled structure with a similar gate to the front, albeit much smaller. This one is roofed in triangular green tiles, and two men stand on either side.

Two men lightly armored in knee-length leather jerkins tightened around the middle with thick belts swing into our path, stalling our horses. Conical hats with fur-lined ear flaps graced their heads, and I wish I would've thought of bringing something like that to cover my own.

"What business?" The one on the right asks, his Stranan accented but clear.

"We've come to meet with the Khan," I say, voice full of a strength I only partly feel. "I am the Pale God's champion and I've come to him with a proposition."

The left guard's eyes are trained on Chinua, taking in her loose hair tugging in the wind, and the tight line of her lips. He leans over to his compatriot and whispers something I can't hear, and the right guard's gaze finds Chinua's, too. I don't look over at her, refusing to let the guards see I'm acknowledging their whispers. After long moments, the guards nod to one another.

"This way," says the guard on the right.

He leads us into the courtyard before a two-story building shaped much like the homes outside, a single long ridgepole with a sharply dipping roof, corners upturned toward the sky tiled in the same green triangles as the gate. A magnificent tree of lovite sits in the center, branches wide and permanently in bloom with delicate leaves and milky-white flowers. It's the most magnificent sculpture I've ever seen. One of the guards notices my gaze.

"A gift from Czar Ladislaw twenty years ago. Called it a gesture of goodwill," he says.

His comrade scoffs, saying something in Adaman I don't understand. Chinua leans in.

"He says it's more like a warning since Ladislaw refused to gift them ore."

My mouth turns down as the guards pull to a stop before

a steep set of stairs, the same beautiful white brick as all the other structures in Adaman so far. Chinua swings down from her horse, so I follow, having to struggle into sidesaddle with the awkward weight of my *letnik*. I'm just contemplating how to get down in a way that is semi-dignified when Alik steps into view, placing his hands on my waist. I slip down along his chest, and though I know it isn't exactly the mark of leadership, a warm shiver runs along my back. He smiles before pulling away.

As soon as we are all on the ground, people take the reins of our horses, leading them off to the left where a low, open-air stable sits. I turn my gaze to the tall stairs and take in a deep breath.

Today I will see if I am ally or foe. Today I will see if I can best Luiza and Ladislaw at their own game.

FIFTEEN

WE ASCEND THE STAIRS. ME first followed by Chinua, Sera, and Alik, then the little group of guards we'd taken more as a show of our force than for actual protection. The steps empty onto a wide stone platform that frames the palace in a square. During the warmer months, I'm sure it's a lovely spot to meander and talk politics, but a bristling wind winds its way through the stone balustrade and spits hard flakes into our faces.

I make my way toward the open doors beneath a felt awning, relishing a break from the wind. Inside, a long hall greets us, held aloft by beautiful columns of silver and gold. They run the length of the hall until they reach a dual set of stairs that curve upward to a platform with a cobalt silk canopy. Beneath it, outlined by a decorative mural of curling whorls, is a man.

Two slightly lower platforms sit on either side of him, filled with people I can only assume are advisers.

The man watches us approach, his face an unreadable mask. As we grow closer, I realize he's much older than I expect, his dark hair and neatly trimmed and pointed beard shot through with streaks of silver. His careful, dark eyes study us as we come to a stop, running over me before snagging on Chinua. His mouth thins, the only outward sign that betrays his emotions.

"I admit when I received a missive saying I'd be receiving an envoy from Strana, this was not what I expected," he says, voice surprisingly deep for his small stature. He stands on the pillowed dais, striding forward to get a better look. I lift my head, my heart beating in my throat.

"We do not come from Ladislaw," I say. "I represent myself and the rest of the Zladonians the Czar has kept imprisoned for the last ten years."

Khan Temujin clasps his hands behind his back before inclining his head. "I will hear your words. Please."

He gestures to a small stool beside him on the dais. I clench my teeth hard, squelching the wriggle of fear in my stomach and the voice in the back of my head telling me I have no idea how to do this. I ascend the stairs, careful not to step on the hem of my *letnik*. The Khan waits for me to settle onto the furred-pillow-topped stool before taking his place. It seems odd to talk to him like this, face-to-face at the same eye level.

Ladislaw held his courts far above everyone else, clearly demonstrating the line between citizen and ruler.

"Tell me, why have I heard nothing about Zladonians this past decade?" Temujin asks.

"Ladislaw has made sure to keep it quiet. We were punished for the fall of Knnot and the plague that followed. Ladislaw wanted someone to blame, and he found it in us."

Temujin's brow pinches and he looks to Chinua, asking her something in Adaman. Chinua steps forward and nods, responding in a clear, hard voice. She keeps her stance wide and her shoulders proud, betraying none of the discomfort I know she must feel. The Khan turns back to me.

"Chinua backs your claims," he says. "Her parents are trusted advisers to me, and so I will believe her words. We do not hold with the imprisonment of one's own people, and as such, we will listen to no treaty on Ladislaw's end."

Relief flows through me from crown to toes in a rolling wave.

"However," he pauses, "we have never allied with Strana. We trade with all the countries of the east, with Drangiana in the south, yet Strana refuses our goods, refuses to give us things in return. Why would I hear the pleas of a girl claiming to be a champion of the gods if nothing will change for my own country?"

I bite the tip of my tongue. "I'm not *claiming* to be a champion. I am one."

"Why would a god choose you? You're nothing but a half-grown child." Temujin doesn't say the words unkindly, but a bitter taste comes to my mouth. I may be young, but there have been czars who took the crown even younger than I am now. Their rule was not questioned.

I tug on the very faint strains of Kosci's power, so small they might have been wisps of smoke, but they fall readily into my palm. A tiny tree of ice and snow mimicking the one outside grows in my hand, the last vestiges of power Kosci gleaned from the guards who'd followed us to Adaman. Temujin looks at it for a long moment before I let it fade, already feeling how unstable the magic is in my veins.

"I know you've heard tales of the champions, and I know most of the world believes them to be nothing but myths. But I do carry the soul of a god within me, and I will use the power granted to me to overthrow Ladislaw for what he has done. Our country is nothing but a ghost of its former glory, lost to greed and poverty. I come before you now to ask for your help, and I do not come empty-handed."

I gesture to Sera and Alik who both step forward, though Sera does so begrudgingly. From pouches at their waists, they produce raw lovite, crude and unprocessed, and set it before the raised stairs.

"I am willing to give you what Ladislaw never would. I control Knnot now, the lovite trade is mine and mine alone. All I ask is that you ally with us."

Khan Temujin's eyes haven't left the lovite since it came out of the bags. It clearly was the very last thing he expected from me, and I can practically see the wheels of his mind turning, any attempts to remain stoic lost to the luster of lovite.

"You wish to overthrow Ladislaw, you say? Will you destroy his bloodline as well? He has a son and comes from a long line of powerful rulers. And, if your stories are true, where is the Bright God's champion? Does he not rise with the Pale?"

My mouth dries at his unexpected questions. In truth, I'd barely thought about Ladislaw's son since the day I saw him before the *tyur'ma* outside Oleg. If I did manage to kill Ladislaw, what *would* I do with Yuri? No matter how much I want to destroy his father, I don't think I have the will to kill a child.

But in not killing him, I leave myself open for Yuri to gather a force loyal to the old crown with a legitimate claim to the throne. My stomach churns as I realize I will have no choice but to step into Ladislaw's place as ruler. Instead of answering questions of Yuri and what I will do once I kill Ladislaw, I address the issue of the Bright God.

"The Bright God's champion sides with Ladislaw. His name is Matvei, a farmer's son, from all the intelligence we've managed to gather, though he's been in possession of the Bright God's power for quite some time, eight years at least." I smooth the *letnik* across my knees to give my anxious hands something to do before adding, "We do have weapons that can be used against him, ones made of lovite and blessed by me."

That part is a lie, but it stands to reason that if Matvei can do it, I can too. I want to send the question to Kosci, but he is nothing but a dull muttering at the back of my mind. I try not to let the feeling unsettle me. It's been so long since my mind was quiet that I don't know what to do now that he's gone. Temujin's eyes shift back to mine.

"It's an interesting proposal," he says, rubbing his chin for a moment. "What say you?"

He turns to the men and women on the small platforms on either side of us. Instantly, they spring to their feet, all of them raising one finger, speaking when the Khan nods their way. I don't understand the discourse and mark it in my mind to learn languages other than Stranan. If I did intend to rule after Ladislaw, I would need to deal with Strana's neighbors.

The idea of ruling sits both like a stone in my stomach and fluttering bird in my heart. When I began this, I thought nothing of the crown and only of freeing Zladonians and getting rid of Ladislaw. I can't turn a country upside down and just leave it behind to suffer in my wake.

"What evidence do you have that you can run a successful campaign?" the Khan says.

"I have already taken one of Ladislaw's prisons and destroyed a battalion of Storm Hounds threatening Ludminka."

"But no open warfare?" He asks with a raised brow.

"No," I say as heat rushes up my neck.

"Do you have an army of your own?"

"It's being trained," I say.

"But they aren't ready," Temujin says it as a statement. Again, that uncomfortable heat curls up my back and sends prickles along my scalp.

"No," I say, "but they will be."

Khan Temujin waves his hand at that, like its nothing but a trifle. A slow tingle laces over my body, lingering in my legs before turning them white hot. I try to breathe through the anger now pulsing at my core, but there is no barrier to stop it anymore. Kosci's voice doesn't ring out in my mind, reminding me to bide my time. I shoot to my feet, and the crowd around us goes silent.

"I know how we must look to you, stumbling along, still finding our feet. But Adaman began the same way, did it not? It wasn't until your great-grandfather united everyone under one banner and began his rule that your country started to gain power. You trained and you fought and you won because it is what you wanted. Now look at your kingdom." I gesture around us like we are looking at all of Adaman instead of the interior of the Khan's palace. "We *want* this, the people I train want this. We will do whatever it takes to see Ladislaw deposed for all he has done."

Temujin's mustache ruffles as he inhales. "Wanting and wishing do not move mountains, Pale champion. You can wish a blizzard gone, but does it move?"

"It does for me," I say through gritted teeth.

"She is worth hundreds of soldiers," Chinua says, stepping forward, proud and fierce. "I have seen her freeze a man solid, call monsters to her aid, craft a wall of unbreakable ice that surrounds an entire village. Valeria *could* will a blizzard to stop, if she so chose. She will change this world, with or without your help, Khan Temujin, but I know how you long for your name to be placed in history alongside your father and grandfather. Being the first khan to ally with Strana, to destroy a czar, would certainly do that."

The room falls utterly still at Chinua's words, the air changing as if by speaking she had taken the breath from their lungs. Temujin begins to speak in Adaman, but Chinua holds up a hand.

"With respect, Khan Temujin, I ask that you speak in a language all here can understand."

For the first time since we walked in the hall, something like displeasure rolls across the Khan's face.

"You did not show me respect when you ran away," he says. Someone gasps in the pulpit behind me.

"As I said to you then, I was not running. I was seeking something worthy of our union, and I have brought it."

Her words fall so smooth and confident from her lips that I could almost believe her.

"Then you will return, now that you have delivered your gift."

Chinua goes rigid and her eyes flick to two men near the

front of the right platform with the same nose and brow as Chinua's. I promised to keep Chinua safe, to keep her family safe. I will not renege on that just because I lack the honey-soaked words of a diplomat.

"Chinua will be doing no such thing," I say, voice as cold and deadly as ice.

"You intend to hold one of my own hostage?" Temujin asks.

"She isn't a captive. She is my general, and the person directing my war efforts. I will not lose her. And you would do well to stop behaving as if she isn't in the room. Ask her yourself, if you don't believe me."

Chinua holds her head high, meeting Temujin's eye with the strength of a ruler. "I follow Valeria. As long as she will have me."

Temujin's gaze slowly moves between Chinua and me as he leans on the arm of his throne.

"Then I suppose we will have no allyship."

SIXTEEN

TEMUJIN'S WORDS SINK IN SLOWLY, the hall quiet enough that the scrape of my beaded *letnik* along the floor is audible as I take a step forward.

"You mean to tell me you refuse because I will not return a person to you who was never yours," I say, the words caustic and hot in my throat. "You take no issue with my quest for power, just my determination to have Chinua by my side."

"Adaman was founded on the backs of people who fought for the right to rule. They were not given it by birth, simply reached. That is what you seek to do, and I applaud your strength," Temujin says, finally rising from his pallet of pillows. "But you are hot-headed, quick to judge, and far too confident in your abilities without evidence of your strength. The proof is displayed before me right now: you're unwilling to negotiate simply because you believe you're right. The honor of being my wife is unmatched in the kingdom. It was a gift I gave her family for years of loyalty. She would have a say in the ruling of Adaman, her own court to preside over. To spit in my eye is a sign of disrespect that I cannot abide."

"Can't you hear how ludicrous this sounds? I offer you the one thing Ladislaw has refused you for two decades and you turn it away because I won't give you Chinua?" I scoff. "And you chastise *me* for my disposition."

Again, the air settles around my shoulders, heavy and thick. I know I should at least attempt diplomacy, that as soon as Kosci regains strength and realizes what I have done he will chastise me for refusing the Khan's offer, but I won't sacrifice Chinua. Not even for the Khan's approval.

Temujin's gaze is steely as he turns to face me, pulling himself up to his full height, which is just a couple inches taller than myself. I don't break eye contact. I will not be seen as some supple willow branch Temujin can bend how he sees fit.

"You may stay and rest yourselves and your horses," Khan Temujin says. "But then you will take your leave. There will be no accord here."

"I offer lovite only this once. If you turn your back on it today, you will never possess it."

It's my last desperate bid to secure an alliance I already see slipping through my fingers. Lovite is the only bargaining chip I have. If Temujin isn't tempted, I can offer nothing else.

Temujin waves a hand at me, as if he is swatting away a particularly annoying fly. It only sets me more on edge, and I have to take a long steady inhale to stop myself from saying something else.

"I will not regret an alliance with a woman who refuses to see sense. I offer you more than you offer me. Lovite is a finite resource. My cavalry, my army, those are things that will be forever growing, forever replenished." He lets out a long sigh, as if almost disappointed. "As I said, you are welcome to make yourself comfortable for a night or two, but I will not discuss this further."

I stand in silence for a heartbeat, too furious to do more than clench my hands into fists. I whirl away from the Khan and descend the stairs to gather with the others. I glare at Temujin before allowing myself to be led away with the others by a man clad in a cotton, knee-length tunic with a high collar.

The rest of Temujin's palace doesn't disappoint. The long halls are finely decorated in large panels of printed golden silk. The floor emanates warmth from pipes beneath the tiles constantly full of hot smoke from fires somewhere far beyond, according to Chinua. Not one of us speaks as the man leads us to a door, opening it with a flourish to allow me inside.

Like the rest of the palace, it's beautiful, the same silken fabric covering the walls, this time in emerald green with bright golden braiding along the ceiling. Beds unlike any I have seen sit in a semicircle around a table in the center of the room. They are all painted bright orange, with high backs along one edge. Small drawers seem to make up the base, every one painted along the edge with swirls curling around diamonds in bright pink, white, and green. Multi-colored blankets lie atop all four, and I want nothing more than to sink into one and bury my head beneath the covers. Instead, I wait for the servant to leave before beckoning Alik, Chinua, and Sera to me.

"That could have gone better," I say in a hushed whisper, too afraid the Khan will have ears and eyes trained on us already. I spent too long being Luiza's little spy to ignore how the game is played.

"You think?" Sera asks, but her voice doesn't hold the vitriol it usually does. Her eyes dart to Chinua, lingering on her reddening cheeks.

"If he's given my father and brother a place in his immediate court, they will refuse to leave." She wrings her hands. "I'd hoped Temujin hadn't gotten to them yet, but the moment I'm alone, my family will try to convince me to accept Temujin's proposal."

I reach out and give her hand a squeeze. "He has no right to claim you, and if I have to fight to keep you where you want to be, then I will."

"Can we finish one war before we start another one?" Sera asks dryly. I'm not sure if she means it as a joke, but a laugh tumbles out of my mouth.

"I would prefer that, yes," I say. I give Chinua's hand another meaningful squeeze before letting it fall. "Temujin will not change his mind, will he?"

"No," Chinua says.

"Then we rode to Adaman for nothing," Sera says, crossing her arms.

"Oh, I'm sorry, would you rather we not try at all and let Ladislaw secure the alliance?" I snap, glad for the outlet to the swirling anger and fear in my stomach. "At least we know Temujin won't agree to any bargain with Ladislaw, if nothing else."

"We could've been in Ludminka, freeing other prisons and gathering more strength to our side. This was a fool's mission from the start," Sera returns.

"Then why don't you lead the revolution, Serafima? Please, take it from my hands, figure out how to rally people to your cause, keep everyone safe and fed, and bring them peace after a lifetime of misery. You clearly feel you would do a much better job than I can."

Serafima's face goes red and her arms tighten across her chest. "You know no one else but you can lead."

"Why don't you start acting like that's true," I snap. "I am trying my best. This isn't a game to me. I care far more than you can even imagine about the people under my banner. I know the risk I took in coming here, but it was one I thought was necessary. I'd hoped it would be beneficial. If Temujin wasn't such a stubborn idiot, it would've been."

Chinua releases a giggle that sounds more like a sob before covering her face with her hands and burying her head into them. Her shoulders shake, but before I can move toward her, Sera steps in and takes Chinua into her arms. She goes willingly, dropping her hands and wrapping her arms around Sera's waist. Sera whispers something soft into Chinua's hair, and I hesitate only a moment before turning away from them. Alik waits beside me and offers his hand, which I take, letting my fingers slip between his. I pull him toward the nearest bed and sit, resting against the tall back of the bed.

Alik settles beside me and I let my head go back, choosing to look at the ceiling, which is also draped in gorgeous emerald silk, instead of the world around me. How had it all gone so wrong? Was I really so impulsive that I wasn't worth allying with? I grit my teeth. I don't care what Temujin could offer me, I will not condemn Chinua to a life of misery just because I want a stronger army.

Alik slips his arm over my shoulders and brings me close, pressing a kiss to my forehead.

"You made the right decision," he says quietly. I look up at him, studying the gentle set to his brow, and a small knot in my chest loosens slightly.

"I promised Chinua I would protect her."

"I know," Alik says. "You are loyal, Val. You always have been. To betray her trust went against your very soul. That isn't something to be disappointed about."

I turn over his words, worrying at the beading on my *letnik*. Across the room, Chinua and Sera separate only to sink onto the bed across from us, mimicking Alik's and my position almost exactly. Chinua's face is wan and pale while Sera's is determined, almost fierce. Despite all her objections, she's grateful for how things played out. It's evident in the way her arm curls around Chinua now, fingers tight on her shoulder like she's determined to keep her from floating away.

But where do we go from here?

Hopelessness tumbles through my body, taking my will with it. Tears burn behind my eyes but I bite my lip, refusing to let them fall.

"We do as we planned," I say into the silence of the room. "We don't need Temujin's army to overthrow Ladislaw. We will free the other *tyur'mas*, then move on Ladislaw himself."

"What of Luiza and Matvei?" Alik asks.

I shrug. "Luiza has bids out for my assassination. She will come, sooner or later, and I will kill her."

Alik straightens at my words, his hold on my shoulder slackening. "Why didn't you tell us?"

"What good would it have done? You know she will strike quick and hard from the shadows before the rebellion can grow beyond something controllable."

"Valeria," Alik grinds out my name.

I narrow my eyes. "I am perfectly capable of protecting myself."

"That isn't the point! You're at risk out in the open like this. There *is* no revolt without you. Luiza and Ladislaw know that." Alik's jaw hardens as we glare at one another.

"We need to get back to Ludminka as quickly as possible," Sera says, breaking the tension in the room. "We'll get you armor and a personal guard to protect you—"

"I don't need a guard," I say.

"I don't care what you say, it's a precaution we're going to take. Alik is right, there is nothing without you. As soon as you die, Ladislaw will swoop into Ludminka and either kill or imprison everyone there. Do you want that? Or would you rather stop being obnoxious for a couple moments?" Sera says, her hold on Chinua never wavering.

I glower, but even I can see the sense of her words, though I wish I didn't.

"Fine," I say. "We leave tomorrow. No use sitting here when there is nothing to be had."

Silence descends upon the room again, and I try to work out the tension in my shoulders. It's impossible in the heavy, sagging fabric of the *letnik*. I drag myself off the bed and toward our carefully stacked packs in the corner, then slip into a beautifully tiled washing chamber attached to the back of the room. Temujin had ideas I wished I could implement throughout Strana, but it would take getting there first. I sigh and start the process of undressing. As I lean forward to slip into fur-lined breeches, the pendant swings off my chest and Kosci's dull muttering becomes louder. Someone must have whispered a prayer to him.

Temujin would've been a powerful ally.

I know, I snap, glad I don't have to pretend away the fearful anger in my heart. *I realize exactly what I have lost.*

Do you truly care for the girl that much?

Do you *not understand the meaning of the word loyalty, or are mortals just pawns to move around your board as you see fit? Some things are not worth the sacrifice.*

It was something you should've considered longer than a moment.

No, I respond, sending the word to Kosci as forcefully as I can. He recoils, and I dress the rest of the way in peace.

When I slip back into the room, the others have curled under the blankets and, though I know it is early in the evening, my bones ache with weariness. I eye the unused bed for one moment before I head toward Alik's. The bed is more than large enough, and he moves over, turning to face me. I wiggle myself closer to him and he throws an arm over my waist, pulling me to his chest. I sigh and press my head into his collarbone.

"Why is this all so hard?" I whisper into the space between us.

He chuckles softly. "You thought it would be easy?"

"No," I say, but my voice hitches a little. "I just thought . . .

I guess I thought I could do it all on my own."

Alik's hand comes up to my jaw, and he tilts my head up so our gazes lock. My heart gives a double thump, want curling through me despite it all. He runs his thumb along my cheek before bringing my chin toward him, brushing a soft kiss along my lips.

"Wars aren't won by a single person," he says, his mouth still only a breath away from mine. "You don't have to be a martyr, Valeria."

I want him to kiss me again. I want him to make me forget everything, the war, Temujin's refusal, the gnawing doubt that always sits at the back of my mind that says I'm doing the wrong thing. I close the distance between us, capturing his mouth before he can say anything else. His hold on my jaw firms, and whispers of longing knot in my stomach. My hand tangles in his shirt, winding it tight around my fingers. Sometimes I wish it could just be us. No Kosci, no deaths, no guild, no Czar. What would our lives have been like? Would we finally be happy?

The thought pricks at my eyes and I kiss him fiercely, as if that can make it reality. His mouth opens against mine, breath warm across my lips, and I fall into him. I know I should care we aren't alone, but as Alik's fingers fall from my chin to trace along my shoulder, then my spine, I can't stop. My hand untangles itself from his shirt to slip underneath and I slowly brush along the muscles of his back.

A small snore sounds from the opposite bed, and I jump, wrenching my mouth from Alik's. The heat of his lips lingers on mine like a heartbeat and I still, listening. No one speaks, but the stolen moment slips away. I can't kiss away the world. I can't melt into Alik and forget everything I'm supposed to be. I press my head into the hollow of Alik's throat. He seems to sense the shift in my mood because he simply brings up his hand to run his fingers through my hair. I let the gentle motion calm me, willing it to relax me into some semblance of sleep.

SEVENTEEN

A SOFT KNOCK AT THE door wakes me in the dark hours before dawn, and I struggle from the warm embrace of Alik's arms to open it a crack, peering into the gloom of the hall. A dark shadow detaches itself from the wall, the figure lowering a hood as they step into the light coming from the small braziers hung on the wall. He's young, maybe thirty years, with a smooth face and well-kept hair. I stiffen as he takes a step forward.

"Stop where you are," I hiss, and he stutters to a stop at the ice in my voice, slowly raising his hands before him.

"Please," he says, his Stranan far more accented than Chinua's. "I just want to see my sister."

I tighten my hold on the doorknob, searching the shadows for another assailant. He's alone, as far as I can tell, and bears no weapons about his waist or within the folds of his robes. Chinua would want to see him, no matter the suspicion clinging in my mind.

"If you do anything to hurt her, I will kill you," I say, injecting every word with venom.

I open the door wider, stepping aside to welcome the man inside. He hesitates for a moment before slipping past me, feet silent and swift in the dim room.

"Chinua?" he says, searching the beds as I add kindling to the dampened fire and bring it back to life.

Chinua sits up slowly, Sera's arm slipping from around her waist as she rubs at her eyes. She stills as soon as her gaze finds her brother's.

"Zhanzhin?" she whispers.

Chinua vaults from the bed, colliding with her brother and wrapping her arms about him. He holds her tight, whispering quick Adamanian words. Chinua slowly releases him, taking a step back with a shake of her head.

"No," she says, switching to Stranan as Sera rises from the bed. "I won't stay here. I can't."

"Please," he says. "Please. Temujin doesn't like being refused. You *know* this. I don't want to see you hurt."

"Staying here would hurt. Why do none of you see that?" Chinua says, lifting her chin. "It would kill me to stay."

Her brother reaches for her, but Chinua takes another step back, inching closer to Sera. The taller girl comes to Chinua's side, putting a comforting hand on the small of her back. Zhanzhin watches the entire affair, understanding dawning across his face. He switches back to Adamanian, words soft and guttural like a summer brook. Chinua's face breaks, brows going up as her brother continues.

Tears leak down Chinua's cheeks as she responds, her voice even softer than her brother's as it catches and breaks. They embrace once again, Zhanzhin curling his arms about Chinua tightly as she weeps into his shoulder. The room remains silent as they hold one another, no one moving, unwilling to disturb the spell. At last, Chinua releases her brother, wiping the tearstains from her cheeks. They exchange a few more words and several tearful hugs before Zhanzhin turns to me, giving a slight bow of his head.

"Thank you for letting me see my sister," he says. "She means more to me than I can say. Perhaps now my heart can rest easy, knowing she has people to take care of her."

"I'll keep her safe," I say. He inclines his head again before making his way to the door, lingering at the handle.

"I love you, *doo*," he says, looking back. "Do not forget about us, for we will never forget you. Keep yourself safe."

"You too," Chinua says, clutching the hand Sera offers.

With a final glance, Zhanzhin slips into the hall, quietly closing the door behind him. Chinua chokes out a sob, collapsing onto the nearest bed, Sera beside her. She pulls Chinua in close as more tears fall.

"He says he understands more than I could know. That he wants me to be happy, but I can't—" Her voice breaks. "I can't be happy without them."

I sit on the bed beside Chinua, patting her back gently.

"We will find a way for you to see your family again. I swear it, Chinua. I never meant for any of this to happen. I'm so sorry."

But Sera had known. She'd fought to stop us from coming and instead of listening, I'd turned her into nothing but an annoyance. I ease back, hating that I ever thought this was a good idea.

"No, I'm glad," she says with a sniff, pulling away from Sera. "I've missed them so much and I got to see them again, to really say goodbye."

"Temujin can't live forever," I say. Chinua lets out a choked chuckle. "But I won't wait that long."

Guilt and apprehension dog me the entire way back to Strana a week later. The frigid wind scrawling across the plains of Adaman has long since chapped my cheeks into bright-pink circles, and my fingers are numb around the reins of my dutiful horse. Not even the slow, growing pulse at my throat brings me comfort.

Our little procession is silent for the time being, the crunch of snow beneath hooves the only sound beside the soft whisper of wind through the fir trees, so deep and dark on either side of us that I don't bother trying to see into the shadows. I lead us onward through the small valley between two foothills, wishing I were already back in Ludminka coming up with a better plan.

My mare's ears twitch, her black mane lifting from her neck with each soft gust. I frown as the hair ripples again. Something doesn't seem quite right. I straighten and, for the first time all day, peer into the trees. The boughs bounce in slow waves, sending delicate flakes raining down on the drifts below, and I realize what seems so wrong.

I can't hear the wind.

There is no whisper, no howl, just evidence that it blows. Heat flashes through me, curling around my chest and squeezing tight. I scan the area slowly, as if that will somehow reveal the answer, and a prickle of unease climbs its way up my neck. I press my fingers to the pendant, forcing Kosci from his slumber.

What? His rankled reply comes before he stills. My heart beats at my eardrums before Kosci speaks. *Someone is coming.*

I spin in my saddle, opening my mouth to speak when something whistles from the pine beside us. An arrow buries deep into the neck of the guard just to Alik's right.

"Ambush," I scream, just as whoops cry out from the trees and an avalanche of black and gold tumbles from the boughs.

More arrows rain down from somewhere high above. I raise my hand, pulling hard on my and Kosci's power. A roof of ice blooms above us like a rainbow, catching the sunlight and throwing strange dapples of murky light across the snow. Thuds sound as arrows burrow deep into the ice.

I don't have time to stop the Storm Hounds from colliding with our horses. Sera swings down at them with a broad ax, connecting with a shoulder and cleaving deep. Alik's steed bucks as a man raises his sword. Alik barely keeps his seat as his horse shies away from the attack. I send a shard of frozen snow straight into the Storm Hound's chest with enough force that it punctures his armor and drives for his heart. He topples backward, and I swing down from my mount, pulling on the threads of magic weaving through Kosci's heart as I go.

They *knew* we would be here. They'd had enough time to scale trees and set a trap where we would be far from any sort of aid. Bataar's information had to have been planted. It's the exact sort of thing Luiza would do—dangle a prize before me and kill me before I could take it.

Chinua stays atop her horse, deftly wielding him away from any attacks while throwing blades of her own. I roll to the balls of my feet, readying to sprint, when someone leaps onto my back. The unexpected weight forces me to the ground, burying me deep into snow and earth. Legs clamp down on either side of my hips and I buck, sending the person tumbling over my head. I wrench myself up as the attacker scrambles to their feet, bringing their blades up to defend, and my breath catches hard and fast in my throat. Standing across from me with a scowl and smoothed chestnut hair is Luiza. As if she doesn't recognize me, she launches herself forward, dual blades trained on my chest. I dodge, but not fast enough, as one of the blades catches my tunic and rips it, sending a searing scratch across my ribs.

Luiza stabs again. This time, I expect it and kick snow into her face. She squeezes her eyes shut, bracing for the impact, and I try to catch the power swirling inside me, but my heart beats too loudly in my ears. She regains her footing and makes to throw a knife. I dive forward, catching her wrist before she can and we both tumble into the snow.

Breath whooshes from my lungs, my chest freezing tight. I curl my fingers into the snow and will a blade to form. The magic slips through my mind for one terrible moment before it finally listens. The now-familiar blade of ice and snow grows beneath my palm. I grab hold of the hilt and roll, parrying Luiza's daggers just in time. She bears down on me.

"Surrender and I'll make sure your death is a swift one," she hisses into my face.

Her familiar voice sends a strange ripple across me. I'd spent all this time hating her for what she did to me. To Alik. I never thought I'd feel the tug of love. I shove it down deep as snow melts into my back, grounding me in reality. I kick out, catching the woman in the chest and sending her into the deep snow behind her.

My breath is ragged and hot in my throat, a stark difference from the icy air I take in. Luiza jumps to her feet before I can move, still so fast after years of doing the same thing. Sweat starts to bead on my forehead as she advances, swinging for my throat. I duck just in time and throw one of my blades. It catches her in the stomach, burying deep. She looks down at it before a slow smile curls across her lips, like she can't feel the pain.

"Clever, clever girl," she croons in the very voice I used to crave to hear.

Sure hands rip it from her stomach, and she palms the dagger I made. I will it to melt, but the magic stubbornly refuses to come, slipping through my panicked hands. She tests the weight before aiming the blade at me. I dodge to the side and it sails over my shoulder. Her blood leaks onto the snow and my vision shutters.

Images of Alik's body, bloodied and gasping on the field before Knnot, form unbidden in my mind. I can't let it happen again, and if I don't gain the upper hand soon, the rest of us are as good as dead. Just as Alik said, there is no rebellion without me. Hot fury pulses through my body, and my power snaps into place.

I whip a bolt of ice into her forearm. The force of it yanks her body back, slamming her hard into a bank of snow. She cries out and gives a vicious tug to yank herself free, but I refuse. I will the ice to grow, curling it up her arm and down her torso, trapping her against the ground. She jerks against the casing, but there is no breaking it.

Dark hair tumbles over her face in soft waves as she strug-
gles, eyes blazing bright. A small smudge of blood clings to
the corner of her mouth and I know if I were to leave her, she
would slowly bleed out in the bitter cold of Strana's mountains.
An ugly part of myself wants to do just that. Instead, I turn my
attention to the others.

The sound of dozens of churning boots ricochets through
the air followed by guttural yells. Storm Hounds lie dead or
dying on the ground, but so do some of my own men. Sera was
thrown from her horse, and she fights for the upper hand from
a man twice her size. Alik spars with a spry, skinny boy, who
kicks at his bad leg. Alik's face goes bloodless as it connects,
and he topples to the ground. Chinua is the only one still on
her horse, but two men grab onto her leg and yank desperately,
trying to get her off.

"Enough," I yell into a growing wind. It sends pelts of snow
and ice into the faces of the remaining Storm Hounds until
I yank hard on the strands of silvery magic I can barely see
dancing through the air. Everything freezes hard and fast, even
Chinua, Alik, and Sera.

I gulp for air, trying to remember myself in the spinning
colors I now make out coursing through the word in front of
me—silver and blue, bright gold and amber. They are so luminescent and real I don't know how I'd never noticed them
before. It's the magic Kosci has been telling me to use. The same
sort that curls through my body from the pendant at my chest.

Spin them. Kosci's soft command rolls from the back of my mind, and I reach for the silvery threads holding Chinua, Sera, and Alik in place. Slowly, the ice and snow melt away. I run to Alik, helping him to his feet. I want to fling my arms around him, but he shudders at my touch and takes a step back, his remaining eye wide and disbelieving.

I clench my hands into fists and turn, marching back to where Luiza lies, still embedded in her tomb of ice. I crouch down before her and consider her for a long moment.

Just looking at Luiza sends lances of pain through my heart. This a blatant reminder I am nothing to Luiza but an enemy. Not her daughter. Not someone she loved. Adversary. Rival. My fingers curl around the icy hilt of my dagger.

"Do you have any last words before I kill you?" I ask Luiza.

She smirks, shoulders shifting in the tight wrap of ice and snow. "You don't have the strength."

"I am not the girl you once knew," I say, but my insides quiver. She meant so much to me before my journey to Knnot. I thought when I saw her again hate would overwhelm me, that sticking a blade in her heart would be full of satisfaction. Instead, a cruel pulse of love beats its way from my heart.

"Then why haven't you done it already, Valeria? You know better than this. I taught you to never leave your marks alone for longer than a moment. You've given me several."

Bright, blistering heat explodes from the ice I'd encased Luiza in. The cocoon shatters and Luiza jumps to her feet, a small, glowing knife in her hands. It pulses with the Bright God's power, sending wisps of glimmering gold magic into the air around it.

Luiza doesn't advance, like I expect. She turns toward the trees and runs. I give a strangled yell and dart after her, but my foot catches on a patch of slick ice left behind by Matvei's dagger and I fall back, cracking my head hard on the earth. Wheels of white edge my vision until I blink, forcing myself up as Luiza's form disappears into the trees.

"Stop," I command Sera as she mounts her horse. "We can't waste time chasing her. We need to know why she was here in the first place."

Sera lets out a frustrated groan, swinging back down from her horse and yanking her ax from the corpse to her right. I rise slowly, making sure to keep my balance on the ice.

"Are any of them still alive?" I ask.

Sera lifts her chin at a man encapsulated in frost, reaching up toward the sky with his fingers curled like he is about to grab onto something. One of the men trying to pull Chinua from her horse, if I have to guess. I move toward him, pulling on the little wisps of light as I go. Kosci hums in the back of my mind as I manipulate each one.

This is your potential realized, Valeria. This is what I've wanted you to see the entire time. The fabric of the world and your ability to shape it.

Is this what you always see? I ask, remembering all the times he spoke of the threads of time.

Yes. The world is layers of multicolored lines on top of one another. We can only change the strands that were gifted to me in the creation of Strana, the ones of ice and death and things left forgotten. The gold is my brother, life and light and hope. They will never be ours.

He says the last line bitterly. I don't have time to respond as the Storm Hound's head emerges from the ice at last. He sputters and blinks as if seeing the world anew. The man isn't old, perhaps thirty at most, with glossy black hair and bright-blue eyes. His entire face hardens as he finally realizes who stands before him, his thin lips going even thinner.

"You aren't much to look at," he says, voice a gravelly rumble.

"I don't have to be," I say. "Who sent you here?"

The man's jaw goes hard. "I won't tell you anything."

"What if I promise to spare your life? You can talk, or I can zip you back up in snow and ice to be forgotten in this pass until the world is nothing but dust and ruin."

More strands of silvery blue appear around him, weaving in and out of his body like a bramble choking a flower. Before I could see the strings, I had been able to see truth inside Bataar's mind. Now, I might be able to see memories. Why shouldn't I be able to? Kosci is a god who looked into the hearts of men every day to take their suffering. The temptation tickles at the back of my mind.

"Tell me," I say slowly. "Or I will take the information by force."

"There is nothing you could do to me that would make me

talk. I spent years training for torture," the man says.

"I do not plan torture," I say. Something in my face must change, because for the first time, fear seep into his eyes.

"Val," Alik says softly beside me. "Don't."

"I will do what I must," I say harshly without looking over.

"It's *wrong*," he insists. "It was wrong when you did it to Bataar, and it is wrong now."

"There is no playing fair in war, Alik," I say. "Now, Storm Hound, tell me everything you know."

I see his refusal before it ever leaves his lips. My hand snaps out of its own accord, catching the man's jaw and squeezing tight. I close my eyes and bend the strings of magic around me until I am no longer Valeria, but Michail Abakumovo, a dark-haired man in the Storm Hounds. Scenes play before my eyes like dreams. Swinging a sword against a wolf, bringing shipments of goods to a *tyur'ma*. Disgust not my own ripples along my skin at the sallow and taut faces of the Zladonians inside the prison, followed by an almost visceral hate. Only one thought plays in Michail's mind as he sees them. *Their fault. Their fault. Their fault.*

I force his mind from that path, turning it instead to Ladislaw. The Czar appears bedecked in his traditional livery, Matvei in brilliant gold by his side. Michail is itchy and hot inside his armor in the great hall of Ladislaw's palace in Rurik, but he stands at attention, dutiful as always.

"Today, we will make a move against the wolf that waits

for us in Zladonia," Ladislaw says, addressing a room full of other Storm Hounds. Michail reckons there has to be around seventy-five, far more than should be necessary for one little girl. "She seeks to sow discord in Strana, to ruin what I've created. We will end this little war before it starts. Half of you will be sent to the Adaman border, where you will wait. Your orders are to kill her before she has a chance to return to the icy fortress she's fashioned for herself."

Silence follows Ladislaw's words, and Michail shifts uncomfortably. Surely the Pale champion couldn't be this much of a threat. Matvei gives a grim smile at Ladislaw's side and steps to the Czar's shoulder.

"The rest of us," Matvei says, slowly scanning the crowd. "Will go to the *tyur'ma* near Zladonia. There, we will cull every last Zladonian. We will not let her add more bodies to her army. We will take a prison, for a prison, perhaps then she will feel the weight of this pathetic rebellion."

I rip from Michail's mind with so much force that he gasps against the pain. My breath starts to come in short, quick pants, and I try to swallow the bile rising in my throat. I back away from the Storm Hound whose head now rests limply against the casing of ice. The bright white of the snow bleeds into the edges of my vision. An entire prison? They can't mean to kill an entire prison.

Alik catches my arm before I can back any farther away. "What is it?"

Concern etches itself into every feature on his face, and I try to concentrate on it instead of the terror now running rampant through my body.

"They're going to kill them," I say, but my voice is a thin, reedy version of itself.

"Kill who?" Alik asks.

"The people inside the prison. The one on the edge of Zladonia. The one we were going to raid next."

Sera grasps my shoulder to steady me, and her firm hand grounds me in reality.

"How do you know?" she asks.

"I looked into his mind. Into his memories. I saw Ladislaw and Matvei give the order."

Chinua's face loses all its color. "All those people."

I rip from Alik and Sera's grip. I can't let them die. I am supposed to be their savior, their champion. I can't sit and do nothing. Perhaps Matvei hasn't reached the prison yet. Perhaps I can get them out before he does. I reach for my horse, putting my foot into the stirrup. Alik calls out from behind me.

"Where are you going?"

"I have to save them," I say, and pull myself up. I gather the reins, but Alik catches the harness. He stares up at me, brows knitted tight over his nose.

"You can't do it alone, Val. We had warriors last time and only barely managed to win their freedom."

I grip the reins so hard the leather creaks beneath my hand. Alik doesn't understand. No one does. This is my fate. I swore to Kosci, to myself, that I would free the Zladonians and kill Ladislaw. Instead, I'd wasted time pursuing an allyship that was never going to happen.

"The prison is four days from here. You'll never make it," Sera says, almost apologetic. Her pity does nothing to stem the ever-tightening clamp in my chest.

"I can and I will. I will use every ounce of power in my body to keep this horse alive and moving until I reach that prison. I won't let them die because of my failings as a leader." I nudge the horse, and Alik releases the bridle. "Return to Ludminka. Or not. I don't care. I am riding for that *tyur'ma*."

"Val," Alik tries, reaching out again. I shake my head.

"I have to," I say. "Please, try to understand."

He retracts his hands, keeping them close to his sides in tight fists. I don't know if I can ever make him understand why I feel like I have to do this. I no longer live just for myself. I live for Strana, for the world. With a deep, painful breath, I turn my horse from him and urge it into a run.

I *will* reach the *tyur'ma* on time. I won't let Matvei win.

I won't.

EIGHTEEN

THE HORSE MOVES LIKE A dark gale beneath me, eating the distance between the prison and myself like a brutal storm. Harsh wind bites at my cheeks, but I keep myself low, eyes always trained on the horizon as Kosci's power feeds into the beast's body. Night falls, followed by a brilliant dawn, a red sun spilling fingers of pink across the frosted ground. Still, I press ever onward until the terrain grows rocky and uncertain and the walls of a prison appear out of a thicket of leafless birches.

I stop the horse abruptly and slip off. Her sides heave and foam coats her mouth, but she stays strong and alive, as if she were magic given form. I pat her neck, releasing her from her rein, before turning my eyes to the prison walls.

Just as at the other *tyur'ma*, this one has a cleared circle of

ground around it, old stumps scattered through the area covered in a fine film of snow. I take in the high wall walk, but no
one patrols the top. I stretch my hearing as hard as I can, listening for something, *anything*, to tell me people still live beyond
those walls. With each silent moment, my chest tightens until
it feels as if I'm being slowly crushed beneath the weight of a
boulder.

Kosci, please.

The plea is desperate, my mind unable to form any words
beyond those. Kosci understands. He says nothing as he extends
our power, reaching through the snowy field toward the high
walls. I can almost feel the snow beneath my feet and the splin-
ters of the wall as the magic crawls over, trailing across icy
grooves. As soon as it reaches the top, it blurs into nothing, like
looking through a dirty window.

*I don't like this. Only my brother has the ability to hide from my
sight. He could be waiting inside.*

I curl my fingers around the pendant, tightening my hold
until the edges bite into my palm. Barreling in is reckless, stupid, but I left all help far behind. If I backtrack now and Matvei
waits inside, I will be nothing but a coward. If I have a sliver of
a chance to save the people inside, I have to take it.

I'm with you, Valeria. As always, I am here to help.

Kosci's steady voice laces through my mind and I want to
take comfort in it, but even with the now-visible strings of
magic dancing on the wind, Matvei has the upper hand. He's

trained with the Bright God for years. I grit my teeth against the building tension in my neck and step from the trees.

I gather my power as I march, forming it slowly into a crackling bluish-white light between my hands. My arms tremble as I attempt to contain it. Before it can explode in my face, I release it toward the gate. It arcs through the air like a shooting star, colliding into the prison with a massive boom.

Snow tumbles from the tops of parapets and buries the small scrub beneath. Rubble and dust rain down as the gate falls, obscuring the courtyard beyond. I inch closer, forming the ice blade, waiting for Storm Hounds to descend or a beam of sunlight to catch me in the heart.

Instead, there is empty silence. No screams of confusion and terror. No war cries.

As the dust settles from the explosion, the courtyard beyond becomes visible.

Blood splatters every spare inch of the yard, staining snow a deep red and churning the dirt into something dark and viscous. Bodies lay strewn across the square, arms splayed wide and large gashes down their backs. My breath starts coming fast as my eyes dart from one body to the next.

Absolutely no one was spared.

Infants and children, adults and elderly. Every last one cut down from behind. There are no Storm Hounds, no Matvei. Just blood. So much blood, frozen and crystallized, still the same bright, beating red as it had been when it spilled from their bodies. Every inch of me shakes as I spin slowly, desperately searching for some form of survival. All I find are more bodies, each and every one brutally massacred, just as I heard Matvei say in Michail's memories.

My gaze stalls on burned wood near the front gate. I can't feel my legs as I force them to take a step forward. Slowly, the jagged lines turn into readable words at least two feet tall.

TOO SLOW.

I lift a shaking hand to touch the word, the wood blackened as if someone had painstakingly burned each letter. Someone like Matvei, who could control the direction of the sun's light.

I rip my hand away from the words, backing away until my ankles connect with something solid. I land hard on the unforgiving ground, a corpse of a girl around my age beneath my legs. I scramble back, entire body giving way to horrible, vicious tremors.

I *was* too late.

I was far too late.

I grind my hands into my eyes as flashes of all the faces in the courtyard beyond play behind my closed lids. The need to cry builds in my chest and throat, but the tears refuse to fall. The ache of it hurts, but nothing I do forces them out. Instead, I scream.

The very ground beneath quakes under the weight of it. Still the tears stay stuck and cold.

This is all my fault.

If only I had seen the trap before it had been sprung. If only I had considered for a single moment Bataar was fed false information. Or maybe he betrayed me himself. I didn't know. The only certain thing was that I failed.

I'd gotten so lost in my bid to outmaneuver Ladislaw that I'd fallen straight into his snare. I scream again and this time a crack rends the air, the cobble beneath me buckling. So many lives lost because of a single stupid decision. A dry sob catches in my throat and my eyes burn as if they might finally shed tears, but still the numbing cold stays beating at my breast, determined to bite until I can feel nothing else. The sensation courses deeper and deeper, nestling its way into my very soul. It mingles with Kosci's home, and he jerks inside me.

He killed them. Every last one of them.

Let me see, he says.

I stand and close my eyes, digging deep into the weaving cords of power hidden inside me. Kosci surges forward completely, and my vision goes white before returning in a hazy blue. Kosci blinks from my eyes, taking in the bodies that lie strewn and broken.

This never should have happened.

I could've, should've, stopped it.

As Kosci returns to his space beside my heart and the crushing weight of the lives before me settles back onto my shoulders, a single thought forms in my mind. Ladislaw ordered this. Matvei executed it. These weren't people to them, just pawns to be used. White hot fury fills every single space in my body, blotting out every emotion until there is nothing left. I'm nothing but a torrent of blistering heat and thrumming energy.

This, I can do.

Anger is easier than guilt, far easier than fear.

And this wrath is righteous.

I will take every single thing Ladislaw has ever loved and ruin it before his very eyes. I will not rest until he has suffered every inch of pain he's inflicted on all of Zladonia. And then, once I'm certain he's suffered, I will kill him. Slowly. Publicly. So the world knows my fury.

Snow crunches behind me and I spin, pulling on my power to send a roaring whip of wind at whoever dares to disturb this miserable graveyard. The gust rips hard at brown clothing and long black hair before recognition dawns.

Bataar.

Surprise whispers through me only to be replaced by a hotter flame of suspicion.

"You." I practically growl the word, eyes narrowing.

I advance, sending gust after gust, pushing him back across the entrance of the *tyur'ma* until his back slams against the ragged wood of the guardhouse door. He holds his arms up against the bitter howl of my magic, and I pull at the threads around his feet. Instantly, the snow does my bidding, crawling over his boots before freezing solid. I let the wind fall away.

"How could you? Look at them, Bataar, look! Did you not

care that hundreds would die?"

"I had absolutely no part in this," Bataar says, voice low, almost ragged. "I overheard Luiza tell an adviser to the Czar they were sending an envoy, and I sent you the information. It wasn't until a few days ago I realized I had been tricked. She knew, Valeria. She knew someone inside was helping you."

"Then why are you still alive?" I spit. "Did she offer you your life if you led her straight to me?"

"No," he snaps back. "As soon as I realized what the real plan was, I pulled every guild member loyal to me and rode here. I hoped . . ." He shakes his head, disgust curling his mouth before he pushes his hair from his face. "I guess I hoped I'd be able to stop it. But I obviously couldn't."

"Liar." The word is so acidic it burns on the way out. Bataar doesn't recoil. He lifts his chin, his eyes never wavering from mine.

"Go ahead and check for yourself. I have nothing to hide."

I don't have to be asked twice. I press a finger into his forehead, gathering the harried strands around us and following them into Bataar's mind. With a horrendous wrench, I fall back into the guild's headquarters. Everything is exactly how I remember it, the worn wood, the secret shadows where initiates like to hide and play pranks on the older guild members. Even the smell follows the memory, leather and dust.

Bataar creeps up the curling staircase in the center hall of the guild, following a shifting pool of candlelight. Soft whispers sound from the landing just above, and Bataar ducks low, practically crawling until he reaches the top. A door stands half open, and someone paces back and forth in the room beyond. Bataar hesitates only a moment before leaning closer.

". . . the envoy to Adaman had better return with good news. We need the alliance more than Ladislaw knows." Luiza's voice rasps from inside, and my heart constricts so hard and fast I'm thrown from Bataar's mind. He pants, sweat beading his forehead as if I'd wounded him. All the strands of magic I'd been holding slip away as I take a step back, pressing a hand to my mouth, catching a sob that claws at my throat. Horses nicker from beyond the prison's walls, but I only barely register the fact Bataar had been telling the truth. We were both too late, and now I have hundreds of bodies on my soul.

"Valeria."

Bataar says my name so softly, so kindly after being assaulted by gales of wind, that a fissure snaps through my chest hard and quick. Another sob finds its way from my body, then another, my eyes burning until the tears are nothing but a misty veil. I shove my face into my hands, turning away from the carnage, desperate to gain some sort of composure. No champion to the gods went down in the annals of time because they wept over corpses. But not crying over all the lives lost seems wrong, too. Someone needs to miss them. Someone needs to grieve.

A hand falls onto my shoulder, turning me back around. Bataar's face is uncertain behind my curtain of tears as he pulls me into his chest and holds me tight. The last bulwark against the pain crumbles and every single tear I've been harboring since the day I began my idiotic mission to Knnot seeps down my cheeks.

Bataar says nothing, just holds me tight, a slow hand running up and down my back as if I am a heartbroken child. I have no idea how long we stand there, my legs weak and wobbling with each sob, but at long last my tears dry. I leave my forehead on Bataar's chest, staring down at my boots and what I'm sure is the only clear patch of snow in the courtyard.

"I thought I'd get here in time," I whisper into the space between us.

"I thought I would, too," he says.

I give a humorless chuckle. "You were truly ready to take on Matvei? For Zladonians?"

I tilt my head up and find that his cheeks aren't dry either. Why did he care so much for people that he'd never known? He'd willingly gone straight into the viper's nest to help and now he wept for the dead, too. His eyes scan the courtyard and his face pinches into something hard and fierce.

"I was," he says, and finally his gaze meets mine. Almost absentmindedly, he brushes away a wet spot on my cheek.

"Why?" The question falls from my mouth before I can stop it. "Why do you care, Bataar? You could leave now, go to Adaman, and never return. This isn't your fight."

Our breaths mingle as I wait for him to tell me I'm right

and push me away. Bataar remains motionless, attention fixed on a place over my shoulder.

"At the beginning of the plagues, before Ladislaw started rounding everyone up, I wasn't old enough to understand what was going on. I was scared, and my parents spent most nights locked in their room, discussing things they didn't want me to overhear. They owned a shop in Rurik before Strana's fall, and they employed a Zladonian woman named Galina. She didn't have to stay after hours for me, but she did, chasing away nightmares and telling stories to distract me from the crashing world around us. I was eight when the Storm Hounds kicked down our door and dragged her out." He chuckles humorlessly. "Do you know what her last words were to me? 'Don't be scared *lapochka*, you're safe. It will be alright.' It was like she didn't care about herself in that moment, even when she was the one being carted away. I've never forgotten it."

His eyes meet mine as he shakes away the memory.

"That is why I want to help. For Galina . . . for everyone who lost someone . . . for you."

I let out a soft breath. "Me?"

"There are few people in the world who see a problem and are willing to fix it. When you find those people, they deserve respect. Admiration."

His gaze never wavers, as if he wants me to remember every single one of his words.

"You will show the world how big a mistake they have

made, and I will help you take your retribution."

"I want to burn it all," I say. "I want to take everything Ladislaw has and make it mine until he is nothing but a simpering man in silks."

"Then do it, by whatever means necessary," Bataar says, taking me by the shoulders. "I know something Ladislaw has hidden away, something he values so much very few know of its existence." His deep brown eyes are bright and intent. "In Yelgarod, deep in the Winter Palace, Ladislaw hides the piece of himself he wants no one else to have. His son."

A cool heat whirls to life in my stomach and my mouth twists into something almost a smile. If Ladislaw seeks to play chess, then I will take this piece.

NINETEEN

IT TAKES NEARLY FIVE DAYS before the others join us at the *tyur'ma*. By the time they arrive, Bataar, his guild followers, and I had managed to move a majority of the bodies to the thin copse of fir trees beyond the prison walls. They deserved to be buried free. It was the very least I could do for them.

Alik is the first to appear on the horizon, and he straightens as he spots us, nudging his horse into a faster gait. He slows as he approaches and slips from the horse, his limp more pronounced after days spent in the saddle. I let him gather me into his arms, but I'm too numb to return the embrace, my eyes trained on the small girl closest to me, her little eyelashes stark against her pale skin.

"There were no survivors," I whisper to Alik. He hugs me tighter.

"I'm sorry," he says.

"Sorry doesn't save them, Alik. I should've been here. I never should've fallen into Luiza's trap."

Churning hooves steal me from Alik's arms as Chinua and Sera stop their steeds beside Alik's. They study the devastation, and Sera's face drains of color completely. She vaults from her horse, scrambling across the slick ground until she reaches a stout body near the edge of the clearing. She collapses beside him as I tread carefully toward her.

"Papa?" The voice that falls from her lips isn't the one I've come to know. It's small, the desperate want of a daughter for her father. Sera buries her face into his shoulder, her own shaking.

I kneel beside her, placing a hand on her back. Chinua falls to her knees, grabbing Sera by her shoulders and heaving her into her chest as a sob rips from Sera's throat. Sera buries her face into Chinua's shoulder. I sit beside them, staring down into the golden-haired man's face, so like Sera's own I don't know how I didn't see it before.

Sera half turns toward me, still clinging to Chinua for support, her cheeks a blotchy red.

"I don't understand. He wasn't one of you."

"He didn't have to be," I say quietly. "He was in Zladonia when Knnot fell, he was selling wares to us. He could've had the plague. And if he didn't, he'd always be sympathetic. Ladislaw couldn't risk that."

My voice is emotionless. For all our arguments, I never wanted this. It was a hurt that would never heal. One I carried with me for ten years until Kosci freed them. Sera jerks away from Chinua suddenly, shoving me hard in the chest.

"Bring him back," she shouts.

"I can't."

"Bring him back! You brought back Alik! Bring him back, too." Tears run in rivulets down her cheeks, freezing before they have a chance to hit the ground.

"I'm sorry, Sera. They'd been gone too long." A knot forms in my throat as Sera's face collapses in on itself, her hands going to her face. "I know it might not help, but I will kill Ladislaw for this. I will ruin him."

Sera says nothing as Chinua gathers her once again. I rise to my feet, unable to offer any other sort of comfort. The guild-lings Bataar brought with him stand awkwardly off to the side, unable to do more than watch. Bataar slips from the shadows beneath the trees, his face a grim mask.

"Did you bring no others to Adaman with you?" he asks.

"No, I didn't want to seem like an aggressor," I say, leaning against the trunk of a tall pine and staring up into the branches above. The blanket of dead needles and slushy snow beneath the tree muffle Bataar's footsteps as he comes to rest beside me. "We can't afford to do nothing. We don't know how long Ladislaw'll leave the *tyur'ma* in Oleg alone."

"What makes you so sure he hasn't already?" Bataar asks,

matching my pose closely enough that our shoulders brush.

"He'll use it as another trap. He knows once I see this, I won't be able to leave them there. But we can't move against them yet. We aren't strong enough, we don't have the weapons. We need a different tactic, one he doesn't expect. I'm tired of him always being one step ahead." I look over at Bataar. "Am I really that predictable?"

His gaze sweeps over my face, studying the planes of it slowly. Carefully. "You are to Luiza. She raised you."

"Then I'm going to have to do something she'll never expect. The information you have on Yuri is too good not to use." I sigh, my eyes going first to Alik, then to Chinua and Sera. "But I know my decision won't be popular."

"Surely they will see the sense in it," Bataar says.

"Perhaps," I respond, eyes stilling on Alik. He will not. I know he won't.

Across from us, Sera finally rises to her feet, Chinua at her side. She takes in the rest of the prison, the additional people, before her gaze snags on Bataar. Her face hardens and she shakes Chinua from her arm, yanking her ax from the belt at her hip as she closes the distance between us.

"How could you have no idea they'd make the raid?" She shouts as she reaches us, pressing the blunt end of her ax into his chest. "You were supposed to be our inside intelligence, and yet we heard *nothing*."

"I didn't know." Bataar's voice lacks any of the warmth I've become accustomed to. Sera opens her mouth, but I put a hand on the haft of the ax, slowly pushing it from Bataar's chest.

"He's telling the truth," I say.

"How do you know?" Alik says coolly, joining the small semicircle now crowded beneath the bows of the pine. My lips thin as I answer.

"Because I lived his memories."

"Valeria," Alik starts, his voice hard as ice.

"Calm down," Bataar says, straightening. "I told her to. If I hadn't, you all would've believed me the enemy."

"I still haven't ruled that out," Sera growls.

Bataar shrugs. "I have nothing to prove to you."

"Everyone stop," I say, and nod toward the growing group of guildlings around us. "I think this is a discussion best had among ourselves."

Sera goes rigid as she looks over her shoulder before giving me a short nod. I lead them into the guardhouse, taking them up the stone spiral staircase at the left of the den. It empties out into what I assume was the commander's quarters, complete with a wide bed full of furs and thick hides of bear and caribou lining the wall to keep out the chill. A fireplace sits on the far side of the room and I cross to it, stoking the embers and tossing on a couple more logs before facing the others.

Sera is the first to break the silence, her cheeks reddening as she pins her eyes on Bataar. "Couldn't manage to do the single job we asked of you."

Bataar's nostrils flare. "I *tried*. Despite what you all may think, I am good at what I do. I stalked Luiza to every meeting with Ladislaw and Matvei. I couldn't hear a thing. It was as if they were talking underwater. When I tried to get closer, I was pushed back."

We don't respond and he forges forward.

"The guildlings were worse. Some of the people I've known for years are nearly unrecognizable. They do whatever she tells them. I've seen partners turn on each other, gladly holding down their hands as Luiza takes their fingers. Does that sound like the people you knew? Something is wrong."

Manipulation, Kosci says. *My brother is quite adept at it. He whispers blessings into their ears and they follow him without question. He gives them just enough to make them feel like he's telling the truth but not enough to let them stray.*

I start to pace, tucking my hands behind my back.

"Zoltoy's manipulating them," I say, putting voice to Kosci's words.

"How?" Bataar asks.

I wave away his question. "It's an ability of the Brother Gods. Just like me being able to go into your memories. He weasels his way in and fans the flames of their beliefs but doesn't give them everything they want. Not yet."

"That's a power no one should have," Alik says, and I stop mid-pace, stiffening at his words. There is an undercurrent to it I don't like.

He does not like the idea of you having such a power. Of you wielding it, Kosci whispers. It's the exact same idea I harbor in a hidden part of my heart that I've never wanted to put words to. That Alik is afraid of me, of my power, of my role in this war. I swallow and force myself to start walking again.

"He's more powerful than I thought," I say.

"He's beyond powerful," Bataar says. He sits on the bed with a heavy sigh. "I've seen what he can do, how he can speak a few words and every person in the area believes him without question. Do you know they burn effigies of you in Rurik, Valeria? He sets them alight with just a look and then speaks to a crowd of hundreds and when he speaks, the entire world listens. He says you kill everyone in your path, that you won't stop until every Stranan is dead and only Zladonians are left."

I don't respond. How can I? Matvei and Ladislaw know if I win the populace, I will win the war.

"He pulled the sun from the sky. Melted every last pile of snow in Rurik. Grass and flowers have started to grow, as if it's spring. No one can touch him."

"I can," I say, certainty thrumming in my bones.

Bataar looks as if he doesn't believe me, but he's smart enough to know when to keep his mouth shut. I study the plains of his face, the high cheekbones and the slow darkening beneath his eyes. Everything about him says he's just as exhausted as the rest of us. If I keep chasing after Luiza's carefully placed leads, we will never get ahead. They will continue to circle ever closer and cut off my head before I can do anything else.

We have no allies, no great army to meet Ladislaw in open battle, and we just lost hundreds of people we swore to save. If I don't manage to do something, to give us some sort of win, desperation will eat away at our core. I tighten my hold on my hands behind my back.

"I refuse to let this go unanswered. Ladislaw knew our plan, Luiza likely knew exactly which prison we would turn to next and made sure to make the first move. They ready a trap for me at the prison in Oleg. They've always been one step ahead of us and it needs to end. We need to strike where they least expect it."

"What exactly do you have in mind?" Chinua asks slowly.

"We are going to take Yelgarod and kidnap Czar Ladislaw's son."

TWENTY

"WHAT?" ALIK SHOOTS TO HIS feet. "We can't. He's a *child*."

"I know exactly what he is. But I also know he's Ladislaw's weakness. He wouldn't have bothered keeping him hidden otherwise."

"We know he's at the Winter Palace," Bataar says, relaying all the information he already told me. "In my reconnaissance at the guild, I found that much. They were all coded missives about the prince's well-being, about his studies and how he improves. It seems he's been there for quite some time. Years, if the documents were to be believed."

"Didn't we see him in Oleg?" Chinua asks. "He stood at the prison with his father. He was just a young boy."

I nod. "Or we thought we saw him."

"Stop being cryptic," Sera says. "You either did or you didn't."

"After listening to everything Bataar found, I think we saw what Ladislaw wanted us to see, a weak little boy who will inherit the crown one day. Someone who is nonthreatening and unworthy of attention. Who's to say he hasn't done exactly that with his own son? Displaying a puppet with one hand while shielding his real heir with the other."

"You think that boy is a body double?" Sera asks, doubt filling every syllable.

"Why not? Ladislaw would've known a true heir was at risk, especially at the beginning of the fall when lovite deposits started drying up and the people started whispering about revolution. He wouldn't have wanted to risk his line ending if Strana did revolt."

The room grows quiet. Only Alik looks around in wild-eyed disbelief. "You all can't think this is a good idea. Even if the boy *is* a body double, the real Yuri can't be more than fourteen," Alik says. He makes as if to reach out to me, but I take a step back. I can't be swayed from this. I refuse to be.

"I'm not suggesting we kill him. We just take him captive and get information from him. Children hear everything," I say.

"I'm not sure I like this idea," Chinua says, moving away from Sera and coming to lean on the back of the chair Alik sits in. "Anyone with children or younger siblings won't want you to take a boy hostage."

"It won't play out well with the army, most of them do have children." Sera agrees. "The optics won't exactly be in your favor."

Anger licks through me like a flame, and I turn my gaze to the three people who've been with me since the beginning. Not a single one seems supportive of my idea to act, all of them too timid, too scared to see the sense of it. Why couldn't they see that the people being buried beyond this prison's walls deserved some sort of justice?

"Who started this war? Me. Now hundreds of people lie dead because *I* didn't act. Not you three, *me*. I refuse to let it happen again, not when I have a card to play. Ladislaw won't move against us if he knows we have his son."

"We aren't ready for that. We don't have the numbers or the skills," Chinua says.

"And that's why we take Yelgarod. Matvei's fervor won't have reached them yet, it's too far north. We can bring them lovite and commerce in the middle of winter. From there, we gather Stranans to our side."

"How?" Alik asks, eye narrowing. "By manipulating them like Matvei does?"

Kosci's and my anger swirl together in a dangerous storm, and I advance on Alik, flicking a finger into his chest.

"Why do you seem so determined to believe Matvei and I are the same?"

"You're the one suggesting kidnapping a child and capturing an entire city."

"Do you have another brilliant plan, Alik? Can you conjure more people to our side? Can you stop Matvei from slaughtering more innocents?"

Alik shakes his head. "You can't do this. Leave Yuri be and continue as we've planned. We'll take the prisons first and—"

"He's waiting for me at the next *tyur'ma*! They will grind all our bones to dust and ash before they let us into another prison. They know we mean to gather an army, and they are taking away our chance."

Bataar rises from the bed, coming to stand at my side against the three opposing forms across from me.

"We have the intelligence. We have the numbers. It's the choice Luiza would make," Bataar says. I send him a grateful look.

"Of course you side with her," Alik spits.

"What does that mean?" I ask, raising a brow.

Alik tosses up his hands. "It doesn't matter. What does is that you are betraying the very thing that made you start this war in the first place! We are better than Luiza. Than Ladislaw! We can't act like him and expect Strana to fall in line. They won't support a tyrant."

"They've been supporting one for more than ten years," I say coldly. "And kidnapping a child doesn't make me a tyrant."

Strained silence descends on the room as Alik and I glower at one another. When Alik doesn't respond, I look to the others.

"Give me a different solution. You all know we need

something to stay the Czar's hand or he'll just keep taking. We tried Adaman. That failed, and it cost us hundreds of lives. If we continue to stumble, we will fall on our own swords before Ladislaw has a chance to kill us himself."

Chinua turns pleading eyes to Sera, who shrugs. They can't deny the truth of my words. Alik's mouth hangs open slightly as his only allies stay silent. He closes it with a snap, his shoulders raising like a cat about to hiss. I hold up my hand before he can speak.

"You know what? I don't want to hear what you have to say. You've made yourself perfectly clear, but I see no other way. This is my decision. At first light, we will move toward the Winter Palace."

I sweep out of the room and hurry down the stairs and back into the open freedom of the courtyard, gulping in the crisp air until my lungs burn. I make my way out into the wilderness beyond the prison's walls, allowing the birches to swallow me, the papery bark peeling back to reveal more white underneath. All the while my heart beats a consistent warning, begging me to find a way to mend things with Alik.

Am I doing right? I ask, closing my eyes and turning my face up toward the dimming sky.

They may think you cruel, but this is necessary, Kosci replies. *This is war. It doesn't come without casualties.*

Why can't they see that? I hate that even in my mind my voice breaks. *War is brutal and cold and heartless. If I felt for every single life I took, I would never swing my sword. Ladislaw will never stop, not when he knows he has all the power. Why can't I play with people like toys the way he can?*

It's the right choice. The boy will be easy to manipulate. Easy to break.

Kosci's calm certainty is infectious, and I allow myself a long inhale, relishing the sharp scent of snow and cold air. I can't doubt myself. Not anymore. My desperation for allies is how this massacre happened. I will force Ladislaw all the way back to Rurik and burn the city to the ground if I have to. I release my breath and open my eyes, watching as the air plumes in a white cloud before me. It doesn't matter what Alik thinks.

I told you the boy would seek to supplant your convictions. Kosci whispers. *He questions you at every turn. He doesn't like what you're trying to do for Strana.*

That's not true.

Isn't it? Kosci says. *He doesn't see the sense in your vision. All he sees is the potential pain of a single child against the hurt of an entire country. Do you think he will agree with you on this? Ever think beyond using the power we wield for fortification and weapons?*

I don't respond because I don't like the answer that springs far too readily to mind. I concentrate on the crunch of snow beneath my feet as I walk even deeper into the glen of birches.

Before the walls of the prison have begun to vanish, quick, uneven footsteps hurry behind me. I pretend I don't hear them.

The last vestiges of sunlight reflect off the pristine snow and purple shadows bloom between the trees like small secrets. It should be beautiful, peaceful even.

"You're not going to talk me out of this," I say without turning to look back at Alik. "My mind is made up."

"Why are you doing this?" He says, voice ragged.

"You saw the slaughter Ladislaw left behind. We could've stopped it if I'd seen through Luiza's plan earlier or if I had refused to go to Adaman at all. I can't lose more lives, Alik. I can't see another prison like that. And if that means playing by Ladislaw's rules, then so be it."

"This isn't you. You'd never endanger a child to get what you want."

"Wouldn't I?" I say darkly, turning to face him at last. "Why does Yuri get to live in comfort, removed from the pain his father has caused? Why does he get to pretend this country is safe and happy? Why is he absolved from the sins of the crown?"

The stony defiance on Alik's face melts away, replaced by incredulity. "Because he is a *child*. He has no power."

"I don't care what he is. What about that don't you understand? I can't let this go unanswered. Ladislaw will continue to take and take until Strana is nothing but corpses and misery." Fury cloaks me again, giving me the strength to push forward. "Don't you see, Alik? Ladislaw, Yuri, any from that line have been tainted by the Bright God. They will never be good for

Strana. But me? Us? We could rule this country. Turn it into the bastion we deserve. You have drops of Kosci's power. How could the people refuse divine rulers?"

Alik takes a step back as if I slapped him, shaking his head. "I don't want to rule. I just want you." For a heartbeat he softens. " The real you."

"This *is* the real me now. This world is sick and I have the power to change it. I can't ignore it." I swallow hard against my next words. "Not even for you."

"Please, don't cross this line. I'm not sure I'll be able to follow."

"Why won't you understand? Can't you see the world burning? It tore your mothers from you. It took everything from me. From us! I can't stop the inferno, Alik. I can only try to control it. Why can't you see that is what I'm trying to do? I just want to protect them, *you*, from this world."

"You are betraying everything you are to do it! You plant memories and rummage around in people's minds free of guilt. Now you want to destroy the life of a child to gain the upper hand?"

"You've hated the fact I have this power since the day I brought you back from the dead. You despise what I can do."

"Because you're hurting people, Valeria! Michail was nothing but a husk of himself after you left and you keep dipping into Bataar's mind whenever you feel like it—"

"He lets me," I nearly shout the words. "He sees the sense of using what I've been given. Why should I ignore the magic in this world to spare your feelings? Do you want Strana to continue to suffer? Or the Zladonians to be rounded back up?"

"You know I don't," he says, mouth thinning into an almost unrecognizable line. I search his eye for some sort of understanding, for a hint of the warmth it usually holds for me, but I find nothing but cold indifference.

"I can't keep telling you to stay your hand when you so clearly want to ruin the world," he says, and his breath hitches. "I can't keep being your conscience."

"I'm not asking you to!" Something between us feels like its shattering and I can't fix it.

I don't even know if I want to.

How can I be with someone who doesn't see that I'm trying to save Strana? Bitterly, Kosci's warning swims into my mind. Why hadn't I listened? Maybe I would have been prepared for this betrayal. For this heartbreak.

"All I want is your support, Alik. For you to see what I am doing and know I am trying my best. This mess was thrust into my hands and all I want to do is right the wrongs Ladislaw has committed. Change *always* comes at a price, and I am the one who must pay. I'm asking that you believe in me, if not my ideas."

A slow tear rolls down his cheek and I desperately want to reach out and wipe it away, but I don't move. I wait for his answer, my heart cracked and bleeding for all the world to see. A blooming ache spreads through my chest as the silence grows between us.

"I love you. I always will." Alik heaves a deep breath. "But I can't support this."

All thought ceases, and my vision narrows until it's only Alik I see. "Why?"

"You aren't the Valeria I fell in love with. You're getting colder . . . angrier. All you wanted when we were in Rurik was your parents. Now, you're taking a child away from theirs. Don't you see how much Kosci has changed you? It's like you're closing your eyes to everything except the outcome, willing to sacrifice every last bit of yourself if it means killing Ladislaw." He lifts a hand, fingers splayed as if begging me to take it. "Please, listen to me. Remove the pendant, sleep on this ludicrous plan, and you'll realize in the morning how wrong it is. Take my hand. Please, Val. *Please.*"

I stare at his fingers, so painfully familiar. I know how he got every scar on them, know how long he practiced using a sword. At one point, we'd known every single thing about each other. I follow the line of his arm up to his face, letting my gaze wander over his chin, his brow, his lips, before stopping at his eye. If I were to take his hand now, everything would be forgiven. But I don't live just for myself anymore. I am Zladonia's sword, Strana's shield.

A sob catches in my throat as I step back, away from his pleading face. Alik's hand drops, his face shuttering tight in a single blink. Every feature hardens until he is the Alik he was in front of Luiza, strong, determined, aloof. It sends a shard of pain all the way to my core.

The clearing around us grows dimmer as the sun sets on the horizon. Alik shakes his head once, hands balling into fists.

"One day, Valeria, all that rage and hate carrying you forward will disappear. That fire burning inside you will die and you will be left with nothing but a hollow heart."

I take in two deep breaths, pushing my tears deep down until I don't remember how to cry.

"I will *never* stop burning."

The distance between us seems more than a few feet. It's miles, an entire country. I can't cross it. He looks as if he'll say more, but his throat bobs and he turns away, his back a rigid arrow. I watch him wade through the drifts back to the prison, knowing if I called out, if I promised to stay my hand, he would come back to me.

But it's not a promise I can make.

A hollow hurt engulfs me as Alik slips between the broken pieces of the prison without a single glance back. I look up to the sky, releasing the trembling breaths I'd been holding back. The first couple of stars have made their way into the world, but they blur together as my throat starts to burn. I squeeze my eyes shut against the tears threatening to fall. They slip down my cheeks anyway, almost painful in the bitter air.

An ache creates a fissure right through my chest and my breath catches in my throat. I curl my arms around my middle, willing the pressure of them to force the hurt away, to dam the welling ache of loneliness.

You still have me, Valeria, Kosci says gently.

Am I making a mistake?

We are doing what we have to. Sometimes that comes with losses we don't expect. Alik swore to stand by your side no matter what. He's the entire reason you agreed to my bargain. You wanted to exact revenge on the people who ripped him from you in the first place. He's never understood that. He would've rather died. All he's done is doubt and fight you every step of the way.

I remember how Alik avoided me in the days after the release of Ludminka. How he asked me not to change, as if I could stop it.

I'd been granted the gift to change the world. The one thing I'd longed for since Ludminka froze. Alik had known that, always had. He'd heard me vow Ladislaw's death more than once as we hid from Storm Hounds. And yet now, he can no longer understand.

I suck in a deep breath as my tears dry to frozen tracks on my cheeks.

Alik didn't want me to have this gift. I could be hero to all of Strana and he would still find ways to fault me. He wants to stop me from being everything I can be. I don't need him.

I don't need anyone.

TWENTY-ONE

I KEEP TRUE TO MY word, refusing to balk at the idea of taking Yelgarod and Yuri. Alik doesn't speak to me the entire time. Not even when we meet my father and the entire army from Ludminka halfway there, thanks to a quick message with Bataar's hawk. I let my plan filter through the army naturally, not exactly eager to declare it to an entire militia that may refuse. By the time the low mountains that house Yelgarod appear on the horizon, it has circulated through every last person. I hear the whispers, and what I can't hear, Kosci supplies.

It's reckless. It's dangerous. Czar Ladislaw will have his revenge for this.

The words are repeated by every campfire, inside every yurt, but no one says I'm wrong. No one except Alik, who disappeared into the crowd as soon as he was able. It hardens my already bitter heart. I guess I should take solace in the fact he didn't disappear completely, but it still feels like a betrayal.

As I turn off the main road and take us into the foothills, following Sera's carefully laid out route, a horse breaks away from the back to trot up beside me. For one painfully hopeful moment, I think it's Alik, but I glance over to find my father instead. Surprise ripples through me, but it disappears as he gives me a warm smile, the craggy lines in his brow hidden beneath a stiff fur hat. His grin disappears when I don't return it, unable to find the certainty I'm supposed to display before my army.

"What is it, *Milaya*? You haven't spoken to your brothers or me since we joined the march."

I wish we were alone so I could collapse into his arms and let his gentle voice tell me I'm doing right. But we aren't, and I don't want my father to know how truly nervous I am.

"I . . . have something I need to do, but I don't know if you'll like it. No one else seems to," I say at last, with a furtive glance in his direction. His calm blue eyes still haven't left my face.

"This plan to take Yelgarod? And Ladislaw's son?" he asks quietly.

I nod, looking over my shoulder casually to see who follows. The rest of the army marches behind us like a luminous blue snake, pieces of lovite armor winking in the sunlight. No one is within earshot, and I allow the tension to ease from my shoulders.

"I wish I could say I wanted you to stay your hand," Papa says. "But after hearing what he did to those people in the prison . . . I don't know. I would never want to lose you or your brothers, but I'd rather you be taken hostage than slaughtered from behind."

My breath hitches a little at his words, the realization I was desperate for his approval crashing down on me like a wave. I grasp his hand, squeezing hard. "Thank you. You have no idea how much that means to me."

My father returns the squeeze before I let my hand drop back to my reins. Stiff-bristled pines start to rise up on our right side, following the incline of the foothills, blocking us from the worst of the winter wind. My father shivers against the sudden absence before giving me a soft smile.

"I love you, Valeria. And the army is loyal to you. You saved us from the freeze and the prison. Not a single one of us will ever forget it."

"You don't believe it . . . too harsh? To inflict this punishment on a boy? To use my powers to do so?" I ask.

"How can I when Czar Ladislaw would not hesitate to take the head of my own daughter? I won't deny I wish there were a better plan, but we will do what we must."

The weight of all the doubts Kosci and I overheard shifts from my shoulders at my father's words. I wish there were another path, too. For all my bravado, I don't want Yuri to suffer as I have suffered. I don't want him to be scared and alone, cut off from the only life he has ever known. Yet I see no other way.

I look back at my father. Part of me wants to tell him everything, from the fear to the desire to rule Strana to Alik. Maybe he would understand. Maybe he'd offer wisdom or comforting words. Isn't that what fathers are supposed to do?

But what will Papa know of ruling or war? He is just as much a stranger to this world as I am, and no amount of parental praise will change anything. As much as I may wish to share this burden, I can't. Kosci chose me and me alone.

"We should make camp," Sera calls out from behind. "We will lose the light soon, and this is as good a place as we are going to find before the palace."

I put up my hand to call a stop to the procession, giving my father a grateful smile before swinging down off my horse. Before I can take my mare's reins, Papa catches them.

"Why don't I take care of your horse tonight? You've got a siege to plan, after all."

A feeble smile touches my lips and before I can second-guess myself, I slip into my father's arms and give him a quick hug.

"I love you, Papa," I say. He grins, his eyes crinkling at the corners.

"Don't you forget about your brothers and me, now. Stop avoiding us and come around our fire once in a while."

I laugh. "I'll keep it in mind."

My father waves as he leads our horses off to a low stand of larch trees, calling to others who break away from the train to feed their horses. As his form disappears into the pines, the light he brought goes with him, and I'm left alone before an army without anyone by my side.

Do not think of the boy. Concentrate on your plan. The rest will fall into place, Kosci says.

Why don't I believe you?

If you suddenly started trusting everything I said, I think I'd believe you were dying.

I huff a laugh and pull a yurt from the sled a team of horses has been carrying. It's almost second nature to set it up now, and I waste no time in hurrying inside as soon as it's erected. It seems so barren, without any of the other cots I'd become accustomed to seeing before the prison. Just mine, tugged near the low-burning fire I'd started in the center. I sigh as I ease onto the cot, warming my legs as best I can.

I stare into the flickering orange of the fire, willing it to eat the horrid knot that has sat in my chest since Alik pushed me away.

I need to forget him as best I can. He made his decision and I made mine. He wants me to cling to a part of myself I can't be anymore. More than anything, I wish he understood. I wish anyone did. Maybe then wearing the mantle of the Pale God wouldn't seem so very lonely.

The flap to my tent opens and I jump, already forming the

blade along my fingers. Bataar steps in, a flagon in one hand and a plate of fish on the other. He barely blinks at the icy short sword in my palm as he crosses toward me to place the food before the fire.

"What are you doing here?" I ask.

"Well hello to you too," he says, smiling as he sits cross-legged on an unused bear hide. He pours mulled wine from the flagon into a small cup and offers it to me. I take it slowly, as if this is some sort of bizarre trick. "Think I'm going to poison you, Valeria?"

"No," I say almost defensively. "But I still don't quite understand what you're doing."

Bataar shrugs, pouring himself a cup. "You weren't coming out. You need to eat, and we need to talk. I'm assuming you want to know the layout of the Winter Palace? The guards? Their numbers?"

I ease onto the ground beside him, taking a long pull of the wine. The acidic taste isn't dulled by the cinnamon and honey, but it warms my stomach and settles my nerves. The truth is, I had forgotten that's what I'd sent Bataar to do. I figured he would've turned over information when we were at the prison, but there would've been no sense in that. I wasn't in the mood to hear it. I down the rest of the wine in another gulp.

"Long day?" he asks, brow raised.

"Long year," I say.

He pours me another cup and pushes the fish in my

direction. "I'm pretty sure I haven't seen you eat all day."

I narrow my eyes at him, uncertain how long he's been watching me or how I didn't spot him, but I take the offered food. He sends a sweeping gaze around the empty yurt and wrinkles his nose slightly.

"Yes, they're all gone. You saw how they reacted to my plan. I think you're about the only friend I have left in camp."

"Some people are afraid of power and the choices that come with it. I find your ability to embrace it fascinating." He smiles and something warm filters through my body. I'm not sure how to respond, so I take another drink.

"What can you tell me about the Winter Palace?"

"I didn't get much of a layout from the letters I found. I know Yuri is inside and that he is guarded, but by how many, I don't know. We will need to send people to scout the area before advancing."

I chew on the inside of my cheek. That had been Alik's job. He'd scanned the members of our army and pulled out the ones best suited for stealth. He'd been training them for a situation just like this, but I no longer know if he will answer when I call. I shove my hair out of my face.

"What about Yelgarod?"

"The city isn't as large as Rurik, but it sits high on the mountainside with the Sayas River at its back. We have no choice but to come in on the road, and I'm sure it's heavily protected."

"So you think we'll need the entire army," I say. I pick at the fish for a long moment, turning over the information before something springs to life in my mind. "But once we have the city, it will be nearly impossible to take. We can turn it into our base camp. It's much farther south than Ludminka, and it'll put us in a better position to maneuver through the kingdom. Plus we can always threaten Yuri's life if Ladislaw tries to lift his hand against the *tyur'ma* in Oleg."

Bataar turns his eyes toward the canvas above, his lips curving into a smile. He meets my eyes again. "Aggressive and ruthless. Ladislaw will never expect it."

The unexpected compliment sends a prickle of pleasure along my spine.

"You don't think it's too much?"

"You're trying to take a country, Valeria. A seat of power would work in your favor. It's ambitious, but it can be done."

I lean back on my elbows, considering him over my cup. "Why did we never talk in the guild?"

Bataar shrugs. "I was hardly there, and you were always busy or with Alik. If I'd known how good of a mind you had for war play, I would've asked Luiza for you to accompany me to Adaman. It would've been a relief to have someone else who understood."

"Now you're just trying to flatter me," I say.

"Why shouldn't I tell the truth?" He raises one of his full eyebrows and smiles. I try to stop the smile spreading on my own lips, forcing the conversation back to Yelgarod.

"What will I do with the citizens, though?" I muse.

"Well, killing them all is out. There has to be at least thirty thousand."

"I wouldn't kill that many people. It's too much work."

Bataar lets out a surprised laugh, and I do smile then.

"No, I think my only option is to turn them to our cause. I need to make them realize I'm a better ruler than the Czar could ever be."

"How do you plan to do that, Czarista of the Pale God?" he asks. I roll my eyes.

"I have my ways." I let my hand drift up to my neck and the pendant nestled there. Kosci simmers at the back of my mind. I'll give the people of Yelgarod a choice, of course. They can aid me willingly, or Kosci and I can make them, using the exact same tactics his brother used on the guildlings. My gut squeezes slightly as I think of Alik's reaction, but I have been given this power. Why shouldn't I use it to spread a little fervor myself? I brush my finger along the stone once, considering.

"Why do you always do that?" Bataar asks, his eyes trained on my fingers.

I look down as I touch the stone again, relishing in the cold spark against my skin. I hesitate for a moment before saying, "This is where the Pale God lives."

"Can you . . . hear him?"

"Always."

"And what does he say about your idea?" Bataar asks.

I say it's a good one, Kosci whispers.

"He says it's the right decision."

"It must get loud, having another person share your mind," he says.

I snort. "It is worth it to be able to do the things I can."

I rise from my elbows and move a little closer. The fire crackles merrily as I cup my hands and put them in the space between us. Slowly, a sheen of ice starts to trickle over my fingers, sparkling in the fire. Bataar watches intently, and I let small snowflakes float toward his face. He reaches out a slow hand, allowing the tiny pieces of ice to collide with his palm.

"Incredible," he breathes. An awed smile crawls across his mouth, and he tears his eyes from the glittering snow to my own. "You're incredible."

I don't know what reaction I was expecting, but this wasn't it. Something about the look in his eyes makes my cheeks heat, and I concentrate on my hands once more, throwing the snow into the air so it falls around us, light and soft. It catches in Bataar's dark hair and long eyelashes as he looks toward the ceiling.

"I don't know how anyone could think you are anything but extraordinary," he whispers as he catches a snowflake on his hand. It melts slowly along with the rest of my fluttering snow.

"I'm sure someone will find a way," I say, thinking of the

other three people who should be in this tent with me.

"Don't worry, they'll come around. Once Yelgarod is ours, they'll see the merit in your ideas," he says.

"You seem awfully certain of people you only half know," I say, pulling a thick log from the pile beside the fire and tossing it on. Bataar catches my hand before I drop it, and I glance at him.

"I'm not certain of them. I'm certain of *you*." He releases my hand. "It's not every day you meet a girl with a god around her neck. You will change the world. Of that, I have no doubt."

TWENTY-TWO

AT DAWN THE NEXT DAY, I hunt for Alik. Yelgarod won't give itself up easily, and I need the city's secrets. The only person who has spies is Alik. I'd given him that role when I thought I could trust him. A solid knot forms in my stomach as I pass tent after tent of laughing men and women. Even the ones we freed from the first prison look hearty, with flushed cheeks and bright eyes.

You've brought them hope, Kosci says, and I jump. *Having the ability to change your fortune is a rare gift. You've given it to them.*

I will give them more.

I know, he says. *Why do you seek out Alik when you could ask Bataar? He is just as capable, perhaps more so. And he's loyal to you . . . to us.*

I need Alik's numbers. Bataar doesn't have the scouts. I say it, but we both know it's a lie.

I want to see Alik. Just because he's refused to believe in my path doesn't mean my heart doesn't ache for him. The memory of his refusal still burns bright in my mind, like a beacon of all I'm willing to give up to ensure Zladonia is free of Ladislaw and Matvei for good. Perhaps he will change his mind. Perhaps he will apologize for doubting me now that he's had time to cool off.

Kosci's uncertainty flickers through my mind, and I shove it back down. He doesn't know Alik like I do. Alik has always been by my side. He can't want to leave now, not when we're so close to having everything we ever wanted.

He told you it isn't what he wants, Kosci says.

I don't think I asked for your input.

Kosci quiets, and I continue my slow scan of the camp.

It takes nearly an hour to find the small group of tents where he hides. His scouts are the first to see me, and they dart into a tiny yurt at the back of their circle. A moment later, Alik steps out.

My heart lurches at the sight of him. He's tied his long hair out of his face, but small wisps still cling to his cheeks in delicate strands I long to push back.

"What do you want?" he asks, his voice cold and distant. I fight to keep my face impassive.

"I need your scouts," I say, gesturing to the people around us who try to behave as if they are benignly eating breakfast.

They gaze up at Alik and me from their small stumps, tin plates in hand. He doesn't move to make our conversation private, so I don't either.

"We aren't helping you kidnap a child."

"I never asked you to," I say evenly. I refuse to let him ruffle me before *my* soldiers. "I need them only to scout the area and tell me what to expect. Any watchtowers or hamlets that might relay our coming to the palace. The sort of thing scouts *should* be doing."

I tilt my chin up, waiting for him to refuse but terrified he will. He stares at me for a long moment before nodding once.

"It will be done," he says. Tension eases from my neck, but I forge ahead with the rest of the request.

"I would like them to report back to me by tomorrow morning. The longer we wait, the more chance we have of being discovered."

Alik performs a sweeping bow, never breaking eye contact. "As you wish, Champion."

I clench my teeth but don't respond as I spin on my heel and stalk away, as all hopes of reconciling shatter around me. Part of me feels like it should make me cry, but the emotion never comes. Instead, I find it's what I expected.

He made it very clear he no longer believes I am on the right path. Alik is, above all things, stubborn. Just like when he believed I knew he was alive and refused to see him. Maybe he still believes that.

Or maybe he was lying when he said he loved me.

I clutch the pendant as I make my way back through camp and into my tent. Kosci's presence instantly calms me. Even if I feel like I'm alone, I'm not.

A moment after I return to my yurt, a solider enters, carrying what I suppose is my breakfast. He smiles and places it into my hands.

"Thank you," I say, looking down at the still steaming food. The soldier nods, but I stop him before he can go. "Can you bring me Bataar?"

The soldier salutes and slips from the tent. I push around the food on my plate.

You were right, I think.

I usually am.

In what seems like moments, Bataar is before me with a small smile.

"You asked for me?" he says with a wink.

"Stop teasing," I say as I pinch the bridge of my nose. "But I do need you. Alik has . . . proved incapable of the task at hand."

Bataar straightens at that. "Still disagreeing I'm guessing?"

"I'm sure the entire camp is guessing by now."

"Perhaps." He shrugs. "What do you need?"

"I need eyes on the palace, details of Yuri's location, and the number of guards who watch him. Any move against Yelgarod without that sort of information is useless, and I know neither Alik nor his spies will do exactly as I ask."

"I'll see what I can do." He slices me a sly grin and turns toward the flap.

"And, Bataar?" I say, and he pauses. "Make sure you aren't seen. By *anyone*."

"I never am," he says.

With that he disappears, and I'm left alone once more.

As night falls, I find myself once again pacing my yurt and listening to the flap of furs on the wind. It howls through camp, beating down on us like it is determined to blow us away before we can reach Yelgarod. Neither Bataar nor Alik's scouts have returned, and worry settles like a hard stone in my gut. I'm just about to extend my power to find them when Bataar stumbles through the flap.

His hair lays limp and wet against his forehead. I shoot to my feet and fling a blanket around his shoulders, ushering him to the fire. I toss on another log and grab an ember for the samovar. I glance at him over the lip of it. The golden brown of his skin has paled, his mouth almost blue.

"What happened?"

"Well, I made sure no one saw me," he says through chattering teeth, inching closer to the fire.

"By doing what? Diving into the river?" I press a cup of hot tea into his hands.

"Yes."

"Bataar, you're—"

"A hero? A true and loyal follower?"

"I was going to say idiot," I say, and he grimaces. "But yes, you're both of the other things, too."

"And to think I almost froze to death for you."

I add another blanket across his lap. "You need to change. You'll catch your death."

I stand and go to the packs at the edge of the tent. I'd given my guards leave to put their items in my tent for safekeeping. I dig through the closest one until I find a shirt and trousers. I toss them over, and they land limply beside Bataar. He stares at them for a long moment. "Don't worry, I won't look."

"I wouldn't mind if you did," he says with a wicked grin.

I wheel about before the heat coursing across my face gives me away. I shift, trying to redirect the conversation. "What did you find?"

The sound of sopping clothing hitting the ground seems far too loud, but Bataar speaks as nonchalantly as ever.

"Not what we expected. I did see someone, dark headed and sour looking, almost a twin to Ladislaw, but he was no child," Bataar says. "All right, you can turn around."

I turn as he slips the shirt over his head. Despite myself, I trace the lean lines of his body before they disappear in a wave of gray fabric. I busy my hands with my own tea before he can catch me.

"What do you mean? Yuri was born just months before the Iovite trade ended," I say.

"The person I saw had to be at least fifteen, if not older. If Ladislaw has used a body double for his son, who is to say he hasn't lied about when that son was born, too?"

I turn over this new piece of information. "It seems like a lot of work. There had to have been staff who knew, midwives present for the birth."

"All people easily disposed of," Bataar says.

My brain pulses with the beginnings of a headache as I slowly start to pace before Bataar. Was it possible Ladislaw had been lying to all of Strana? The effort he would've had to go to was enormous, but it wasn't beyond the realm of possibility. Bataar reaches out and catches my upper arm, halting me before I can start back on the beaten path I've made in the center of the yurt.

"This changes nothing," he says, brushing a strand of hair out of my face. The gentle touch sends a warm shiver along my body. "In fact, it may make it easier. The others won't fight you anymore."

"We don't know it's not just another trick," I say, bearing my single insecurity in a bid of desperation. "I can't afford to make another mistake like Adaman."

"Even if the boy *isn't* the real Yuri, we will still have Yelgarod. Ladislaw will lose his only foothold in the north."

I stare up into his face, the edges of his hair already drying in the warmth of the yurt. He is the only one aside from Kosci who has stayed by my side, the only one who doesn't think I'm cruel for wanting to kidnap Yuri in the first place. I part my lips, wanting to say something to acknowledge everything he's done for me when the flap of the yurt opens again.

We both look over to find Alik framed in the entrance, fires smoldering behind him as the army prepares dinner. He takes in Bataar's hand on my arm and the scant distance between us, his mouth growing tighter with each detail. Bataar's hand slips away, and I turn, clasping my hands before me.

"Yes?" I say.

"You asked me to report when my scouts had returned. I've got the information you want," Alik says without emotion. I try to read him, searching for signs of anger or resentment. He's as blank as the canvas behind him. I tighten my hold on my hands.

"Please grab Chinua and Sera, my father and brothers, too, if you can find them. We've got a siege to plan."

After my brothers, father, and a rather rumpled-looking Sera and Chinua are dragged into the tent, I relay what Bataar saw at the palace.

"So you believe this . . . person is Crown Prince Yuri?" Sera asks. "How can you be certain?"

"I can't be," Bataar says with a shrug. "But he looks an awful lot like Ladislaw. Why would they go through the effort of encoding missives if they weren't hiding something in Yelgarod?"

"It isn't as if this would be the first time you were tricked," Sera shoots back.

"Enough," I cut in before it can devolve. "The fact is, we don't know who he is, but he *is* someone important enough to have guards. Either way, he will be a good source of information."

"Do you plan to rifle through his mind, too?" Alik asks. The air goes out of the room, all of them waiting for my response. I remain planted firmly near Bataar and raise my chin.

"If I must," I say. I pause, waiting for Alik to chastise me yet again, but he remains silent and sullen. "It doesn't matter at the moment what I will do with the boy inside Yelgarod. Taking the city is our best bid for outmaneuvering the Czar. We will maintain power over the north, and if we are lucky, power over his son, too. What we need to concentrate on is the layout of the road and city itself."

Alik stiffens, and for one horrible moment I'm certain he will refuse to give me the information I need. He lets loose an irritated breath before opening his mouth.

"There are three watchtowers, all of which communicate by reflecting a light off a mirror. The first rests a mile up the path, the other two a quarter mile apart after that. The last watchtower reports to a garrison above the city gates."

"What of the land around the towers?" I ask.

"Barren. They've taken out all trees and foliage in a hundred-yard radius around them."

"Any villages?" Chinua asks.

"None that they could see, and they scoured the area well." Alik pulls a parchment from his belt and hands it to Sera. "This is a rough sketch of the land. We attempted to get into the city, but the walls were wide and heavily guarded. It seems Yelgarod is partially carved into a mountain on the north side, with a river at the south. It will be impossible to surround it."

Sera and Chinua crowd around the rough sketch, but I keep back, unwilling to cross the distance between Alik and I.

"If we hope to march on Yelgarod without alerting everyone in the city and the palace, we will need to take out the watchtower closest to the gates first. If we can control that, we can make sure no information on our army is reported back to Yelgarod," Chinua says, and Sera gives her a brief, glowing smile.

"Before we could move," Sera says, "we'd need more information on the terrain from this camp up to the third watchtower. The mountainside has to be steep and nearly impassible. They wouldn't leave their side undefended otherwise."

I swing my gaze to Alik, and I wonder briefly if he will refuse to respond. This plan is being specifically molded to catch Yuri and Yelgarod both.

"Why don't you send your scouts out to document the area?" I ask. His body stiffens, and I quickly scramble for something to stop him from refusing. "Unless you don't feel they are up to the task. Then I'm sure Bataar can manage."

Alik's lips thin as he stands. "I'm sure we can handle it."

He doesn't wait for me to dismiss him, slipping back into camp without another word.

I clear my throat, ignoring the silent question in my father's and brothers' eyes. "As for Yuri, Bataar has informed me there is a way to reach the back of the palace. But it is dangerous. It will need to be a small team, quick and sure. As it is undoubtedly apparent to everyone, I don't think I can count on my little band of spies to handle the mission, which is why I've asked you here."

I nod toward my family. "I want you, Bataar, and a small group of others to follow Bataar's lead and capture the prince before he has a chance to escape. We will send you a signal with the mirror on the watchtower when we plan to break into the city. That should give you enough time to get in position before word reaches the palace the enemy has breached the gates. With any luck, the people of Yelgarod will go quietly and won't know we've taken Yuri."

"Will they even care we have?" Gregori asks.

"That remains to be seen," I say.

TWENTY-THREE

TWO HOURS BEFORE DAWN THE next day, we make our move on foot. My father leaves with Bataar and my brothers to block Yuri's escape, while I follow Sera with a band of thirty people capable of climbing and fighting.

The soft chime of lovite armor and crunch of snow are our only companions as we make our way to the base of the foothills. One look up the side full of fir and birch trees and I know it will take us hours to reach the watchtower.

"Ready?" she whispers.

I nod.

My calves scream as we trudge up the side, clinging to slim trunks to pull ourselves forward. Despite having hiked across all of Strana to reach Knnot, my chest stings with each inhale. The steady soldiers behind me never complain or lose pace, so I keep barreling forward.

We reach a sharp, stony outcropping, the tip of the tower just visible over the top. Tall pines spring up on either side, lending their branches for us to climb. I stare at them, questioning their ability to hold a person in full armor. The rocks are too slick to clamber up, and even if they weren't, I'm not sure anyone could manage and still have the strength to fight whoever holds the watchtower.

I think we can make short work of that, Kosci says.

Strength courses down my hands and tingles in the tips of my fingers. I raise my hands and let Kosci's idea form before me, manipulating the gossamer threads of magic darting through the air. The snow gathered at our knees begins to tremble, slowly building on top of itself to form a ramp right to the top of the outcropping.

I drop my arms and it solidifies with a soft sigh, like snow whispering down tree branches. The forest stands quiet. Even the ragged breathing of the soldiers at my back has stopped. I inhale the sharp scent of fresh snow, gathering every ounce of courage in my body.

"Shall we?"

When no one moves, I take the first tentative step onto the ramp. It creaks beneath my weight but holds as firm as any wooden structure. I ascend, the army following behind me. I crouch before I crest the rise and motion for the others to do the same. The ground before us lays bare, the watchtower in the center.

It isn't much bigger than a cabin, wide pine boards rising twenty feet above us, emptying out onto a stout platform. Five broad backs clad in black stand at the low rails surrounding the platform, all of them facing the road leading up to Yelgarod. A large mirror sits on the right side and a Storm Hound reaches out to wink it a couple times, murmuring to his compatriots.

"Five up top," I whisper back to my squad. "No telling how many are inside the tower. Be ready to fight. We need to reach the top before they can signal Yelgarod we're coming."

I beckon the archers forward. We don't have many, but they should be good enough shots to take out the Storm Hounds up top if we can get close enough. We creep forward slowly, and I curse every crack of snow beneath our feet.

It isn't until we are close enough to see the frost glistening on the edges of the watchtower's roof that one of the Storm Hounds looks over his shoulder. He lets out a strangled shout, lunging for the mirror to signal a warning to Yelgarod. He doesn't get a chance to touch it before a lovite arrow embeds in his throat.

Four more arrows whistle through the air, two lodging in heads, while the others find their marks in the heart. One of the Storm Hounds stumbles forward, knocking into the mirror as he crashes to the ground. It spins wildly, flashing every time it catches the sun's rays.

"Hurry!" I call.

Storm Hounds flood from the small door on the side of the tower. They rush toward us, swords and shields raised, at least twenty in all. They stop, creating a wall with their shields as three behind them nock crossbows. I raise my hand and frost climbs around their boots, rooting them in place. Some struggle against it, but it only makes the frost squeeze tighter.

I yell and race forward, the army crashing behind me. I have to reach the mirror before one of the Storm Hounds does. The crossbows fire with a twang, hitting the person just to my left. They stumble back, but I can't spare time seeing if they fall.

We crash upon the Storm Hounds in a wave. They swing their blades, but they clang uselessly off the lovite armor. They yell something about aiming for our necks as I cut through the man before me. He drops to his knees, blood streaming from his throat, staining the snow beneath his knees a brilliant red.

The squeal of sword-on-sword rings through the air as I dart past the crossbowman and into the building. He follows and I flick my wrist, sending shards of ice at him. They rip through his armor and embed themselves in the wood at his back. I sprint up the stairs two at a time.

I barrel onto the platform at the top and come face-to-face with a young girl, maybe two or three years older than I am. Her chestnut-colored hair is caught up in a tight knot at the nape of her neck, and she gapes at me as I step closer. Her hand inches toward the mirror.

"Don't do it," I whisper. "You don't have to die today."

"It is my duty," she says, her voice soft.

"You can join me. I can give you whatever you want. You have but to ask for it." I take a step forward. The girl's trembling hand hovers above the lever of the mirror.

"Who are you?" Her voice is barely a whisper.

"I am the Pale God's champion. I've come to make a new world, a better world where all can prosper." I'm close enough to grasp her hand and gently lower it to her side. I use my power to search through her mind, gleaning the small, important parts of her life that she holds close. "I don't want to kill you, Anya Demidova."

"How do you know my name?" she asks.

"I know much. One of my gifts as a god's champion is seeing what a heart truly wants. I know what you wish for, and I can give it to you. I will give you your family back."

"My . . . my family?"

"I see what the Czar did to them. Tossed them in a prison because they didn't pay their debts. They languish with the Zladonians in Oleg's *tyur'ma*. You hoped this post would earn you enough renown and money to free them," I say, and she goes completely still. "Aid me now, and I will make sure you are reunited."

"What do I have to do?" Her voice trembles.

"Kneel now and swear fealty to me. Join my army on our quest to usurp the Czar and I swear to you, I will grant your family freedom and every happiness I can afford. I will even bless you, if you ask it of me."

Anya stares at me, her brown eyes like a fawn in the forest. I hold her hand and wait for her decision. Time stretches indeterminately around us. She licks her lips once. Twice. Her body coils tight, and I know her plan before she acts. She attempts to lunge forward, a small dagger in the palm of her hand. I sidestep her easily, allowing her momentum to carry her into the wall of the watchtower. Anya slams hard into it before wheeling about to face me, eyes constantly flickering to the mirror at my back.

"You don't have to do this," I say, voice calm and sure. "Why fight for Ladislaw? What has he ever done for you?"

"I gave him my loyalty," she says, and slashes out again. I take a single step back, avoiding it completely.

"Is that worth dying for?" I ask. Kosci's power beats rapidly through my body, the vine-like tendrils curling through my sternum and winding around my ribs. Magic suffuses every part of me now, lending my bones strength, my mind certainty. "I offer you a chance at a place within the new Strana, one where you are with your family again."

Anya cuts viciously through the air, and I slip away from her with fluid grace, hands clasped behind my back. Her movements are all anger and desperation.

"You are nothing but a witch. You offer promises you can never deliver. Ladislaw warned us you would tempt us, and you will find no willing ally in me."

A cold, angry surety washes over me.

"I will offer mercy only this once," I say, dancing around the mirror as Anya lunges again.

"I don't want your mercy," she snaps.

"Then you won't have it."

With a brutal efficiency, I grab the lip of the mirror and ram it up, the opposite side connecting with Anya's jaw. She stumbles back, leaving her chest exposed. With a single snap, I send three crystalline blades into Anya's heart. Her face goes slack, and she collapses to her knees, wavering for a moment before falling forward, barely catching herself on her hands. I cross the small platform toward her, crouching to get a better look.

"I gave you a chance. I didn't want to do this, Anya."

In a final moment of defiance, she spits blood into my face. I wipe it away slowly, doing nothing to stop her collapse to the floor. I consider her body for a moment before shaking my head and rising to my feet. I gave Anya a choice. That's more than the Czar ever gave to the people of Zladonia.

I look out over the battlefield behind the tower. Blood trails across the snow like broad brush strokes, but the bodies being dragged to the center of the empty field are predominately those of Storm Hounds. Only a few of my own soldiers fell, and something like pride bubbles in the pit of my stomach.

Even now, my army trudges up the mountain path with Chinua at the helm. Yuri cannot escape me. No one can. Power crackles and pulses through my body in every breath. I will see a new Strana built if it's the last thing I do.

TWENTY-FOUR

I CAN TELL WHEN THE first watchtower on the road to Yelgarod falls. The wind dies, the world inhaling as the true war begins. Wild, bright flashes come from the second watchtower, sending a message of attack, possible invasion. I do nothing aside from grip the rails of the observation platform and wait for the second tower to fall. Their decimation is louder, the chime of lovite armor and the cries of terror are closer, almost visceral. I wait a few more moments before trudging downstairs to the storeroom where Sera watches the squadron eat dried meat and drink small sips of honeyed wine.

"Finish up," I say as I shrug back into my cloak. "Our army marches up the path now."

By the time we all manage to filter from the tower and onto the street leading to Yelgarod, the army is within sight.

Chinua leads them, her head adorned in a magnificent helm of lovite scrolls and steel.

I hail her, and her horse trots forward, pulling to a stop just before me. I catch its nose, giving it a rub before looking up.

"Any issues?"

She shakes her head. "They fell quickly. It's clear they weren't expecting a force this size."

"Any survivors?" I ask.

"None."

I nod as a soldier brings me a steed of my own, a pretty white mare with black socks. I swing up and pull beside Chinua. We march forward, the slow incline of the path blocking Yelgarod from our sight. My stomach tightens as the road steepens, deep grooves of erosion marring the center.

The broad gates are the first thing to appear, followed by the small yurts outside the wooden palisade, clinging to the sides as if they might gain the walls' protection by proximity alone. The ramshackle tents are still and quiet as we pass. Occasionally, I catch sight of small children poking their heads out tent doors with wide eyes and open mouths. Some adults grow bold enough to stand with flap raised to watch me pass. Each one is lean and starving, each one weighted by the last ten years.

I wonder how many times they've seen a procession like this pass through their community. Did anyone ever stop? Did they ever care?

I put my hand up as a small girl tumbles into the road. Her mother hurries out and gathers the girl in her arms. I swing down from my horse and crouch until I'm eye level with them. Gaunt hollows sit where the mother's cheeks should be, every bone on her hand painfully visible.

"I'm so sorry, my champion. I swear it will never happen again." The mother's voice is tight, but my body prickles at the title. I look to the little girl cowering inside her mother's arms and smile softly.

"You look hungry and cold," I say, and she nods. I stand and beckon Sera forward. "Pass out as many blankets and cloaks as we can spare. And give them some of our larder. I think they need it more than we do."

Sera quickly relays the message back, and I offer my hand to the mother.

"You have nothing to fear from me. I just want to help. Hopefully, the little we can offer now will make the coming weeks more bearable."

The woman presses her forehead to my hand, clutching it tight. "We can never thank you enough."

She catches her daughter's wrist and hurries her back into the closest yurt, her hands already flitting about as she speaks to her partner. I meet the glances of all the others who had braved peering out into the street. I'm not sure what to do, so I lift my hand in an awkward wave and get back into the saddle.

Word from the woman in the street must travel along the

rows of tents because soon a small crowd swells around us. They cheer and weep as we pass out what we can. Everyone in Strana had been affected by the loss of lovite. For years, the citizens have scraped by on what little we could trade to our allies while Ladislaw did nothing to help his country. With each blanket given, bubbles of laughter and relief are shared through the crowd. It's infectious, turning the mood into something almost festival-like. I don't need an army or bloodshed to win this city. I just need to give them hope that I can change their lives.

Slowly, the yurts outside the walls of Yelgarod are replaced by the stark and firmly fastened city gates. I glance up to the long balcony above to see arrows trained straight at my heart.

"You'll turn back if you know what's good for you," cries a male voice.

"Open these gates, or I will blast them down myself," I call.

"We will never let the city be taken!"

"Then you've made your choice," I say.

My power springs easily into my hands now as I gather the tiny strands from the air. A blast of winter wind blows from behind me, slamming hard into the door. With a sharp crack, the gate snaps inward. I pull back and send another blast. A bolt flies from above, catching me in the shoulder, but I hardly feel it as the magic radiates around me. Ice forms along the broken boards and shatters, sending shards of wood into the cobbled square beyond.

I let my horse pick its way through the fallen gate, keeping my head held high. A twang from a bow sounds above me. I raise my hand without looking back, forming a solid shield of ice and snow. Alik's little demonstration taught me that one. I look over my shoulder to see a terrified soldier with bow raised. I flick my hand, and quick gust of wind sends him toppling off the palisade. I grasp the bolt in my shoulder and grit my teeth as I yank it out. Blood seeps down my clothing for a heartbeat before I seal the wound with a single thought.

Heavy footfalls sound from behind us as armored soldiers pour out of a garrison attached to the high walls of the city. They circle the small battalion that followed me, cutting us off from the rest of the army.

The long spears of the soldiers around us part as a tall woman strides forward bedecked in the feather pauldrons of a commander. She lifts her head high as she comes to a stop at the beginning of her squadron, as if that will force me into submission. Bright flecks of blue and silver magic dance through the air, begging me to grab hold and mold them to my will.

"You will stop your attack on this city at once," she says with all the authority given to her by Ladislaw.

"I have no wish to attack the city," I say, my voice as clear and loud as I can make it. "I want its help, and I plan to help it in return."

Beyond the garrison and the small courtyard lie a wide street with tall houses on either side. People hang out windows and seep from buildings to watch the play before them. I speak to them now, not to the Storm Hounds I know will never surrender.

"For too long the Czar has taken from his citizens and never given back. We have suffered for ten years while he throws lavish parties and wastes lives trying to reopen Knnot. I tell you now, it is I who reopened the mines."

I gesture to the soldiers behind me dressed head to toe in lovite. It catches the wan sunlight above and throws watery blue light across the snowy cobble at our feet.

"I am the Pale God's champion, Valeria. With me at the helm, I can reclaim Strana's glory and I won't forget the citizens who sacrifice to make this country what it is. Lay down your weapons and swear fealty to me. I have no wish to kill any of you, but I will if I have to. The Czar cannot remain in power. He is poisoning this country, and I will see it righted."

The spears of the Storm Hounds around us wobble at my words. My soldiers raise their swords and the world seems to still. I will not make the first move against the Storm Hounds. I cannot be seen as the antagonist if I hope to convince any of these people follow me.

"I'll never let you pass."

The commander springs forward, the Storm Hounds on her heels. A piercing cry rings out behind me as one of the spears catches one of my soldiers in the throat. He collapses to the ground, and I tug hard on the silvery threads hanging in the air, gathering them into my body. An icy tendril bursts from the ground, circling around the waist of the closet Storm Hound. I tighten my hold, and he screams in pain as it squeezes into his ribs.

The commander slashes toward my horse, who rears. I barely manage to keep my seat as we come down with a jarring thud. I manipulate the strands of magic around the commander, calling tendrils with glinting thorns from the ice. The commander's own momentum impales her on the nearest spike and she goes limp, sword clattering to the ground. I slip from my horse and the ice brambles fold away from me, opening onto the city street. I leave the forest of overgrown briars, allowing them to grow and lace together overhead like a twisted archway. Blood seeps down the sides, tainting the tips of the thorns, and I inhale, a cold smile slowly forming on my lips as I look into the massing crowd, faces painted with a mixture of awe and horror.

"Enough," I order, loud enough it echoes off the city's walls. "Drop your weapons now, or I will have no choice but to command the ice to crush the rest of you."

The sounds of wooden spears and short swords falling on ice rings through the courtyard, arms raising above heads to signal their surrender. I nod to Chinua who pulls several foot soldiers from our army.

"Round them up. We can't let them run free until they vow allegiance to us," she says.

Sure Chinua will manage the last of the Storm Hounds, I face the street full of people once more. They part before me as I start forward, and my body hums with Kosci's power. People reach out to brush my hair or shoulder, reverent whispers spreading through the narrow streets.

I keep my face set in a mask of indifference, but inside me a bubble of hope grows. I hadn't had to slaughter a city to take it. Yes, some of these people may escape to tell the Czar of what I have done. I hope they do. He needs to know I have his son and his city.

I will give these people what they need. Food, warmth, money, and the thing Stranans want above all else—lovite. It's the symbol of wealth and security. The guarantee that they won't languish impoverished and dying for years beyond counting.

As soon as I give them that, the entire city will be mine.

I have never been to Yelgarod. Luiza never gave me a mission here. What Alik said of the city is true. A towering peak grows out of the city's side, the walls a luminescent dolomite. The sheer cliff disappears into a sea of peaked roofs in muted blue tile. The buildings are just as tight as they are in Rurik, pressing up against each other until the streets appeared to be one long house instead of multiple smaller ones. I follow the sea of silent people, hoping the wide street will deposit me before the Winter Palace.

The cobbled streets are in ill repair, buckling and rolling

from years of frost and warmth. I feel more than see the small crowd following my movements, and I smile as the pitched towers of the Winter Palace finally come into view over the rooftops. The road empties into a long thoroughfare before the castle, running horizontally along the thick, iron fencing circling the palace.

A clean courtyard with a fountain of charging horses sits in the center, ice clinging to their wide, unseeing eyes. Despite already giving the people of Yelgarod a display of my power, I can't resist the urge to do it again. I pull at the small bits of magical fabric encasing the fount. The ice breaks away and water spouts, fresh and warm, from the fountain, steaming in the cold air.

A chorus of gasps rings out and my grin grows. Once I'm sure my army has gathered around me, I turn to face the city with the palace at my back.

"I will bring you glory, Yelgarod," I say with all the authority I can muster. "In a week's time Iovite will flow into your coffers and flourish through your city. All I ask for is your help. I can bring this wealth to all of Strana, to your brothers and sisters, parents and cousins, but I cannot do it alone. I need an army and capable hands to help mold new weapons and armor. I expect nothing for free. You will be paid for all you do. So what say you, Yelgarod? Will you join me in overthrowing Czar Ladislaw and taking back Strana?"

The echo of my voice rings in the streets, and the villagers are a mass of blue-and-black cloaks. My heart hammers as I wait for a response, transported back to the horrible moment when Ludminka had refused to follow me.

"Valeria!" Someone calls from the back of the crowd. "Valeria!"

The chant starts to gain speed, traveling through the citizens like a wildfire. I can't help it. I raise my arm above my head in victory.

The crowd responds with a resounding roar and a tingle begins in the tips of my fingers, quickly consuming me. This is what it means to rule. Kosci knew before I did the power I could hold, not just his, but a power of my own. The ability to turn people to my side. To have them believe my promises and risk their lives to defend my cause. At last, I have arrived at what I am meant to be.

I will take every village and town from here to Rurik. I will stir up the people's fear, free them from their suffering. Enough hate the Czar to be willing to fight against him.

A slow smile starts to crawl across my face. It's a new dawn, and I am the sun.

TWENTY-FIVE

ENTERING THE PALACE IS FAR simpler than I expected. The gate lock comes away easily in my hand, and I step into the wide field before the castle. Snow covers the topiaries that dot the courtyard and hides the curling paths beneath.

The Winter Palace stands three stories tall, painted a light aqua with gold trimmings. Thick bands of interlaced gold twist down every available edge and trail up tall chimneys. It spans even larger than the palace in Rurik, with two wide wings that connect back to two other wings, forming a box.

I lead the soldiers through the courtyard and into a vast foyer, the ceiling soaring in high arches overhead, carved of white wood and golden filigree. Two staircases lay at either end of the foyer, curving up to meet on a landing high above my head. Before me is a long hallway with rounded ceilings and bright gold lights twinkling along the walls.

It's more opulence than I have ever seen.

I move forward into the hallway. It runs the length of the palace, splitting off into grand ballrooms of red and gold, music rooms with hand-painted pianos and ivory violins. At last, I am deposited into the kitchen. A roaring fireplace takes up the entirety of the wall to my left, while a thick whitewashed wall with small windows looking out onto a kitchen garden spans the length of the wall opposite me.

The fire still crackles away, the smell of fat on flame permeating the room and making my stomach growl. A half-dressed goose lies in the center of a wooden island, a pie without a top crust sitting beside it. The cooks left in a hurry, and not too long ago. For the first time since I stepped into the Winter Palace, worry twists at my gut. I hope Bataar and my father managed to catch Yuri before he escaped.

Soldiers chatter and laugh behind me, spreading out through the palace's vast halls. I can't imagine what the Zladonians think. It's more than we've ever seen, and we were the ones harvesting the lovite to make Ladislaw his fortune. We should've been the ones to live in grand halls of marble and glass. A vicious satisfaction worms its way through me. The castle is ours now, and I will make sure all of Zladonia is given what it is owed.

I follow the windows to the left, past the fire and into a

darkened hall. The condensation on the window freezes into beautiful whorls of frost as I pass. It empties into yet another wide room whose purpose I can't even begin to guess at. The palace seems never-ending, and I don't know where to start looking for the prince or the party I sent to stop his escape. I open the frosted door and exit into the courtyard.

Trees hug the corners, surrounded by waist-high stone walls and dead ivy. The paths intersect in a tight cross, strict lines of herbs and vegetables in each quadrant. The snow in the center has been stirred up, footprints leading toward the back of the garden and through the door on the other side.

I follow them, picking up my pace as I enter yet another dark room. This one appears to be a private library, with tall bookcases and a small fireplace tucked into the corner. I turn right, toward the slightly open door in the middle of the wall, and enter some sort of bedchamber.

The room sails above with a tray ceiling painted sky blue and gold. A wide, canopied bed with white curtains sits in the center with a cheerful fire popping away to its left. If I had to guess, this is where Yuri was staying. Stray papers sprawl across the desk pushed up against a high window, and wooden practice blades sit abandoned in the corner.

But where would he have gone from here?

A quick peek inside the door to the left of the bed reveals a tub built above a large fire, and another room for steaming. I close the door and plant my hands on my hips. There has to be a secret way out. He left too quickly to be sure of covering his steps, that much is certain by the ajar door to the library.

I scan the velvet paneled walls, the seams buttoned down by golden wood. At last, my eyes catch on a ripped piece of velvet to the right of the bed. I push on the panel and a small door swings open. It's far too small for me to walk down, so I fall to my knees, wincing against the cold bite of the roughly hewn stone.

The palace is a palpable weight around me, the creaking timbers and wet stone reminding me far too much of our days trapped inside Knnot for me to linger.

A dim outline starts to form before me. Another small door, with bright white light around its edge. I shove it open and fall face-first into a snowdrift. I scramble to my feet, squeezing my eyes shut against the blinding brilliance of white snow. When I finally blink away the dots, I make out figures standing on an open river, a lean boy with a group of black-cloaked men.

Yuri.

I race toward the others, the scene becoming clearer the closer I get. My small team surrounds the Storm Hounds and Yuri, their swords at the ready with Bataar and my father shoulder to shoulder. The group of Storm Hounds stand in a circle around the boy who can be no other than Ladislaw's son. He has the same pointed jaw, the same heavy brow and gray eyes. The resemblance between him and the younger boy Ladislaw had been using as his son is startling, but this Yuri is clearly older, clutching a saber of his own, poised to strike if anyone got near enough.

"Why have you stalled?" I say as I slip into the space between Bataar and my father.

"The *prince*," Bataar sneers the word, "has decided he will end his life before he allows us to take him."

A tic starts in the boy's jaw as our gazes clash.

"If he truly meant those words, he would've done it already," I whisper to Bataar.

With a jerk of my finger, shards of ice explode from the river and pierce through the feet of the guards before Yuri. They howl with pain as blood wells over their boots, steaming where it meets the snow. It's all the distraction my men need. They rush into the fray, cutting down Storm Hounds and parrying their blows. I watch my brothers and father, trying my best to protect them against low blows and flying daggers with thin barriers of ice.

Yuri wheels toward me out of nowhere, connecting with my upper arm. The sword bites deep. I jerk away, hissing as the frost on the blade makes the sword stick. With another wrench, it comes free, and I stagger backward, readying my icy daggers.

"You've already lost this fight," I hiss. Yuri's gaze narrows as he resituates the blade in his hand.

He darts forward, and I barely manage to slide out of his way. I throw my daggers. One sails over his shoulder while the other finds its way into his bicep. He winces, but it doesn't slow his movements. His sword work is brutal, lunges and slashes deadly accurate. I parry his next blow, but the sheer force of it snaps my blade in half. Yuri smirks, and my blood boils.

"Enough," I shout. As if coaxed by my voice alone, pillars of ice shoot from the ground, trapping Yuri in a cage of frost. With a growl he levels a swing. His blade connects with a hollow ping, vibrations traveling up the blade and into his arms, causing him to drop his sword.

I step forward, curling my hands around Yuri's icy prison bars. "You are mine, princeling."

Yuri's hand snaps out like a viper, curling around my throat. He squeezes, yanking my head into the ice bars, and my world explodes into bright stars. I blink them away before grasping Yuri's forearm. A biting cold rolls from my hand, searing across his arm. He releases me with a yelp, taking several steps back, cradling his arm.

"You will pay for that," he says.

I smirk. "I very much doubt it."

Before he can respond, I return to the battle waging behind my back.

My father bashes a Storm Hound with his shield, and Anton darts in, sinking a short sword into his middle. Bataar stands to the side, leveling arrow after arrow. A flash of silver catches my eye, sailing straight toward Bataar, and a dagger sinks deep into his shoulder. He cries out, clutching it, blood pooling between his fingers. The Storm Hound who threw it darts forward, raising his sword high. I lash out, sending an ice shard straight into the man's back. He topples forward, landing on top of Bataar and sending them both crashing to the ground.

I rush to him, shoving the man from Bataar. He sucks in a breath and stares up at the sky.

"I thought I was going to suffocate," he says.

"I could've let him kill you. Would that have been better?" I ask.

"Maybe," he says. I roll my eyes and haul him to his feet. He reaches for the blade but I catch his hand.

"Leave it until we can get you to our infirmary. You don't want to lose any more blood than you have to."

"You didn't take your own advice?" he asks, nodding toward the crusting blood on the right side of my chest.

"I'm not you," I say. "I can handle a little blood loss."

He scoffs as I scan the river. Storm Hounds lie limp across the ice as one of my women pulls her axes from another's back. Yuri still stands in his cage, anger rolling off him in near palpable waves. I rise to my feet.

"Grab our new prisoner," I say to my brothers. "Let's see what Ladislaw's hidden son has to say."

TWENTY-SIX

YURI SITS SILENT AND SULLEN in the chair before the fireplace in the library. Three guards stand at the entrances to the room, their eyes never leaving him. He'd proved himself capable enough with a blade that I don't trust leaving him to his own devices. In all my plans of taking Yuri and Yelgarod, this was the last thing I expected. A little boy might have been scared by a couple cheap tricks and the threat of no dinner. The stubborn silence from the young man perhaps only a year younger than myself is much harder to break.

I turn from him, finding Bataar in the shadows beside me. Bandages circle his shoulder and hold his arm tight to his chest. Even still, a small patch of blood forms on the linen. I cross my arms and lean against the doorframe.

"He's refused to say anything," I whisper.

"What did you expect? He's loyal to his father."

"Why can't he see what Ladislaw has done?"

Bataar shrugs, wincing. "Such is the way of loyalty."

I huff, my eyes slipping back to Yuri. He stares back as if he senses my presence.

I sigh, turning away from the boy to stare into his room. Perhaps there is something in here that will force him to open up. Documents or missives from his father, evidence of subterfuge from Luiza. Something I can use as pressure. It would be so simple to reach into Yuri's mind and pluck what I wanted, but the gnawing guilt fueled by Alik still clings to my interior, staying my hand.

"Are you ever going to clean yourself up?" Bataar asks. He nods toward my arm, and I glance down at my bloodied tunic and cloak. I frown, stupidly trying to brush it away. "Sit."

Bataar points to Yuri's bed. I don't want to admit how comforting the downy blankets look, so I turn my nose up instead.

"I'm fine," I say, but he pushes me toward the blankets anyway. I sit with an exasperated sigh, and he crouches beside me. "I feel like you need to be here more than I do."

"This isn't the first time I've managed to find myself at the wrong end of a dagger," he says, unclasping the cloak from my throat. The material flutters to the bed, revealing the large stain at my collarbone and blood oozing from the still-open wound in my upper arm.

I turn toward him, my expression flat. "This isn't the first time I've been hurt either."

He looks up, and I become very aware of how close we are. A wry grin tugs at his lips.

"Ah, but this *is* the first siege. It's a special occasion."

I give half a laugh and relinquish my arm at last. He carefully draws the shirt up over the wound on my arm and shoulder and gives a soft exhale. He turns it carefully in the firelight.

"It can't be that bad," I say. "I took care of the one in my shoulder."

He rolls his eyes. "It's not good either. Did they get you anywhere else?"

I shake my head. "Just the blood you see."

His eyes dip toward my collarbone, taking in the puncture scar the bolt left behind. In spite of myself, my breath catches in my throat. He tugs his eyes away, returning his attention to the wound on my arm. A divot appears between his brows and he leans closer.

"Do you even know how deep this thing goes? Seriously, Valeria, you should've come to the infirmary with me."

I reach out and smooth the crinkle between his eyebrows, pushing gently to send his head away from me.

"I'm *fine*. If I wasn't conserving my power, I would heal it, but I don't want to risk not having it if I need it," I say.

He crosses his arms over his knees and nearly glares. It's the most serious expression I've ever seen him wear. He slaps his legs before standing. "Stay here."

"Oh yes, I was in a hurry to argue with a spoiled prince," I say as he slides outside.

I sit in the quiet of the room, already missing his chatter. He makes me feel far less alone. I toy with the end of my shirt, wondering what I will do if Yuri refuses to answer any of my questions.

You already know the answer, Kosci says. *Simply slip inside and rifle through his memories, as we have done before.*

And if I don't want to?

Do you refuse for yourself or because of someone else? Kosci sends a swirling image of Alik into my mind's eye, watery and unsure, as if looking at his reflection in a puddle. It sends a sharp twinge through my heart. *You cannot let the opinions of others sway you from the right path. Especially the beliefs of a boy who has never wanted you to have this power. He would rather we suffer than use our might to crush Ladislaw and my brother.*

I run a hand over my face, hoping it will wipe away Kosci's words. I'm saved from answering by Bataar slipping back inside, bandages and antiseptic in one hand and some sort of tincture in the other. I make a face.

"If you want to lose your arm to infection, please, be my guest," he says, sitting beside me once again.

"I can do it myself," I say. I reach for the antiseptic, but Bataar dumps the fluid onto some of the bandages instead.

"I know, but I want to help," he says, keeping his hands

busy. "Hasn't anyone ever taken care of you before?"

I open my mouth to say yes, but specific memories of it never come to my mind. My parents did when I was small, but Luiza certainly never did. All our cuts and bruises were to be nursed in silence. And Alik . . . well, it seemed I was always the one doing the nurturing. Bataar says nothing as he presses the cloth gently to my arm, and I wince at the burn. With practiced fingers, he wipes away the crusted blood and spreads the tincture carefully around the gash. Bataar cradles my bicep, taking the long bandage beside him to slowly wind it around my arm. The warmth of his fingers and the soft pressure of his palm sends a curling tingle up my arm, and I have to bite my tongue to keep from shuddering.

"It seems like you've done this a lot," I say to break the silence.

"The courts of Adaman aren't for the faint of heart. You learn a few tricks."

"And you want to go back?" I ask.

His hands slow, and he finally glances up. His deep-brown eyes catch glints of russet light, and for the briefest moment, he isn't the lighthearted, confident person I've come to know. Shadows hang from his shoulders, dragging them down.

"My . . . parents are there. Somewhere." His eyes move back to his work. "It's why I never turned down an opportunity to go to Adaman, no matter what Luiza was having me do. I thought for sure I'd be able to find them, but the country is vast, far bigger than even Strana. I didn't hear so much as a whisper."

"I'm sorry," I say softly. "It's hard, to not have your family."

"I'm sure you know the feeling," he says. "At least you found a happy ending."

"For now," I say.

"For now," he amends.

"How did you end up in Strana without them?" I ask, watching his sure hands as they reach the end of the bandage.

"I was born here. My parents moved to make their lives in Rurik as spice traders. They had all the contacts they needed and, let's be honest, Strana isn't known for its seasonings."

I laugh, and he gives me half a smile.

"But after Knnot fell, people didn't have extra money to spend. They quickly went into debt, far more than they could ever hope to repay. The people they owed money to swore to take me as leverage. Before they could, my parents sought out Luiza. They'd heard she offered sanctuary to children and begged her to save me. She agreed to keep me hidden from my parents' debt collectors so long as she got to keep me." He shrugs. "They wanted to keep me safe, so they agreed. I went to live at the guild the very next day."

Bataar says it all so flatly I can almost believe it doesn't bother him. Except his fingers tremble as they tie off the bandage knot. I gather my feet beneath me and lean onto my knees, tossing my arms around his neck and hugging him close. He goes rigid beneath me only a moment before curling his own around me. His hair tickles my cheeks, but I hold on tight.

"I'm sorry," I whisper.

"It was a long time ago," Bataar says, and his voice rumbles pleasantly through his chest.

"Not long enough," I say. I give him a final squeeze before rocking back onto my heels. "After this is over, I can help you find them. If you want."

"I think you'll be a little busy," he says with a smile.

"I'd find time to help you."

He recorks the tincture, the curve of his mouth never faltering. "If I knew all I had to do to get your attention was to tell my sad story, I would've done it a long time ago."

"Well you did tend my wounds, too," I say.

His eyes flick back to my shoulder, tracing along the line of my bone. "What's this?"

"What?" I ask, looking down.

Bataar's fingers trail down a line of bruises, following the slow curve of my collarbone. The slip of his calloused fingertips along my skin pulls a shudder from my body.

Something shifts in the air between us, the distance between our faces suddenly seeming much closer than it actually is. I try to keep my eyes trained on his but his gaze flickers down, so fast I almost don't catch it. I wet my lips as his hand drifts toward my hand. Our fingers graze for just a moment and a cool warmth rolls through my chest. All I would have to do to touch my lips to his is lean forward.

A cough sounds from the room beyond and I jump, whirling to my feet. The library sits as I left it, half hidden in shadows, a guard on either side of the door. I close my eyes, curling my fingers into fists. I never should've let myself forget what I have to do. I slip my injured arm back into the tunic and take a steadying breath.

"Would you mind going to the kitchen to get some tea?" I ask Bataar without looking back at him, afraid of what I will find on his face. "I think I will need it after this."

TWENTY-SEVEN

I STEP INTO THE ROOM, and Yuri's eyes barely flick to me before going back to his hands. I sweep into the chair across from him, casually leaning back as if I interrogated princes every day.

"I'm not going to tell you anything," he says calmly before I can open my mouth. "You can save whatever words you have. You can offer me nothing I want, and I've no intention of betraying my father for a false queen."

I cross my legs, saying nothing for a moment, allowing Yuri to study me. I assume he wants anger, perhaps even embarrassment from me, but I feel neither.

"I find it interesting you expect me to offer anything," I say. "You live only because I intend to use you as leverage."

Yuri's jaw tightens. "I can assure you, you'll receive nothing from my father in exchange for me."

"You admit that your father cares so little for you that he would not risk himself to save you, and yet you're willing to keep all his secrets to yourself?" I lace my fingers, steepling them as I have seen Luiza do so many times.

"This crown belongs to my family. I will not give it up just because my father isn't what I wished for."

"You will let this country suffer further because of some archaic belief that you deserve to rule because you were born to it?" I ask, annoyance tainting my words for the first time since we started talking.

"And hand it over to you?" Yuri raises a brow. "How are you any better suited to rule? You're just a girl who was gifted the powers of the Pale God and decided she was strong enough to overthrow an empire."

"I did not start this war to destroy Strana. I want to save her. Your father has done nothing but ruin it since the day Knnot fell. He will continue to let Zladonians rot in *tyur'mas*, content to let them bear the burden of his wrongs. It is his fault he couldn't maintain trade agreements, that he turned all his efforts into reclaiming Knnot instead of finding new things to export, and it is his fault that he refused to listen to the truth: the Zladonians had nothing to do with the fall of Knnot or the plague. If that were the case, the *tyur'mas* would be empty." I narrow my gaze. "This war is your father's fault."

"You hide behind my father's mistakes, using them as a

277

shield for what you really want. You think you're the first person to want to lead a revolution, Valeria of the Pale God? There have been dozens in the history of Strana, and in the end, they all wanted the same thing. Power. You don't care about the Stranans or the Zladonians. You want this country for yourself."

The room goes cold, the fire struggling to stay alive, sputtering and clawing at the logs until finally snuffing out. Yuri's breath plumes before him, but his eyes do not leave mine.

"I lead this army because I want what is just. Your father has sins to answer for, and I will see them paid in blood. And once I've finished with him, I will destroy your precious Bright God. He has done nothing but help maintain the crown's power. He seeks to supplant the Pale God and take his magic for himself. *He* is what you accuse me of being. Do you really think your line would've survived as long as it has without the grace of Zoltoy? He pulls your strings and lets you believe you are the puppet master instead of marionettes."

"I would rather watch Strana fall than give it to you," Yuri spits.

"You are a fool," I say, my voice as cold as the room around us. Despite his efforts not to, Yuri shivers, breath releasing from between chattering teeth. "You will give me what I want in the end. Whether you want to or not."

In spite of the cold and the obvious fear in his eyes, Yuri leans forward. "You may break my bones and brand my skin, but I will *never* help you take Strana."

"Then you've made your bed," I say, and rise. With the motion, the room returns to its normal temperature, the fire slowly crackling back to life. "Now you must decide if it was worth it."

I walk from the room, lingering at the door leading into Yuri's chambers. "Take him to the cellars. Let him rot there until his tongue loosens."

I pace through the unused rooms of the Winter Palace, each one more infuriating than the last. So many large rooms, so many expensive things, and for what? It was wealth that could've been given to Zladonians, it was space that could've kept everyone safe who fled Zladonia ten years ago. It makes the anger in my gut twine even harder around my soul.

The long corridor I'd been stalking down ends in a dim, quiet room. It takes a moment for my eyes to adjust to the soft light pooling from the sconces around it. Towering bookshelves at least ten feet high line the walls. A second level sits above that with long, delicate looking ladders leading up to the platform circling the room above. The center of the library holds plush chairs and tiny tables. I run my fingers along the book bindings closest to me, letting the papery softness soothe my soul. I could never afford books in the guild, and my parents only had a couple in their house.

I follow the shelves, my fingers never leaving the books.

There is something about the scent of paper and ink that calms the storm in my mind. Perhaps because it reminds me of Luiza's tiny office, an alcove tucked in the back of the guild where she couldn't be disturbed. I wonder if she's there now, plotting how best to slit my throat.

"Have you found anything?" A female voice says from above. I still, cocking my ear up toward the voice.

"No," Alik responds from right above my head. Shock ripples along my nerves at the sound of him. We haven't spoken once since I took Yelgarod.

The other person sighs. "We've been at this for hours. Can't we go make camp somewhere? We need to sleep at some point."

"Fine," snaps Alik, and the sound of a book closing follows. "But we will return as soon as we can. I know something is hiding in these books. I just need evidence."

I bite the corner of my mouth. Evidence of what? I didn't ask him to do any reconnaissance. Footsteps make their way to the ladder nearest me, and I dart back, wedging myself between two bookcases. I steady my breathing. The last thing I need is for Alik to think I am spying on him.

"Even if you manage to find it, what makes you think she will believe you?" the girl asks. "She seems to care less and less for you the farther into Strana we get."

I swallow. The girl is clearly talking about me, and despite myself, I want to know how Alik will respond.

"I've known Valeria a very long time. The girl I know would listen to sound evidence, even if it said something she didn't care for. I know she doesn't seem like that person anymore, but she is in there. I know she is." Alik's voice is full of a hollow hurt that pierces all the way through my body.

"You said that when she wanted to kidnap the prince, but it didn't stop her from doing it. The person you knew is gone, Alik," the girl says as her feet hit the ground. "She is ruthless and will do everything in her power to win, even if that means hurting the people closest to her." The last words are said softly, as if the girl isn't sure she should say them at all. "What will you do when you can't stop her? Have you even considered it?"

Their slow footsteps draw closer to my hiding spot, and I press myself even farther into the corner.

Alik releases a long, low breath, and my heart tumbles down into my stomach along with it.

"If she won't listen to reason, I have my own power to stop her. I'll challenge her before everyone, to ensure she agrees to the duel."

Cold fury runs straight through my veins, and Kosci stirs at the spike. How *dare* he? Even in all of my worst nightmares, I never expected Alik to openly oppose me. We've disagreed hundreds of times, but now he seeks to challenge me before an army *I* built? With power he shouldn't even have? That he *told* me he couldn't call upon?

I warned you, says Kosci. *You put your faith in the wrong people. Love is fickle. It comes with contingencies and compromises. You are trying to win a country, and he can't be bothered to see the sense of your plans. Or all the things you've sacrificed so Zladonians can be free. So that he can live.*

I don't want to believe it. My chest feels as if it might crack in half. Alik, my Alik who has been by my side through every up and down in my life, is now willing to betray everything for Ladislaw's child.

You should cut him out now, before he has a chance to do you real harm.

He would never hurt me.

I think the words, but I am no longer sure I believe them. What else has he done besides hurt me? He laced doubt into every single one of my thoughts, every action. Even the sacrifice of saving him from death was a point of contention.

I don't know if I have the strength to push him away.

With me, you have the ability to do anything. I will not leave when you need me most. Unlike he has. Remove him. He is a loose brick in our foundation.

At last, Alik and the girl stride by my hiding spot. Neither look over as they pass, both of their gazes locked on the path before them. Alik doesn't seem as if he regrets what he says; a cold determination highlights every angle of his face. He will challenge me if he feels I've transgressed, as if he is some sort of moral scale that can judge what is right and wrong. If he does, and it is before the entirety of my army, I will have no other choice but to accept. The very idea makes me want to press deeper into the shadows, away from the threat. If it comes to an all-out duel between us, I will win. Alik may have somehow retained shreds of Kosci's power, but he has no idea how to wield it, nor is he connected to the source.

Perhaps Kosci is right and I should uproot him before he has a chance to move against me. There is no doubt that it would be a display of strength, a warning to anyone who would dare to supplant me. But I can't kill the boy I love.

Can I?

TWENTY-EIGHT

FOUR DAYS AFTER MY CAPTURE of Yelgarod, I find myself descending the spiral staircase to the deepest part of the palace. Two soldiers, a dark-haired man and woman, stand on either side of the brittle wood door. Beyond is a root cellar, cold and damp—perfectly uncomfortable enough for a prisoner. I nod and they part to let me inside.

Yuri sits with his back against the far wall beside an empty barrel, an uneaten bowl of porridge at his heel. He kicks it at me as I enter, but I push it to the side with a blast of wind. It spills across the ground and freezes. He doesn't so much as twitch at the magic, and I come to a stop, staring down my nose at him.

"Have you changed your mind?" I ask.

"No," he spits. "You will have to try harder than a little

cold, thin gruel. And here I thought the Pale champion would have more tricks than a discomfort. I suppose the rumors about you are false."

"Do not mistake my kindness for weakness, Yuri. I can make you talk if I want to."

"What are you waiting for? Permission?"

The comment wheedles its way along my spine. In truth, I don't know why I am waiting. I know what I have to do, and yet I let Yuri linger here instead of taking the memories by force. The only thing that stayed my hand before was the idea that Alik would hate me for doing it. But it seems he will resist no matter what I do.

"Very well then, if you wish for pain so badly, I will give it to you," I say.

With a simple twitch of my fingers, I manipulate the strands of magic in the air, sending rock and ice up from the dirt floor to circle Yuri's wrists and hold him tight to the ground. He grunts, surprised by the action, but his face remains annoyingly blank. I kneel before him, reaching out a single finger. He attempts to pull away from it, but there is nowhere to go. I press my index finger into the middle of his head and push.

I let magic course through my body, the silver and blue strands from my soul breaking through the barrier between Yuri and me. He takes in a sharp inhale as my magic twists into his mind and flashes of his life flow from his memory into mine. Yuri and a kind-faced woman sipping tea and laughing over silver spoons. She gives him a soft smile and smooths his hair before landing a light tap on his nose. His mother, if I had to guess. I dig further, wrenching his mind from her and onto his father.

There are fewer memories here. A gruff voice demanding he swing his arm again, a darkened shadow full of curling smoke where the outlines of Ladislaw were barely visible. Whispered words conjure themselves toward the forefront of Yuri's mind.

"Too many eyes have turned to you. There is no choice but to send you to Yelgarod to finish your studies," Ladislaw says. A bright room comes into focus, tall windows on the eastern side catching the green lawn outside the palace in Rurik. "Rumors already circle that you are my son. I cannot contain them for much longer."

"Please, Slava," the woman behind Yuri whispers, gripping his shoulders tight. "I want him to stay with me."

Ladislaw's eyes go to the woman and the memory version of Yuri looks up to his mother. Auburn waves cascade over one shoulder, her proud aristocratic nose lifted high.

"He is our son; he deserves to stay here."

Ladislaw's hand slams onto the table and they both jump, Yuri's body coiling back as his father stands.

"You know the risks as well as I do. He cannot remain in this palace, not with whispers of uprising on every street. He goes to Yelgarod tomorrow. Say your goodbyes."

The heartache in the memory suffuses into my soul, but I push past it, too, searching for memories of Matvei. The very thought of the name pulls me deeper into Yuri's memories, blotting out the heavy, pained pants coming from the boy. I tumble down deeper until I slam hard into a burnished gold wall. It circles as far and wide as I can see. I slam against it, using all the strength within me. Yuri's body jerks against the movement and he cries out.

What is this? I think to Kosci.

Defenses, his voice seems louder in this space. *My brother has protected any mention of himself or Matvei. You will see nothing Zoltoy doesn't want you to.*

I rip from Yuri's mind, heedless of whether it hurts him or not. His head slumps forward at the action, blood dripping from his nose. Of *course* they had planned for this. Even when I make a move the Czar doesn't anticipate, he finds a way to block me anyway. I cannot force Yuri's mind to my will without killing him, that much is obvious from the ragged way he breathes now. I give Yuri moments to recover before crouching before him again. He winces, and a remorseless beat of satisfaction rolls through me. Let him be afraid.

"You will tell me what your father is planning," I say calmly. "Tell me what he is doing with Luiza and Matvei and I will release you, no questions asked. I'll even give you a horse to run all the way to your father. All you have to do is talk."

Yuri's chest heaves with each breath as he forces his head

up. "How do I know you're telling the truth?"

"I never lie," I respond.

He laughs sourly. "Every ruler lies."

"Not this one." I brush invisible dust from my shoulder.

"Then you admit that's what you want. My crown. My kingdom."

My gaze snaps back to Yuri's. The drips of blood have stopped coming from his nose, and he holds his head high with every ounce of regal importance he believes he's entitled to.

"I will do what is best for Strana," I say.

"And what if that isn't you? What if you bring a different kind of ruin to this world? One where people hide in the streets, too fearful to pray to the god that gives you strength?"

"There is not a single reality in which that is true," I say. "I bring Strana what it needs."

"Lovite?" Yuri asks, raising a dark brow. "And what happens when that runs out? What happens when our neighbors see our crumbling kingdom with an untested girl at the head?"

"I will crush them just as I will your father. There is no one who will be able to stand in my way. Not Adaman. Not Drangiana. And certainly not you. I will take your crown even if I have to cut it from your father's head. This world deserves better than what your line has given it. It is time for the sun to set on your dynasty and rise on mine."

Yuri gives another bitter laugh. "You sound just like my father."

"Never"—I growl the word, letting an ice dagger form in my palm—"compare me to him."

I slam the blade into his exposed calf. He screams, the sound echoing off the chamber. I catch Yuri's throat, just as he had mine days ago, and bring my face close to his.

"By the end of this day, you will tell me everything I need to know." I whisper the words, and Kosci's power surges through me, deadly and certain, while another blade forms in my hand.

I place it to Yuri's collarbone, following the line of it to the hollow of his throat. I'm just about to cut when a loud bang sounds behind me. I shoot to my feet and find Alik in the doorway, chest heaving, blade in one hand. A sneer curls my lips.

"Now you finally decide to show yourself," I hiss, my voice cold. "I should've known."

"You aren't Valeria," he says.

"I am."

"You *aren't*."

Alik stands rigid and sure before me. The guards no longer loiter in the corridor outside. One sweep with my power tells me they huddle upstairs beside a dying fire.

Cowards.

Betrayers.

I will destroy them all for this.

TWENTY-NINE

ALIK MOVES BEFORE I REGISTER it, slipping through my defenses and yanking the leather strap at my neck. I punch his chest, sending all my fury into it. His grasp loosens as he doubles over, but the pendant crashes to the floor and bounces toward the door. I scramble for it, desperate for the strength around my neck.

My hand closes around it only to be kicked, hard, by Alik. The pendant shoots from my grasp and slides across the room as my hands burn from the pain. He grabs my shoulders before I have a chance to dart after it.

"Let go!" I say.

"Stop this and I will." Alik shakes me.

"I'm doing what I have to." I put every ounce of steel I can into my voice. "I'm making the hard decisions no one else wants to."

"Look at what you were going to do." Alik's finger flies toward Yuri's bloodied form. "You would've never done that before. You didn't want to so much as rough up the marks Luiza sent us after. You are not yourself."

I keep my gaze from straying to the pendant, ignoring Alik's words. Kosci understands what it means to carry this burden. Alik doesn't. He won't even try to.

I need the pendant back.

I let indecision cross my face, convincing Alik that I'm considering his words. He slowly eases away from me, and I let my hands hang limp and useless by my side. I need him to believe me tame, malleable, but as soon as he turns toward Yuri, I bolt and sweep the pendant into my hand, cradling it close to my heart. I sling it back around my neck and glance back at Alik.

"Why are you doing this?" His voice shakes as he straightens.

"Because no one else will. Freedom is always a fight, Alik, a battle that we have to win. Ladislaw will never release his yoke."

"If you keep on like this, you'll destroy this country as easily as Ladislaw did."

His words slap me much harder than when Yuri said the same thing. It is more difficult to dismiss when it is the person you used to love. Yet despite his professed love, he paints me the villain, as if Ladislaw hasn't done things hundreds of times worse than this.

Boiling fury laces down my back. I reach out my arm and

yank. Alik skids away from Yuri, tugged by invisible strings only I can see. I pull him through the door and slam it closed, locking it tight before I release Alik. His chest heaves as he does his best to swallow his emotions.

"I have done nothing, absolutely *nothing*, close to what Ladislaw has done. I bring food and warmth to the hundreds suffering outside Yelgarod's walls. Everything I've done is to make this country better for everyone. All I ask is for help to overthrow the man who made Strana what it is now. How dare you liken me to him!"

"This isn't the right way," Alik says.

"What is wrong with this idea now? He isn't a child like we thought. He's just as old as we are. He could've stood up to Ladislaw by now, declared his intent to right the wrongs of his father, but he hasn't. He blindly gives his loyalty to a man who would rather hide him than claim him as heir."

"It doesn't matter if he's not a child, you still would've taken him if he was." Alik throws his hands in the air. "You are using your magic to manipulate him, just like Matvei does. What's next, Valeria? Stringing up bodies of skeptics on the palisade for all to see? Storm Hound heads on pikes?"

"And what if I did those things? It's what they'd deserve. Anyone who stands against me stands with the Czar and what he's done." I make my voice even colder. "And I'll do it to any who betray me within my army. A line you're walking dangerously close to, Alik."

"How have I betrayed you?" he practically shouts. "Because

I disagreed? Because I didn't want to be part of a group that would kidnap a child and force him to pay for something he didn't do?"

Yuri's memories of his mother float unbidden into my mind. He was just a little boy when Strana collapsed, not old enough to do anything aside from have tea parties with his mother.

Alik senses my hesitation. "You have your city. You have lovite and an army that would follow you into the sea if you asked it of them. You don't need Yuri. Release him."

"I can't," I say softly. "He'll run straight to his father. They'll know everything."

"Then let him free of the cellar. He needs a bed."

"He could gather people loyal to the Czar to him, get a message out somehow, and bring Matvei down on us before we're ready."

"You're being paranoid," he says.

"I'm being logical! Since I can't count on you for more than chastising and acting like a child. You've been hiding ever since I first laid plans to take Yelgarod and Yuri," I spit.

"I wasn't hiding," he snaps. "I was working. I've been sending my scouts out for days looking for the Czar and trying to find a weakness for the Bright God's champion. Kosci is not telling you something. I don't know what, and I don't know why, but he is. I've been searching every single book and stray piece of paper for what's happening to you, for what happens to any of the champions."

I recoil, grasping the pendant tighter. "Kosci is the only one in the corridor right now who hasn't lied to me."

Alik's jaw hardens. "I've admitted my mistakes. And the god you think so highly of *has* lied to you. Do you forget he was the one who froze Ludminka in the first place?"

"He did it to protect himself. To protect the world from Matvei's desperation for Kosci's heart."

"Valeria, *listen* to yourself. You are telling the same lies he is."

"They aren't lies," I shout. "You can't see what I can."

Alik makes as if to reach out but lets his hands fall. Why can't you see what you're becoming? You care so much about this world, but you do nothing but destroy it to get what you want."

I swallow back a knot in my throat, trying to remember that the boy before me was the one person I used to call home. The piece of me I'd spent a year of my life mourning. But I can't. Hot anger sears down my legs until I can no longer feel them, and the pendant in my hands flares a brilliant white. Alik's eye snaps to it instantly. His face breaks.

"Drop it. Please. Give yourself a break."

"Make me," I snarl.

Alik's hand clenches into a tight fist. It's the only warning I get. He dashes forward. I sidestep him easily. He's always been bad at hiding his intentions in a fight. It was something Luiza harped on constantly. It takes him a moment to stop on his unsteady leg, but he swings back to face me.

"I don't want to do this," he says.

"Then stop."

He lunges for me again, and I step to the side. Kosci's power curls around me like a protective shield. I'm not sure if Alik would truly hurt me, but I don't want to find out.

"Someone has to. You refuse to listen to reason," he snarls.

"The way I see it, you're the only one who has a problem," I say.

He manages to snag my wrist. I twist the fluttering magic around me, turning my arm into something blisteringly cold. His face tenses and he drops it, angry red welts already starting to form. He shakes it out and takes a deep breath. The corridor seems to shrink and grow dimmer. Tighter.

The same blue glow I saw that night in the *tyur'ma* with Alik starts to form around him once more. It shouldn't be possible. I am the one chosen by Kosci. I should have all of his power. Yet here Alik stands with a modicum of the strength I have, ready to fight.

"Just drop it. Don't wear it for a week. A month!" he shouts.

I don't respond. Instead, I step into range and throw a punch. He dodges and tosses one of his own. We've done this dance a hundred times, always striving to be better, perfect, just so Luiza would pay attention to us. His movements are almost as familiar as my own.

I hate the reminder of our past. I hate that we're further apart than ever. I hate that he fights against me at every turn, that he doubts me. That we'll never be the same.

The thought makes my next punch go off target. He easily counters it and barrels forward, pinning my shoulders against the rough wall behind me. Power swirls around us both in fits of blue and white. My chest heaves as I stare into his eye. His breath matches my own, and I realize this is the first time we've been close in weeks.

Almost automatically, my eyes flick down to his mouth. I'd spent nights thinking about it. The feel of his hair through my hands, the press of his lips across my neck like a caress. Suddenly, more than anything, I want it to be a reality.

I grab the back of his neck and pull him toward me. He doesn't resist. Our lips crash together, and his hands wind up my body to tangle in my hair. He pulls it gently, tilting my neck back and pressing a kiss to my jaw, then my neck.

I catch the gasp before it leaves my mouth. I crush the pendant in my fist, refusing to release it, but also wanting this so bad it hurts. Alik finds my lips once more, mouth hungry and insistent. He traces the seam along my side and, stupidly, tears prick my eyes. I pull back from him and look up into the face of the boy I made a deal with the devil for.

"I miss you."

The words fall pathetically from my mouth, not doing justice to the swirling mass of confused emotions brewing in my heart. Alik gently runs a finger down the side of my face.

"I miss you, too."

"Please come back." I grip the back of his tunic and twist the fabric in my hands so he can't back away. His body goes taut at my touch.

"Stop wearing the pendant unless you need it, and I will," he says. "There is something wrong with it. I can feel it. Even the things I've seen about it in the history texts mention something about its power."

Alik's words slowly sink in, and I study his face, searching, *hoping*, to see a lie. Even when we were younger he was always the more cautious, the one more likely to think and plan than rush into the world. It's why we had worked so well together. He would do the calculations; I would handle the rest. If he truly thought there was something wrong, then maybe there was. But without the pendant, without Kosci and his mutterings, I wouldn't know how to do any of this. I have no mind for tactics and war. I've never been good at planning ahead. Kosci keeps me steady and sure. He provides the power I need to take prisons and rule cities. Without it, I have nothing.

"I . . . can't." My voice breaks. "I never know when I might need his power. We could be attacked at any moment."

Alik steps away from me, the fabric easily slipping from my hands. He shakes his head.

"Val, I am begging you. Let it go. Let *him* go."

"He's the only thing that makes me strong enough to destroy the Czar."

"You are strong by yourself."

"No, I'm not." Hot tears pool in my eyes, and I angrily brush them away before they can fall. I don't want to seem weak, not even in front of Alik. "I've never been able to stop a thing happening in Strana. Not the freeze, not Luiza's manipulations, not the Czar throwing every last Zladonian into prisons for the simple act of existing. Now I can. Because of him."

When Alik doesn't respond, I slowly brush his cheek. He closes his eye against the touch, leaning into my fingers, and I try to memorize the feeling of it.

"I'm sorry I can't be who you want me to be, Alik."

His eye opens, so painfully beautiful that I have to look away. I'm doing this for Strana. For Zladonia. I cannot falter. Not when I am closer than I've ever been. Before Alik can say anything else, I turn and walk away with my shoulders straightened. I want him to call out. I want to run back to him and let him gather me into his arms. To kiss me until I forget about the war, and the Czar, and Kosci.

But I can't.

If I don't fight, no one else will.

THIRTY

THICK, SWOLLEN CLOUDS DARKEN THE sky the
following day as I sit at the small desk in my room, looking
over the papers Sera sent me of soldier numbers and rations.
It all seems fine to me, but I'm the first to admit I have no
idea what I'm looking at. My mind wanders to Yuri, and my
stomach clenches tight. What would I have done if Alik hadn't
stopped me?

Gotten the information you needed, sniffs Kosci.

I'm trying, I say.

*Try harder. Time is ticking. You haven't been quiet about your move-
ments. My brother and the Czar will not hesitate to attack. If I had more
strength, I could search them out, but I am trapped inside you.*

I'm so sorry that's such a burden, I snap. *It isn't always a pleasure
for me either.*

Dark spots float through my vision for a moment as Kosci's

annoyance overwhelms me, and I get lightheaded and weak. I swat him back with such force a spike of pain drives its way between my temples. I wince and cradle my head on my desk. A knock sounds on my door.

"Come in," I say without looking up. Quiet steps enter, ones I can't quite place. I look up just as Bataar's hand slips onto my shoulder.

"Are you okay?" he asks.

I study him for a moment, wishing I could share this burden with someone else. What can I say? That I'm terrified Kosci's power is growing? That I have no idea what happens if I can't contain it? Before a single word can leave my mouth another knock sounds. Chinua and Sera slip in together, both of their faces drawn.

"Tell me," I say.

A heaviness in the air settles as the people around me exchange glances. Without a word, Sera pulls a vellum parchment from her vest and passes it to me. The smooth texture of the paper almost makes me shudder, far too reminiscent of pure lovite for my taste. I flip it over and study the broken seal. It's the Czar's, embedded in a deep-black wax. I slip the letter from inside and take in the large, proud script rolling across the paper like a thunderstorm.

Pretender,
Release my son and the city of Yelgarod or I will burn another

tyur'ma to the ground. You think I don't know how to deal with children pretending to be king? You aren't the first to try to take my throne, and you will not be the last. I refuse to deal with usurpers and traitors. Surrender now and I will allow Zladonians to continue their lives inside a tyur'ma together on the islands in the Northern Sea. You, of course, will be beheaded for treason. It is your life for the lives of all Zladonians. Make your decision quickly. I am not a patient man.

Ladislaw's signature curls large and ornate on the bottom of the letter, taking up nearly half the parchment. I scoff and throw it to the side. No doubt he hadn't even bothered to write it himself.

"How far is Oleg from here?"

"Three days' ride, maybe more if the Czar has sent patrols."

"I'm sure he has," I say. "And if he wants to make threats, I'll deliver mine. Ready a small battalion. We leave in two days' time."

"You can't rush into something like this," Chinua says.

"Do we have troops ready?"

"Yes," she replies.

"Do we have the weapons?" I ask.

"Yes," she says again. "But aren't you worried Ladislaw is planning for exactly this? What if you are rushing straight into a trap?"

"Ladislaw will do nothing because I have Yuri. He seeks

only to intimidate us into submission. If, somehow, he finds the courage to face me in Oleg, I am ready for him. I am not the person Matvei remembers from Knnot."

"We don't doubt that," Sera says, and I blink. It isn't what I expected to come from her mouth. She registers the surprise on my face and sighs, crossing her arms. "I know we've had our differences, Valeria, but you've proven yourself a capable leader. I'm proud to follow you."

Her words warm a small part of myself I thought I buried. Alik's staunch refusal to believe in me had leaked into every area of my life. To hear someone actually thought I was doing right, that I was making this world better, was more a balm than anything else could've been.

"Thank you," I say, giving Sera a smile. "It means more than I could say."

"Don't you go soft on me," Sera responds.

"Never," I say. Chinua glances over at Sera, giving her a wide smile that makes her cheeks redden. Sera clears her throat.

"Have you decided what you will do with the Czar's son?"

I let out a long sigh, collapsing back into my chair and running a hand over my face. "He won't talk and my attempts to look through his memories failed. It seems Matvei and Ladislaw thought something like this might happen."

"So he is useless?" Sera asks.

"Hmm," Chinua says, tapping her chin. "Not useless.

Tactically, he could be a good distraction. If Ladislaw believes we will harm his son, or already have, he might be more willing to meet us in open battle."

"And," Bataar adds, "if we can crack him, we will get all the information we need to outmaneuver Ladislaw."

"Fine," I say, glad for once I am not alone. "We will break Yuri and take Oleg. After that, Ladislaw will have to answer to us."

Bleary-eyed citizens of Yelgarod stand near their doorways, watching the slow procession of my army. Even in the dim of dawn, we look magnificent. Me astride my white horse, breastplate gleaming, the people behind me armored from head to toe in Iovite, with sharp-edged weapons that will never dull. Now it is time to send my warning.

I left Sera and Chinua behind to oversee the city while I am gone. They are more than capable, and the recruits still need more training. I haven't seen Alik since our fight, but Bataar rides behind me on my right, with my brothers on the left. I told my father to stay with my mother. She would need someone if the worst should happen.

"You know, I think my nose is the thing women admire most," Gregori says to Anton as we clatter out the city gates and begin our descent.

"I think women don't care about it at all," Anton says. "Besides, mine is clearly superior."

"Right," Gregori scoffs. "Look at it. Like a stubby toe."

"At least mine has personality. You have a beak."

"You're both wrong," I call over my shoulder. "You are just the mistakes before perfection."

"Hey," Gregori calls out. "I thought you were supposed to raise our morale. Clearly you need to learn how to compliment people."

I laugh as I let my nervous mare trot forward, more confident than I've felt since I started this war. I'm in control now, staying Ladislaw's hand with the thing he wants more than lovite. Taking the prison in Oleg will be easy, swift, and we likely won't be met with much resistance.

Descending the mountain is much easier than going up. As we follow the hard-packed snow out onto the low foothills, I catch Bataar's eye and give my head a jerk. He allows his horse to draw even with mine.

"I need you to take three people you trust and scout ahead. I want to know where the Czar has his men. He wouldn't let us leave Yelgarod. He'll have people stationed somewhere."

"It will be done," he says.

Before I can say another word, he melts back into the mass behind me, pulling three people I recognize from the guild with him. They give their horses rein and break into a gallop, disappearing into the rolling hills beyond.

I keep our pace slow and steady. There will be no hiding one hundred and fifty horses moving through the forest no matter how hard I try. All I can do is wait for Bataar.

It's midday before I hear the heavy beat of hooves charging through the forest. Branches break beneath the heavy footfalls and I tense, waiting for an attack. Instead, Bataar bursts from the thick firs, head bleeding and eyes wild.

"They're coming," he manages to gasp before an arrow whistles overhead.

"On me," I call to my soldiers. "About-face, they are in the trees."

I peer through the thick boughs for a hint of black and gold. I can't see a thing between the clinging snow and dark-green needles. With a deep breath, I gather my magic. It pools around me more readily than ever, throbbing in time with my heart, lacing through my bones, my soul. I send it forward. Harsh wind whips from behind, kicking up my hair. It slams into the trees, dislodging the snow in sheets of white. Still, I push until treetops break and needles rip from their branches. The pine closest to me starts to fall, roots sending a shower of hard earth and snow tumbling across the road.

With a jerk, I let the wind die. The world around us is silent and still. A group of men stand huddled in the center of the now-empty forest before me. There can't be more than thirty.

Easily destroyed, Kosci says.

I charge, my soldiers behind me. We break past the naked trees and crash upon them.

I run a spear of hardened snow through the first Storm

Hound I encounter. He falls to the ground with it embedded deep in his gut. I form a blade of ice and start swinging. We more than have the advantage. They didn't expect horses and fine weapons. They believed us nothing but a group of vagabonds playing at war.

I grin viciously as I fell yet another Storm Hound, watching him collapse on top of his brethren. Hot blood streaks down my face, but our charge isn't over. Not yet.

I wheel toward Bataar. "Where is the camp?"

He doesn't respond, just turns his horse to the east and starts off at a trot. I follow, the army close on my heels.

It doesn't take us long to get there. They planted the camp in a small valley between two foothills, no doubt thinking the terrain would hide them. It also put them at a disadvantage. I spin my mare in a circle as my soldiers gather behind me.

"Leave no one alive."

With that, I let my horse go. She gallops down the hill, gaining speed and throwing snow with her decent. A white cloud billows around us as we reach level ground and jump the small barricade they half-heartedly erected. A loud cry tears from my mouth as I rip a hole through the first tent I come to.

The canvas falls like a leaf from a tree, illuminating two forms inside. I send my sword in, catching one in the heart. His comrade scrambles from the tent and yells the alarm. People flood from the tents around me in various states of undress.

They manage to raise their weapons before the rest of my battalion descends.

It's a massacre. Storm Hounds fall with every stroke of my army's swords. Horses trample across tents and knock over crates. With no armor and no warning, the Storm Hounds crumble to dust around us. Mere minutes later, the camp lay silent except for the heavy breathing of our charges.

I slip from my horse. "Look for supplies. Anything usable, we take. Burn the rest."

Piles of food and medicine grow at the edge of the camp as each tent is systematically ripped apart and checked. I'm the first to take up a stick from the low-burning fire in the center of camp and set it to one of the canvas tents flapping in the breeze. It takes a long moment for it to catch, but once it does, the flame quickly eats its way along the oiled surface.

The crackle of other things burning soon permeates the air. I remount my horse and move the army from the camp, back up the hill we'd come down. Once at the top, I look at the wasteland below. Everything burns, a massive black cloud billowing into the sky.

Ladislaw doesn't know what he's awakened.

THIRTY-ONE

WE MAKE OUR WAY SLOWLY to Oleg, taking the time to root out every Storm Hound encampment we can find. By the time the city lies like an inky mark on the horizon, we have enough supplies for double the number of soldiers I have with me. Not a single person escaped.

I made sure of that.

I let the soldiers rest miles away from Oleg under the cover of the very trees we walked through months ago on our way to Knnot. We hide among the pines, our tents camouflaged to mirror the white earth and deep wood. I lie on my stomach beneath a particularly large evergreen, the dead needles crushed beneath me, sending plumes of pine through the winter air.

I monitor the *tyur'ma* as best I can over the top of the

barricade, studying the spill of smoke from each narrow house. This prison seems to be primarily set up for fishing. The back of it opens onto the Iron Sea, and small figures stand knee deep in the water with nothing more than a couple layers and a net.

My blood burns.

I roll from my spot and stalk back to camp, mind whirling with possible infiltration plans and anger at the Czar's cruelty. The very last thing I expect to find when I throw back the flap of my tent is Alik.

I freeze, the flap falling gently behind me to brush against the snow outside. The large tent I'd been given to house the table of maps Sera sent with me and the wood-burning stove in the center of it suddenly feels far too small. I swallow and steady myself.

"I didn't expect you," I say.

"I didn't tell anyone I was coming."

"And why is that?"

"Because it's information I didn't want anyone else to know."

This catches my attention. I chance a step closer with an eyebrow raised.

"Well, you didn't ride four days from Yelgarod just to stare at me," I say.

Suspicion still whispers in my mind, and I monitor his movements. How long had he been in this tent? Had anyone seen him come in?

"First, I want you to remove the pendant and put it on the table," he says.

I balk. "And why would I do that?"

"Because what I have to say is for your ears only. In Ludminka you promised to keep our secrets. Do you intend to be true to your word?"

I fiddle with the pendant, turning over his words. Kosci's hesitance runs through me like a steady stream. I don't want to let him go, not when we are so close to having everything we want. But a part of me still longs to be with Alik. I can't deny that my thoughts at night eventually turn to him, his easy smile and bright laugh. In the end it's my heart, instead of my mind, that wins.

I lift the pendant over my head and shove it deep into my pocket. It's close enough that if Alik was to try anything, I could hold him off until the pendant was back around my neck.

"There," I say, when he doesn't immediately speak. "I've done it."

"I honestly wasn't sure you would," he mutters so quietly I almost don't catch it.

I should be affronted, but I punched him the last time he tried to take it from me. I'd never wondered about that until now. It seems so stupid in retrospect.

Or was it?

I hate that I can't tell anymore.

"While you've been busy building an empire, I've been

trying to uncover what I could about the champions to the Brother Gods," he says, stepping closer to me. It sets me on edge, my body drifting between anxiety and desire. "You know it's been hundreds of years since the last champion, and more than that since there have been two. Do you know why?"

"You know I don't," I say.

"I don't know what you know anymore, Val. You made sure of that."

I press my lips together, refusing to be baited into another argument. The air stays heavy between us until Alik sighs.

"It took a lot of searching through Vestry archives and the libraries in the Winter Palace, but it sounds like every champion before you also had a stone that held the hearts of the gods. It is in every painting of champions past, every scribble in the margins of journals. The stone is the conduits' connection to the gods, and removing it severs that connection. The gods must keep their hearts close to their conduits if they hope to access their magic. Without their hearts, the gods can do nothing."

"I don't see why any of this matters," I say.

"*Because,*" Alik stresses the word like I'm missing some huge revelation. "It means if we can destroy the conduits, we can destroy the connection to the Brother Gods."

A strange shiver runs over my body, and dread settles hard into the pit of my stomach. I want to pull back from him and hide my pendant somewhere he will never find it.

"It's impossible," I say.

"Not if we trap them together," he says. "They only care about war with one another. They've used humans as their pawns for centuries because they could never find one another. The Pale God was buried too deep, strung throughout all of Zladonia. The Bright God could never hope to find him. But if we manage to get Matvei's conduit, we can cast them together and they can battle their war over life and death between themselves alone."

I shake my head. "What you're saying doesn't make sense. If this was the case, why would no one have done it before? Why isn't it in the sermons or written throughout every legend on the Brothers? How has no one ever reached this conclusion?"

"Because the gods don't want their secrets told." He searches my face, pinching his lips together at whatever he finds there. "I knew you wouldn't believe my word, so I brought you proof." He gestures to several old tomes and scrolls on my cot. "It also warns of a madness that comes with being too close to the conduits. That they whisper poison. I told you Kosci wasn't telling you something, and this proves it. He is *changing* you, Val. Warping you until you're the exact type of host he needs."

Color races along Alik's cheeks as he stops speaking, breathless and so sure I would see the marvel of what he had found. It's a way to ensure there are no other champions. A way to end the war between the two that has raged for a millennia. But if I gave up my own conduit, I would never take Strana, let alone hold it. Things would fall right back to the way they were. Worse, even, now that Zladonians had shown their strength.

"What are you asking me to do?" I say slowly.

"Find Matvei's conduit and destroy it with your own. Toss them into the sea or crush them with one of your lovite weapons. I don't care. It will all be over."

The world seems to swing sideways, and my entire body trembles. I can't give up Kosci. I won't.

"No, you can't be so naive as to think the Czar will let an entire rebellion slide just because he no longer has the help of his champion. He will destroy us, Alik. He will make sure we never see a day beyond a prison ever again. Ladislaw told me so himself. He wants to send all Zladonians to the north, on a barren island in the middle of the sea! He doesn't want us to flourish. He wants us out of the way so Strana and all its lovite can be his."

"Then destroy their hearts after you defeat Ladislaw. Just get rid of it, Val. *Please.*"

"And leave me vulnerable to attack in an unstable country? Who knows which country would try to move on Strana once they hear the Czar is dead. We'll need strength after the war. A country can't survive on hope alone."

"You *want* to rule after this?" He draws his head back quickly.

The tent suddenly feels too hot. Yuri's words repeat over and over in my mind. *Then you admit that's what you want. My crown. My kingdom.* I hadn't realized it before Alik's question, but it *is* what I want. Things can't go back to the way they were. Not now, after so much has changed. We can no longer be ruled by Ladislaw, and Yuri would only follow in his father's footsteps. Who did that leave but me?

Now that the idea has grown, it branches into my mind, blooming with the endless possibilities of all I could do. The world lies before me asking for a leader, and I can answer. I will.

"Yes." The word slips through my lips like a vow.

"There are dozens of people better suited to rule. You are just a seventeen-year-old." The words spill from Alik's lips, running together in their hurry to get out.

"And? There have been younger Czars." I tilt my chin, willing the sweat rolling down my back to stop. I want my pendant back. Kosci has the words to make Alik understand.

"This isn't a task that has to fall to you, Val. You don't have to change the world and rule it, too."

"If I don't, no one else will."

Alik crosses to me with a speed I don't expect and catches my arms gently in his hands. He gives me the smallest of shakes and I look up.

"You are killing yourself," he whispers. "I can see it even now. You've got no color, you're freezing to the touch, and you try to hide the bruises but I see them, too." He runs his fingers down my arm, catching my wrist and turning it over so the discoloration catches in the firelight. He caresses it with this thumb. "I'm afraid if you keep going, you'll never come back."

I rip away, putting several steps between us. "Why do you care anymore? You made it clear you couldn't love what I've become."

"Because I don't think you're wholly *you* anymore, Valeria! You hardly look the same. You don't even sound the same. Maybe the others have missed it because they haven't spent as much time with you, but *I* see it. I know you down to your core, and have since we were children. You've changed. And I don't mean your attitude or your morals, I mean everything about you." Alik pushes his hair from his face. "Why can't you see that I'm trying to protect you?"

"You'd say anything to prove your point," I snap. "And I am the last person in Strana who needs protecting."

With a frustrated groan, Alik rips open the pack at the foot of my bed and pulls out the small mirror I always carry with me, tucked in the same pouch of my bag as it always has been. It used to be to check for white hair while on missions for Luiza. I hadn't thought to look at myself in a very long time.

He raises it to my face, and I stumble backward, shoving his hand away.

"This is a trick," I say.

"No, it's not. It's been happening since the day you reopened Knnot," he says and lifts it closer to my face. I turn away, but he doesn't stop. "At first I wasn't sure. It seemed ridiculous, but with each passing week I grew more and more certain."

My back presses against the table of maps, rocking the lantern on top dangerously. I don't want to look again, but there is nowhere else for my eyes to go. They slip onto my reflection, and I don't know the person who looks back. My cheeks are hollow, almost gaunt. High cheekbones I don't remember cut up my face, and raised purple-blue bruises ink along my chest, curling from a circle of white flesh right where Kosci's pendant usually rests. The biggest difference, however, lies in my eyes. They gleam cobalt, and the thing I see inside isn't Valeria of Ludminka.

It's something far more ancient.

I lash out at the mirror again, hitting Alik in the wrists. It topples from his hands and shatters across the ground.

"Leave," I growl, far more feral and dangerous than I ever have been in my life. "Never come back."

"No," he says. "I'm tired of being without you."

With a look, the shards of the mirror fly into the air and train themselves at Alik. His eye goes wide and I advance on him, feeling larger and more powerful with each step.

"You think I just control snow and ice? Winter wind and rock? No. I am so much more. The cycle turns and all return to me, to suffering, pain, and death, no matter how much they fight. You will be no different. If I ever see your face again, I will strike you down where you stand."

Alik goes deathly pale. For the first time in a very long time, he looks truly scared. I try to grasp my anger, to pull it back to myself and stop stalking toward him, but my body doesn't respond. It moves forward undaunted, the shards following right beside me as if I'm not in control at all.

I beat at the inside of my mind, begging for it to listen. I don't want to kill Alik. I willed my life away for him. The last thing I ever want to see again is his lifeless corpse in my arms. I knew that to be truer than anything in the world.

Pain lances through my muscles and the shards drop to the ground with a horrible splintering sound. I follow right behind them, barely catching myself on my knees.

"Run," I gasp, and stare up at Alik. "Now."

THIRTY-TWO

ALIK SPRINTS FROM THE TENT without looking back. I curl my fingers into the hard dirt beneath me and try to breathe around the pain lancing through every inch of my body. It feels like being burned alive or swallowed in a freezing river. The bruises I'd seen appearing slowly over my body the last few days ache, throbbing in time with my heart. Blistering cold burns along my thigh, right where Kosci's heart sits in my pocket. I rip it out, slamming it on the ground beside the shards of broken glass. An eye both mine and not mine catches in the largest fragment, stilling my frantic motions.

"What are you doing to me?" I gasp.

Exactly what you asked for, Kosci whispers in the back of my mind.

I grasp the broken piece of glass so hard blood wells around it and slides down the reflective surface.

"This isn't what I wanted."

Oh, but it is. You wanted the power to destroy your enemies, to rule an empire. Do you think that sort of magic could be contained in your fragile mortal body? No. A caterpillar must shed its skin to become what it's meant to be. You must too.

I did want the ability to destroy the Czar and Luiza, even Matvei. I couldn't do it alone. Not without his power and surety. I grit my teeth.

This is the cost of your war, Valeria. Do you want to free the Zladonians or not?

"You know I do," I say between ragged breaths.

You will transform into the thing you desired most. A woman to be feared and respected. A girl cloaked by the power of a god, but it won't be without pain. Your emotions run from you and my power follows. I cannot direct the flow, only you can do that. Take what I've given you, Valeria. Destroy this world.

Doubt still lingers in my mind, and I swallow.

"Is what Alik said true?" I finally manage to ask the question that has been dancing on my tongue. Kosci's silence is my answer. Everything Alik said, from destroying their hearts to the sickness that flourishes through the champions, is true.

If you do not hold up your end of the bargain, if you do not find a place for me to thrive, I will ruin this world. I house myself here because I made you a promise. If you refuse to pay, I will rip from your body without a second thought.

I don't doubt the truth of his words. Shakily, I pull myself to my feet. My muscles still cramp, but I force myself to release the shard of glass.

"I never should have accepted your deal," I say.

If you hadn't, you and everyone you have ever loved would be lying in a pool of their own blood. You may not like the cost, but you have what you wanted. Revenge is just a single grasp away. Will you turn away now that you are so close?

With every ounce of my strength, I push Kosci down as far as I can. I hate that his words make sense, that I can't deny this is exactly what I wanted. I want Strana, I want the awed stares and reverent whispers. In my heart of hearts, I more than want Strana. I want to crush it. This country has done nothing but watch the suffering of Zladonians for ten years, content to turn over a *malozla* in exchange for a few coppers and bread. Why shouldn't I take this country? Why shouldn't I ruin it?

I drop heavily onto my cot and cradle my head in my hands. I hadn't fought my way through Knnot to give up. I know what Kosci is now, what he truly wants from me. I can harness his power to fulfill my promises and still be rid of him at the end.

Or would he find a way to snake through my mind and pull my plans from me as I slept? How could I hope to outwit a god who lived in my own head? I can't deny that I craved the strength that flowed through me every time I wore the pendant and wielded our power. I was a god to them. The Storm Hounds the Czar sent to trap us never had a chance because of me.

Because of *us*.

I can't give that up.

Not yet. Our war would be lost as soon as Matvei stepped onto the field.

I stand and do my best to straighten my disheveled clothing. I glance down at my palm, intending to wrap it, but the wound heals over as I watch. I clench it into a fist. Even without the pendant strung around my neck, Kosci's power flows through me, following the bruising along my bones. Alik was right, I am changing.

But it's necessary.

Moonlight clings to the all-too-familiar buildings of Oleg. The village is as I remember it. Still run-down and hopeless, practically the personification of Strana's destruction. Not a single window holds a candle. No one has the coin to spare. The streets are empty, the weather far too cold for even a beggar.

We steal through the silent streets of Oleg like stray cats. I'd made sure each soldier tamped down their armor, ensuring the lovite in it wouldn't chime and alert everyone to our presence.

Dark clouds brew overhead, blotting out the half slice of moon that had hung there.

I lead us through the city to the very cobblestone square

I'd stood on with Ivan not more than four months ago. Then, I'd been helpless to stop the Storm Hounds. A scared little girl who couldn't control a single thing in her world.

Now, I was the vengeful ghost all of Strana should fear, and I relished it.

The gate of the *tyur'ma* looms before me, but I'd already brought down the gate of Yelgarod. What was one more? I let the power grow around me, fashioning it into the perfect weapon. The soldiers inhale as I shoot it forward, smiling as it crashes into the gate with a boom that shakes the entire town.

Surprised shouts come from inside, but before they can do more than grab their weapons, I send my soldiers in. I race over the broken pieces of wood and jump into the prison courtyard. This one is larger than the others, expanding for nearly a mile down to the sea.

Rage courses through me and I aim it at the stark, slanted building before me, releasing all of the pent-up hatred within me into a wave of ice. It devours the building, freezing the Storm Hounds in the doorway mid-charge.

It's just like the day Ludminka froze, only this time I'm in control. I tighten my grip on the building, squeezing until I feel it give way. The garrison explodes into thousands of ice shards, wood and flesh indistinguishable as it falls like snow around us.

"What are you waiting for?" I snap at the slackened soldier beside me. "Get everyone out now!"

He shakes himself and darts toward the closest narrow house, the others around him following his lead. I march toward the sea. Storm Hounds fly from side streets and shadows, weapons raised and eyes wild. The soldiers behind me meet their blows, stopping them long before they can ever reach me.

The storm bruising the sky darkens and the wind grows wilder, cementing my presence in Oleg. This city will be mine, just as Yelgarod is. The fear around me is intoxicating, the power of it fanning the flame in my breast. I extend a hand, sending a shard of ice straight through the Storm Hound about to pounce from the eaves of a nearby home. He collapses to the ground.

I don't look back, continuing down the street, passing rows and rows of houses. I can feel the suffering of all the people inside: children with gnawing bellies and parents with failing hearts from years of being overworked with little food.

This is what I feel. Every day I have walked this earth, this is all I feel. Kosci's voice rings at the back of my mind. *My brother profits from life, from happiness. He doesn't see the true soul of mortality. The endurance, the tenacity, the drive to survive. He will never understand your power and will never lend his support. Not like I do.*

With an invisible hand, Kosci reaches out to the nearest house. Four heartbeats sound from inside, each one bleeding and tired. He siphons the pain, drawing it away like poison from a wound. It courses through me and I shiver. It beats inside me, mirroring their hearts, and I feel when Kosci releases them from their pain. It sheds from them and the flame of their souls glows brighter.

I can do that? I ask.

We can.

More, I say.

I know I shouldn't tempt him, but I have the power to take away the pain and hurt of the past ten years with a snap of my fingers. Don't they deserve that?

The suffering crashes down on me like a wave and I spin along its eddies, seeing snatches of memories. Men forced into freezing water, not allowed to come out until their fishing nets were full or their fingers blackened by frostbite. Women made to give birth in tiny, dark corners, laboring for days only to produce a dead child because no midwife had been there to help.

It hurt. By the gods did it hurt, but I can feel their burden loosening. By the time I reach the ocean, my entire being seethes and aches. I want to forget. I want to always remember.

I fade between myself, Kosci, and the hundreds of voices swirling through the winter air. Snow pelts my face and waves rush up over my knees as I step deeper into the sea. The burn of the freezing water does nothing to ground me. I float among the Zladonians and my soldiers alike, feeling hope and pain and fear mingled together into an overwhelming wall.

I cannot let this continue.

I will not.

When the sea reaches my waist and the water pulls at my clothes, I extend my hand and gather water into my palms. The salty scent cascades around me. There will be no Oleg when I'm through. Why should it continue to exist when it turned a blind eye to all those behind the thick walls of the prison? They should suffer as they've made us suffer.

I let the power I collected rush out into the sea, zigzagging along frothing waves and arching past secret dens of eels and squid. It races past the walls submerged in the ocean and straight toward the piers of Oleg.

Oh, how I hate those moldering wooden things. Still the image of Alik's blood dripping through the slats of them burns in my mind, a memory I will never forget. I will bring them down. I will bring the entirety of Strana to its knees.

The magic barrels into the piers with the force of a winter storm, and the water freezes as it laps over the long boards. I pull the storm overhead closer, stirring the merciless waves until they roll over Oleg's quay and reach the first of the warehouses.

Ladislaw claimed to leave a fortune of goods there, all for the land the *tyur'ma* had been built upon. And the greedy hands of its citizens took what was offered with no questions asked. I force ice and salt water into the building, easily tearing aside the rotting boards.

The world glows a hazy blue and the walls go transparent, funneling my vision through homes and broken shops and forgotten greens. I shift as pressure builds within my chest.

It's too much.

It's all too much.

I scream as power lances out of me, seeming to gleam from every pore, every piece of hair. The sea rises around me, revealing dark sand and hiding clams. It hangs suspended for a moment before exploding outward.

I feel more than hear the screams of the citizens in Oleg. The world flickers between darkness and light, and the only thought in my head is of vengeance.

At last, it is mine.

THIRTY-THREE

I COME TO ON A foggy beach. It takes me a long moment to realize I can no longer feel . . . anything. Not the wind tugging at my hair or the grit of the sand beneath my fingertips. I sit, expecting to find frostbite across my legs, but they are still swathed in the dark trousers I'd put on yesterday.

The world stands still and silent around me. I rise and take a blind step forward, trying to determine where I am. Something cracks beneath my boot. I glance down to see a crab, its shell broken by my foot. My eyes widen as I take in the sand around me. It lies flooded with fish and sea creatures of all types; upended, empty clam shells and dying lobsters, desiccated seals and, far before me, a dying whale.

I walk from the sand and onto the rocky shore, following

what I hope is the road through the prison, cocooned in a swirling fog that never dissipates.

"Hello?" I call out.

My skin prickles as I pass the first narrow house. Blood splatters the whitewashed side, but there is no body to claim it. I push forward, finding shards of frozen wood speckling the ground. I remember in a flash the blinding explosion of the garrison. I barely recall doing it.

In fact, I don't remember much from last night.

Something rises out of the mist before me. Dark, languid forms piled on top of one another. My heart hammers in my throat as I catch a bit of white hair, a piece of lovite armor.

I let out a breath. The bodies before me are Storm Hounds, entirely encapsulated in ice. They almost look like they might blink if I were to reach out and touch them. It's so similar to Ludminka that I clutch Kosci's heart tight, like it is a talisman against the memories.

With trembling legs, I move past the broken prison gate and into Oleg. The streets are silent and bare as I move away from the prison and into the city proper. Whispers of wind curl through the homes, tugging at the mist and pulling it from the ground.

Where *is* everybody?

The road empties into the small square, dotted only by a well in the center. Crystallized waves of salt water stand hip high, rolling along the thoroughfare to the sea. People half hang out of windows, clinging to their shutters, staring open mouthed at the water pooling around their homes.

Each and every person is frozen stiff, trapped in an unbreakable sheet of ice.

I stare down at my hands. This isn't what I wanted. I may have hated the people of Oleg, but I didn't want to curse them like Ludminka had been.

Oh, but you did. Kosci's voice slithers forth for the first time since I woke. *You wanted all this and more, remember? You wanted to paint their blood through the streets, rain sorrow and suffering down on them like a vengeful storm. You showed the world your teeth, Valeria, don't deny your pride.*

"No," I whisper as memories of the night before streak through my mind.

I *had* wanted them to suffer.

I'd wanted to burn the world and them with it. Why did they deserve to go unpunished after years of watching the suffering of others? A lightning flash of a memory sears through my mind. Stumbling into the sea, the swirl of pain and power flowing through my body, and burning so brightly that I combusted.

I had no longer been able to contain Kosci's power.

I steel myself as I make my way from Oleg, passing more frozen homes and horrified faces. The scene is so achingly familiar. This time, though, I made sure no one was able to escape.

From the rise at the edge of the village, I finally make out the faint outline of the forest. A dark curl of smoke floats over them like an ink spill, and I know at least some of my army made it out. I make my way toward them slowly. No need to rush. They won't go anywhere without me.

A wild call sounds, echoed through the trees until culminating in a roaring yell. Dark shapes hurtle through the forest toward me. It takes me a moment to realize they hold raised swords. I throw up a hand and time slows to a crawl. Their feet hover above the ground, caught in mid-run, their mouths set in slow cries.

I walk among them, studying their flowing white hair caught beneath helms of lovite. My own soldiers, faces filled with determination. I touch the man closest to me, watching as the warmth of my finger sticks to the hard metal of his breastplate. I'd never been able to do this before.

That's because you always resisted me. Now your power matures, and still you can do so much more.

His voice makes me shiver, Alik's warning ringing through my mind. I release my hold on time and their feet crash to the forest floor. They spin, confused as to where they are. As they finally find me, they lower their weapons and kneel, hands pressed tight to their chests.

"We hoped you would return," says the woman in front, her face covered by a heavy helm. "We praise you, Czarista."

A ripple of pure pleasure rolls through me at the title.

Ruler, empress, queen. I beckon for them to rise, and they do so immediately.

"What happened last night?" I ask.

"We liberated the prison and took its residents back to base camp," reports the woman with brisk efficiency. "You stayed in the village as we left. I've . . . never seen anything like it. You shone like a star, Czarista, and you cut our enemies down before they had a chance to raise a fist."

A smile curls across my face. "Let us go back to camp."

The woman takes the lead, the two others flanking me on either side as if I need a personal guard. The camp is just as I remember: tents lie scattered around the trees, pitched wherever there is enough room. The only difference is the burning pyre in the center.

It wasn't often we burned our dead, preferring the sanctity of earth. But I hadn't been here to carve the ground open for them and they'd made do. Soldiers and freed prisoners alike surround the logs. Some chant tearful songs while others look on with clasped hands and lowered heads. These people gave their lives for me, for Zladonia. If I can't bury them, I will at least give them a proper sendoff.

The crowd parts for me as I stop close enough to the pyre to feel the tickle of warmth along my skin and smell burning hair. I don't need to raise my hands, but it feels like something I should do to signify importance.

"We thank all who sacrificed for the good of Zladonia.

Your names will be remembered, written in stone so the world may never forget what it cost to win our freedom. With all the power within me, I bless you. May you rest in eternal peace."

With a flick of my wrist, a wind roars through the brush, fanning the flames and sending them higher until they seem to touch the treetops. I make myself watch them burn.

It takes nearly half a day for the pyre to burn to ash. I remain until the last bit of sinew has burned away, leaving nothing but a pile of charred, smoking bones. All of this death could've been spared if only I had fully accepted Kosci's magic earlier. I stalk back to my tent, snapping at a soldier to send a message to Bataar. He arrives before I do and holds open the flap without a word. Once we are doused in the comfortable dim of the tent, he speaks.

"Are you all right?"

The question catches me off guard. "Of course I am."

"You seem . . . different." He takes a single step forward. "And what I saw last night was something out of a legend."

"We're living in the middle of a legend, Bataar. We were as soon as the champions were chosen." I study the maps on my table, ignoring the large stack of scrolls and books Alik left behind. There is nothing more information can do for me now. I'd made my choice. Kosci and I will remain together until the bitter end.

"How did you do it?" Bataar asks, my fingers still on the soft edges of the map.

"I . . . don't know. It was like the entire world became nothing but strings I could manipulate. I could feel every hurt, see memories of horrible things that had happened." I curl my fingers in, staring hard at the inked lines of Strana to stop those memories from consuming me. "It all collected in my soul and I just . . . shattered. Everything became possible, all I had to do was think it and it happened. It was . . . glorious."

And I want to feel that way again. In that single moment, nothing could stop me. Not Ladislaw, not even Matvei. The world became mine and Kosci's, one we could mold how we saw fit.

"I wasn't sure you were even alive after that." The words are soft enough to be a prayer. It drags me from my thoughts, and I turn toward Bataar, noticing for the first time the dark circles beneath his eyes and the sharp tug of his mouth. "I searched for you. Even as the ice took the town."

"For me?" My brow wrinkles. "Why?"

"You aren't immortal, Val."

"Have you ever read a tale where one of the champions died by mortal hands? No. They always fade into the darkness of the world, never to be seen again, only to be remembered in songs and stories," I say, a hollow pit opening in my stomach. One that feels terribly close to loneliness. "I suppose that is what will happen to me one day."

Bataar's fingers tighten around my hand at my words. He looks as if he wants to say something, and in that single beat, in

333

that one flicker of fear not for himself but for me, his devotion writes itself across his face. Bataar goes still as I raise a hand. Slowly, I trace the lines of his face, trailing down his jaw. I'm not sure what I'm doing, or even why, but I like the way warm excitement dances its way through my chest. I let my thumb smooth over his cheekbone.

"It was kind of you to search for me," I say into the still air between us. "I'm certain no one else did."

His lips part slightly as he reaches up to caress the braid near my shoulder. Almost timidly, he moves from my hair to my cheek, running his thumb across it until it catches softly on my bottom lip. His breath hitches, and the stroke of it whispers along my lips. The sudden hunger for his mouth against mine swallows me. I close the distance between us and let my mouth rest against his.

The warm press of Bataar's mouth on mine sends a roll of pleasure down the entire length of my body. I lean against him and his hand goes to my lower back, trailing across my hip. Somewhere, almost far away, I think I should feel guilty. He isn't Alik.

But he is such a beautiful boy, isn't he? He respects and loves the power you wield, Kosci whispers. *Why deny yourself the simple pleasures?*

At the gentle prod, the feeling vanishes and all I can concentrate on is the way Bataar's arms circle me, warm and sure. I draw my fingers along his arm until it reaches the nape of his neck and the hair caught into a bun there. My fingers tug at the leather strand holding it in place and it falls like a sheet of black ice, spilling over my fingers silky and smooth.

Bataar shudders against my touch. As he deepens the kiss, I pull my fingers along his hair, twisting into it, hungry and desperate for the cool flame that blooms to life in my belly at his touch. He cups the back of my neck, bringing his lips back to mine. I let my mouth open and his tongue flickers inside. I gasp and grind against him. Needing him, wanting him.

"Valeria?"

Instantly, I freeze. Alik stands framed in the doorway, the tent flap caught in his left hand. I become acutely aware of Bataar's arms, one around my waist, other hand still cupping my face, my own still caught in his hair.

Alik takes a step back, blinking rapidly as if he can clear away the image before him with enough concentration. When it doesn't fade, his face cracks open, horribly raw and painful, before he shutters it with a breath, locking himself away from me and the rest of the world. It pulls at the deepest part of my heart and finally, *finally*, my numb fingers untangle from Bataar's hair and I step away.

"I saw what happened last night, to you, what you did to Oleg. . . ." Alik's voice is hollow. "I wanted . . . well, it doesn't matter what I wanted."

"Alik," I say, but he shakes his head and lets the tent flap fall between us.

My heart starts to hammer in my chest, then moves to my throat.

"Please," my voice breaks. "Please go."

Bataar doesn't argue. Just puts a hand to my face, brushing it gently, before ducking outside.

What have you done?

I let all the anger, all the fear and loathing and pain fall onto Kosci's shoulders, the barrier between us melting away to nothing. I know it won't matter. He's felt worse. There are far more horrible things in this world; I had seen them for myself, but it didn't stop this from hurting.

Nothing at all, Kosci says. *Do you assume every decision you make is swayed by my hand? You saw something you wanted and you took it.*

You let me. Encouraged me!

And? Kosci's voice rises, a thunderstorm in my mind. *You are still holding on! You cling to a boy who refuses to support you, hanging on his every word and begging for his forgiveness. You can be so much more, Valeria. He is the last thread of your old life, the one thing holding you back from becoming all you can be. Why bend to the will of a boy who never saw your potential? Who never wanted you to have power in the first place?*

I reach for the pendant and, with a scream, tug it from my neck, throwing it as hard as I can against the canvas wall. It strikes with a dull *thwack* and falls to the floor.

I don't think it truly makes a difference. Kosci's magic still shifts inside me, and I can no longer tell the difference between us anymore.

I'm not even sure there is one.

THIRTY-FOUR

FOUR DAYS LATER, SERA AND Chinua meet us at the entrance to Yelgarod with pale, strained faces. I follow them back to our headquarters at the Winter Palace, not bothering to stop for the citizens who ask for blessings.

Once settled before the fire with a hot cup of tea, they hand me a missive. This one thick, the printing inside written so hard, the outline shows on the backside of the paper. I open it slowly.

The destruction you wrought on Oleg is more than a crime. It is the act of a purely evil soul. I refuse to allow your chokehold on this nation to continue. I don't care if I have to cut through every last Zladonian in the world to reach you—I will do so. You can take my cities, you can take my son, but I refuse to

let you take my crown. I am coming for you, and I will not
stop until I see your head on a pike before me.

Ladislaw didn't bother to sign it this time. With a sigh, I toss it into the fire.

"Why did you do that?" Chinua asks, scrambling forward and grasping the poker. The vellum curls and disintegrates before she has a chance to dig it free.

"We have no use of it. He's just throwing a tantrum," I say. Kosci thrums beneath me, infusing every emotion with his own.

"He blatantly stated he is going to murder you," Sera says.

"It's not the first time," I say with an eye roll. "Besides, he'll be too terrified to try anything right now. Not after Oleg. He'll send someone else to do his dirty work, likely Matvei. We will double the guard around the city and send out spies to look for tracks."

"No, we won't," Sera says. "Alik returned three days ago. He took his entire team."

"What?" I look up, jolting so hard that tea spills onto my hand. I wipe it on my thigh.

"Alik left the city. We watched him go," Chinua says and reaches out for my hand. I wrench it away.

"You didn't try to stop him?"

"We did! He wouldn't listen. He said he was no longer needed and he wouldn't put his people in danger any longer."

Chinua shivers and Sera takes an unconscious step toward her.

"I'm tired." I settle my cup onto the table beside me and stand, brushing trembling fingers down my tunic. "I'll make arrangements with the former guild members we have left to work as scouts. We don't need Alik to protect ourselves."

"Are you sure you are okay?" Chinua asks hesitantly. "I know . . . things have been difficult between the two of you, but he loves—"

"I'm fine," I snap. "I simply wish to be alone."

I don't wait for their response. They likely don't have one. As the long, shadowy halls of the Winter Palace overwhelm me, the cold, hard beat of fear rolls over my body. I'm not afraid of the Czar or Matvei, not even Kosci's growing control over my senses.

But of being utterly and totally alone.

I haven't spoken to my brothers or father since Oleg and made that choice purposefully. The closer the people I love are to me, the more danger they are in. Kosci has made it clear he seeks to sever the relationships of the past. He believes they make me weak, that they hold me from the transformation he so desperately craves.

Now Alik is gone.

And Bataar . . . I felt something for him and one day, I believe I could grow to love him. But was it a fair thing to ask? Slowly, I'm losing everything I sought to protect, left with only anger in my heart and a cold god in my soul.

My chambers are almost stuffy when I enter, evidence no one has been in them for a while. I draw back the heavy velvet curtains, opening the small window just a crack to let the bitter winter air in.

I sink onto the too soft bed, head in my hands. The Czar will come for me. Of that, I have no doubt. I've proven I'm a threat, someone to be taken seriously. I can't stop now even if I wanted to. I will have to meet him on the battlefield, and to do that, I need Kosci's heart. We are nothing without the power of my pendant. I am nothing without the heady beat of magic coursing through my system. With Kosci, I will win this war. I can't give that up.

Despite myself, I pull Kosci's small lovite pendant from my pocket and let it dangle from my fingertips. It looks so unassuming in the dull light, just a piece of uncut lovite, no bigger than a coin. Yet it holds the entirety of a god. I slip it on and Kosci practically purrs.

Need something?

Where is he?

With a flash, my eyes go dark and I'm greeted by a long, desolate road, plains on either side. Horses tramp along beside me and as I look down, I realize I'm in Alik's body. I can feel the ache in his leg, pulsing and cruel, but worse is the invisible crack in his heart. If it could bleed, surely he would be stained red.

A balaclava sits over his nose and a hat is pulled low on

his head, but tears still freeze on his cheeks as he rides ever onward. I can't sense a plan or a destination in his mind, just a desire to be away. Far, far away. But he also longs to come back, to be close. To me.

I rush back into my body in a whirl of white smoke, and when I open my eyes, my cheeks are wet, too.

"Well, you got what you wanted," I say into the still air. "He's gone."

It is better this way. No chains bind you to your mortal life now. You can be elevated into something so much more. You can be my equal in all things.

"You can't make me a god, Kosci. You don't have that sort of power."

Once I kill my brother, I will have the power of life and death, the cycle of the world in my hands. I can do anything I wish.

Even through the ache in my soul, the thought tempts me. Me, a scared girl from a broken village, uplifted to the status of a god. Not only will I have changed the world, but I will be revered, respected. If I will always be on the outside, I might as well bask in the glory of being a god. But the path of divinity is lonely. Cold.

"I'd never see Alik again," I say.

You aren't going to anyway, he replies.

"You're certain?"

If you truly wish, I can show you the threads of time and you can see for yourself. Your strands will never weave together again.

Grief breaks over me in a wave, and my chest goes so tight it hurts. I want to cry. I want to scream.

I open my mouth, but the only thing that comes out is a horrible moan. I sink down to my knees and the entirety of everything—of the last ten years—presses down on me. A sob rips from my throat and tears burst from me like water held too long in a dam. It wracks my entire body until my tears mingle with snot and saliva.

It's pathetic. Disgusting. I can't do anything to stop it.

This is worse than when I thought Alik died, because he is still out there, but I will never, ever have him.

I want to call Kosci a liar, to deny what he says is possible, but everything he's ever seen has come true. He has always been right. Why would this time be different?

I hate this feeling, of being so powerful, yet so powerless. When I accepted Kosci's deal, I thought I would have the ability to do anything I please, that I would never be help-less again. Yet here I am, weeping on the floor like I had any number of nights when the frost came too close to the guild headquarters. All because of one stupid boy.

A boy who sought to control you himself, Kosci says, and the air around me moves, as if another person stands in the room with me.

"Stop," I say, my voice cracking.

But isn't it the truth? From the start he told you not to use the magic I granted you. He whispered words of dissension to soldiers loyal to you, he even used your own power against you. Who's to say that isn't what he is doing now? Running to Ladislaw to tell him everything he knows about Valeria of Ludminka.

"Alik would never betray me." My words sound so pathetically empty. I blink through my tears as the air around me stirs again and shadows jump and twist in bizarre shapes.

Don't be naïve. When you interrogated Yuri, what did Alik tell you? That he wouldn't hesitate to stop you if he felt you were doing wrong. As if he is judge on the morality of the world.

I grit my teeth even though Alik's voice, his determined face outside that root cellar door, springs crystal clear into my mind. He had said that.

This isn't some assumed betrayal, Valeria. It is one, pure and simple. Alik left and he took your people with him. He knew his role in our war, knew what you were trying to do for Strana, and still he left. And why? Because he saw you kiss someone else when he'd made it clear he could never love you?

I swallow the next sob, choking on it before it falls from my lips. Everything Kosci says is true. Alik hadn't wanted me to have Kosci's power, even when I was using it to free Zladonians, or when we'd found his mother, or when I'd brought him back to life. He'd never understood the intoxicating draw of it, the way if I tried *just* a bit harder, I could control whatever I saw fit. He'd never tried to understand, asking me to be rid of the pendant at nearly every opportunity.

Now he deserts me when I need him most? When we are so close to victory?

There wasn't a single time when Alik felt as if I'd made the right choice, when he realized how much I gave up to ensure Ladislaw paid for what he did. He'd wanted me to be selfish, to ignore the suffering of hundreds. I rock back onto my heels and dry my face. Slowly, the hole in my chest bleeding for Alik begins to sew shut, threaded by betrayal and anger.

How *dare* he?

If Alik thought me so wicked, then wicked I would be.

I will destroy the Czar and I will use his son to do it.

Alik can't stop me now. I will bring this entire world to its knees, and if anyone tries to stop me, I will smite them where they stand. Who are they to question a god? Magic courses through my very veins, painted with notes of Kosci's approval.

I will no longer play this game of cat and mouse. If the Czar heard of Oleg's destruction already, he is close. I will make a move he has no choice but to notice. Then Strana will be mine.

THIRTY-FIVE

I BARGE INTO THE ROOT cellar, the door banging off the stone wall with a clap. Yuri sits where he has been, tucked against the barrel in the corner. He rises slowly, eyes scanning me from head to toe.

"You seem . . . different," he says, seeming almost bored.

"Listen, you spoiled little brat," I advance with each word. "You are going to—"

Yuri holds up a hand, and I'm so shocked by the interruption I stop speaking.

"I know what you want and I am willing to give it to you." He pauses, as if he knows I need time to process what he is saying. "No more tricks, no more wasting away in this cellar, no more prodding into my mind."

I cross my arms, scanning him exactly as he had me. "And

what do you want in return?"

"I give you the information to find my father, and you give me the crown." He leans against the wall, crossing his feet at the ankles. "That's my deal."

"So you can do exactly what your father has done? You would turn the blades of the Storm Hounds back on me the moment I showed my back."

"Despite what you may believe about me, I am nothing like my father. I've spent more time here with tutors and nannies than I ever did at the palace with him. He and I live in different worlds. As such, we think differently."

"You honestly expect me to believe that?" I ask. "You could've made this deal when I first captured you. Why wait?"

Yuri tenses and in the silence of the room I hear him swallow.

"I believed my father would come for me. That he would rescue me because I meant something to him. Clearly, I do not," Yuri says, never stirring from his casual posture. "I hear what the guards outside my door say. He hasn't even attempted to come to Yelgarod. Not so much as a spy or assassin. I suppose he believes I'm not worth the effort. The world already thinks the boy he parades around Strana is his son. If I am lost, he will simply replace me, as he always has."

I don't want to believe his little speech, and yet a part of it tugs on my soul. I, too, was a pawn, used by Luiza to get what she wanted, easily replaced when I was gone. All I'd done during my time in the guild was hide in the shadows and hope one day I would be allowed to walk in the sun. How much of his life had Yuri wanted the exact same thing?

He is playing you, Kosci's cool voice slithers from the back of my mind. *He knows enough about you to twist your feelings. Your emotions have always been easily manipulated. Do not let another boy do it.*

Despite the sense I can see in Kosci's words, something about it doesn't feel quite right. This is a path to peace. When I began this, I didn't want the crown, I simply wanted freedom. If I can achieve that, why shouldn't I take it?

You would trust the words of Ladislaw's child? He may speak of growing up far from the shackles of his father, but he was still raised in the ways of ruling. All kings do is lie and cheat to maintain their power. You cannot trust him. You can trust no one but me.

Yuri cocks his head, finally straightening from the wall. He takes a step closer and I tense.

"You know, Matvei did that. It was like he was dreaming while awake, lost in a world only he could see." Yuri takes another step closer. He catches my wrist and turns it over, yanking up the sleeve of my shirt. "And he had these."

Yuri's finger trails up the bruises on my arm, a strange blue, almost luminescent in the light from the single torch in the hall beyond. They follow the path of my skeleton, the twin bones of my arm connecting at the wrist in a myriad of small bruises. I rip my arm from his grasp and shove the sleeve back down. It apparently breaks whatever curiosity had taken hold of Yuri as he blinks, his eyes finding mine.

"His aren't blue, though. More like amber. The more he used his magic, the more obvious they became."

"And how would you know this?" I say.

Yuri shrugs. "My father would send him to check on me. He was here not more than three weeks before you arrived, sealing up the secrets in my mind. At the time, he said it was just a precaution, the result of Luiza pressuring them to take pains to cover their assets. I should've known then I was just a commodity."

"You will not win my sympathy," I say. "We all have sad stories."

"I'm not asking for your empathy. It's clear you have precious little to give, but you have something I want and I have something you want. I am asking for a bargain, nothing more."

My lips thin. "Haven't you heard about making bargains with gods? They never go the way you want them to."

"I can see what it cost you," he says without pity, without fury, just a pure statement of fact. "And still, I will make this trade. I know where my father harbors his army and I know what he intends to do. Do you want this information or not?"

I fly through every other possibility. I could continue to slam against the golden wall in his mind until either it, or he, falls. Or I could shake on this deal.

And double-cross him before he does it to you, Kosci says.

We do not know if he will do that.

The chances are too high. The only way to protect yourself is to maintain your control. Take his deal, then slay him in the middle of the battle. No one will know who swung the blow that ended him.

I grit my teeth. Kosci gives me an out if I need one. It would be as simple as letting a couple daggers slip through my defenses and find their way into Yuri's heart. I lick my lips and extend my hand slowly.

"Very well," I say.

Yuri slips his hand in mine. We shake but I don't let go, tightening my grip.

"If you attempt to renege on your promise, I *will* seek retribution."

Yuri gives a smirk. "As will I."

I make my way into a small drawing room where Sera and Chinua have been preparing. Papers lined with numbers and tactical movements hang tacked to the wall and examples of Chinua's explosives lie across empty side tables. They both sit, Sera cradling Chinua's hand in her own, running the length of her arm with her fingers. They jump as I enter, and a sharp pang of hurt rushes through me. They deserve to be happy. Someone does, in the middle of all this bloodshed.

Their eyes slip from me to the slender form following just a few steps behind. Both rise to their feet, Sera's hand going for a weapon that isn't there.

"It's fine." I sit down. Yuri promptly takes a seat beside me, immediately scanning the maps strewn across the table. Sera notices and slaps her hand on top, glaring at Yuri.

"You bring him straight into the heart of our army?" she says.

"We've come to an agreement," I say, gently slipping my hand onto Sera's and moving it from the maps. "He will help us find his father and tell us what he knows about their battle plans, and in exchange, I will give the crown of Strana to him."

"And you believe him?" Chinua asks as she studies Yuri. "It seems too convenient to me."

I sigh, pinching the bridge of my nose. "Listen, I could not have asked for a better war council. You're both smart, determined, and more than loyal, but we can't continue to linger. The longer we stay in one spot, the more time Ladislaw has to weasel his way into our defenses. We need to move soon. Yuri has offered the very thing we need. Besides," my eyes slip to him, "despite Matvei's defenses, I can still tell when he is lying. That much the Bright God cannot hide."

Sera's mouth doesn't fall from its firm line, but she gives a tight nod, slowly sinking into her chair. Chinua also eyes Yuri, her face more unreadable than Sera's. She taps her fingers on the table for a moment.

"We are waiting for what you have to say, Yuri," she says at last.

He studies each one of us in turn before setting his jaw and placing a finger on a barren part of the map.

"Here." The spot rests just beyond Oleg, apparently flat and empty based off the map beneath us.

Sera looks up. "You truly expect us to believe he's chosen to train his army out in the open? Or that he would ever tell you what he has planned?"

"My father didn't tell me, Matvei did," he says, leaning back in his chair and crossing his arms. "The Bright champion always took a special sort of interest in me. I think I reminded him of his younger brother."

"Please excuse us if we don't believe you," Chinua says.

Yuri shrugs. "You can choose to think me a liar if you want. Win or lose, I will still retain the Stranan crown."

"He's telling the truth," I say. Kosci's power hums like an undercurrent in the room, swimming along the threads of shimmering magic. It is easy enough to see the truth in words now. False ones crack and crumble as they leave a liar's lips. Truth floats pure through the air, harmonizing with the magic around it.

Chinua shakes her head. "Surely you can't believe this is a sound tactic. We cannot trust him."

"I don't," I say, mood darkening. "I trust my magic. It has never led me astray and it doesn't now. Yuri speaks true. His father sits in the plains outside Oleg, ripe for the taking. If we move soon, he will never see us coming."

Chinua scoffs, but its Sera that answers.

"Ladislaw is likely far more prepared than we are, and we

would be taking the fight to him. Who is to say that isn't exactly what he wants?"

"There is no better place for a battle than open ground. We are away from prominent cities and Ladislaw sits behind no fortifications. The more time we give him, the more provisions he will make," I say.

Both girls look at one another and a silent conversation seems to pass between them.

"In the end," Chinua says, her eyes not leaving Sera's, "I will go with you."

"And I with you," Sera responds, voice soft. There is a beat of silence before both turn toward me.

"War is coming, whether we want it or not. We can either meet it in the open or risk a siege. If you believe Yuri, then we believe you. When do you want to move out?" Chinua asks.

"We make our final push at dawn in three days' time," I say, clenching my hand into a fist.

At long last, Ladislaw will be mine.

THIRTY-SIX

AT FIRST, I'M NOT SURE what wakes me. The chamber is pleasantly warm, the fire having died out some time ago. The dim light of predawn leaks from between the sliver of curtains to my right, throwing a strip across the foot of my bed. I blink again, not daring to reach up and rub the tiredness from my eyes. I can sense the oddity, as if the chamber came to life just to hold its breath in this moment.

A flash of silver is the only warning I get.

I roll to the side and a dagger embeds itself deep in the pillow I'd just been resting my head on, feathers falling from the tear. I scramble to a crouch and find the all-too-familiar eyes of Luiza. I bare my teeth and slip from the bed as she lunges again. She sails into the bed, landing with an audible *oompf.* Luiza may have caught me off guard last time, but she doesn't know what she's awakened now. I snarl and let Kosci's power lower the temperature in the room.

Our breaths plume before us and I'm certain she must be freezing, but she slashes at me, movements still sharp and quick as if she doesn't feel the cold at all. The blade of ice is in my hand without a second thought.

Her eyes dart to it and I use it to my advantage, sending a stab toward her gut. She dodges at the last minute.

"I see you still retain what I taught you," she says.

"I see you still play lapdog to Ladislaw," I say. "Was my last warning not enough?"

I slice again, this time at her face. She catches my blade on her own and a high-pitched whine echoes through the chamber. Luiza shoves me back, a move she's performed a hundred times. I plant my feet, anticipating her next move. As always, she drops and attempts to sweep my legs.

She encounters nothing but the sudden rock of my ankle. I let Kosci's power fade once more. This is my fight. I could freeze her on the spot if I chose, but I want the satisfaction of ending her life myself.

"What do you think you're doing, Valeria? You were never meant for this," she says as she darts away. "You were supposed to die. The Bright God said you would."

"He can't see everything," I say. "Not without his brother. Not without me."

I swing and catch her forearm before she has a chance to

pull away. The ice sinks deep, blood already surging over the blade. She sucks in a deep breath, eyes hardening.

"Was I ever anything other than a pawn to you?" I growl as I rip it out. "Did you truly take me in because you saw a suffering girl? Or because you knew I was something to be used?"

The burning questions I'd had for months pop from my mouth before I can stop them.

"I never made it a secret I use my guildlings."

She slides forward and catches me above my knee. Hot blood bursts from the wound to roll down my leg. Taking advantage of her bared back, I stab. It sinks deep into her shoulder. Before she can move, I wheel around her, shoving her to the ground. Luiza bucks and my weakened knee gives just enough for her to roll onto her back. I leap on top of her, conjuring a new blade and shoving it hard into her left bicep. It lances straight through, pinning her to the floor.

She gives a muffled cry and writhes beneath me, but I hold tight. In the dim glow from the fireplace, she looks almost fragile, her pallid skin translucent enough that I can make out the vein that runs through the center of her forehead. So weak, so mortal.

"I won't give you the answers you're looking for," she hisses.

"We don't need them from your lips. We will rip the secrets from your brain." I lean forward, my lips brushing along her ear. "And I'll make sure it hurts."

Luiza goes utterly still. I count her ragged breaths and

recognize the familiar pattern she'd taught us all in the guild. She wants to lure me into complacency, make me believe she's unruffled in the changes she's found.

"Why don't you?" she asks.

"I want the satisfaction of killing you myself," I say. "You manipulated me. Made me believe the only thing I had ever cared about in the world was dead, when you knew all along Alik lived a week's ride from me. How could you stand watching me cry? Did it not twist your heart at all to see me in such pain, *Mother*?"

I hiss the last word and shove my thumb into the open wound on her shoulder. She squirms beneath me, and I bare my teeth. Let her hurt. Let her suffer all the ways I suffered. Let it pour into the ever-widening pool of power in my soul.

"You made me feel like you loved me. That I was something special to you, when all along you knew what I could be if only I accepted Kosci's deal. You sent me to Knnot on purpose. You knew the Pale God would let me in, but you hoped I would die in the process, leaving you and Ladislaw all the profits. I was the sacrifice. The lamb you raised to slaughter. Did you not care for the girl you said you loved?"

She stays silent for a beat before forcing her eyes to meet my own. "It was always the truth. I do love you, Valeria."

"Liar!" I shove another blade into her right bicep. She cries out, surprise and pain mingled as one.

She bucks beneath me. I clamp my thighs tight, refusing

to budge. When that fails, she settles once more beneath me.

"I did know what you were. Matvei had long been in the Czar's service and warned of your coming. A little girl with snow-white hair who survived Knnot. When I found you, I couldn't believe fate would be so kind. They wanted to murder you, but I knew you'd be of use. I convinced Ladislaw of it. He wanted Knnot reopened and if the Pale God faded, so too would his brother, and he'd lose all chance of Iovite ever flowing through his coffers again.

"At first you were a tool. So easy to manipulate, so desperate to be loved, to be useful. You did all I asked without question. I couldn't have asked for better. But then you had your Alik, and you no longer needed me. I tried to separate you, send you on missions that would divide you, but you stupidly clung to each other."

"So you had him killed."

"He was supposed to be, but the Storm Hounds, as usual, can't get a job done."

I'd known Luiza cared little for us, but to hear it so blatantly from her mouth cuts deep down into the bottom of my soul, leaving a fissure so wide I can't see across it.

She sighs beneath me. "But I knew you'd do anything to find him."

"*You* were the one who sent the Storm Hounds after us, to make sure I died before I could take my power as champion." The revelation slowly rocks me. All this time, I had thought the Storm Hounds followed Ivan because he was a traitor. I'd blamed him for being trapped inside Knnot, when really it had been me all along.

"What are you doing, Valeria? A war for the crown?" she croons, like she did all those times she comforted me after nightmares of Ludminka. "You aren't meant to rule. You're just a girl, a puppet on strings for a god. You can never hope to be anything of consequence."

Fire snaps through me at her words, my body recoiling, readying to strike. I realize my mistake too late. Luiza uses my backward momentum to roll me from her hips, ripping her arm from the blade with a scream before tugging the icy dagger from the other. She staggers to her feet, teeth glinting in the dull light of the embers. I grapple for the power to create my own, but it slips from my fingers. Once. Twice.

Luiza lunges at my throat, tackling me to the ground. I catch her wrist as the tip of her dagger caresses my neck, leaving a stinging line behind. My muscles tremble as Luiza bears down, and our eyes lock as I grimace against her weight.

Her face slackens, the weight on the blade lessening as warmth floods her eyes for the barest heartbeat. It's the same sort of affection I'd seen as she cared for my illnesses and brushed my hair as I cried after I thought Alik died.

It is the moment I need. With my free hand, I craft one of my swords and bury it to the hilt in the place between her sternum and her ribs.

Her mouth falls open as she catches the hilt of my sword with her hands. With a single glance down at it, she collapses to the side. She lands with a hard thud, her eyes going vacant and blood pooling around her on the plush carpet. I draw in several strangled breaths, unable to tear my eyes from the glassiness of hers. I scramble to my knees and reach for her, only to stop myself with my hand trembling mere inches over Luiza's corpse.

Blood seeps into the carpet, turning it a deep black in the light from the embers. I wait for the numb apathy to dissipate, for the tears to come, but I feel nothing, not even satisfaction.

She'd used me, manipulated me, tried to kill me not once, but three times. She said she loved me, but it was a lie. One she likely even told herself. She didn't know what love was. All she knew was power and control.

I should be glad she's dead.

I should feel *something*, I want to, but I can't manage it. Luiza is just another life lost to this war. And there will be more. There will always be more.

Soft warmth cradles me, almost as if a set of arms encircles me. No one else lingers in the room, but I feel a presence as surely as if there is. A gentle hand strokes my hair.

"It will be all right, Valeria."

It's Kosci's voice, but instead of being inside my mind, it rumbles from the space before me. I blink and a soft outline materializes before me. Kosci stands, translucent but firm before me, hair unbound in long sheets on either side of his narrow face. His sharp cheeks are rosier than the last time I saw him beneath the mountain, his eyes brighter. I reach out and my fingers brush through the apparition.

"How—"

"You are keeping your promise. It gives me shape, makes me real in this world, if even for a little bit."

Seeing him, so real in this world, melts the apathy that had descended upon me at Luiza's last breath. My hands begin to tremble as my throat tightens. "The world will never be the same again, will it?"

Again, the soft warmth filters around me and takes my hands. Pins and needles run along my fingers at the touch.

"No," Kosci whispers. "We will make it far better."

THIRTY-SEVEN

THE DAY WE MARCH FROM Yelgarod dawns blindingly bright, stark rays of winter sunlight reflecting off the mountains of snow around us. Still the people of the city come to watch us leave, applauding and crying out for us as we pass. They are happy, their homes full of coin from trading lovite with Drangiana. They believed in my promise to restore Strana to her rightful place and so will follow me no matter where I go. And if they don't, Luiza serves as a warning, her body tied to the iron fence surrounding the Winter Palace.

The days journeying south are long. Kosci and I try to keep the weather at bay as best we can. By the time we steal past Oleg, a numb hollowness has seeped into my bones. For so long I had worked for this moment, and with Yuri by my side and Luiza dead, Ladislaw can't refuse me a battle. His only piece left to play is Matvei. The champion is his only hope at retaining power, and I'm certain he will use him.

I slow our troops as we ride closer to the unnamed town Ladislaw has quartered. Even on the wind I can hear the unsettled sounds of horses and smell the stink of unwashed bodies and manure. If Ladislaw sought to hide, he is doing an extremely poor job. I straighten as hooves ride up behind me. Sera sits brilliant and fierce in Iovite armor similar to my own with a broad ax strapped tight across her back.

"We should camp with our backs to the sea. There is a small cove not too far from the village that should house us. The fewer angles for infiltration, the better."

I nod, allowing her to take the lead. The ground rolls and falls in soft hills before leveling out. It seems as if I can see for miles, the land stark and unmarked. It's such a difference from the high mountains and forests I'm used to that it almost makes me feel vulnerable. There is no hiding out here.

But I am through hiding.

True to her word, Sera leads us to the coast, following the slow curve of white sands. The iron-colored waters churn wildly in the winds, and Sera turns toward a gulch of a small stream feeding into the sea. We follow it in silence, the fervor in the air almost palpable.

She reaches a narrow part in the valley. We have to squeeze between the granite cropping three by three, a perfect choke-point for the Czar's army if he tries to take us at base camp.

When it widens once more, Sera stops. Fallow fields lie on either side of the small stream, easily hopped over if it hadn't been frozen solid. The walls of the valley rise high on either side. Few would be able to climb down, though artillery could rain from above. I'll have to station a watch.

It is easily defensible, out of the harsh wind, and hidden from eyesight. It will do. I tell the soldiers to fan out and establish camp. I'll send an envoy to Ladislaw in the morning, demanding he surrender and telling him that I have Yuri. If he refuses, we will destroy him.

It all seems so simple. I don't know why I felt nervous before.

I take stock of our supplies in the infirmary set up on the east end of camp. The vast white tent stretches nearly the entire expanse of the valley. Long cots line the walls while people busily ready medical supplies. We are as ready as we can be for a war.

The flap at the front pulls open, and Bataar strides in. We haven't spoken since that night in my tent, and I find my stomach in a riot of flutters.

He locks eyes with me and strides forward. "My scouts already returned. Ladislaw has a barricade around his camp, a shallow moat of angled spikes outside it. Seems he prepared for this."

"A risk we knew coming here," I say. "Did you see where Matvei was?"

"He and Ladislaw are on opposite ends of camp. We can't take both at the same time easily. Splitting our army would leave us too vulnerable. We don't have enough troops for that sort of attack."

I pinch the bridge of my nose, willing the tension between my brows away. "We need the others."

Bataar nods. "I've already asked them to meet in your tent."

He brushes a thick strand of dark hair over his ear and my heart lurches a little. I look away, pretending to straighten a blanket over the cot nearest me. As I smooth it, he takes my hand, slowly, as if he's afraid I'll bolt. The warmth of it almost makes me shudder.

"Valeria, you don't have to keep avoiding me. Do you think you're the first person to fall victim to this pretty face?" He gives me a smile.

"I could slap you," I say.

"You wouldn't be the first to do that either."

I huff a laugh. Part of my heart still pangs desperately for Alik. But Kosci told me I would never see him again. He ran away. He never supported the person I needed to become to win this war. Bataar does. I give his hand a squeeze.

"After this is all over," I say, "maybe we should give it another try. Just to make sure."

The side of his mouth quirks up. "I think I'd like that."

I slip my fingers from his, wishing I could keep them there.

"Come on. Let's go meet the others," I say.

We make our way through camp, which buzzes with something like excitement. People attempt to keep themselves busy, but their eyes stray toward the cliffs above us, as if waiting to see an encroaching army. I slip into my tent, Bataar behind me. Chinua and Sera already rest on the low stools before the oven in the center, and I take my place beside them, waiting for Bataar to sit before speaking.

"We've got the layout, but it's not much to work with," I say, and gesture for Bataar to relay the information. Sera's and Chinua's faces grow paler by the moment, and Chinua shakes her head as soon as Bataar is through.

"We can't let the barricade stand. They'll always have the tactical advantage."

Bataar nods as Sera considers the topographical map before her.

"The land is mostly flat and open here, and he's kept the sea at his back. We can't lay siege to battlements, we don't have the supplies or the fortifications."

"Then we move forward with our third plan," I say, riffling through the stacks of papers until I find the ones I'm looking for. "We knew this was possible. We'll take out the battlements and maneuver our army to the low rise to the north."

"The only way plan three works is if we get close enough to place the *tersh-ek*," Chinua says, pointing to her careful scrawl in the margins.

"We will," I say. "You can't guard a camp if it's too cold to go outside. Not even Ladislaw will risk losing soldiers before a battle. I'll bring the temperature down, and we'll place the *tersh-ek*. Then, in the morning, I will ask for war."

At dawn, I remove some of the thick vellum from Sera's supply and sit before my small fire, quill in hand. Up until now, I'd refused to respond to Ladislaw. What was the point? Now, however, he has a choice.

Ladislaw—
I will no longer let you control the people of Strana. You've
caused nothing but suffering and pain for ten long years. I will
not forgive you. I will not forget either. Your son is mine, and
if you ever want to see him again, you will surrender now.
This is a war you've no hope of winning. Luiza is dead.
Yelgarod is mine. You run thin on allies. If you think Matvei
will save you, you'll be disappointed yet again. He weakens
beneath my strength, and soon you will be crushed alongside
him. If you wish to avoid this war and save your people, accept
my challenge to battle one on one. If you chose the path of the
coward, which I assume you will, I will meet you on the field
before us at noon.
Choose wisely.

I reread the note, and Kosci nods his approval. I set the ink with powder and find the closest person capable of riding a horse. I look up at the aged man, studying the lines in his forehead and the set of his jaw.

"You do me a great service," I say at last.

"It is my pleasure, Czarista."

I hand him the letter, followed by a white sheet. "Wave this above your head when you're close enough to be seen, but not near enough to be shot at. They should know you bear a letter and let you pass."

He nods, clutching the reins tight in his hands. As soon as the letter is tucked safely in his breast, he takes off toward the rising sun. I pace the camp, too restless to sit and too distracted to do anything important. I check to make sure Yuri is still secure in the tent farthest from the entrance. He slumbers away, as if he doesn't care his father may die by my hand. Perhaps he doesn't.

The morning ekes by, the camp slowly awakening and going about the morning chores. Some sit with wet stones and blades, silently sharpening already razor-edged lovite, while others cook or polish armor. Again, I make the long trek from one end of the valley to the other, my path through the snow now stained with mud. I'm about to turn around and walk toward the sea when a shout echoes from the cliffs above, panicked and tight. I quickly climb the snow around me to the scouts I'd placed along the cliff's edge.

"What is it?" I demand.

The girl besides me lifts a finger toward the horizon.

Sunlight spills across the white snow, momentarily blinding me. I squint and finally make out a lone figure drifting forward on a horse. He rides at an odd angle, tilted hard to the left and flopping as if unconscious.

No. Not unconscious.

Dead.

The horse draws near enough for me to grab. The man I'd sent out earlier sits tied to his horse with the same white sheet I'd given him, stripped of all his armor, a long gash across his neck.

Cold rage settles upon me. I cut the bindings from the man and catch his body as it falls, slowly lowering it to the ground. The girl comes to a stop next to me, her face even paler than usual.

"Bring me Serafima, Chinua, and Bataar," I say. She doesn't move, her eyes still trained on the man's gray face. "Now!"

She scurries away from me without a backward glance. I bend down, allowing my knees to sink into the wet snow, and brush the graying hair out of the man's face. This is my fault. If I hadn't sent him, he would still be alive. It wasn't fair.

Nothing is fair in war, Valeria. You should know that by now.

Perhaps I should've gone.

So you could be the corpse instead of him? You are necessary.

I bit the tip of my tongue at Kosci's words. I can't deny they aren't true, but my heart still aches for the man before me. I wonder if Ladislaw even read my letter, or if he'd dismantled my soldier on sight and threw the envelope into the flames.

The crunch of snow beneath boots makes me turn, and I stand as the others approach. Sera's lips thin as she takes in the man at my feet.

"Your scout to the Czar?" she asks, and I nod.

"I think we have the only answer we'll need," Bataar says. "He has no intention of avoiding an all-out war. He'll sacrifice everyone to kill you and keep his throne."

"Then I suppose we should make ready for war," I say, and turn my eyes to the rising sun.

THIRTY-EIGHT

WE LEAVE THE CAMP BEHIND not more than an hour later. I take the lead, Sera, Chinua, and Bataar at my back, the rest of the army following. We trudge the slow rise out of the valley and double back toward the fields where Ladislaw hides.

I ease the procession as the many tents of Ladislaw's encampment appear before us on a hill. Black and gold banners flutter in the breeze, encased behind thick timber walls, spikes exposed toward us before them.

Chinua rides up beside me. "We'll form a line. Put cavalry in the front, archers behind them, foot soldiers next."

"What of me?" I ask.

"We keep you secure until Ladislaw or Matvei is on the field. We can't take the champion without you."

I nod and she spins toward our soldiers, barking orders. Our soldiers fall into line, a wall of shimmering lovite. I shield my eyes as I turn my gaze toward the encampment.

At first, I don't think they've moved. Perhaps Ladislaw wants to wait us out, make us come to him. Slowly, ever so slowly, soldiers crawl out of their hiding places. Some dotting the homes of the village to our left, others mounted on horses.

No sign of Ladislaw or Matvei.

Sera reins her horse in tight behind me, bringing her helm down over her head.

"They have to outnumber us two to one."

"I know," I say. "But we can't go back."

"I never said we should. Strana will change after this, and I'd rather it change for the better. You've done by right by us, by everyone you've freed. I will follow you to the end."

I reach over and clasp her armored shoulder. "I couldn't have asked for a better person to have by my side."

My heart thunders in my chest as the gates to the barricade open, and a small contingent emerges. They jeer and cry out Ladislaw's name. Sent to mock us, then, like that small force alone could destroy what I've built.

A high-pitched trumpet calls out over the knoll, and the soldiers give a mighty yell, banging their swords against bright shields of Zoltoy-blessed lovite. I wheel my horse around to face my amassed forces. Fierce eyes and hard-set jaws stare back at me. Ready. Determined. I lift my sword high and use magic to throw my voice.

"At last we look into the eyes of our enemy. You see their numbers and may think there is no way we can win, but they lack something we have in abundance. Hope. We've seen the worst they have to offer and spit on it. They lost themselves to greed, leaving our country to rot. I say no more! We will take this field and destroy our enemies. You have followed me this far, and for that, I thank you. Now, let us make one more push, one more attempt for a better world. And for years to come, people will remember who fought here, who claimed this land, and who laid down their lives for freedom. You are not people to be broken and used! You are fierce. You are strong. And you will change the world!"

A cheer rings at my words and a thrill rushes through me. At last, it is time to take my vengeance.

I spin my horse around and lower my helm. Chinua and Sera take their places on either side of me. The world seems to go still. Both armies stare each other down, wondering who will dare make the first move.

I will answer the question.

I nod at Chinua, who lifts one of her arms. The archer beside her takes aim. Instead of turning her eyes toward the army across from us, she angles herself toward the nearest barricade wall. Someone beside her lights the tip of her arrow. With a steady hand, she takes in a deep breath and aims.

It arcs high overhead. Laughter and calls come from the other end of the field, more shield bashing filling the air. The arrow flies through the brilliant sky before embedding itself deep into the thatch of the nearest wall. It burns slowly, emitting the faintest curl of smoke. I send a whisper of wind to fan the flames.

It takes off, climbing down the wood and sizzling along its base. A moment of silence flows through both armies before a massive boom rings out across the field.

The wall explodes upward, casting fire and debris on the pieces next to it. The soldiers before the wall scramble away, but another explosion destroys the gate, bringing more fire.

More pain.

The army across the field rushes away from their fallen comrades, scrambling to retain formation as the walls smolder behind them, occasional explosions sending belches of fire from the rear walls. Yells start from inside, followed by quick commands.

In the disorder, I make my move, directing my army toward the Storm Hounds. My troops stampede around me, gaining momentum with the slow slope of the hill. I urge my horse into action, bending low over its neck as bitter wind curls around me. The horse glides over the frosted field of broken wheat, its sides heaving. I release the wind, sending it at the first line of encroaching soldiers. It rolls over the field like a wave, crashing into them with such force they stumble backward.

Heavy hoofbeats fall behind me, and I force my horse to

slow, allowing the cavalry to descend upon the decimated first line. Crashes ring out as swords meet metal shields. Lovite blades bite through flimsy steel, connecting with the men beneath them.

Soon the field is filled with the cries of dying men. Horses trample across fallen bodies and their riders hack at the men beneath them. I scan the battle. There should be a cavalry of the Czar's. Where were they?

A cry rings out from the low rise to my left. I look just in time to see hundreds of men descend on horseback, kicking up billowing curtains of snow. They slam into our exposed flank. Their horses are more battle ready. They kick at offending steeds, knocking men from horses and pushing their mounts to the ground.

"Archers!" cries Chinua over the sound of squealing horses.

The twang of bowstrings fills the sky as arrows start to rain down on the Storm Hounds. With practiced ease, they lift their shields above their heads, taking the brunt of the arrows. I grit my teeth. I will not let our army go so easily.

With a deep inhale, I reach for the vast well of Kosci's power deep inside my soul. I pull on it until it feels as if my body may burst. Clouds quickly build over the tents of the Czar's encampment, sending the banners ripping in the wind. With a tug, I pull the clouds in tight. Snow bursts from overhead, gales of wind sending it pelting into the eyes of the opposing army. I manipulate the dancing lights of magic, building the storm, bringing more snow, more ice, more frigid wind.

Arrows fly again, and I order the storm to carry them. It sends them sailing like ballista missiles into waiting shields, piercing straight through the metal and into the eye of the man before me. He crumples to the ground.

More, Kosci orders. I obey.

I tug the swirling blue mist inside my chest to the surface. It leaks over the field, curling around the legs of charging Storm Hounds. With a crack, it freezes solid. Cries ring out as knees dislocate and ankles break. I grin as Sera chops the arm from a charging Storm Hound.

Our foot soldiers raid behind us, taking out stragglers or those who hope to attack from behind. I push forward, past the low spiked barricade and toward the first of the tents. Ladislaw has to be here somewhere.

The ground beneath me starts to rumble. My horse falters, then tries to bolt. I can't hold on. I fall to the right, landing on the ground hard enough to knock the air out of me. I try to inhale and get to my feet as people whirl around me, each one caught in a battle of their own. No one notices me. Stray feet trample across my hands and kick my cheek, pushing me deeper into the bloodied snow beneath me. Blood pools in my mouth and I spit it out as a member of my army falls over my prone body. They land hard on top of me, the weight of their armor combined with their body pushes me deeper into the snow, tightening my lungs until I can hardly breathe. I attempt to push up as a Storm Hound aims his blade for us, but the man is too heavy. Snow swallows my harsh pants, and I can do nothing but watch as the Storm Hound's sword descends toward the man above me. It connects with a sickly squelch and warmth rolls down my back, collecting in the nape of my neck.

It can't end like this, lost beneath a corpse until I suffocate. With a yell, I claw into the ground, ripping myself away from the corpse and into the freedom of churning boots and clashing metal. My biceps scream in agony as I draw myself forward one painful inch at a time. Kosci sends a hot burst of strength through my body, and finally I emerge onto the battlefield. I swallow the blood in my mouth and allow the ice sword I've become so familiar with to form. I pull myself up, stabbing into the Storm Hound attacking my soldier beside me. He crumbles and I start forward, lungs burning with fresh air.

Arrows not our own hail down on the soldiers behind me. Some plink harmlessly off the lovite armor, but others find their mark. A helmed Storm Hound rushes. I duck under his blow, bringing my own up, cutting deep into his waist. He falters before falling to the ground.

Chinua calls another order far behind me, sending more arrows down on the Storm Hounds. Some find our own men instead. Three more of my soldiers drop. I clench my teeth and try to fight my way through the press of bodies whirling around me. Find Ladislaw. Find Matvei. End this before more soldiers are lost.

Grunts fill the air as swords meet shields and axes break pommels. One of my soldiers stumbles into me, the Storm Hound in front of him nearly double his width. I dart toward his knee. It moves away, coming up to collide with my nose.

I stagger back, already feeling the pulse of blood down my lips. I lick it away and throw the blade in my hand. It whirls end over end, embedding itself in the man's chest. My soldier runs the Storm Hound through.

I re-form my blade, hacking and slicing where I see black and gold. The field is absolute chaos, the only thing differentiating the people before me is the color of their armor. More of my soldiers fall, some with wounds to the neck, others missing hands or with deep wounds in their legs. They cry out for my blessing, but I can't give it to them. I can't spare the magic.

I fend off another attack as sweat pours down my back. Despite all my training, my muscles still wobble under the combined weight of my armor and weapon. I draw upon Kosci's power, willing it to filter through my body, to give me strength.

He answers. With a surge of energy, I rush forward, tumbling out of the way of a broad sword before coming up behind the Storm Hound to bury my blade in his neck. He falls to the ground, giving me the first uninterrupted view of the battlefield since the beginning.

My lungs burn as I take in the wall of black and gold pressing against my army. Chinua stays on her hill with the archers, sending commands when she can, Yuri by her side, but the Storm Hounds are far more powerful than the militia I cobbled together. There is only one way to end this. I have to find Ladislaw and kill him. I take in as much air as my body can hold and shove Kosci's power into the earth. It shifts beneath my feet, sending a rolling wave toward the Storm Hounds on my left.

As if in answer, another rumble sounds from beneath and a crack appears below my feet, running toward my army. I try to throw my voice, desperate to be heard.

"Move out of the way!"

Only the closest soldiers hear me. The fissure widens, swallowing Storm Hounds and my soldiers alike. I spin as something sears its way up my back, eating away at my armor.

Matvei stands before me, brilliant and golden as the sun, his face hidden behind a lovite helm of his own, the veins a burnished bronze. He spins the blade in his hand and readies his stance.

"I told you to leave it alone, little girl."

"I'm no longer alone," I growl, Kosci's voice beneath mine.

"You think my brother can save you?" he says, his voice far deeper than before. Matvei's mouth quirks into a smile. "He's been locked in my prison for centuries beyond counting. He will never be anything but a plague to this world. Someone to speak about in hushed whispers."

"Isn't it better to be feared, Brother?" Kosci says. "You

continue to walk this world, too weak to return to the heavens and too scared to take the power you so desperately need from me to go back."

"I'm no longer afraid." Matvei darts forward far faster than I thought possible for a man of his size. I slide to the side with ease, coming down on his exposed arm. It nicks him just above the elbow.

First blood is mine.

Matvei whirls with a roar, bringing his sword down on my head. I barely have a chance to parry, my entire body vibrating as our blades connect. He bears down, and my arms tremble.

Allow me, Kosci says. I release the dam holding him in. Power flows through my body, and I shove Matvei off hard enough he stumbles backward. His eyes narrow.

"Is that how you want to play?" Matvei's eyes go dim before returning a honeyed amber color. "No longer content to allow your champion to work on her own?"

I want to snarl, but my face no longer responds to my command. Instead, a numb haze descends over my mind, dampening my view of the world.

"You've never allowed yours any rein. I don't see why I should."

The words fall from my lips, but it isn't my voice. Wasn't my thought that was spoken. For the first time since the battle started, panic flares through me. Kosci's irritation bats me back like a child.

We dart forward, catching Matvei off guard. Without a

second thought, we slice at his exposed thigh, pressing deep into the muscle. The man wobbles for a moment, blood spilling down his armor to pool around his foot.

We stab the blade upward, and I can feel Kosci's joy. He means to connect with Matvei's exposed throat. The part of me still present inside my body notices the stone embedded in Matvei's armor on his right breast.

Zoltoy's heart.

I want to grab it. I want to slam an ice shard straight through it, but no matter how hard I fight, my arms don't respond.

Matvei slides back just in time to avoid the tip of our blade. His great chest heaves as he inhales, then he chuckles, his eyes flicking for a moment to my left. We roll as a large broadsword swings down from above. We look up into the eyes of Ladislaw from our spot crouched on the ground. He sits astride a beautiful white horse bedecked in tack of black and gold. He stares down at us, the sun breaking through our storm behind him as if he is a prophet come to deliver the world from evil.

"Where is my son?" he demands.

"Somewhere safe," my voice along with Kosci's says. This, at least, we agree on.

With that, I send a bright burst of blue ice into the sky. Ladislaw looks up at it, then back at me with a cruel smile on his face.

"You missed," he says.

"Did I?" A cruel smile of my own twists across my face.

Ladislaw's nose wrinkles as he stares down at me, broadsword still clutched tightly in his armored hands.

"It isn't too late to surrender, *girl*." Ladislaw says the last word like an insult.

"As always, I'm the little girl," I say, every ounce of hatred and malice I built up spilling from my lips, pushing Kosci into the back of my mind. I am the strength. I am the fury and the storm. "You seek to wield the world like a blade when it is my armor. I am here because you never thought a girl could challenge your world. I'm your pretender, your usurper. The one that turned your people against you. The girl you couldn't kill."

Ladislaw's lips curl and he swings down from his horse. He advances on me, raising his blade.

"This country is *mine*. I was born to rule. You . . . you are nothing but an insect beneath my boot."

Ladislaw lunges along with Matvei, and it's everything I can do to keep their blades from landing. Matvei seems to move faster and faster, the pendant above his heart glowing so bright it hurts my eyes.

A horse gallops by, and Ladislaw's eyes snap to it. Astride it sits Yuri, blade raised. Ladislaw turns toward him just as the flat of Yuri's blade smacks against his helm. I use the distraction, just as planned. I plant my blade deep into Ladislaw's back, the metal of his armor crumpling beneath my blow.

He roars and wheels around, taking my blade with him. I

make another just in time to catch his attack, Matvei's right behind it. They push me back from the camp and toward the smell of hot blood and anguish of the battlefield. Screams of the dying ring out, battering me, fueling me.

I throw back Ladislaw's next blow and spin, landing a long slice across Matvei's armor. Blinding light explodes around him, reflecting off the snow until the world becomes nothing but white.

Kosci fumbles for control of my actions, panic lacing his movements. I refuse with every ounce of my will, stumbling into a barricade, the sharp wood digging against my spine. I release the frozen blade and conjure a shield of ice above my head as Matvei hacks again and again.

"Matvei, pull back," Ladislaw says through labored breaths, his lips bone white. Blood seeps from the dagger protruding from his back and he sways on his feet. "Heal me. Do you hear? Heal me this instant."

Matvei doesn't listen to the obvious command. He continues to rain blows down, forcing me to the ground beneath the punishment of his strength. His bleeds golden light, streaming from his eyes and the wounds across his body like rivulets of rain.

He moves far faster than any mortal man should, seeming to take up more and more space, blocking the world until it's just me and him in a swirling storm of light and snow.

Matvei screams, his chest jerking forward. I scramble back, putting a singed piece of the spiked barricade between us.

His chest jerks again, this time toward the sky, and a bright beam of light shoots out toward the sun, tearing a hole the size of a fist through his chest. Massive hands from within grasp the sides of the fissure in Matvei's chest, tearing and pulling until a head emerges, followed by a broad torso.

Matvei's body shudders then falls to the ground, revealing the man in the center. As he steps from the corpse, Matvei's body fades away, floating on the wind like ash.

THIRTY-NINE

"YOU SEEM SHOCKED, LITTLE GIRL," the man before me says.

He has the same eyes as Matvei did, honey amber with thick eyelashes, but everything else is changed. Long golden hair swings down his back, nearly obscured by his broad shoulders. His wide mouth is set in a harsh, jagged line, a scar cutting into his upper lip.

"Who are you?" The words come out hushed, small. I don't know why I asked. I already know the horrible answer.

"Zoltoy, Bright God, giver of light and warmth."

Barely, Kosci whispers. *He is nowhere near full strength. He still remains tethered to this earth by the heart beating at his breast.*

My eyes drop to the pulsing gleam of lovite stone in the center of his chest. It's tiny, not much more than a pebble in the expanse of his body. It's the same shape as the pendant at my neck. His heart. His soul.

All I have to do is destroy it, just like Alik said.

Ladislaw's weapon droops to his side, mouth slung open as the color leaks from his face. The battle raging around us slows until it dies completely. Soldiers on both sides have stopped, their arms slack at their sides, their eyes trained on the Bright God before them. He radiates summer heat, the slush around his feet drying as we watch.

"Did my brother not warn you?" He swings his honeyed eyes to me. "Did you never question why there were no tales of champions beyond the battles they fought? You are nothing but vessels. Useless sacks of flesh to siphon strength from until we can emerge anew."

With each new word Zoltoy speaks, something in me falters. How many times had Kosci likened me to a butterfly? How many times had he said I must transform to use my power? It was never me who was metamorphosing. It was Kosci.

Everything Alik said was true. *Everything.* Kosci was hiding something from me. Something bigger than the strange numbness that slowly seeped into my body, or the noxious thoughts I never knew were mine or not. If I thought Alik's betrayal horrible, this was so much worse.

I had trusted Kosci, given everything to him. He was the one person in this world I believed I could truly count on, and in the end, I was a pawn. Just like I had been to everyone else. In my determination to be free of Luiza and Ladislaw, I had fallen into an even worse trap. One that ended exactly where Matvei's had.

"No." I shake my head.

"Come now, Kosci. Show the host your true colors," croons Zoltoy.

Kosci surges forward inside me, his hand pressing at my chest, desperate for release. My ribs bow, aching to give way to the pressure, but I put my own hand to it and push down. Tears sting my eyes, but I hold my hand over Kosci's, the sharp prod of his hand against the inside of my skin sending a wave of utter wrongness coursing through me. I am more than a host to a parasite. He may have siphoned my emotions and stolen my strength, but I refuse to give him my life. I will not die a prisoner in my own body.

"No," I say again, bearing down hard until his hand recedes and I feel only my sternum beneath my touch. "My body is my own. My will is far stronger than your host's ever was, Zoltoy. I retain control."

"Bright God," Ladislaw says, giving a small bow before the man. "Kill this pretender. Strana is rightfully mine. She has no place in this world."

"No. Strana is mine." The Bright God reaches out and grabs Ladislaw around the neck and squeezes. With a horrible snap, the Czar's head falls to the side, his eyes wide and unseeing. The Bright God tosses Ladislaw like he is nothing but a rag doll. His cold eyes move to the crowd.

"My brother and I built this world. You were mere mistakes,

things created to be forgotten. I will take back what is mine."

With a flick of his hand, Zoltoy sends the soldiers nearest us flying. They collide with the barricades, long spikes cutting through their armor to stab through their chests. I grab the snow before me, willing the cold to keep me grounded. This is my body. I didn't live through the past ten years to lose my life as a prisoner.

Release me, Valeria, Kosci commands, his voice rumbling through me like a storm. *My brother will burn everything you love. I'm the only one who can stop him.*

"Liar!" I scream into the earth.

Ice explodes around me in jagged spikes. Something like fear emanates from Kosci. The power I wield now does not come from the pulsing pendant at my neck, it comes from my bones. With each heartbeat, the bruises along my hands gleam, just like lovite had in Knnot.

A dim realization settles over me. Lovite had been Kosci's bones, the remnants of the divine, harvested by Zladonians for generations. So long, in fact, its dust had worked its way through our bodies, giving us bone-white hair and papery skin. With Kosci's power strung around my neck, my own body absorbed the magic he so desperately craved. Just like lovite.

No, he says, but I can feel his emotions now. Panic. Surprise. Fear.

Kosci may have given me his power, but it was no longer his. I control it. It hums in my bones, vibrating at a frequency

I can't hear but can certainly feel. I do not need Kosci. Not anymore. Just like everything else, my dependency on him had been a carefully constructed ruse. A manipulation into feeling alone and rejected by everyone else so I had no other person to lean on but him.

I bear down harder on the fury in my heart and the ice shoots out farther, catching the Bright God in the leg. It pierces the flesh of his thigh. Ichor pours from the wound, bright gold and viscous. He turns his wild eyes to me, breaking off the icicle in the process.

"You dare stand against me?"

Light blasts from his hand, searing the ground as it makes its way toward me. I jump to the side and the light catches the tent behind me, sending it into a column of flames.

Sera calls from somewhere in the fog behind the Bright God. A surge of soldiers breaks from the mist, arrows filling the sky as if both armies now fight as one. They rain down on Zoltoy. A bright beam of sunlight bursts from his hands and the arrows erupt in flames, disintegrating into useless ash. He stomps at the encroaching army and a ripple of earth flows from his foot, sending them flailing.

Release. Me. Kosci says again. He pushes hard at the inside of my body, and the bones inside my hand gleam bright blue beneath my skin. I force his soul back into the piece of lovite around my neck, into the ground beneath my boot, making him as small and fragile as I can. His will battles against my own, but I will not lose.

Not now. Not ever again.

You used me!

Of course I did! Did you ever truly think a mortal could defeat a god? I needed you and you needed me. We were a perfect match. I freed Strana, now you free me so I can destroy my brother for once and all.

You planned on killing me? This entire time?

What else is there for mortals to do besides serve the gods who made them? You were important, Valeria, powerful. Your name will be remembered throughout all time as the girl who revived the Pale God. The one who changed the world. Isn't that what you wanted?

I wanted to live *in the world I created.*

What have I told you this entire time? Change requires sacrifice, and that sacrifice is you.

Zoltoy throws another bright beam toward the advancing army. It sears along their skin, and it cracks and bubbles, blackening before my eyes. He turns back to me. The sun seems to move closer, melting away every bit of snow, turning the field into nothing but mud.

"You have no hope. This is a war meant for gods," the Bright God says. "Refuse and I will devastate the people who dare defy me, the very people you want to save."

He gestures toward the soldiers around me. Most lay elbow deep in mud, struggling to regain their footing. Chinua clutches Sera to her chest, blood pouring down the larger girl's forehead to mingle with her blond hair. Tears stream down Chinua's ruddy face, and she brushes a kiss to Sera's lips.

They are dying. Everyone.

But if I release Kosci, what havoc will these petty, jealous gods wreak across the world without a host to contain them? They will destroy it in their quest to best the other. Worse than any war humans could ever wage.

"If I release him, will you leave us in peace?" I ask.

"I swear it," the Bright God says.

I look down at my hands, bloodstained and covered in muck. Perhaps this was all I was ever meant to be. A sacrifice for the people I love. I catch on to the truth of those words, forcing them through my mind until Kosci can see nothing else.

You are alone anyway, Valeria. You have no one left who loves you. He whispers.

He's right. Matta and Papa, left behind at camp. Gregori and Anton no doubt dead on the field.

And Alik. He'd tried to warn me. He'd begged me to listen and I hadn't. Likely all part of Kosci's plan to make me completely and utterly alone.

Oh, Alik . . .

I wish I could've seen him. Just one last time.

"Well?" the Bright God says.

I look up at him, tears streaming down my face. "I will save this world if it's the last thing I do."

Kosci bubbles inside me; a numbing cold starts in my toes, slowly working its way up toward my heart. I hope Strana will survive. I hope the people will endure, despite everything. A ragged cry sounds from my left, and Bataar races forward. My heart stutters and stops. The bright lovite blade in his hand catches Zoltoy in the back of the neck. More ichor splatters from him, staining Bataar's dark hair with flakes of gold.

As if destroying a fly, the Bright God's hand whips out and hits Bataar in the chest. His body soars across the field, colliding with a wall of soldiers. I close my eyes against it. That stupid, stupid boy.

I can't stop Kosci's slow pull on my body, his rising form going for my chest, right where the Bright God had crawled from Matvei. I let him think he will make it. That I will allow myself to be the lamb Luiza raised me to be.

A strange horn calls out over the field. At first, I think I failed, that it is some herald of death, but it bleats again, insistent. Angry.

I force myself to turn and there, on the far side of the hill, sits hundreds and hundreds of people. With another horn call, they take off into a gallop, their long strides eating away at the earth, angled straight toward the Bright God.

At the head is Alik.

FORTY

I BLINK SEVERAL TIMES, CERTAIN I'm mistaken, but his white hair streams wildly behind him as he lifts a long spear.

Yet again, Kosci lied. Alik hadn't left me at all.

Heady relief floods through me as the herd bounds closer. The Bright God's attention shifts as they gallop onto the field, readying spears of gleaming lovite. They sail true, one burying itself deep into his shoulder. With a snarl, he snaps the spear off and more ichor oozes down his body, flowers springing to life where it falls. The wound heals over as he advances.

Frost curls across my collarbones, and I hiss at the pain. Kosci's pendant beats in time with my heart, insistent. Demanding.

Now.

I must move now.

I rise from the ground, my legs unsteady as Kosci whirls inside me, surprise and annoyance rolling through my mind. A fist bangs on my skull, and my hands go from feeling too hot to numb as Kosci tries to take control.

You cannot double-cross the gods! You promised me this, Valeria. You made a vow.

And you broke it, I think back.

I did no such thing.

You promised me strength, power, and survival. I will not survive this. You are mine, Kosci, not the other way around. You broke your own oath.

I take a step, and Kosci jerks inside me, trying and failing to take control yet again. I keep my eyes fixed on the Bright God as I stumble forward, gripping Kosci's pendant tight in my hand as if that will stop him from taking control once more.

Zoltoy's back stays toward me as god and calvary crash together. Hooves collide with Zoltoy's chest, the horse's Adamanian rider thrusting a spear toward Zoltoy's thigh. The Bright God catches the rider about the middle before the blow lands. The god curls his fist tight around the rider, hoisting their body high above his head. For a single, achingly clear heartbeat, I can make out the rider's face: brows high, mouth open in a cry I can't hear. Zoltoy casts the rider into the approaching horses with a roar and the body collides with them, sending the riders toppling to the side.

I struggle into the chaos, taking up Bataar's fallen sword

as I go. I'm close enough to smell the sweat of the horses and hear Zoltoy's measured breathing. Close enough to kill him. I shove the blade into Zoltoy's side, wincing as hot ichor pours onto my hands, sizzling where it meets my frost-covered limbs. Zoltoy turns toward me, his bright eyes blaze with every inch of holy fire in his soul, but Kosci's words hang in my mind. He is not a god. Not yet.

"What do you think you're doing?" he growls.

"Killing you," I say, grasping the burning amber lovite embedded in his breastplate.

The Bright God laughs and catches me around the throat, squeezing tight as he lifts me to his face. "Do you think you are the first to try such a trick?" He sneers down at me, gaze tracing the leather strap of Kosci's pendant to his heart beating frantic bursts of blue in time with my heart. "But I do believe I will be taking this."

Zoltoy's thick fingers pluck at the pendant and sickly hot pain claws through my chest, Kosci's heart fused with the delicate skin of my neck. My vision goes bright white and I'm certain I'm going to die.

His hand goes slack, and I drop to the ground, gasping for air. The Bright God falls to his knees, revealing Alik behind him with golden ichor splattered across his face. The blade melts in his hands, the last vestiges of Kosci's power fading from Alik's body. It had found its way into his bones too, just a touch of it, but enough for him to wield a portion of the magic I did.

"Do it," he yells as wind starts to whirl around us.

I crawl forward, each movement sending bursts of pain through my chest, until I reach the Bright God. He glares at me, desperately trying to regain his footing. I still clutch Bataar's sword in my hand. With a yell, I drive it toward the frantic pulsing stone in Zoltoy's chest. The Bright God's large hand grasps my forearm, melting away the metal of my armor. Kosci screams in my mind and rattles inside the prison I'd placed him in, shattering bars, clawing his way toward his brother, toward the freedom he so desperately longs for.

Hot tears spill down my cheeks as every part of my body screams in agony, but I bear down harder until the blade catches the tip of the stone. Zoltoy gasps, his hold on my arm slackening. I take the opening and pierce the Bright God's heart.

The world erupts into a sheet of bright white. Screams start all around me as I fall backward. I land hard on my side, and Kosci's heart burns at my chest. I squeeze my eyes shut against the light now emanating from Zoltoy and work my hands to my neck. Kosci catches hold of my muscles as I cling onto his necklace.

You need me. You can never hope to rule without me by your side. Without me, you're nothing but a mortal girl. Powerless. Empty.

"I am powerful enough on my own."

With a scream, I rip Kosci's heart from my neck and throw it to the ground. Taking up the same blade I used to kill his brother, I slam the tip down on Kosci's heart. The lovite cracks, a blue light shining along the fissures. I stab it again, putting all my weight behind it. The mud sucks at the stone, and I'm certain I'm not enough. That Kosci is right.

A loud snap rings out and the heart shatters. Blue light pours from the stone in beating waves, rolling across the battlefield to mingle with the dancing white of the Bright God. They surge around each other, nipping and biting, screaming and fighting. They spin in a column, twisting and winding until they are almost indistinguishable.

Howls of wind pull toward the twining column, sucking my hair forward, tearing my body toward it. I try to grab anything to stop myself, my nails breaking on wood and slicing on blades. Still I slide across the ground, ever toward the light.

My muscles give way, limp and useless, and the cyclone of the Brother Gods consumes me. I spin like a leaf caught in a breeze. The magic now biting at me, sipping will from my marrow, taking all I have left to offer. I don't have the strength to fight it. Let them feast on my bones. At least Strana is no longer a battleground for the gods.

We are finally free.

FORTY-ONE

SWIMMING FROM THE DARKNESS IS one of the hardest things I've ever done. Every thought pulls me deeper, attempting to keep me in its numbing embrace. Hadn't I done enough? it asked. Don't I deserve a break? But something keeps me pushing forward. A steady, stubborn thud drawing me out of a world unknown.

Blinding light slices through my eyelids, and for one horrible second, I'm certain I'm dead, everything is far too bright, too white, to be real. As my vision clears, a rippling canvas yawns overhead, thick poles holding it aloft.

Every single part of my body hurts as I attempt to move my arm. Nausea rolls through me, and I let out a muffled groan, squeezing my eyes shut. Hurried movement sounds to my right, followed by a strangled gasp. I try to turn my head, but the act forces bile up into my throat and I empty my stomach onto the floor beside me. A long shadow cuts across the blazing light, further blurring my vision between light and dark. A gentle hand caresses my face, the smell of fresh snow and pine following it.

"Alik." It sounds almost like a sigh, my voice is so strangled and soft.

"Go back to sleep," he says. "I'll keep you safe."

Again, my vision goes dark.

When I next open my eyes, I'm not sure how much time has passed. The canvas tent still looks the same, my body still aches, but my vision is sharp. I test my head slowly, pleased when it doesn't throb.

I glance around, taking note of my familiar belongings; the low little chimney fire, the wooden table with maps still strewn across it, the buttery yellow quilt from my house in Ludminka. And there, in a low chair to my right, sleeps Alik.

I test my arm, wincing as it brushes against the heavy covers. A bandage twines from wrist to elbow, the gauzy white marred only by deep-red splotches in the vague shape of a handprint. The Bright God's, seared straight into my flesh for all eternity.

I manage to reach Alik's knee, brushing it softly with my fingertips. He jolts awake, his eye darting instantly to me. Alik drops from the chair and gathers me into his arms, burying his head into my hair. My body cramps at the sudden movement, my injuries flaring to life in painful stabs, but it is worth it to feel his arms around me again. Alik holds me steady as I bring my arms around his neck. A strangled knot forms in my throat as I let my fingers curl through his hair, hot tears burning down my cheeks.

"I thought you were going to die," he whispers, breath hitching.

I gasp a sob, pressing my cheek into his shoulder. "I thought you'd never come back."

We cling to each other, both of us poorly containing our quiet sobs. With the last of my strength, I hug Alik tight, memorizing the soft brush of his hair along my cheek. My arm gives a sharp jab of pain and I wince. Alik slowly lowers me against my pillows, settling me slightly upright. A hot rush of guilt tumbles through my body as our gazes connect, and I force my eyes to the orange glow of the oven, my mouth drying as I searched for words I didn't know how to say.

"Alik, I—"

"I don't care." He cuts me off and presses the softest kiss to my forehead. "I don't. I choose you, even if that's not how you feel about me, even if we can never be what we were. I will always choose you. When I . . ." He swallows hard. "When I saw you after the Bright God's attack, pale and bleeding and broken, I thought I might as well break, too. I finally understand what it's like to think you lost the person you love, and I understand why you took that deal. In that moment, I would have, too."

My breath catches as Alik gently grasps my hands, cradling them in his own.

"I was certain . . ." I inhale shakily. "I was certain you hated me."

Alik's face softens. "I never hated you, Val. I don't think I could, even if I wanted to. I knew you were still in there, even if Kosci had used the conduit to control you. I could see it from time to time, instances of mercy, your love for your family. And I swear to you, I never abandoned you. I knew you needed Temujin to win this war, and when you still intended to attack Ladislaw, I returned to Adaman."

Tears prick my eyes again, and I turn my face away to hide them from Alik. He gently grasps my chin and turns it back toward him.

"You don't have to hide from me," he says, and slowly, ever so slowly, presses his lips to mine.

Something inside me explodes, cascading in warmth through my entire body. I kiss him back until my injuries spasm. Reluctantly, I break away and lie against the pillow, still feeling his lips hot along mine.

"How long has it been?"

"A week."

"What?" I try to sit up. He gently lays me back down.

"It's okay. Everyone's okay."

"But what happened? How did you get Temujin to help you? Is Sera alive? Where are the Storm Hounds? Yuri? Bataar?"

"One question at a time," he says with a smile. "Temujin was against it at first. He was still very slighted by your refusal to hand over Chinua. I told him you'd granted me the position of envoy and that I was to come to an agreement by any means. It was a lot of haggling, but in exchange for Temujin's help and Chinua's freedom, I agreed to trade raw lovite with them exclusively for three years."

A long, wobbling sigh leaves my lips. Alik had always been better at charm than I had.

"And the rest?"

"Sera is fine. She'll have a scar, but Chinua has told her it makes her much more attractive."

I chuckle, wincing as it pulls at my ribs.

Alik's hand tightens once before he forces it to relax. "Bataar lives. Broken ribs and a punctured lung, but he lives."

I bite the tip of my tongue even as relief washes over me. That idiot risked his life for me. Again. And I wasn't sure where any of us stood. Alik barrels forward, determined to ignore the stillness in my body.

"The Storm Hounds went back to their families, for all I know. The Czar is dead, and so are the gods. The country doesn't know what to do anymore. They need someone to rule."

"Yuri will take his father's place," I say, exhaustion tugging at my mind. "It was our agreement. He would lead me to his father, I would give him the crown. He more than made good on his word. I ask only that we keep Zladonia, and I think Yuri will be amenable to that."

"You no longer intend to rule?" he asks, his hands motionless.

"I will not rule Strana," I say, lolling my head in his direction. "But if Zladonia wishes it, I will take care of her."

"Then let me be the first to offer my pledge of loyalty, Czarista." Alik presses a kiss to my knuckles.

"Valeria?"

The flap of my tent rips back, revealing my family crowded around the entrance. They fall into the tent one after another; Matta putting her wrist to my head with pursed lips, Papa stoking the fire back to life, Anton tossing more logs in as Gregori places another blanket across my lap. By the time they're through, sweat beads on my brow.

"I better never see such a thing again," Matta pulls her wrist away, giving it a shake. "You nearly died."

"She was trying to save us, Matta," Gregori replies, leaning on the desk.

Matta sniffs, going to the samovar beside the oven, evidently through with the conversation. I scan every single one of them, checking for any missing limbs or gashes, but I find them all as hale as ever. They busy about the tent making tea and readying a small meal of broth and bread, chattering all the while over the outcome of the battle. Many had been spared the brunt of it, Matvei's shattering of the earth had separated a majority of the army from the opposition. It had taken them nearly an hour to find a way around, and by the time they'd arrived it was mostly over.

Not much remained of the battlefield besides a broken, scorched bit of earth that crumbled away into the sea and blackened lumps of melted rock. One thing was certain, in all their rambling there was no trace to be found of the Brother Gods. They had twisted away into the heavens, disappearing in a burst of oranges and silvers.

I am no longer Valeria the guild member.

Or Valeria the champion.

I am just Valeria.

EPILOGUE

THE SEASONS CHURNED FORWARD, MELTING snow from the land and replacing it with a sea of grass. Trees budded and leafed, wildflowers grew, and Strana healed.

My burn from Zoltoy faded with the seasons, going from bright, angry red to dull pink. It blazed across my forearm in the bright early summer sunlight streaming from above, painting the palace of Rurik in splendid colors of blue and white. The citizens of Rurik who had gathered to see the coronation of Crown Prince Yuri parted for me like a wave, whispering in my wake. Some painted me a daring hero, others a disgusting usurper.

The rumors decimated me in the first months after the separation between Zladonia and Strana, burrowing into my fragile heart until I believed them. Now I hold my head high as my family smiles at me from the lawn lining the palace's pathways, Gregori arm in arm with the blacksmith's daughter, who he'd promptly confessed his love to as soon as he returned from the final battle. Seeing my brothers happy and alive, my parents proud and beaming, the Zladonians free and healing, those things mended the tear in my soul created by Kosci.

I followed the same graveled path I'd taken all those months ago to steal into the Vestry. It sat in ill repair, no one wishing to pray to the Brother Gods anymore. And they were no longer there to hear us. Kosci's absence was nearly visceral, a strange blank spot in my mind full of a deep nothing I didn't dare to linger on. I don't know where Kosci and Zoltoy found themselves. If we were lucky, maybe they were dead, gone to wherever gods go when they are no longer needed. I preferred they stay there, refusing to give them any power from my thoughts.

My beaded *letnik* drags along the ground, a soft swish sounding after every step, and I trace the edge of the palace, hiding from prying eyes and allowing the walk to calm my heart, the twittering birds and gently waving flowers bringing a sort of peace nothing else ever seemed to. I mount a stone staircase near the back of the palace, finding my way onto a wide balcony paved in flagstone. It overlooks the royal gardens, a maze of hedges and carefully kept roses. Ladislaw had locked the beauty away for himself, but as one of his first decrees, Yuri ordered it be shared with everyone. People of all walks of life now promenade through the paths, chatting and laughing as if the world hadn't been upturned just six months before.

Alik leans against the stone balustrade of the balcony, sunlight playing off the silvery white of his hair, and despite it all, or maybe because of it, my heart surges. He turns as I approach, pressing a fist to his heavily brocaded jacket.

"Such formalities," I say, tossing him a smile as I cross my arms and peer at the couples strolling arm in arm in the gardens below.

"You are the face of a country now. I have to show my Czarista respect," Alik says as he leans on the rail beside me, his shoulder resting gently against my own.

The blistering cold of my imprisonment has faded, taking the bruises with it. I am more myself than I have been in months, and I smile out at the sea of blooms waving in the summer breeze.

"We made it," Alik says. "Yuri will be crowned Czar, and all our agreements will fall into place. Zladonia is its own country now."

I release a contented sigh. "The world has righted itself."

Alik turns, placing his lower back against the rail and leaning to get a better look at me. Sunlight clings to the edges of his hair, turning them a burning orange as he cocks his head to the side.

"What will you do? Once this is over?"

I bite the inside of my cheek, considering my words before

I speak. "I'm accompanying Chinua, Sera, and Bataar to Ada-man. Chinua intends to introduce Sera to her family, and . . . I told Bataar I would help him find his parents. I don't want to break that promise, even if I don't have the power I did before."

"I see," Alik says slowly, considering his hands for a moment. I tense, bracing myself for his response as he looks up. "When do we leave?"

I jolt up from the rail, hope bursting through my chest. "You'd come?"

Gingerly, as if afraid I'll race away, he rests his hand along my cheek. "I told you, Valeria. I choose you, in this lifetime and the dozens to come. So tell me, when do we leave for Adaman?"

A smile breaks over my face, and I fling my arms around him, hugging him tight. We had made the world whole once more, now I could finally live the life I wanted, without Ladislaw, or the Brother Gods, or Luiza telling me all the ways I didn't deserve what I had. Perhaps I would be labeled hero, perhaps I would be villain, but at the end of my story, no one could say I didn't change this world.

ACKNOWLEDGMENTS

Storytelling has been a passion of mine since I was a little girl listening to my dad tell stories of fairy trees and monster-slaying dolls while my mom wrote novels in her office at work. You could almost say storytelling is in my blood, a foundational part of who I am. I am beyond thankful I have gotten the chance to share two novels now with the world and can confidently say I would've never gotten this far all on my own.

I will forever be grateful to my parents, for not only for sharing their love of fantastical stories and faraway places with me, but for encouraging me to pursue what I loved even if it was unconventional. Thank you for always listening and supporting me in every way. I love you both very much.

Thank you to my sisters, who were semi-willing participants in my elaborate imaginary games that fostered my love for fantasy and storytelling even more. You both mean the world to me, and I am so grateful I get to call you both my sister. I can confidently say I would've never become an author if not for your constant encouragement. I love you.

Thank you to my husband and forever best friend, Mark,

who has believed in me since I first told him I wanted to be an author at seventeen. You've spent years upon years listening to my wild ideas, tears, and complaints and deserve some sort of award for most patient person on the planet. If not for you, I would've given up long ago, so thank you from the very bottom of my soul for choosing me.

Thank you to my children, who never missed an opportunity to help me work whenever they could. Your silly jokes about my characters, fantastical ideas about plot points, and hugs kept me going when times got tough. You both bring so much joy and light into my life and I am so proud to call you both mine. Never stop being your curious, wonderful selves.

Thank you to extended family near and far on both my side and Mark's. I am so fortunate to be a part of families so warm and supportive. I am thankful for every single one of you who shared your excitement about my debut and eagerly asked about the sequel. Your enthusiasm helped remind me why I love to write, and I am so very grateful that you all took such measures to let me know how much you care.

Of course, neither *The Bright & the Pale* nor *Wrath & Mercy* would be in the world today if it weren't for my fantastic agent, Sarah Landis. You saw the potential in my stories and helped me hone them into something I can be proud of. You are a relentless champion for your authors and a dedicated friend. Thank you so much for all you've done and continue to do for me. To many more books together!

Thank you to my editor, Karen Chaplin, for honing *Wrath & Mercy* into what it is today. I am glad we got the chance to work together as you've taught me so much about the industry and how to edit a novel for publication. It has been quite the adventure and I am pleased with everything we achieved together. I would also like to thank Celina Sun, who did an incredible job as editorial assistant. Your notes were invaluable to me on *Wrath & Mercy*, and I look forward to seeing all you will accomplish! Thank you for all your help.

Another massive thank-you to my copy-editing team, Jill Amack and her production editor, Jon Howard. Without you both, my books would be nothing but grammatical errors and syntax problems. I would also like to thank Harper's publicity team and especially Lauren Levite for all your hard work. I am so grateful for you getting my novels into the hands of readers.

An enormous thank you to my Monsters and Magic team: Jessica Olsen, Sam Taylor, Courtney Gould, Kylie Lee Baker, Margie Fuston, Candice Conner, Laura Rueckert, Cyla Panin, Vanessa Len, Lauren Blackwood, Nicole Bross, and Tori Bovalino. You all made debut year manageable, and if it weren't for all of you, I likely would've cried a majority of the year. Having friends to turn to when things get hard is absolutely invaluable to me and you have all helped more than you know.

A special thank you to Lyndall Clipstone and Sue Hong. You two are the reason *Wrath & Mercy* is as strong as it is.

Without your help in dusting off the bones I had created, I would've never uncovered the true heartbeat of my sequel. I will be forever thankful for your assistance and support. I couldn't have done it without you!

A hearty hug to my snug room pals: Gabby Taub, Dani Moren, Rachel Greenlaw, Ellie Fitzgerald, and Kylie Freeman. You keep me smiling and your support means the absolute world to me. It's so essential to have friends to turn to in the writing world, and I am beyond thankful to have you all.

And last, thank you from the very bottom of my heart to every reader who has picked up my book. The amount of love and excitement from you all has helped me realize exactly why I want to write professionally, and I will never stop being humbled and thankful for every new reader.